M000190544

SUDDEN ONSET

TOM DARDICK WITH **CHRIS DARDICK, PH.D.**

Immortal Works LLC
1505 Glenrose Drive
Salt Lake City, Utah 84104
Tel: (385) 202-0116

© 2021 Tom Dardick and Chris Dardick, Ph.D.
www.suddenonsetbook.com

Cover Art by Ashley Literski
http://strangedevotion.wixsite.com/strangedesigns

All rights reserved, including the right to reproduce this book or portions thereof in any
form whatsoever. For more information email contact@immortal-works.com or visit
http://www.immortal-works.com/contact/.

This book is a work of fiction. Names, characters, businesses, organizations, places,
events and incidents either are the product of the author's imagination or are used
fictitiously. Any resemblance to actual persons, living or dead, events, or locales is
entirely coincidental.

ISBN 978-1-953491-20-6 (Paperback)
ASIN B094F6GVNX (Kindle Edition)

This work is dedicated to the scientists who devote their lives to understanding the mysteries of life, the educators who inspire the next generation with a spirit of stewardship and a deep appreciation for life on earth, those of Faith who seek to understand what science has revealed about God's magnificent creation, and to the students who will someday deepen our knowledge about the amazing world we live in.

EXCERPT:
THE NECESSITY OF PRECURSOR COOPERATIVES

Wallace, M. D.[1,2] *and Weingartner, J. A.*[1]

1*University of California, Berkeley, Dept. of Plant and Microbial Biology, 311 Koshland Hall, Berkeley CA, 94720.*

2*National Interagency Biodefense Campus, Fort Detrick, MD 21702*

Section #1: Cooperatives

Among the most important primordial events that have ever occurred, this one happened without spectacle. It didn't matter that no one was there to bear witness. Even if directly witnessed, this creation would seem unremarkable. Molecular building blocks are invisible, but far from insignificant.

It began so modestly that it wasn't much of an event at all. A better way to think about it is to picture a string of small stepwise occurrences struggling for order within a sea of chaos. As such, this was far from unique—similar occurrences happened countless times before in similar places.

Somehow, against impossible odds, this particular succession distinguished itself. To say this curiosity was created may be correct, but also misleading. It wasn't fabricated in the normal sense of the word. This was more of an unintentional inevitability given the right circumstances; a specific set of conditions more or less fashioned to ensure that it would come into being. Whether created or a random occurrence was merely a matter of perspective.

A DEEP FREEZE

D r. Mira Wallace slipped and nearly fell as icy gusts buffeted her. She steadied herself with the handle on the outer door of the Antarctic science pod to compensate for her numb legs. The near fall barely registered. The physical dangers posed by the storm didn't matter to her. If she found what she sought, the most fundamental of all life forms, she'd transform the understanding of evolutionary science. She could find the key to unlock one of the great mysteries.

The team doubted her. Not as a microbiologist, Mira knew. She lacked other qualities needed to be a leader in this kind of expedition. They weren't wrong. But they put themselves into this mess, too.

Their opinions of her weren't mission critical, she told herself. The withering effects of the windstorm soured the attitudes on the team. Once the gales harried them ten days ago, the onslaught refused to relent. The resulting equipment failures and hardship could not be reasonably attributed to Mira, but blame had to land somewhere. If it helped them better cope, she could carry the burden. Along with everything else.

Besides, she shared their sentiments. Her frustration had long metastasized into fear. But their words still stung. Earlier, she'd overheard the geologist say Mira didn't care about their sufferings. The astrophysicist suggested she could withstand the cold better than the rest of them because her blood was already ice-water. She'd heard such comments her whole life. Distant. Uncaring. The perception resulted from her focus on her work. That's what she'd always told herself. Maybe it was, in part, her earbuds. People assumed she didn't wish to interact with them. Maybe they had a point.

Marcel, the climatologist, was a problem. He made sport of stirring the pot. He would find fodder for complaint, storm or no storm. She needed to take action to squelch his degradation of team spirit. What could she do, though? Over the wind's howl she heard his muffled voice through the thin walls of the pod, his thick French accent unmistakable.

"She has, how you say? The head of a pig, this is what she has."

The wind calmed for a moment, and she heard the others guffaw. One, she couldn't tell which, went along. "You mean to say she's pig-headed? If you mean she's stubborn, you've got a point."

Her cheeks would have flushed in anger if the weather hadn't already reddened them. Personal discomfort, technical glitches, and logistical challenges she could handle. Those challenges were made up of sequential duties. She could reason her way to advantageous outcomes. That part of her duty posed enough troubles. She needed no more, especially avoidable self-inflicted ones. Why didn't the others show the courtesy to tell her their specific complaints? If she could address them, she would. If she had to guess, well, higher priorities required her attention.

Their assessment of her was uncharitable. Matters always clarified in hindsight. And she suffered right along with them. The too-real risk of losing the generator meant, well, they all knew what that meant. Fear has a way of erasing courtesy. And compassion.

What was best for the mission? Not stomping in and causing a scene. Measured against her goal, insults didn't matter. Mouths snapped shut and faces grimaced protests in response to the whistling whoosh of crazy-cold air ahead of Mira as she entered the science pod. The flimsy structure creaked and swayed under the press of the polar tantrum. Thus far, the pod's fiberglass walls conferred enough insulation to stave off death at the hands of Antarctica's fury. The place had become more cramped, more crowded, and more locker-room-pungent every day over the past three weeks. The single common area was supposed to boost team spirit. It hadn't worked that way.

A modest kitchenette occupied the middle section and featured two pushed-together collapsible-leg tables used for both meetings and meals. Bunks and workstations per each scientists' particular discipline encircled the space. The one place in the entire camp where she could get a modicum of privacy was the airliner-sized commode attached on the far side of the structure like an afterthought.

Mira held her tongue as she stomped the snow from her boots and hurried to her station. She stripped the polar gear from her wiry frame. Room temperature was under 15°C, but in contrast to where she'd just spent the last few hours, it felt like a sauna. She grimaced at the tedious procedure of cycling through the layers with fingers aching, necessary only because of the call of nature. She'd already began to perspire as she threw one item after another toward her bunk. One glove, her fleece hoodie, and her thermal pullover landed on the floor. When she got to the last layer, a glint of light shined from a silver-and-gold-begemmed charm bracelet on her left wrist. She slowed so the fabric didn't snag and risk damage to the dangling charms. Her hand unconsciously checked to be sure.

None of the others spoke. Eyes darted to Marcel. They urged him on with gestures. He rose and approached her.

"Well, what happens out there?" His s's and th's sounded like z's due to his thick accent.

"The temperature drop is negatively affecting the secondary generator."

Marcel didn't disguise his exasperation. "This we know. This is not what I am asking."

"Kyle's working on it." She continued to remove her weather gear.

"I hope you are now ready to listen to reason," he pressed.

"Reason is the only thing worth listening to." She increased the volume on her piano and violin playlist and hurried to the kitchenette, ripped open a protein bar, snatched an energy drink, and barricaded herself in the restroom for as long as she needed to consume the snack and relieve herself.

Try as she might, Mira couldn't keep the pestering doubts at bay. Their window of opportunity would stay open a short while longer as the Antarctic summer ended. If the weather didn't break, there was no choice to make. If they couldn't get the drill equipment working again, and soon, there'd be no point in remaining. She knew what the team wanted her to do. She couldn't bring herself to do it. Did she have the right to risk the others? To what degree? Each person knew what they signed on for.

Still, she wrestled with the decision. If she called for evac, they'd never get this chance again. She knew better than to entertain hunches. Hunches were not scientific. Yet, she couldn't shake the feeling that the microbe she'd spent her adult life searching for was down there, in the lake two miles below her feet. Her fate rested with Kyle now. If she ever prayed, this would be the time.

Mira didn't pray. Instead, she rubbed her temples and berated herself. She could have more fully considered contingencies should the worst happen; she could have requested more fuel, another backup generator. She might have even received approval for those requests—what's another few hundred thousand compared to the $25 million this expedition had cost? A venture this far into the interior continent to a virgin site multiplied the expense and difficulty of doing anything. All decisions involved a trade-off. This she knew from experience. Truth was, as always, her mission plans were meticulous and thorough. This despite the fact she'd never before ventured to Antarctica. None of those realizations assuaged her.

She re-entered the main area. Her freckled brow wrinkled and her cracked lips narrowed in a frown. Marcel stood right where he had last stood and waited for her.

She did not meet his eyes. She rarely met anybody's eyes.

"I told you this, did I not?" He took two steps closer. "Take out those things from your ears, s'il vous plaît. Climate change, she not only means more extremes in weather, she also limits our ability to predict those swings. You should be hearing my words."

She spun to face him but left her earphones in and the mellifluous atmospheric music on. "What are you saying? We shouldn't have undertaken this mission at all?" He risked being smashed with the entire force of her pent-up frustration. To avoid so doing, she talked past him. "Tell me there's some hot *c. canephora*."

"If we had not, this mess, she would not menace us so, no?" Marcel pressed.

Mira's gaze found his left hand and his two fingers missing nails. She frowned at the white and blue discoloration on his fingertips, the signature of the onset of frostbite. Unlike some, he hadn't camped out in relative comfort the whole time; he'd spent nearly as much time in the elements as she. Still, she wanted to say what she really thought of him. Even a few years ago, she might have done so. Instead, her eyes remained upon Marcel's injuries. "Your discomfort is regrettable."

She pushed past him and filled a thermos with coffee. She returned to her living space to don a fresh set of thermal underwear. Mira showed no modesty in revealing the skin—blotchy from the conditions—of her thin, taught limbs.

Mira re-geared. Marcel resumed his protest, incredulous. "You are not going back out there? Every time you open the door, more power goes poof, out the window."

As if to emphasize his point, the lights flickered again. Mira managed herself with a deep, calming breath. He wasn't the issue here. Not really. She met Marcel's glare, her clear gray eyes conveying neither warmth nor malice. He was like everybody else in her life—he didn't understand. She defiantly slipped on a dry hood, shoved her arms into her parka, fixed her mask in place, put on dry gloves, and left without reply.

"Ça me soûle!" Marcel exclaimed in the face of another icy blast as he waved both arms in frustration.

A DEADLY AGENT

The features that distinguished the odd patch of ground from the rest of the high desert's surface were easy to miss. Unlike the surrounding hard-packed, coarse pebbly terrain, the patch appeared to be fine sand of a dull gray hue. Except sand is crystalline. Light reflects and refracts off of each grain's tiny facets. This substance was different. It seemed to spit photons back at every angle.

Most notably the patch lacked the saltbush, greasewood, pickleweed, or other spiky brush that dotted the salty Utah basin. A geologist or botanist might notice their absence, even though the patch was smaller than the average suburban driveway. But most people would never notice it. Surely not someone in the throes of crisis like U.S. Army Ranger Ed Roberts, despite the fact he landed facedown an arm's length away.

Duress made him miss the condition of the tequila bush next to his feet. The plant's spiked radiating leaves wilted and fell away at unnatural speed in dull gray flakes. He concentrated on the effort to expand his diaphragm as every muscle in his body screamed for oxygen. With disturbing reluctance, air worked through his nose and mouth, through the experimental TPF (Tracheal Particulate Filter), and into his burning lungs while, two feet away, the plant's biomass crumbled, flaked, and fell into the growing patch.

Roberts didn't care about test results or what the Brainiacs learned. The TPF encumbered him. Though it was small and didn't initially produce discomfort, he now felt like he was a snake trying to swallow its prey. The device might keep soldiers safe from airborne toxins, maybe even save thousands if, God forbid, some ideologically enslaved terrorist set off a dirty bomb. The TPF could've made him bulletproof and his mind wouldn't change. What good was the protection if you couldn't breathe and nobody understood a word you said?

Not that he wanted to talk to anyone. He lay still and waited to recover. He couldn't. His power to concentrate vanished. He kept thinking about the one person who mattered most to him: his daughter, Chloe.

He obsessed about one question: how could she reach the point where, halfhearted though it may have been, she actually tried to end her life? His marriage was in tatters, but she had to know he and her mother loved her more than life itself. She had to know that, didn't she?

Lines of thickening red streaked his cheeks and neck, the work of cruel thorns along his sprint through the brush. He paid them no mind. The paucity of air in his lungs and Chloe's well-being left no room for such minor issues.

Focus, Roberts, he admonished. He fought the urge to rip his glove off, stick his fingers down his throat, and pull out the infernal slimy TPF—test or no test, orders or no. After all, what did this experiment matter? He pictured Chloe's face as he had playfully smeared her nose with frosting. He remembered her self-conscious, snark-laced laugh.

Her laugh. Hers alone. Nobody laughed like her. No, thirteen is not too old for pink, or for horsing around, sweet child. How did it all get so bad so fast? Her pleas to stay tortured him further.

As if he had a choice. Another wave of guilt for even being in this place slapped him. He loved being a soldier—the responsibility became his identity.

Too much; that was clear now. This was a young man's work. Not the occupation of an engaged, present father. This was the last place he needed to be.

He wished with all his heart he could magically transport to his daughter's side. But orders were orders.

Fifty yards away, a desert-camouflaged jeep slid to a halt and contributed another cloud of dust to the thickening haze. CSM (Command Sergeant Major) Rain Somerdale, the man entrusted to supervise the entire three-day exercise, jumped out and ran to the test area's boundary. He glared in Roberts' direction.

Roberts didn't see him and couldn't make out his words because of the distorted TPF-buzz of his voice, but he knew who shouted in his earpiece, *"Roberts! You're out of bounds, Ranger."* While the words were garbled, he understood Rain's tone, *"Get back to the field."*

Roberts' arms protested as he struggled to push himself upright. He raised his head as he fought the TPF for adequate air. This exhaustion was absurd. As he willed himself to his feet, one of the wilted tequila bush's fronds fell on his desert-camouflaged pant leg, directly above his boot.

Roberts' couldn't clearly see the landscape and the action around him. The desert dust kicked up by tire treads and the impacts of less-than-lethal foam projectiles, along with the aerosols used in the test, obscured his lines of sight. Skidding pursuit vehicles and shouting test participants appeared ghostlike as they blinked in and out through the violet-gray haze. The air partially cleared and Roberts caught the movement of a yellow boundary flag as it flapped weakly in the stray breeze.

Another distorted command from Rain buzzed in his ears, *"Get over here, soldier. Move."*

Roberts straightened, spied Rain, and gave half a wave to signal compliance. On his first step toward the closest boundary flag, he winced. Had a desert thorn worked its way into his boot? Before his next footfall, he knew his guess was wrong. He bent to see what could produce such a strange sensation.

"What are you doing? Back to the zone!" This time Rain's voice resounded clearly as he removed his TPF.

Roberts' pain grew in both his foot and his calf. His eyes became bloodshot and bulged in disbelief as his pant leg disintegrated. Fabric fell away in flakes of gray. The same phenomenon happened to his boot. Roberts' alarm skyrocketed as the process moved into the flesh of his foot and leg. The agony intensified as the sensation spread. Roberts bellowed in pain, fell to his knees, and onto his back.

Those of the Red Team and his fellow test participants within earshot did not know what they heard. The TPF gave Roberts' scream an eerie buzzing quality, like shouting into a fan. They collectively paused. The muffled echoing pops of foam bullets ricocheting and the revving engines of pursuit vehicles all quieted.

Rain donned a rebreather mask as he sprinted to Roberts' side. Others followed, but he admonished, "Get behind me!"

Rain crouched to scan Roberts's body for clues about the man's distress. His eyes widened as Roberts' flesh underwent the same process that wilted the tequila bush fronds. "Hold on, Ranger. We're going to get you out of here."

Roberts didn't comprehend the words. His mind could only register pain—white hot and relentless.

Rain radioed, "Medical. I need immediate evac. Contamination protocol." He lifted Roberts from behind under his armpits but stopped when his right leg below the Ranger's knee fell away in a pile of gray flakes.

He gently laid Roberts down, removed the man's helmet, and stroked the stubbly hair of his military cut. "Hang in there, son. Help is on the way." His eyebrows raised in alarm as he spotted the patch. He pulled Roberts a few more yards away.

Roberts had known pain. He'd survived battle conditions, both simulated and real, that'd make most anyone shudder. But nothing in his experience prepared him for this. As his flesh transformed, amid the storm of firing neurons, he managed to mouth five TPF-distorted words. They were his last. "Chloe. But...she needs me."

A REVIEW

I n the anteroom of the Base Commander's office suite, CSM Rain Somerdale sat in a lone padded utility chair, its cushion exposed through weathered cracks. Veins in his forearm bulged as he clicked his gold pen open and shut. The faded taijitu—people called it his 'Yin-Yang symbol'—tattooed on his left triceps peeked out from under his rolled-up shirtsleeve. The curves of the design rippled as his muscles flexed; it still had most of the definition it had when he'd got it as a rebellious 18-year-old. The wear of twenty years of strenuous military service and his graying crew cut told his age more than anything else.

He crossed his legs the opposite way in a futile attempt at comfort while he ruminated on the events of the previous day. Weariness showed under his eyes as worry had cost him his habitual seven and half hours of sleep. His toughened body contrasted with his blue eyes that wandered to the inscription on the pen and narrowed. *Ever Vigilant.* Hmph.

During the past six weeks before the incident, groundwork for the TPF test dominated his focus. Like the handful of others in his profession privy to the concept of the prototypes, the potential for protecting military personnel, first responders, or civilians in chemical, biological, or radiological exposures excited him. None of his enthusiasm remained.

Another handful of officials entered and walked past without so much as a glance at him; two more civilians in navy suits led by an Army officer in dress uniform. Rain stood and saluted. A subtle nod was the most pronounced response. Even the people he knew well, the senior officials at Dugway, uttered not a word to him when they filed into the adjacent office.

Even so, the assembly buoyed his spirit. These new faces were accomplished people who journeyed far and fast to help. They represented considerable federal resources. Years of flat budgets and disastrous PR eroded resources at Dugway; his staff withered to a mere skeleton crew. Despite his extensive experience, Rain had encountered nothing like the mysterious substance that had so appallingly stolen Roberts' life. Cleaning this mess would require help. Lots of it.

The door opened and his Commanding Officer beckoned him in. "Ready, Command Sergeant Major?" His deep voice resonated sympathy.

Colonel Garrett Potteiger commanded the U.S. Army's Proving Ground at Dugway, in the position for less than a year. Rain held him in higher regard than most of the nine previous base Commanders. Rain's first priority was to ensure safety for those who used Dugway's extensive facilities. He found Potteiger more aligned with that objective than his predecessors.

They walked past the unattended assistant's desk and into Potteiger's office. Framed pictures on the wall behind a large walnut desk stood out among the sparse appointments. Cheerful family photos were flanked by images of Potteiger posed with various dignitaries, including four-star Generals, several CEOs of Fortune 100 companies, and even an ex-President of the United States. Though spacious, the room was now cramped with a dozen bodies situated around a conference table and in chairs along the wall. Potteiger motioned, "Please have a seat, Command Sergeant Major."

Rain complied. "This is CSM Somerdale," Potteiger continued. "Among his other duties, he heads our Chemical, Biological, Radiological, and Explosive training operations and supervised the drill when the incident occurred."

Grave expressions darkened the faces around the table. Rain

shared glances of acknowledgment with Dugway's Chief of Staff Victor Lyden, Director of the West Desert Test Center Robert Harrison, and Technical Director Dr. Jerry Griffin. He'd worked with each for years.

Rain's eyes did a double take at one of the faces among the visitors. He dropped his pen, astonished. "When did you get here, Connie? I sure wish it was under better circumstances, sir." He retrieved his pen.

"Me too, son." Colonel Constance Yanoviak had long gone gray. His face lacked the admonishment of some of the others; his smile showed warmth. "I look forward to catching up with you later."

Rain did too. He hadn't contacted his mentor since Connie's assignment as Military Deputy at the Edgewood Chemical Biological Center at Aberdeen. Rain was never particularly close with his own father. His hippie parents hated the military, and he lost contact with them when he enlisted on his eighteenth birthday. Connie filled that void and provided guidance Rain needed. Seeing the man here lifted his spirits. For a few moments, anyway.

"I see you already know Colonel Yanoviak. These other folks are from DTRA, ATEC, and the office of the Undersecretary of the Army.[1] You're aware, I'm sure, this will not be our usual AAR." After-Action Reviews were generally simple meetings. "Just tell this panel what you told me yesterday."

"Yes, sir." Rain spoke faster as he spewed the distasteful details. "Exercises went more or less as planned up to the point of the incident." He straightened. "There were complications that led to the Ranger's—Roberts'—death. It was my fault he strayed out of bounds. I failed to anticipate the difficulties we experienced. Visibility was poor. Verbal communication was impaired by the TPFs. These issues were foreseeable. They compromised safety."

Some expressions on faces around the table softened, apparently in response to Rain's acceptance of responsibility. Aaron Moore, Chief of the Advanced and Emerging Threat Division at DTRA, remained severe, unblinking. "We will take a closer look at your precautions in due course. We understand you were in charge of the sweep. Why was the hazard not identified prior to the exercise?"

Rain blinked. He self-recriminated again. "It was technically outside of the safe zone. But I routinely cover a larger perimeter as a buffer. I don't know how I missed it."

"From what I understand, it wasn't much to see," Connie said. "When had you previously inspected that area?"

"Last month."

"And you missed it then too," Moore challenged.

"Obviously, no one knew it was there," said Connie.

"That has yet to be determined." Attendees shifted in their seats in response to Moore's remark, and its tone. DPG's senior leaders shared nervous glances.

Rain straightened. He knew the vast stretches of the surrounding desert better than anyone. Whatever that substance was, it had to have recently appeared. His thoughts accelerated and clarified. "It wasn't there three days ago, before the exercise."

"How do you suppose it got there, Command Sergeant Major?" Moore's tone became accusatory.

"I don't know. I have no idea what it is or where it came from. I'm much more concerned with our more pressing problem."

"And what is that?" Moore pressed.

Rain looked at the faces around the table. "How do we clean it up?"

In response, the officials shared glances with one another. Moore pressed on. "We have the same concern, Command Sergeant Major. And you can help by being as forthcoming as you can."

"That's what I'm here to do."

"We shall see."

"I don't appreciate your attitude, Mr. Moore." Potteiger held his ire under control, but barely. "This man is the best there is at his job. If not for the CSM's actions yesterday, others might have died. Bad enough I had to call Roberts' wife and tell her not only had she lost him, but she couldn't even have a body to bury. I never want to have a conversation like that again." His countenance shifted from anger to sadness. His eyes watered and his voice cracked. "The man had a thirteen-year-old daughter."

Moore never took his eyes off Rain. "We appreciate your service, Command Sergeant Major. I too have a job to do. And I also consider it important." His lips smiled, but not his eyes. "Now, if I may continue, I'd like you to share your ideas, however rudimentary, for the cleanup operation."

"The area has been cordoned. The contamination is spreading. We don't know how or why. We're deploying a containment tent while our scientific team concludes their assessment."

"Good, I'm glad to hear that." Connie remained sunnier than everyone else. He wasn't happy, Rain supposed, but more like he wasn't as fearful. "I'd like to inspect the site as soon as practical."

Moore interrupted. "Until our people have done so, I want no further actions taken."

DPG was a U.S. Army installation. This guy acted like he outranked Commander Potteiger. He didn't. "Why?" Rain challenged. "We have a hazmat crew there now."

Moore turned to Potteiger. "Tell them to stop whatever they're doing." He was still adversarial. "Right now." He paused and looked the DPG officials in the eyes, one by one. "This is a crime scene."

Potteiger stammered an unintelligible objection. It was not an argument, and the Commander let it drop. Rain's focus remained on his personal failures. Moore's point could be valid.

Moore's gaze returned to Rain, inquisitor-style. "You placed a mask over your face when you ran to the aid of the victim."

"Yes."

"Why?"

"S.O.P." The Standard Operating Procedure for any potential contamination included a mask.

"Did the victim have one?"

Rain leaned back and deliberately slowed his pace. "No, sir."

Moore's tone grew more severe. "Anybody else in the field?"

"No."

"Why were you the sole person equipped with a tactical gas mask?"

Rain's throat tightened in recognition of what Moore intended with these questions. He measured each word. "Sir, I've done this kind of work a long time. You could say I'm old school. This was a test of a new kind of respiratory protection, and masks were not required. But mine hung by my side, as always. If you'd seen what I have seen, seen what happens to a child exposed to mustard gas, or some horror show like that, you might know why. When it became clear to me the ranger was in crisis, I put it on without thinking about it. I couldn't help him if whatever affected him got me too."

Moore's face revealed neither acceptance nor rejection. "But the mask would've made no difference, correct?"

"Apparently not. The substance seems to corrode by touch. It was a small miracle I wasn't infected, too."

If Moore intimidated Connie, it did not show as he said, "I'd like to zoom in on the issue of contamination."

Moore maintained eye contact with Rain. "Where do you think the substance came from?"

"I haven't any idea, sir."

"Give us your best guess."

He wrestled with the matter ever since he witnessed the substance eat Roberts' clothes and flesh. He wanted to cooperate, to help as much as he could. "Old waste? Buried underground—maybe a leak? Maybe a toxin became exposed, perhaps by erosion. It doesn't rain much, but you'd be surprised by the wind erosion in the region."

"What do you know about disposals in the area?"

"Disposal areas are marked and remote. The exercises were not near any such area. If it turns out that is the issue, then it's a mistake."

Connie reasserted himself with a lean forward and a raised voice. "Disposal of hazardous material is handled judiciously, people. Always has been. The cause is probably something else."

"The material got there somehow," Moore challenged. "How could such a mistake happen, CSM Somerdale?"

"I don't know. Improper records, maybe? Though I agree with Connie—it's improbable."

"We have yet to exclude anything, Sergeant Major. This is just the beginning of the investigation." Moore's tone remained adversarial. "What you suggest is the consensus view. It is curious, though."

"What is?" Potteiger grimaced, testy.

Moore again scanned the room as he established and held eye contact with each of the DPG personnel who sat at the table: first Potteiger, followed by Lyden, Harrison, and Jerry, before he circled back to Rain. "Nobody around here seems to know what this stuff is or where it came from. But the likelihood is someone put it there. Our job is to ascertain who that was and what their purposes were. And I want this matter kept quiet until we do so."

After an awkward silence, Rain spoke. "If there's one thing Dugway has built a reputation for, it's keeping secrets."

---

1. See Supplement for explanations of various U.S. Government agencies in the story.

A GENERATOR

C ontrary to her colleagues' accusations, the frigid conditions sapped Mira's body and soul the same as theirs. Against the bullying wind, she willed her aching limbs across the drifting snow along the path now worn flat, mostly by her boots. Storm or no storm, she was responsible for this operation. Though she lacked the power to change their situation, what she wouldn't do was sit around the science pod and wait. The gray-black mass of fog that plagued them earlier dissipated. At least the gusts were good for something. Now sky and horizon melded together behind the worksite in a blinding diorama of white.

Absorbed by their work, and under pressure to get it done as fast as possible, none of the drill crew acknowledged her. She sighed in exasperation when she found the drill boss, Kyle Newman, right where she had left him forty minutes prior—still at work on the generator. He should have been back operating the rig by now.

The generator spit and sputtered. Kyle knelt and leaned in. "Piece o' dung would run better on penguin farts!" He thumped the Caterpillar-yellow metal casing with a blow of his gloved ham-fist. The clang reverberated as the drive motor groaned back to speed. "Don't just stand there like a pack o' morons, get another preheater on that blasted tank!" Kyle shouted loud enough for the crew to hear through their insulated headgear and over the din of droning equipment and howling wind.

Two of them turned the generator off. Again. Despite gloves

stiffened and heavy with ice, they expertly spliced a black canister into the fuel line. One of them reluctantly said, "Last one, Boss."

"What's the problem now?" Mira shouted over Kyle's shoulder. On his knees, he could still look her in the face.

"Fuel's at the blasted cloud point!" Kyle spit back. He didn't bother to turn around.

"What does that mean?"

He wrenched a boot through the crusty snow to hoist his 370 lb. frame. Clad in a thick yellow and black jumpsuit, he looked like the generator itself had grown arms and legs and come to life. He towered over her. She couldn't see his face behind his headgear and beard; ice crystals clung to every bit of fabric and hair. "Paraffin wax crystals precipitate from the class four winterized diesel fuel and clog the blasted works," he rumbled. "Alright with you if I get back to it now, ma'am?" He did not wait for a reply and resumed his work.

Kyle's gripes didn't bother her months ago, in the planning stage and the first days on the ice sheet. But his demeanor remained morose no matter what. He eroded what little remained of their morale. Though the reasons baffled her, she'd observed in her many past expeditions the spirit of the team constituted a commodity as precious as fuel or food. And they needed to hang in there for at least another week. Maybe two, Antarctica willing. Provided Kyle's team could keep the secondary generator alive.

No one among the deferential group of scientists and technical crew would criticize him. Not to his face. Neither would Mira. She knew the leeway could not be ascribed solely to his imposing physique and frontier manner. Universally respected among those knowledgeable about the drilling industry, Kyle belonged to a handful of people who had ever drilled into a subterranean Antarctic lake—though not this one—and not this remote. The crew had come to count on his guidance for every matter. Getting him here was no simple matter for Mira; she first had to talk him out of his early retirement, then justify his price on the grant. Kyle had all the autonomy he wished.

The mission wasn't supposed to be like this. Summer in West Antarctica offered a few weeks' window to carry out their work. Average temperatures in the region in late January hovered around a tolerable -25°C. But they got walloped with plunges to below -50°C. Even more problematic were the endless gusts. They often exceeded 100 kph.

Mira's American hosts at Palmer Station had strenuously advised them to reschedule. She refused. She preferred the counsel of their Russian counterparts, successful at Lake Vostok on the other side of the continent. "It is now or never, Dr. Wallace. If you leave now you don't come back," said one. Another added, "Antarctica obliges no one."

One of the crew restarted the generator. Kyle coaxed up the throttle. After it whirred to a stable speed, another crew member reactivated the drill rig. The massive spool resumed its slow, steady turn and the flexible pipe snaked into the ice. Water bubbled up around the hole; it flowed out and refroze into a slick glassy teardrop.

Mira clasped her arms together, lowered her chin and leaned close to Kyle. "The laser drill. Did I mess up?" She hadn't experienced doubt like this since her earliest expeditions. "Was the steam rig the right call?"

Kyle's tone moderated, his gentleness atypical. "Doc, you've done a fine job. Better than others I've seen. We could've gone with the steam. But I couldn't be sure we'd get 'er done the way you wanted; no contamination, right? Not sure steam would a' done 'er."

"We're consuming too much fuel."

"You stop that, right now. Hear me?"

She nodded, half-hearted. She'd made the decision long before. To second guess now wasted energy.

Her eyes found the depth gauge. They had to be close now. She spotted Jeff Weingartner, her post-doctoral assistant who worked with her for the past couple of years at UC Berkeley. He helped the crew unwind the coils. It wasn't his job, but it didn't surprise her to find him out here. In his drab outer-wear, he looked like he belonged more with the drill crew than the scientific team. Over the past couple of weeks, he had spent more time in the drill crew quarters. He seemed to prefer their macho camaraderie, replete with rough talk and gambling to the comparatively austere environment of the scientists' quarters. She admired him anew. Antarctica had yet to dent Jeff's spirit.

She waved him over and he loped to her side. "Yes, Mira?"

"Inform the others we're about to join the boreholes. Marcel should bring his camera."

Jeff hopped to. She envied his youthful energy. Ten minutes later the scientists assembled in silence around the drill crew. Kyle worked the control panel. He examined the readings. His thick gloved fingers flitted over the buttons as he made fine adjustments.

Nobody uttered a word over the next few moments. If Kyle could connect the pressure-equalizing hole to the main borehole, they'd surmount the last remaining (and most difficult) technical hurdle. The task was akin to threading a needle blindfolded while dangling the strand from ten feet above. The scientific work of their various disciplines depended on Kyle's skill.

Mira reminded herself to breathe. A wave of awe washed over her. The lake below was one of the last places on Earth uninvaded by humanity, or any other living creature (well, not for countless millennia.) A memory filled her mind: as a young girl, she scampered along a dry creek bed and picked up every rock she could, hoping to find a salamander or hellgrammite. Her current situation dovetailed with the image; like she was about to pick up the last rock on Earth to find a remarkable creature underneath.

The generator sputtered again. Over endless minutes the only sounds were its spasmodic drone, the incessant whistling wind, and Kyle's off-color gripes. Finally, he grunted in satisfaction. "That should do 'er." A second later, the hole belched with a muted pop. A massive spray of water followed and shot high into the air. The droplets instantly froze into prismatic ice crystals which swirled all around them. The dim sunlight dappled a brilliant rainbow against the pure white landscape.

Jubilant whoops erupted. They hugged one another and offered congratulations and gratitude to Kyle. He ignored them as his attention, along with grumbles afresh, turned to pulling the drill head out of the hole.

Mira shared his thinking. It wasn't yet time for celebration. Space and weight limitations, along with environmental factors, prevented him from casing the holes. That provided a small window to swap the laser head with the sampling bore head, get it down the main hole, and into the lake below before this secondary hole froze shut.

Mira stood alone with her thoughts. The giddiness of the others floated past her like the settling ice crystals. They swirled in the wind, in perfect rhythm to the piano arpeggio in her ears. Kyle kept at his work. He must feel similarly. The peculiar emotional mixture was familiar, part fear of failure and part thrill of potential success. This was the intense satisfaction especially longed for by scientists, a rush not unlike what a gambler experiences between the sound of the gun and the moment the horses' noses stretch over the finish line. Soon, she'd be able to act. She'd be the first person to find microbial life in the lake 3.4 kilometers below her feet. More important to her personal crusade, if she found those exotic life-forms, she'd examine their DNA. Because of the pristine environment, she knew the observations she'd collect would help her fill in missing pieces in a four-dimensional puzzle that had more than a trillion pieces. She'd be closer to the answer to the biggest question in biology—how did life begin? The scientist in her told her to temper her emotion. She'd find what she'd find. But the rest of her couldn't help it—she believed the keys were down there. It pleased her to take personal responsibility to unlock this mystery. She couldn't count the sacrifices she'd made in that pursuit. Gone more often than not, she didn't really have meaningful relationships with her colleagues at Berkeley. Her ceaseless trips were never to a comfortable, pleasant destination. It was always to the harshest conditions the planet offered. The exposure took a toll on her, most evidently in the weathered skin and deep lines on her face. Small prices.

AN INTERESTED PARTY

Rain Somerdale shut the door to Potteiger's office when Dr. Wesley Quon descended upon him. Though not six feet tall, he moved like someone much taller. He did not merely walk. Quon's smooth and silent strides startled Rain as he appeared behind him.

Quon tilted his perfectly coiffed hair in a polite but impersonal greeting. If he remembered they had met three days prior, when they had a detailed conversation about the Tracheal Particulate Filter exercise, it didn't show.

"Good morning Dr. Quon."

"Yes." Quon put his hand on the door handle to Potteiger's office. Voices came from the other side of the door, barely audible.

"Unless you were just summoned, I wouldn't recommend you go in there."

Quon removed his hand and smiled. "You were just discussing the—accident, I presume. When will testing on my device resume?"

"I'm afraid I can't say."

"You cannot say, or you will not say?"

Quon's smile struck Rain as odd, inconsonant with the man's challenge. The exchange with Moore left Rain irritable. "What difference does that make?" he snapped.

Quon remained unfazed. "As a paying customer, I deserve answers. I have a strict timeline, and this delay, whether an accident or mere incompetence, is unacceptable."

"Incompetence?" Quon's callousness shattered the last of Rain's patience. Heat radiated at his temples and sweat beaded in his scalp.

He stepped closer to Quon and raised his voice. "A man has died, sir. Whatever killed him presents an ongoing risk. Your device is not a priority."

Quon's smile vanished. "That will not do."

Letting his anger get away wouldn't do, either. Rain bit down on his lip and cycled his pen once. "That decision is above my pay grade. I can tell you this. There will be no more TPF tests any time soon."

Quon's face darkened further, but just for a brief moment. His wide, toothy smile returned. Rain presumed he'd formulated a retort. Instead, Quon grabbed the door handle and rushed into Potteiger's office, so fast his head was through the door before Rain could react. Should he physically stop Quon? No. Let Moore deal with him—it would serve them both right. Rain shrugged. His regard for the TPF and its inventor fell. He hurried down the hall. He had reviews of his own to conduct.

QUON GAVE no thought to barging in. As eyes shot toward him, he proclaimed, "I have not yet had the pleasure of meeting all of you. Please forgive my intrusion, but I have serious concerns about how this blunder will affect the evaluation of my device."

Most anyone else who opened that door would have been invited to leave. Quon knew his status made him an exception. He owed his reputation not to the TPF device, but rather his bio-electric GreenCar.[1]

As he'd explained to Potteiger upon his arrival to DPG a week prior, "The key component is a unique species of algae only found nearby in the Great Salt Lake. It drifts there in large slimy balloons. It is an ingenious survival strategy—they contain fresh water that nourishes the algae, even though the salinity of the lake, ten times that of the ocean, would otherwise make it uninhabitable for them. The algae itself actually desalinates the water in the interior. When I noted this process creates an electrical potential, I naturally sought to harness that power. I developed a semi-permeable conductive membrane upon which the algae can grow and continually renew the electrical potential by pumping salt from one side to the other. The algae only require sunlight, hence the clear plexiglass outer casing. This consistently produces up to twenty kilowatts per hour, sufficient to charge the vehicle's batteries with no need of a charging station."

"It is an impressive achievement, Dr. Quon," Potteiger had replied. "I see your GreenCars everywhere. They look like you're riding in a polished emerald. Pretty hard to miss. You must feel like Elon Musk."

Quon had heard the comparison before. It always made him bristle. "Musk created nothing new. He merely bought a company. Tesla and similar technology were no innovation. They add to our dependence upon carbon-based fuels. My GreenCar is a true breakthrough." Quon's tone and body language shifted as he cackled. "Perhaps a more apt comparison is Henry Ford. You can have any color you like, as long as it is green."

This Potteiger was different from the one who had first greeted him. Quon saw Potteiger's lips thin and eyes narrow in agitation. But the man's tone remained polite. "With all due respect Dr. Quon, that is not a fair characterization of what happened."

"Please forgive me, Commander. I hear a man died." Quon pulled the door closed and strode to the table. "I also know his death had nothing to do with my TPF. What on earth went wrong?"

The representative from the Undersecretary of the Army stood. "This is a classified matter. We are not at liberty to discuss it further."

The statement had no visible effect on Quon. His eyes went from face to face and zeroed in on Moore. "Of course. National security. Secrets." His voice grew conspiratorial. "You know my TPF is classified, too, I am sure. And I understand perfectly—I have high-level clearance myself."

Potteiger rose and stepped towards Quon. "I'll be happy to discuss your concerns when we're done here, Dr. Quon."

Quon remained unfazed. "I do not wish to be immodest, but in reality, I comprehend more than all of you. If the grapevine can be trusted, and I realize this is not always the case, what you encountered was an aggressive biological agent. This is a field in which I have, as you might know, some small amount of expertise."

"Of course, thank you, Dr. Quon. We'll keep that in mind." Potteiger's tone was both irritated and diplomatic. He grasped the door handle. "We'll talk more later."

Quon didn't flinch. Face impassive, there were no wrinkles to reveal he approached fifty years of age. "It is obvious this agent is previously unknown. There will be few people capable of providing timely discernment."

Potteiger opened the door. "Yes. Now, if you don't mind?"

"Wait, Commander." Moore's lips curled in what some might call a smile. "Dr. Quon makes a good point. Do you have scientists here at Dugway with his level of accomplishment?"

Harrison said, "The West Desert Test Center has ample capability—"

Jerry talked over him. "Well, maybe not of Dr. Quon's notoriety, but—"

Moore focused on Quon. "If you'd be willing, Dr. Quon, we could use your help." He glanced back to Potteiger. "I'm sure it'd be a mere formality to accommodate Dr. Quon's participation."

Potteiger responded by shutting the door.

With no invitation to do so, Quon took Potteiger's seat at the table. He again flashed his wide, signature smile. "I am honored. Please, tell me all you know."

---

1. For more on Quon's GreenCar, see Supplement.

A NEW PAGE

Quon stumbled on the way into the Bio-Safety Level-3 (BSL-3) lab in the Salomon Lothar Life Sciences Facility (LSF).[1] Clumsy in the hazmat suit, he scanned his surroundings. Biohazard stickers on a clear plastic container caught his eye and drew him to his subject. He hesitated as he reached out, equally giddy and fearful about the procedure. He grasped the vial and held it to the light. What was this material, really? Whatever the answer, it was special. Special was good. If it could be properly managed. It had to be biological. This procedure would tell him for sure.

It hadn't taken much to convince the authorities to allow him to conduct the electrophoresis (SDS-PAGE) test procedure.[2] Quon hadn't personally worked in a lab in a few years, but he remembered this aging technique. He smiled as he recalled his argument to gain permission. Inferior minds. They had no idea what they were dealing with here. They foolishly saw only threat. Fear. Such a limiting emotion.

The required solutions awaited, prepared earlier by DPG technicians. He tolerated that much. He double-checked their prep work, anyway. He did so with a pH meter and added a few drops of hydrogen chloride to lower the pH of the buffer.

The Polyacrylamide gel was ready, submerged in a small tank filled with the same clear liquid buffer. He gently gripped the thin plastic comb, its square teeth about the same size as those of a human adult. With a slow rocking motion, Quon removed the comb from the gel to reveal ten rectangular wells.

He placed a tube filled with a viscous dark blue liquid marked 'sample buffer' in the fixture in front of him. Quon's hand hesitated again as he reached for the biohazard box. Inside was a milk-white plastic tube marked with a bright red dot. He lifted the small tube with his gloved fingertips.

Sweat trickled into his eyes. The hazmat suit prevented him from rubbing them. Annoyed less by the irritation than his anxiety, he gingerly unscrewed the lid. He transferred the contents into a flask and added the detergent mixture to extract any proteins present in the sample. Next, he drew up 0.03 ml of the processed agent, less than a tear drop, and added it to the sample buffer. He stirred it in with the pipette tip.

Quon leaned closer to view the gel against the bright room lights. He squinted through the thin fog of his face shield while he submerged the pipette tip into the SDS solution until it hovered above the first well. He ejected the mixture. The liquid seeped into the well and formed a blue square suspended in the top of the barely visible gel. Quon repeated this process eight more times.

In the tenth well he added a different liquid, colored the same 'Coomassie' blue as the solution in the other lanes. Labeled 'marker,' this one contained ten different proteins of known sizes.

Satisfied with the preparations, Quon attached a red gator clip to the positive terminal and an identical black clip to the negative terminal. He decided on a low voltage and an eight-hour duration. He'd have results in the morning. He flipped the switch and electricity flowed. He again leaned close and half-hoped to see something dramatic. He saw nothing but a thin sheet of bubbles emanating from a thin platinum wire which signaled the flow of electrical current. He shrugged and left containment, anxious to get back into his suit and tie.

"What in Heaven's name is this?" Jerry frowned. He squinted at the image Quon had just handed to him. The lanes in the gel were supposed to be checkered by bright blue lines from the Coomassie stain, lines designed to indicate the exact proteins that comprised the agent. He examined one lane, then the next. Each was unstained and shriveled, even the marker lane—entirely unreadable.

He passed the photo to Xi Shu, a staff microbiologist at the West Desert Testing Center. As she examined the image, her knitted brows mirrored Jerry's reaction. They shared a puzzled look between them, leaned close, and whispered words too low for Quon to discern.

Quon did not share their reaction. He appeared happy for the result. "Is there an issue we need to discuss?" His smile didn't match the challenge in his tone.

"No." Jerry's tone sounded defensive. "It's not important."

Quon suspected they blamed the result on him—that he'd botched the procedure. Maybe he should let them continue to believe that.

Harrison, Potteiger, Connie, and two other scientists, fresh arrivals from Edgewood also attended the briefing in the conference room. One of the Edgewood scientists asked, "How could the marker lane be compromised too?"

Potteiger didn't apparently know enough to even wonder that much. "Somebody want to explain to a non-scientist what we're looking at here?"

"Electrophoresis is a process that allows us to visualize proteins," Jerry answered. "This tells us if this agent is biological."

"Did it not work?" Potteiger pressed. "Was there a problem with the procedure?"

"That, Commander, is an important question." These people had some nerve to question him. Quon summoned his patience. Though these were lesser minds, he needed them. For now. "I assure you it was not an experimental error."

"Then can we conclude it is not biological?"

"No, we cannot," Quon stated. Was that a hopeful tone in Yanoviak's voice?

The other Edgewood scientist spoke. "Maybe expired chemicals? Anybody check the labels?"

"No one throws anything away around here." Jerry scratched his head. He turned to Xi Shu. "I hope Dr. Quon wasn't given any of our old chemicals in error."

"I don't think so," she murmured, "but I'll make sure."

"Likely we'll need to try a different extraction method," offered Connie.

These people grasped at straws. They could not see the obvious when it sat right under their noses. Quon wanted to say so. Instead, he moderated. "Do so if you wish. But it will not matter. The problem is not with the chemicals. There is only one conceivable explanation. The agent did this. There can be no other cause." Remarkable.

Jerry objected. "But it was chemically processed with organic solvents. And besides, the detergent in the buffer should have rendered it inactive."

"Yes." The man raised valid points. Quon paused for a moment. Fascinating. "There are particular proteins that feature internal chemical bonds which can keep them from unfolding and being inactivated by the detergent."

"Interesting speculation, Dr. Quon." Harrison seemed unmoved. "But that gets us no closer to useful answers."

"Oh, but it does." Quon held one of the photographs closer. "Just not the way we expected."

Connie appeared the least worried of any other than Quon. "What do you propose we do next?"

Quon placed the photo on the desk. "We must use alternate formulations for our buffers and matrices. We will also test the full spectrum of variables. Of course, we shall also conduct spectroscopy. But I wish to bring in additional expertise."

Potteiger's voice inflected up, anxious. "Who do you have in mind?"

"I would like to invite another researcher to join us. She is most unusual, as is her work. I have followed her career closely. Her perspective could prove revealing."

---

1. See Supplement for explanation of Bio-Safety Levels.
2. See Supplement for explanation of the SDS-PAGE procedure.

EXCERPT:
THE NECESSITY OF PRECURSOR COOPERATIVES

Wallace, M. D.[1,2] and Weingartner, J. A.[1]

1University of California, Berkeley, Dept. of Plant and Microbial Biology, 311 Koshland Hall, Berkeley CA, 94720.

2National Interagency Biodefense Campus, Fort Detrick, MD 21702

Section #1: Cooperatives, cont.

It began with an audacious organic compound called a peptide. They were in great abundance in that place, a location where most of the light took the form of high energy ultraviolet radiation. The intensity of the UV light severed the bonds of most of the peptide molecules, which had incalculably short lifespans. But this particular peptide was a fusion of the amino acids alanine (A) and cysteine (C). Cysteine contained an atom of sulfur that formed a strong double covalent bond with other Cysteines, making this new A-C-C more stable. But the stability of A-C-C was not entirely of its own merit.

This other factor was a function of tremendous and unlikely fortune, or intention. It formed an unwitting alliance with another molecule that stabilized the peptide. This improbable partner, Cytosine, was not merely altruistic in granting longer life to A-C-C, but their relationship was mutually beneficial. Cytosine was also unstable and might have disappeared altogether if not for its partnership with A-C-C.

AN EXTRACTION

Room temperature in the science pod fell below 10°C. Nevertheless, sweat streaked Mira's freckled brow, cheeks, and neck as her heart beat a disconsonant rhythm against 'Song for Sienna' by Brian Crain in her earbuds.

She placed the track-etched bacteriological filter on a piece of double-sided sticky tape, affixed it to a metal cylinder, and inserted the assembly into the sample stage of the cryo-scanning electron microscope. Countless objects flashed in and out of focus on the monitors in front of her—a dizzying jumble, a blue-gray mosaic of cellular structures, clumped together in haphazard clusters. The image didn't appear that way to Mira.

The list of people who'd spent time working with her included fellow professors, students in her classroom, a select few of whom she supported after their graduation, peers on various panels on which she'd served, and fellow researchers who accompanied her on numerous expeditions to collect microbial samples in the planet's most extreme environments. This diverse group all saw Mira the same way—she struggled with emotion, both hers and that of others. The attribute caused problems. It was also one of the reasons she was such an exceptional scientist.

She agreed with the assessment. In science, observations either were real, or they weren't. But it never seemed to work that way. Teams, all teams, included people who often couldn't agree about what was true and what was not. The dynamic was a continual source of frustration for her. Emotion was the culprit.

She was not inclined to change. To the contrary, she cultivated her dispassion. As a scientist, she valued objectivity above all else. The discipline paid dividends beyond objectivity, focus, and reliable memory. She had developed rare observational power, especially details about microbial structures and behaviors.

The weather at Lake Ellsworth normalized, and as a result, so had the reliability of the generator. They still needed to conserve fuel, and therefore they lowered the temperature in the pods. But stable electricity meant they could run their equipment. She could conduct her work. There wasn't a moment to lose.

Her eyes darted up and down, back and forth across the monitors. Her left hand jumped between mouse and keyboard as she panned and zoomed in on specific cells. She rapidly clicked, captured, and categorized the freeze-frame images.

Jeff meticulously prepared each sample, taken at incremental depths of the lake. His work required near constant running of the centrifuge. In the claustrophobic atmosphere of the science pod, the loud whir aggravated their fellows, especially when they tried to sleep. Of course, Mira paid no mind. And Jeff took his cues from her.

Once Jeff readied samples, he brought them to her station in regular intervals. His movements mirrored the repetitive precision of Mira's. The two of them worked in efficient synchrony like an automated factory.

Mira lost herself among the myriad of shapes—spherical, rod-shaped, spiral, filamentous, sheathed, square, stalked, star-shaped, spindle-shaped, lobed, and trichome-forming—all revealed in exquisite detail. How technological advances changed her life! She was right; this subterranean lake teemed with unique life-forms. Hours passed as minutes. To her, the microscopic world was the real world. Humans were just beginning to comprehend this universe. Scientists and non-scientists alike egregiously underappreciated this truth—ours is a microbial planet. Microbes were the source of all life; and nothing could live without them. She regarded non-microbial life-forms as combinations and arrangements of specialized microbes. Her students were often fascinated to learn for every cell in their bodies there were ten microbes—technically foreign life forms. Their bodies were in fact, like every living environment on Earth, cooperative ventures.

Mira's mind thrummed. Was it here? She didn't know the exact thing she searched for, but she'd know when she saw it. Well, not exactly. The real work of microbiology was not well-suited to human minds. Computers did the heavy lifting. Life boiled down to math: A Universal Code, manifested to navigate the physical world in every way chemically feasible. Processing power was more important than imaging in piecing together the many millions of combinations, the life-forms that comprised The Tree of Life.

Mira enjoyed neither popular entertainment nor casual conversation. The excitement in her life came in moments like this, moments both precious and fleeting; products of months or years of painstaking toil. But in those sublime flashes of genuine insight, no words could describe the experience. Those were the moments when she was fully alive.

One by one, the other scientists gathered behind her. This was a shift. The same people who'd disparaged her work as a fishing expedition and who'd doubted her hypotheses, even saying she was on a quest for a microbial Bigfoot, were now riveted to the screens alongside her. Even Marcel, who earlier insinuated Mira held to emotion over evidence. He couldn't have insulted her more if he'd tried.

The extraction of samples from Lake Ellsworth set all manner of activity into motion. Mira's colleagues fought through their Antarctic fatigue and busied themselves with the work of their particular disciplines. Their studies were more fashionable (and thus, in their minds at least, more important) than hers—astrobiology, climate science, and bioenergy. They'd never say so out loud, but they resented Mira's authority on this project. This despite this extraordinary opportunity being due to her leadership, determination, and, more importantly, her reputation in the scientific community for delivering results. She conceived and planned the mission. More importantly, she acquired most of the grant money from the National Science Foundation and the U.S. Department of Energy for the high-risk expedition.

Mira's discovery of life-forms previously unknown to science melted any remaining negativity in the science pod. The team marveled at her handiwork. Though they didn't know what they looked at, excitement built as she marked one microbe after another 'UNCLASSIFIED.'

None were more enthusiastic than Marcel. "This is difficult for my belief," he said, ignoring the earlier tension between them, "that so many creatures live entombed in absolute darkness for two million years. You were right."

The geologist corrected him. "More like four hundred thousand. And it's only isolated relatively speaking. The water recycles every seven hundred years or so."

"Quoi?!" Marcel spat. "Why do we suffer here, then? I thought we were looking for something ancient."

The exchange snatched Mira from the tiny world inside the first sample ever extracted from the bed of Lake Ellsworth. She smiled. Excitement left no room for irritation. Painful stiffness in her arms and back inspired a pleasant stretch. "We're looking here because the environment is extreme, not because it's old. Cockroaches lived 400 million years ago and today they still look the same. We search for older life forms in extreme environments because when life first appeared, the environment was extreme. Microbes can still be found inside volcanoes, floating in the upper reaches of the atmosphere, buried under mountains, and the floors of the oceans. Even the toxic Dead Sea."

She needed a break in more ways than one. She knew the time of day only because she had to record it for her lab-book entries; time zones in Antarctica were a formality. It made no difference.

She wasn't sleepy. But she was bone-weary. Beyond the harsh elements, there was no night; the sun never set. It threw off her circadian rhythm. She wasn't alone; difficulty with sleep schedules was a source of tremendous physical and mental stress for the entire team.

She stood to extend her stretch. She started at the sound of a distant multi-pitched hum. The scientists glanced at one another, perplexed as the sound grew into a roar. The sound grew so loud they had to raise their voices to hear one another before the rumble dopplered away. The sound built again as an airplane circled above.

"Anybody order out for pizza?" Jeff's attempt at levity was unsuccessful. None of them expected an arrival. It was not safe to land at the site until the Antarctic weather, at least in the part of the continent around Lake Ellsworth, calmed. Even if a team member had been injured, there wasn't enough time for a plane to arrive so soon.

"Keep working, Jeff. I'll see what it's about." She put on her mask and hood and then exited the pod while Marcel and a couple of others dressed.

THROUGH THE BLOWING snow and ice, Mira spotted the silhouette of the large transport as it landed on the white expanse. The ski fittings on the landing gear created an engulfing white horizontal cyclone of snow crystals. She marched to the perimeter of the camp.

Kyle joined her. "You know about this, Doc?"

"I haven't the slightest. I'd have expected radio contact first, whoever it is."

The plane skied to a stop a few hundred meters from them. At the rear of the plane, a ramp lowered. A loud boxy Nodwell Turbosquid, a nimble climate-controlled snow machine, exited. It sped towards them; the segmented treads kicked up a smaller snow-cloud in its wake than had the plane. The machine jerked to a stop nearby; the cab rocked back and forth as the doors opened. Three arctic-camouflaged soldiers climbed out.

The tallest marched directly to Mira. "Are you Dr. Mira Wallace?"

"Um—yes."

"I'm Lieutenant Banks, United States Army. Ma'am, your services are needed. We're here to take you with us."

She balked as she processed the man's words. "What?"

"We come by direct order of General Marcus, Commander of the United States Army. This is a matter of national security."

Mira and Kyle shared dumbfounded glances. Why would these soldiers be here? Military. Some sort of attack? Bioweapons? "I'm afraid I'm a little busy here."

"We are sorry to interrupt you. But this is a matter of utmost importance."

"Why me? What am I supposed to do?"

"I can't answer that, ma'am. My orders are clear. I am to bring you with us. Time is a factor."

Mira clamped her mouth shut. Bank's face was stern, serious, and concerned. She appraised the soldiers next to him. Strong, purposeful, professional. She knew well the risk and cost it took for them to even be here. As much as she wished it were, refusal was not an option. Not really. "I don't like airplanes."

Banks stared stonily at her.

Mira wasn't intimidated, but also knew there was no point in arguing further. "Can I at least go to the bathroom first?"

She re-entered the pod without undressing. She stayed long enough to make sure Jeff understood her instructions to continue the survey, properly pack the living samples for transport, and save their work. Jeff knew what to do, so the review was unnecessary. Still, she felt better doing so. The review helped her digest the unwelcome development. She was being arrested—not for wrongdoing, but the opposite. To be pulled from her work at this moment felt like being taken to prison. She stuffed a few essentials into a backpack as she tried, without success, to formulate an argument that would send Banks away.

"What is this?" Marcel reverted to his old self. "You are leaving? Now?"

"I presumed you'd be relieved." She turned to Jeff. "You're in charge of the sampling. It's your decision when to conclude the surveys." She returned to Marcel. "Kyle's now in charge of the logistics. Should you have any more issues—talk to him."

Marcel clenched in anger. The others huddled around him; their faces similarly incensed. "You put your assistant above me? Only a postdoc? I do this longer than he's been alive—"

Mira opened the door, stopping Marcel mid-sentence. She again turned to Jeff. "I'll text you when I know more. Get the samples safely to Berkeley. Can you do that for me?"

"You can count on it, Mira." Jeff's voice held discordant notes of confidence and doubt.

She rejoined the soldiers and Kyle, now ringed by the drilling technical crew. "Jeff will be responsible for the scientific team. I expect you to make the calls about extraction procedure. You good with that?"

"Sure, doc."

She faced Banks. "Any way I can get two more days?"

"I'm afraid not, ma'am."

"How about one?"

"No ma'am." He pointed to the Turbosquid. "Right this way, if you please."

"I really don't like airplanes." Her breath grew short. She'd had to fly countless times for her work. She'd flown to get to Antarctica in the first place. But in all of those cases, she'd had time to work up to it. Now she didn't, and she didn't want to leave. She couldn't make her feet move.

"Ma'am?" Banks lifted his arm toward the plane. "I must insist we go now."

She looked at him blankly as her entire body clenched. Banks nodded to the other soldiers who flanked her. She managed to move her feet as they guided her forward, each one held one of her arms.

Kyle called to their backs, "Hey! Easy with her!" They marched on without acknowledging him. "You fellas got any fuel line preheaters on that bird?"

A REACTION

Gigi Patilla's face-shield fogged. The weight of the bulky air tank registered on her back, knees, and the soles of her feet. As a lab technician with plenty of experience earned in Dugway's LSF over the past five years, she appreciated the need for precautions. But the claustrophobic sensation from this particular hazmat suit, one she'd not had to wear previously, one made for someone larger than her, inspired anything but a sense of safety.

The discomfort didn't dampen her spirit. It was part of the job, that's all. There were few others at Dugway as skilled as her; when Jerry called her in and briefed her on what happened in the TPF test and the potential ongoing risk, she didn't hesitate to volunteer.

The procedure was only one of uncountable possible permutations and approaches that spectroscopy offered. The study of unknown materials was a complicated proposition, one that presented mind-numbing numbers of variables. The team discussed them all: what technique to begin with, for instance, or the best build for the column (for those methods that required such decisions.) The truth was that nobody knew enough to be sure about any of it.

None of that concerned Gigi. She knew in general terms what this particular mass spectrometer did and how it functioned. This quadrupole orbitrap spectrometer would gasify the subject substance and collect ions along the length of a tube.[1]

The resulting signature would indicate the chemical makeup of the tiny amount of hazardous material in a vial now sitting in the cabinet in front of her. Her job was to make sure the machine ran the way the scientists specified.

She sat in the analytical chemistry lab and regarded the vial with the red biohazard sticker. Along with it in the isolation cabinet was a rack of pipettes, another vial, and a special metal plate. There were two rubber hands that protruded into the chamber to enable researchers to manipulate items with one last layer of physical separation. Despite the friction from the gloves of her suit, she easily slid her petite hands in and grasped a pipette. She transferred droplets from the red vial into small round depressions in the plate. In the next step she covered each droplet with a detergent to facilitate protease cleavage of the proteins. Quon selected various concentrations of sodium deoxycholate (SD) for this first trial.

"That's fifteen minutes, Miss Patilla. Time for more air," came Jerry's voice in her headset.

"Hold on to your horsies, why don't you?" She leaned closer and increased her pace. "Almost done. Just a couple...little boogers left." She pipetted the last bit of SD. "There. Whew!"

Behind the station where Gigi conducted the transfer was the device, the size of an industrial oven, that would do the work. She withdrew her hands, lifted the shield, and gently lifted the metal plate. Uneasy on her feet, she steadied herself as she turned to load the plate into the auto-load sample stage of the mass spectrometer. "All set," she chirped as she clicked the input stage door shut.

There was more for her to do. At the computer monitor, she selected the specified tune file, entered the data file name, and pressed the green 'start' triangle. She hurried because she knew she pushed her air supply.

As she hurried out of the lab and into the chlorine dioxide shower, her breath grew short. She needed seven more minutes in the suit, three for the chemicals and four for the steam rinse. Though the observers knew of her risk, they paid no attention as the shower sequence commenced. All eyes were on the lab.

Smoke spewed from the mass spectrometer.

Jerry shouted. "Shut it down!"

"I didn't start the cycle yet," exclaimed the technician at the control station, "it's not ionizing!"

The technician, Jerry, Connie, two other staff scientists, and Quon observed from outside of the BSL-3 labs and monitored via an audio/video feed. They shared wide-eyed glances of puzzlement and alarm. Black smoke thickened as it billowed out. Their view became obscured. A loud klaxon alarm sounded and the fire suppression system activated. Fire-suppressing Halon gas filled the small lab.

Connie blinked in disbelief. "The mass spec is burning," he exclaimed to nobody in particular, "what the heck is going on?"

Quon didn't appear alarmed. "Fascinating." If anything, he looked enthusiastic.

The technician's voice rang out, a desperate edge to it. "Jerry—Gigi's not responding!" He switched the view to monitor the shower exit. The floor outside the shower was dry.

Jerry spoke through the com. "Miss Patilla, are you all right in there?" No reply. "Gigi?" He turned and commanded, "Get her out of there!"

Three suited figures appeared on the monitor and buzzed the shower door open. The steam cycle continued, thick clouds obscured vision. Gigi lay unmoving, crumpled on the stall floor. Two of them reached to lift her. Though she weighed well under 100 lbs., they struggled. Their inexperience in the bulky suits evident, they both found footing difficult on the slippery wet tile. At last they managed to maintain their balance, slide their arms under hers, and get her to her feet.

"Wait," the technician shouted over the intercom, "the shower cycle has to finish. Fifteen more seconds." The men's loud breaths through the com marked the long seconds. "Okay—go!"

The suited figures carried Gigi to the containment area exit door. "Emergency!" One of them radioed. "Open the airlock!"

"*Can't do it right now. Event in the analytical chem lab. Area on lock down,*" a voice over the radio intercom announced.

"Hurry!" yelled the technician, "She's out of air!"

The eyes of one of the suited men who helped Gigi widened in fear. "Are we sure she's not contaminated?"

His colleague offered calming words. "We just showered—she needs air. I'll give her mine."

Another suited figure rushed in. "No. I have a spare." Rain moved gracefully compared to the others, at home in the hazmat suit. He took Gigi from their grasp and gently laid her head back to the ground to improve blood flow to her brain. "I got her. Go, evacuate now." He installed the new air supply tank.

The others followed his orders and retreated as Rain picked her up and followed them out. He laid her down again and opened the stubborn hermetic zipper. He pulled the hood from over Gigi's head and removed her headgear. "Come on, girl." He compressed her chest at 120 bpm.

Robert Harrison rushed to Rain's side. "Please tell me she's all right."

Rain didn't answer. He checked her pulse. Long tense moments passed while he tried to resuscitate her. At last, Gigi's eyes opened, and she gasped for air. Her body convulsed with the effort; the spasm shook the fine locks of her hair.

"Thank God," Harrison exhaled.

"Relax, Gigi." Rain brushed the red-tipped dark brown strands from her eyes. "Just breathe. Easy, now."

She gradually regained her senses and complied. The playful spark relit her deep brown eyes. After a few breaths, she tried to speak.

Rain and Harrison couldn't hear her. They leaned close.

Gigi winced in pain as she spoke in a weak whisper. "You. Forget...about me?" Harrison and Rain looked at each other. Their eyes returned to Gigi. She smirked.

After another uncertain moment, the men grinned.

"You? Who could forget you, Gigi?" Rain let out a relieved chuckle.

She tried to sit upright but fell back. Pain sparked fear. Rain saw it replace the mirth in her eyes.

"Easy, girl, you're okay. I probably cracked one of your ribs. Sorry about that."

She winced. "No worries, Rain. We girls have one to spare, I'll have you know."

RAIN LEFT the lab area emotionally and physically drained. He had lost track of the time of day. It didn't matter; he absolutely had to go home to get at least a few hours of sleep or he'd be useless. Once the mass spec stopped smoking, Harrison decided to have the building cleared until they could formulate a restoration plan. They could make no progress until the machine and facility were back in operation. As usual, Rain was the last to leave. He summoned the energy for one final check and walked the halls. He pulled a few open doors shut. On his way out, he heard a voice from behind the closed door of the reception office. Not one to eavesdrop, Rain nevertheless hesitated at the door. He should have known. Quon was the only person who would've remained in the building despite Harrison's directive. Rain frowned with disapproval.

"I am well aware, Marvin. No, I will handle that matter myself. Tell them there has been a development."

Quon's tone lacked its usual haughtiness. He sounded irritated, maybe even unsure of himself, a contrast from the other interactions Rain had with him. Rain listened. "I am not at liberty to elaborate... We need more time... They will have to be patient... See if you can find a buyer for some of my shares... I do not know that... There is no timetable yet... I cannot explain why the testing has been delayed. Enough of this. Do not worry about that, Marvin. I will find an answer. I always do, do I not?"

Rain considered backing away and re-approaching loudly so

Quon wouldn't know he'd overheard. Instead he rapped twice and opened the door without invitation.

"The building is to be cleared, Dr. Quon. That includes you."

Quon's face went blank, and he ended his call with his thumb as his hand dropped to his side. "Of course. I was just on my way out."

"I'm sure. Let's go." He held the door and watched Quon glide out.

"Is this necessary?" Quon protested. "Time is of the essence, you know."

"We'll be back to work as soon as possible. Probably in the morning. Even you have to sleep sometime, right, Dr. Quon?"

"I wish it were not the case, but you are correct." He turned and exited; his gait noticeably slowed.

---

1. For more on mass spectroscopy, see Supplement.

EXCERPT:
THE NECESSITY OF PRECURSOR
COOPERATIVES

Wallace, M. D.[1,2] and Weingartner, J. A.[1]

1University of California, Berkeley, Dept. of Plant and Microbial Biology, 311 Koshland Hall, Berkeley CA, 94720.

2National Interagency Biodefense Campus, Fort Detrick, MD 21702

Section #1: Cooperatives, cont.

The chemical conditions that allowed Cytosine and A-C-C to cooperate were also a consequence of a chance event—a sudden and unlikely change in the environmental pH. The well-timed pH change initiated two important additional processes. First, urea favorably reacted with Cyanoacetaldehyde to replace the depleting Cytosine, and second, the sulfur atoms in A-C-C catalyzed a reaction between Cytosine and its cousin Thymine.

This growing supply of building blocks led to the formation of long polymers—molecular strings made up of the two cousins. The accumulation of these polymers sparked yet another chain of chemical reactions. Some catalyzed the formation of new peptides, which in turn formed new partnerships. In a relative instant, complex chemical reactions flashed in and out of existence like a microscopic Fourth of July finale.

A CLEARANCE

If she'd fully known the clearance process, Mira would've insisted upon first being allowed a night's sleep. She assumed the 127-page Standard Form 86 was all they needed. She completed the document during most of the ten-hour flight via Gulfstream C-37A from Santiago. Her fatigue made the effort even more grueling, accentuated by the headache she battled for much of the way. She couldn't even comfortably listen to her playlist. Without it, concentration came harder. That added to her stress. She hadn't lied to Banks either. She hated to fly. Air travel was another price she had to pay if she would find the object of her life's quest. Her fear was real—it caused her sweats, indigestion, and sometimes even worse symptoms. But she flew, anyway.

Hers was as uneventful a trip as a day-long dash across hemispheres could be. The liaison assigned to accompany her was pleasant enough, save for a bothersome lack of information. She told Mira their destination, the importance of the required paperwork, and nothing else. The ache in her temples and at the base of her skull debilitated her less when they transferred from the rumbling LC-130 turboprop to the quiet, lithe corporate jet. It was a small comfort, but sleep eluded her.

She couldn't pry her thoughts from the preliminary findings in the Ellsworth samples. Could it really be among those isolated life-forms? After all, the polar conditions weren't that old. She nevertheless felt she was close—she would identify the code that started it all. But a sense was just a sense. It wasn't science. Neither were her incessant doubts. But that did not mean her feelings lacked effect. The steady state of anxiety they created certainly was real. It drove her. That and the desire to accomplish what her parents tragically did not. If she could, all the sacrifice would mean something. If she found the very first microbe, the Tree of Life would finally have its root. The picture of how life came into being would become that much clearer. Again, she tried to calculate the odds that the object of her search still existed. It was a pointless exercise. Not enough data. Yet she firmly believed that if somehow the microbe had survived the eons, it would likely persist in an extreme environment. Somewhere. Only there would it avoid the extinction events that changed or eliminated so many of its descendants. That hypothesis increased the risks in her exploration efforts. And not only physical risks, but professional risks too. The scientists in Antarctica were not alone in their skepticism.

Bumpy turbulence broke her reverie. She indulged one last thought about Jeff and Kyle. They would competently wrap the mission. She believed that. Yet her anxiety would not go away. Pictures of the worst filled her mind. Would the samples survive? Were they properly documented? Would the weather hold?

Once the jet landed at the Michael Army Airfield at Dugway, she rode to the HQ building in a white late-model jeep. The crisp winter air felt balmy against her skin. A contingent of people in desert-camo Army fatigues and business suits greeted her.

The tallest among them extended his large hand. "Dr. Wallace," he beamed, "a pleasure."

Mira looked at his hand blankly but did not take it in hers; her arm was just too heavy. Besides, his friendliness was inadequate. He'd taken her from her work.

The man returned his arm to his side, his enthusiasm otherwise not visibly lessened. "Thank you very much for this. I'm Garrett Potteiger. Somebody apparently thought it was a good idea to put me in charge of this place." His attempt to lighten her mood failed. She avoided eyes as he offered introductions to the others circled around:

Col. Connie Yanoviak, Dr. Jerry Griffin, and Robert Harrison. "We have urgent need of your expertise. We'll get you briefed as soon as you're through the accelerated clearance protocol." Unsteady on her feet, she blinked and continued to avoid eyes. Potteiger's voice grew more empathetic. "I know you've had a long journey and you must be tired. We need you to understand how time-sensitive this matter is— we hope you can get started right away. Are you up to it?"

She wasn't. The trip she'd endured tired her. On top of the privations of Antarctica and not getting more than a few hours of sleep for—she didn't know how long—the word exhausted didn't suffice. Raw and sore, the skin of her face and extremities belied the tolls of the brumal weeks. She appeared skeletal. She didn't need a mirror to know it. "I guess."

The others shared glances around the semi-circle. Evidently, she was not what they expected. "I'm going to hand you over to my most trusted man." Rain stepped forward. "This is Command Sergeant Major Rain Somerdale. He will help you settle in here at Dugway."

She gave him no more acknowledgment than she had any of the other men.

"Ma'am, if you'll kindly follow me?" Rain gave her a friendly smile and took her backpack.

She'd had enough of soldiers and their orders. She shuffled along behind him, anyway. It was the only available path back to her work.

THEY ENTERED the building and found a kitchenette where Rain offered her coffee. As was her habit, she searched her memory for the scientific classification: *coffea*, a genus of flowering plants in the family *rubiaceae*; class *dicotyledonae*; sub-kingdom *angiospermae*. She sipped and recognized the brew as the common species *c. arabica*. She preferred other blends, but she was glad for it. Hoping to sleep, she'd refrained during the long journey. To be at all coherent, she needed the caffeine boost.

Rain explained the remaining clearance process as he made himself a cup. She sipped hers, which she always took black, and speculated about what it implied about him as Rain filled his mug half full of coffee, half full of cream, and stirred in four sugar packets.

She didn't, however, appreciate what she heard about what lay ahead of her, especially the bit with the psychologist. Mira looked at Rain, a silent plea in her eyes. Were his cheeks flushed? Did that mean he was sympathetic? She shook her head. It didn't matter whether he was or wasn't. This wasn't his call. Bureaucracy. She placed her earbuds in her ears and turned her music on its usual low volume.

Rain's voice gentled further. "I'm afraid you won't be able to wear those during this clearance process."

"It helps me concentrate. I'll do better with them."

"I'm sorry. I'm afraid it's not optional."

"Really? What difference does it make?"

Rain didn't respond, but kept his eyes locked on hers, insistent.

"There." She yanked them out in exasperation and stuffed them in a pocket. "Satisfied?"

"Thank you. Bring your coffee. We'll leave your backpack here."

The psychologist awaited them in a small conference room with no windows. His polygraph device occupied the center of the table, upon which was also a thick manila folder, a yellow legal notepad, and a gold pen. He greeted her with an extended finger toward the subject chair. "Please have a seat."

Resigned and silent, she collapsed into the chair perpendicular to the table and next to the polygraph. The rumple-suited psychologist indelicately placed a blood-pressure cuff on her left upper arm, wrapped two rubber tubes around her chest and abdomen, and placed two sensors on the index and ring fingers of her right hand.

Mira often felt an urge to pull away when someone touched her. That impulse was particularly strong with this man. Psychology. Barely a science; at least as practiced by most she'd encountered. She squirmed as he made the connections.

"This will be easier if you sit still."

Mira caught a whiff of the man's breath, acrid with tobacco smoke unsuccessfully covered by a green and white striped mint he slid from side to side in his mouth with his tongue.

"If you're going to work so close to people, you should use an activated mouthwash after your coffee and cigarettes." She said it the same way she'd state the time of day.

"Noted. Are you always so free with advice?" The man's motions were clinical and deliberate. The exchange didn't speed them.

Mira's scowl deepened at the sounds, close to her ears, of his slurps and the clicks as the mint struck his stained teeth. She faced away to escape. When he finished, he took his seat on the opposite side of the table. She examined the sensors on her fingers and the wires that tethered her to the device. "Polygraph tests are pseudoscience, you know."

The man remained detached. "The procedure is required to finalize your clearance whether you find it scientific or not. Now, I will ask you a wide variety of questions. Just respond truthfully, to the best of your knowledge. Let's begin."

Mira never lied. Not even white lies. This time was no different. He concluded the baseline questions and went on to cover allegiances, associations, personal tastes, professional milestones, and even her doctoral thesis. She bristled when he suggested she might be more successful if she didn't shun the spotlight. "What is that supposed to mean?" she challenged.

"You're recognized by your peers as one of the world's most accomplished microbiologists." He picked up her file and thumbed through the pages. "Says here, winner of the Selman A. Waksman Award, FEMS-Lwoff Award, several American Academy of Microbiology awards, and a two-time Nobel prize nominee. Such achievements open many doors. Says here you've rejected numerous invitations to speak publicly, to appear on prestigious broadcasts, and even turned down a lucrative book deal. If you accepted those kinds of opportunities, you'd be more well known."

"According to you, this is a problem?"

"I didn't say that." He wiped his brow, put the file down, and glanced at his notes. "Let's focus more on current events. You worked closely with Dr. Sergei Chulkov in Antarctica. Is this correct?"

"Not closely. We spent the first two days in Antarctica with him in Vostok as a part of our orientation. He was our host there."

The man read the output of the polygraph and scribbled another note. "You did not know him well?"

"No. He gave me good advice."

"Are you aware he is a person of interest?"

She scowled at the suggestion Sergei could be associated with espionage—and somehow this implied she might be involved in something of the sort. She wanted to rip off the sensors, bolt, and never see this man again. Instead she inhaled, long and slow. The polygraph's needles jumped around, but she neither knew nor cared what they might convey to him. "I know he's a respected and accomplished scientist. I believe he remains in Antarctica. He's an expert on working in that environment. That's all I know about him."

He again showed no reaction to the sharp tone of her response. "That is all I have for now." Mira again frowned as he rose, came to her side, and leaned over her to disconnect the sensors. He packed the polygraph and left without a further word.

Rain approached her. "I'm sorry ma'am, but we have a bit more to go. You doing okay?" She responded with an unenthusiastic nod. "Good, cause next we have a bunch of required paperwork."

Mira's head swam as she digested an alphabet soup of acronyms and signed countless papers. Eventually Rain put the stack of forms to one side. Her heart sank when the psychologist reentered the room, along with a fresh dose of smoke-smell. He explained he'd next conduct a thorough psychological evaluation.

He began by burying his head in her file. "Let's go back to your reluctance to appear publicly. People around you describe you as a loner. Why do you think they say that?"

"It's their opinion." She'd heard this before. Noise. "I spend the bulk of my time either on expedition or in the lab. Some people think it's strange, but I don't believe the assessment is accurate."

"Your colleagues report you don't share information about your personal life. Why is that?"

"What is it I'm supposed to share?"

"Relationships, for instance?"

"They usually know who I know."

"You don't like to talk about your past, your experiences?" The man's manner remained the same no matter what direction the conversation took—detached and unexpressive.

"I share what's relevant."

"They don't mean that, and neither do I."

"What do you mean, then?"

The man ignored her question as he jotted a note and continued to thumb through her file. "It says here when you were seven years old, your parents were killed in a small plane crash in northern Thailand."

"I was almost eight."

"Yes, well, those of your colleagues who were interviewed, every single one of them, didn't know about it. That doesn't strike you as odd?"

"Why? That happened almost forty years ago."

"Still, an experience like that weighs on people. People process grief in conversation with others."

"It surprises you I don't talk about my parents' deaths? You must not be very good at your job."

If he had a reaction to her slight, he didn't show it; his tone and pace did not seem to change no matter what. "They were scientists, like you. They died on an expedition. It doesn't strike you as notable you now do the same?"

"I come from a long line of explorers. I suppose that is unusual."

"Yes, it is. Let's move on. You were subsequently raised by your grandmother. Tell me about that."

"What do you want to know?"

"What was your relationship like?"

Mira took some time as she struggled to form an answer. She looked at Rain, who sat still, impassive.

"Well?"

"I don't know. She packed me a lunch and made me dinner. Sometimes I liked what she gave me, sometimes I didn't."

"That's it? No personal memories? Did she ever read you stories? Teach you things?"

"I made my own breakfasts—well, if you consider pouring bowls of Honey Nut Chex making breakfast."

"She didn't take you places?"

Mira ruminated for another short while. "The zoo. I always wanted to go to zoos. I didn't care which ones; they were all interesting. I'd have gone every day if I could have. Sometimes she took me."

"Sounds like you may have had some pleasant memories."

"She could never keep up. I'd leave her on a bench so I could observe more animal behaviors." She reflected again. "She gave me a gift once. I still have it. She surprised me when she did that; she never gave me presents. It was okay. I never wanted toys, clothes or such, anyway. I wanted a microscope, a real one. She didn't think it was a good idea. I did get one eventually—from my science teacher. Gramma wasn't mean to me, but she didn't like the time I spent in the woods. She wasn't obliged to go out of her way to give me gifts." Mira paused yet again. She hadn't considered this time of her life in a long while. The memories were accompanied by surprising emotions. "But that one was—well, I really liked it. The occasion was my graduation from UPenn, where I earned my doctorate in microbiology. She died not long afterwards." Loss and regret spiked. Also, gratitude. Her emotion showed in the welling in her eyes—not enough to result in tears; but enough to make them glisten.

"What did she give you?" The pitch of his voice inflected higher, the first sign of any interest whatever. Rain leaned closer too.

"She gave me this." She extended her arm to reveal her charm bracelet.

The psychologist regarded it with a slight frown. He glanced at Rain, who had the opposite reaction. He pressed on. He listed complaints about Mira, some from students, some from fellow professors. "How do you feel when you hear feedback like that?"

She could guess the sources. They shared one common trait—they weren't passionate about microbiology. Consequently, she cared not at all about their opinion of her and said so. The conversation reminded her of exchanges with Marcel. "Are we about finished?"

"Almost. Are you aware people with profiles such as yours, who lack what might be considered close friendships and the people around them regard them as hard to get to know, are often diagnosed as sociopathic?"

Mira snapped to Rain. "That's it. I'm done with this." Her cheeks flushed red and her voice wavered. "You people bring me here to help, at a most inconvenient time to say the least, and I'm subject to interrogation and insult?" She pulled her earbuds out of her pocket, put them in, and turned on her playlist.

Rain stepped toward the psychologist. "Dr. Wallace has a point. I believe you've been plenty thorough. It's time to wrap this up."

The man sighed. "Fine. Time for a smoke, anyway." He took the file and notepad and left without another word.

When he shut the door, Rain shrugged. "We're almost done, ma'am."

"You've got to be kidding me. What more could there be?"

"It's an orientation video required of those who will be doing work in the laboratory facilities at the West Desert Test Center."

"How about we skip that? There is no need for me to do any laboratory work at the West Desert Test Center."

Rain's demeanor hardened. "You don't yet know what this is all about; I get your reluctance. But you need to understand right now. This is serious. The scientists here believe you can contribute. I know this has been difficult; I know you're exhausted. But frankly, ma'am, they're going to put you to work. And you're going to agree to do it."

She met his eyes. Though his jaw was set, perhaps in anger, something else flickered in his eyes. After a tense moment, Mira muttered, "Just get on with it."

"Tell you what. You can leave your earphones in." Rain played the video and walked to the doorway. He looked back at Mira who now concentrated on the program. "I'll be back in half an hour." He left the room.

Mira speculated this video, which outlined safety requirements and procedures, was intentionally as dull as humanly possible. She rubbed her eyes as it ended.

Shortly thereafter, Rain came back. "Thank you, Dr. Wallace. The hope was you'd be able to join the scientific team for a situation report at this point. We call it a SITREP; I'll do my best to not talk in acronyms." He handed her a lanyard with her new credentials. "I'm guessing you'd prefer a shower and some sleep. Am I right?"

"Yes."

"My orders are not to discuss any details with you until after you've met with the scientific team. But I'll give you an overview on the drive over to your quarters. Fair?"

"Fair." She added softly, "thank you." Other than from her postdoc Jeff, maybe a word here or there from Kyle, this was the first genuine kindness anyone had shown her in months.

A DRIVE

Mira lacked the energy to undress and collapsed on the bed in the clothes she'd worn for two days. She slept, unstirring, for ten hours. She still rose before the sun. She left her wrinkled clothes in a pile and noticed an outfit laid out on the dresser for her—a solid pale green blouse and a pair of black tattersall slacks. Her wardrobe included items of only four colors—black, brown, gray, or beige. She owned no dresses or skirts. Her slacks and shirts featured no patterns. These clothes weren't what she'd buy herself, but at least the color was sufficiently subdued so that it wouldn't distract her.

The heat of the shower penetrated her pores. She closed her eyes and tipped her head back as the steam cleansed weeks of crud from her skin and cold from her bones. She towel-dried her hair and ignored the streaks of gray that grew more prominent with each of her expeditions. She never considered getting it colored and never used a stylist. She simply cut off the end of her ponytail whenever it got in her way. She supposed that time had come as she pulled back the chestnut strands and looked in the mirror. Antarctica had further weathered the tanned, freckled skin of her face. Her eyes were still bloodshot and a bit puffy, the skin along her cheek bones, tips of her nose and ears still angry from the onset of frostbite. She rubbed her sore thin lips and wished not for lipstick, but Chapstick.

She had always been thin. She frowned as she looked positively skeletal now, more concerned with her health than her appearance. She shivered and pulled the clothes on as fast as she could. They fit well, or would have at her normal 115 lbs. She made her way down the creaky carpeted stairs. The small townhouse was built economically; cookie cutter and unimaginative. Stark, it was at least clean and comfortable. She noticed a box of cereal and a bowl on the little table in the kitchenette, a handwritten note beside them:

Dr. Wallace—I heard you mention your craving for Honey Nut Chex yesterday. I took the liberty of getting you a box. Milk's in the fridge. I hope 2% is okay. I'll be by at 0700 to bring you to the facilities.

P.S.—I also hope the clothes are to your liking. We'll make sure to get you properly supplied for your stay with us. Again, welcome —R.S.

Mira grinned. The cereal, the clothes—this kind of attentiveness towards her personal needs felt unnatural. Did he want something from her?

She poured herself a bowl and enjoyed crunching as much as she had the shower. Her strength returned with each swallow. The simple act of eating her morning childhood favorite soothed her. She rose and explored the townhouse. She stopped, shifted her weight to her right leg as she brushed her foot along the carpet. The plushness of the pile against the sole of her foot and toes comforted her. Carpet. Softness. Warmth. No other detail about the place caught her interest, and her thoughts gravitated to Jeff in Antarctica. No carpet there. Nothing but MREs to eat, too. Had the weather relented for the evacuation? She willed it were so.

She examined the handwriting on Rain's note. Neat. Legible. An organized mind. Someone who paid attention to detail. His sketchy summary of what lay in front of her raised interesting questions. He mentioned a deadly outbreak. He couldn't say what it was, where it came from, what it did, who was affected, or what they hoped she might be able to do to help. Whatever the cause, she knew it had to be extraordinary for them to bring her here like this.

Rain knocked at 0700 sharp. Mira collected her belongings into her backpack. She looked for her phone to start the day's playlist. She searched her pack. It wasn't there. She cracked the door and continued her search with increasing urgency.

Rain noticed. "What's wrong, Dr. Wallace?"

"I can't find my phone."

"I'm sorry. I told you yesterday I had to hold on to it until you were cleared and briefed." Rain shrugged. "It's at HQ. I'll make sure you get it back this morning."

Mira sighed in relief, but also flushed, peeved. She remembered no talk about her phone. "Please do. I'd like to get an update from my team. Plus, it has my music."

"You said it helps you concentrate. Tell me more."

"Without it, it's hard for me to filter out certain kinds of stimuli. It gets tiring."

"Hmm. And that works, huh?"

"Yes. I don't put it on loud, just enough to occupy a particular part of my brain. People sometimes don't like me doing it, though. Like you didn't yesterday."

"It was protocol, that's all." He grabbed the door handle. "Ready to go?"

She nodded. He guided her to his jeep where he opened the door for her.

The drive from the English Village to the West Desert Test Center HQ in Dugway's Ditto Area was nine miles.

"*Atriplex confertifolia.*"

"What did you say?"

"Sorry, bad habit. People tell me it annoys them."

"What annoys them?"

"When I classify living things. Sometimes I blurt it out without thinking."

"That's not what I'd call annoying."

"We'll see if you still see it that way once you've been around me a while."

He grinned in response as they drove another mile. Mira took in more of the scenery. Though desert, the landscape looked lush in contrast to barren Antarctica. She classified more plant species but did so in silence.

"What was it you said?"

"The plant I saw? There's another one right there." She pointed. "You'd know it as shadscale: family *amaranthaceae,* order *caryophyllales.*"

"Okay, I can see how that could be annoying."

"Oh." Her chin dropped.

Rain glanced sidelong at her. "I'm kidding." He grinned.

"Oh. Yeah, I'm not good at that."

"No? Good. Maybe there's something you could learn from me. I had thought that might be impossible." He seemed to await a response, but she offered none. "So, I suppose you're familiar with the region if you know the plants around here."

"I am. I've conducted surveys not far from here."

Even she could hear good nature in his voice. "So, tell me this. Why do all the plants around here have thorns, spikes, or needles?"

Mira ignored the joke and answered in earnest. "In harsh environments, life-forms need every edge they can get."

If Rain felt disappointed at her answer, he didn't let on. "Iron sharpens iron."

"What?"

"Never mind."

They approached the Ditto area. "That was kind of you—the clothes, the Chex."

"My pleasure."

She noticed the taijitu on his left triceps and the Cross on his right. "Are you Buddhist, Christian, or confused?"

Rain's brows raised, puzzled.

"Your tattoos."

"Oh. Yeah." He let out a little chuckle.

"Well?"

"I'm Christian." He pulled a small gold cross out from his

undershirt, flashed it, and tucked it back. "The tattoos are old. But that doesn't mean I don't think Chinese wisdom is valuable."

"How so?"

"Good question. I'm still trying to figure it out." He became pensive. "What happened the other day. It makes you think—tests your belief."

"Belief." Mira's tone was dismissive.

"You're not a believer?"

"I believe in reality. That's what I believe."

"Reality, huh?" They arrived at the West Desert HQ building and Rain parked by the front door. "What you're about to learn is gonna impact your view of reality."

A NEW TEAM

Mira followed Rain upstairs, down a well-lit hall and into another conference room, three times as spacious as the room of her previous day's ordeal. The austere space included multimedia equipment for in-house briefings and teleconferencing. Through three big windows, the room offered a view of the airfield and mountains beyond. Harrison, Xi Shu, and the two Edgewood scientists sat at the table.

Harrison said, "Welcome. I prefer to wait until the others arrive before we discuss the hazard." Light conversation stumbled along, sporadic and stilted. Harrison asked Mira about her work and her journey; her answers were short and non-specific. At 0800 Potteiger finally arrived with a contingent of attendees from Rain's review meeting. The representatives from DTRA and ATEC were absent. Quon entered last. He spotted Mira and hurried to take her hand in both of his.

"I am so very delighted to see you again, Dr. Wallace. I apologize for allowing so much time to go by without reaching out to you. As you may be aware, I have been rather busy."

Mira's eyes widened as she fought the urge to pull her hand away. Sure, she knew him. And she had indeed worked with him—briefly—prior to his notoriety. She'd reviewed some of his scientific publications—content, by the way, that she criticized not because of its conclusions, but its methods and Quon's liberal appropriation of the ideas of others without sufficient citation. The way he acted, the others might assume she'd been his close colleague for years.

"You're not like I remember." His manner and meticulous style were not what they were back then. Always bright and ambitious but also self-conscious and awkward, he was not someone you might consider stylish. Now he was a different person, and not like any scientist she had ever worked with, for that matter. She rarely watched television, but she had seen enough in passing to form the impression he seemed better suited for the camera than the lab.

"I hope that is a compliment." Along with perfect teeth, Quon's smile revealed that he believed it was. "I am very much looking forward to working with you again."

"I'm looking forward to finding out what's going on around here."

Quon beamed. "That this question is difficult to answer is specifically why you are here. We require someone with specialized knowledge. You came instantly to my mind."

"Thank you, I suppose." Her tone had an accusatory edge. "I'd like to know why you believe I am the one person who can help."

"For one, Dr. Quon claims you're uniquely qualified." The handsome older man extended his hand. "Colonel Constantine Yanoviak. Call me Connie."

She took his hand in a brief, warm shake. She rubbed her hands together afterward, unsettled by all of this hand-shaking. Thankfully, the people in her circle had fallen away from that social convention. She knew it wasn't universal. What was this obsession people had with touching one another?

"Have a seat, everyone." Potteiger's manner was graver than when Mira met him. He took the chair at the table's head. "Let's get to it—the clock is ticking. During a recent field test, we lost a good man. Calling what happened to him tragic is an understatement. An abomination is what it was. We don't know much about the contaminant other than it's spreading and standard protocols for remediation are not working. It's on us to make sure what happened to him doesn't happen to anybody else, people." His eyes found Harrison. "Bob?"

The only part of Harrison that moved was his mouth. "The substance appeared in the desert, within the perimeter of the Proving Ground. A soldier came into physical contact with it. That contact catalyzed a violent reaction, first with his fatigues and boot. The reaction ate through those materials, then did the same to his epidermis, causing express necrosis in the subcutaneous tissues and penetrated to fibrous and calcified skeletal structures."

Mira interrupted. "You're saying this agent reacted with his clothes and ate through flesh and bone, like some kind of acid?"

Harrison mumbled a response as Connie interrupted. "I'd say it like this: the substance appears to break down organic material, whether it is living or not. It ate through the victim's boot and worked its way into the tissues of his foot and leg in a matter of seconds. The man's flesh, and even his combat fatigues, were all but dissolved. Before he could be evacuated, there were no remains left to work on —not a trace that could be used to identify him or send to his family for burial."

"I've seen some awful stuff in combat." Rain swallowed. "Been through some nightmares. But not like this. No weapon—chemical, biological, or anything else I could imagine—could produce those effects. Worst experience of my life."

Rain's reaction Mira could understand. The rustle of papers on one end of the table, the squeak of a chair on the other side, and multiple intakes of breath by people on both sides momentarily distracted her. "You've brought me here to help. But what you describe is in fact outside of my expertise. Microbes can't do that, and I'm not a chemist."

"Yes, Dr. Wallace." Quon's smile contrasted the grim mood of the others. "That was my initial reaction as well. The team has conducted preliminary tests. The results are inconclusive. This is troubling. And intriguing."

Mira needed a lot more information before she'd be able to offer anything useful. "What experiments have you run?"

"We attempted a chemical analysis using mass spectroscopy." Harrison's voice cracked. "The sample compromised the input stage before we initiated the ionization."

"Compromised?" Mira's confusion rose. "What do you mean?"

"It appears there was some reaction with the matrix material. This damaged the input stage."

An Edgewood scientist offered another hypothesis. "Maybe that's the same reason our attempts at electrophoresis fail?"

Mira's mind churned as she processed. "It doesn't sound biological. I'm not sure I can be of any help with this."

"I believe you can." Quon's smile widened. "After all, this is a billion-dollar question."

"Clearly, I'm missing something." Mira's fingers tightened.

Quon leaned toward her. "The question of whether this substance is biological."

"How could that be so difficult to answer?"

Xi Shu's manner was, as usual, soft-spoken, almost timid. "The polyacrylamide gel lost integrity when the sample was loaded. This happened whether we used SDS or urea denaturing conditions. We also tried microfluidic protein separation using non-polymerized acrylamide. This also failed. We can merely speculate the agent reacts with the acrylamide itself."

Xi's suggestion captured Mira's imagination. "How could that happen?"

"We do not yet know." Xi offered Mira a small smile, but it did not register.

"This substance appeared in the ground?" Though dismayed by the lack of information, Mira perked at the prospect of a new mystery. She wanted to know the answers to the many questions that popped into her head. "I'd like to inspect the site."

Potteiger interjected. "I'm afraid I can't authorize that. It's not safe."

Mira didn't expect this response. Before she could object, Quon beat her to the punch. "Of course, Dr. Wallace will need to examine the site. We shall need to conduct tests of a wide variety. This will include biological and chemical inquiries as well as seismic, infrared, and other geological means of subterranean surveyance. Our progress will be all the more effective if we are not met with resistance at each request."

"Sooner is better." Mira glanced at Quon. "I don't know anything about seismology or the other disciplines you mentioned. But I want to observe the exact conditions under which the incident occurred; collect samples of the surrounding environment for analysis. From what you've said so far, we should be able to rule out a biological cause." And she wouldn't have to be here any longer. She made a mental note to ask Rain to get her phone back as soon as the meeting concluded.

"I understand this is inconvenient." Potteiger remained stoic. "But procedural protocol is established for a reason. The guidelines are there for the protection of personnel and property and have been considered. They can't just be capriciously changed. Our first priority is the restriction of exposure for civilians."

"Colonel, under normal conditions you'd be right," said Connie. "But Dr. Quon makes a valid point. This will be an extensive operation. We'll have a lot of civilians involved. There's no avoiding it."

"Yes. I must emphasize the importance of allowing the scientific inquiry to go where it must." Quon puffed himself up and spoke as someone accustomed to authority. "It will not be without risk. We will generate numerous requests during this investigation. Some may strike you as unusual or against protocol. If we are to get the answers we require, I humbly request we not be impeded."

Potteiger looked at Quon with brows raised in suspicion. He turned to Rain, who shrugged. "I will escort her, sir. I will be responsible for her safety. Okay?"

Potteiger considered for an extended moment. He faced Mira.

"Very well, Dr. Wallace. But do me a favor. Do exactly as you're told."

"Isn't that what I've been doing?"

"Yes," Rain interjected. "But some do that better than others." He glanced at Quon.

EXCERPT:
THE NECESSITY OF PRECURSOR COOPERATIVES

Wallace, M. D.[1,2] and Weingartner, J. A.[1]

1University of California, Berkeley, Dept. of Plant and Microbial Biology, 311 Koshland Hall, Berkeley CA, 94720.

2National Interagency Biodefense Campus, Fort Detrick, MD 21702

Section #1: Cooperatives, cont.

The original alliance between Cytosine and A-C-C folded quickly. What sprung in its place were more sophisticated symbiotic relationships, each one brought about by a series of unlikely events. Ever more complex molecules were produced and devoured, the survivors being just a bit more capable than their predecessors. On and on, without end, this constant change continued to be a necessary and inherent property.

At this point it is not accurate to describe it as a thing in itself, but rather a loose collection of chemicals. To become a describable singular entity, it had to grow beyond its dependence on chance events. It needed to move away from spontaneous chemical reactions, harness those most beneficial, and then improve upon them. It needed to become self-sustaining and adaptable. And it needed to store new information.

In other words, it needed the ability to evolve. Absent that, its progress would have been derailed, as had happened elsewhere innumerable times before. Against incalculable odds, it came to be at this one time, in this one place. And nothing would ever be the same.

A CRUEL EXPERIMENT

They assembled in a designated prep area near the Life Sciences Facility. "I still don't like it," Potteiger exclaimed to nobody in particular. "She's not trained for this."

"Thank you for your concern, Colonel." Mira made no attempt to disguise how little she meant it. "I've heard that before."

"Yes, well. Whatever you've done before—you haven't had the necessary biohazard training." His objection lost conviction as his voice softened.

"You've brought me here as a scientist. I need to observe."

Potteiger's brow wrinkled, but he relented. "Just make sure you do as the Sergeant Major instructs."

"Don't worry. I know how to follow procedure."

She and Rain climbed into a desert-camouflaged jeep. Suspension worn, the vehicle lurched and bounced as they made their way over rough terrain to the site, about a mile and a half west of the Ditto Area. "I hope you didn't take all that the wrong way. The Commander didn't mean anything."

"It's not the first time."

"He just wanted to ensure your safety."

"I know."

"Good." Rain paused. "I want you to be safe too."

They rode in silence for the rest of the drive. Rain stopped the jeep a quarter mile out. "Time to suit up. You won't be able to wear your headphones."

She frowned but stuffed them into her pocket. Mira had spent significant time in the BSL-3 labs at Berkeley. But she had never worn a hazmat suit like this before. She tried to relax as Rain taped her socks to her scrubs and her inner latex gloves to her sleeves. His touch unnerved her, as any such procedure might. Yet the urge to recoil wasn't so pronounced. Strong, rough hands. But gentle. He helped her into the bulky air tank harness and outer suit. Finally, he helped slide on her outer boots and gloves.

"They claimed the substance ate through a man's boots and pants. How are these suits going to protect us?"

"You're the first person to ask me that." Rain placed her intercom headset, fixed her air supply mask in place, and tucked a towel into the top strap. "The fiber is not organic. It's made from silica—asbestos. It's been tested, and it doesn't react."

"Asbestos? So now I should worry about lung cancer?"

If Rain knew she joked, his answer didn't show it. "It's a non-particulate fiber."

"I'm holding my breath, anyway." Mira's attempt at humor revealed her lack of practice.

"Oh, we're joking now. I wasn't informed."

"What's the towel for?"

"To wipe the inside of your visor."

He connected the headset to the two-way radio and the air supply hose to the front of her mask and fastened her hood. "Good?" She nodded approval. Rain next attended his own preparation.

So suited, standing in the desert, she daydreamed about Antarctica and the status of her samples. Jeff's competence consoled her. He'd get them back to Berkeley intact. Though she'd left a mere two days prior, she missed not just the work, but the team. Even Kyle's cusses. Even Marcel's complaints. She hoped everyone was okay, that nobody lost any more fingers or toes to the cold. But she also reckoned if the object of her search turned up there, it was a price well worth paying.

"Ground Control to Wallace. Ready?"

She snapped out of her reverie. They drove the remainder of the distance to the site.

She pictured the kind of tent used for shelter on her surveys. This one was more on the scale of those used in an old-fashioned traveling circus. Seven figures, clad in the same suits she and Rain wore, busied themselves. Two of them expanded an outer perimeter as they unwound more yellow caution tape and pounded metal stakes into the hard ground. The echoes of their hammer blows reverberated around them. Others examined computers and less familiar equipment on folding tables ten meters from the tent.

Rain greeted one of them. He was the tall, thin, graying man whom Mira had met when she had first arrived. She remembered neither his name nor his position. The man's mask fogged around the edges.

"How's it going, Jerry?" Rain placed a gloved hand on the man's shoulder.

"Not good. There's more of it. We can't figure out where it's coming from. Not much room left in there."

Rain's eyes met Mira's. His held alarm; hers, scientific dispassion. The substance spreads? "I'd like to look inside."

"Excuse me, Jerry; you met Dr. Mira Wallace yesterday." Rain turned to Mira. "There were so many people you've had to meet in such a short time. I want to make sure you get to know Dr. Jerry Griffin. He's our Technical Director here at DPG."

"I looked over a couple of your scientific publications since I learned you'd be joining us, Dr. Wallace." Jerry didn't extend his hand. "Intriguing work you do."

"Thank you." Mira's eyes remained on the tent. Where most people might see fabric and a zipper, she saw access to information. "May I?"

"We have monitors for that purpose right over here." Jerry pointed in the direction of the technicians who busily wired and calibrated the equipment.

"I'd prefer to see for myself."

Jerry looked at Rain, who head-tilted approval. "Be my guest." Jerry stepped aside. Rain opened the outer door, and they stepped into the modest portico that granted access to the airtight inner-layer. Rain zipped shut the outer door and opened the access flap.

"Don't go in," Rain commanded. "Just look."

Mira nodded and stuck her head into the aperture. The sight struck her as anti-climactic. She hadn't known what to expect, but she thought it would be scarier. More sinister. Instead, there wasn't much to look at. Caged utility lamps hung from the ceiling at points along the tent's lateral support struts. They cast harsh light to reveal a near featureless floor of dark gray. She noted the perimeter retained some semblance of the surrounding desert, with rocks of various sorts and sizes, but no vegetation. Her eyes scanned the surface as she looked for some detail that might give her something. Nope. Maybe its texture held a clue? She fought the urge to bend and put her hand in it.

She leaned back out. Rain took a turn, but his head came out almost as fast as it had gone in. He resealed the inner layer and the two of them exited the tent.

"What are you doing to the atmosphere in there?" Mira asked.

"We're replacing it with pure nitrogen."

"Why nitrogen? Have you tested other gases?" She was there as a biologist. If this entity was biological, surely any number of chemicals would devitalize it.

"No. The working theory is nitrogen may deprive it of reactants and stop or at least slow its spread."

"Is it working?"

"I don't think so." Jerry shot a tense glance at Rain.

"Chlorine gas might be better." Mira saw Rain's worried expression, maybe in response to her suggestion. "Chlorine destroys cellular membranes and kills microbes. If this agent is biological, that should reverse the spread."

"Despite what Dr. Quon has already concluded, we don't know

that yet. We do know it isn't cellular. Chlorine gas could make the situation worse."

"How?"

"It introduces another hazard to people and wildlife."

"Whatever we're going to do, we better do it quick," said Rain. "The contaminated area was a lot smaller the other day. If it keeps going like this, we won't be able to contain it, no matter what we pump into the tent."

Mira felt a shiver. She couldn't deny—this situation was scary. What was this substance's nature? "I want to feel it in my hands. It looks granular, like fine dust."

"It isn't," said Jerry. "It looks like that, but it isn't crystalline."

"Could I take a small sample back to the lab?"

"We have plenty of samples in process already. We'll be able to provide you with what you need for whatever studies you have in mind."

Mira considered what those experiments should be. How could this agent be so reactive? Lost in thought, she failed to notice the approach of a three-truck caravan that rolled to a stop not far away. A group of isolation-suited people emerged.

The loud squeal of a small pig broke Mira's concentration. One of the new arrivals lifted a small cage out of the back of one of the trucks and carried it toward them. She realized what they had in mind. Revulsion spasmed in her gut. "*Sus scrofa domesticus*," she whispered. Her brow furrowed and her lips tightened. Judging by what she'd heard about the effects of this agent, what they were about to do was beyond cruel.

Rain stepped close. "You okay? We don't have to watch."

"Is this why Potteiger didn't want me out here?"

"Of course not." Rain noticed as she stared at the mountains. "What is it?"

"I was just thinking—why not start with a rhododendron?"

"That's what they did. Or something like it, anyway. They've tested plants and rodents. More such tests are being set up in containment. So far, the same effects happen every time. But they said this test will tell them more about exposure specifically on humans. Pigs are the best model for that. Apart from chimps."

"Yes, that's true." She flashed back to a particular zoo visit, this one to the National Zoo in Washington, D.C. She sat on the window ledges in the primate pavilion for hours, fascinated with the behavior of the chimps, orangutans, and especially the gorillas, while fellow visitors crowded around to get glimpses themselves. The similarities between the animals in the cages and the people who jockeyed for a better position formed an indelible impression.

"We don't have to stay."

"In my work, there's no need for animal testing. I recognize it's sometimes necessary." She steeled herself. "I came out here to observe. That's what I intend to do."

Rain pointed. "We'll observe on the closed-circuit monitors."

They joined the others at the control station. Rain leaned close to speak with one of the new arrivals, Robert Harrison. Jerry joined them. Mira heard him say, "How do we know this pig won't go berserk and compromise our tent?"

"That's not going to happen," said Rain.

They huddled around the control station. Among the instruments that displayed the vitals of the piglet and atmospheric readings within the tent, three rugged laptops displayed video feeds from various angles.

Two of the team flanked the man who held the piglet. They took measurements, skin and hair samples, and conducted a final check on sensor integrity. The animal calmed and oinked in earnest, perhaps in expectation of a treat. The animal nuzzled the crook in its handler's elbow. When the technicians finished, one of them opened the access flap. He nodded to the handler who looked to Harrison, who signaled the go-ahead with a wave of his hand. The piglet quieted, resigned. Its handler entered with the piglet and exited without it.

All eyes went to the monitors. The piglet wandered around the perimeter for a short while and oinked in curiosity. It wandered deeper into the interior and froze, long enough for Mira to entertain a passing thought: maybe this whole issue has been overblown. The piglet's squeal shattered that notion.

The plea grew louder and louder; more and more panicked. The observers all leaned away in revulsion. Mira was no exception; her stomach turned strong enough for her to picture how unpleasant it'd be if she vomited inside her suit. Yet her eyes remained fixed on the monitors. The necrosis initiated on the poor animal's hooves and legs. It worked up to its side, nose, ears, and eyes. The process appeared akin to stop-motion photography of withering leaves, sped to an impossible rate. The piglet tried to escape, but its legs failed and it fell. Though it thrashed back and forth, it could no longer move. The squeals changed in character as the animal's tongue and snout crumbled away. Its innards became visible and were similarly consumed. The sound became dull, weak, but more besought.

Mira couldn't resist the impulse to look away. She quelled the revulsion by noting the readings on the monitoring equipment. The body temperature of the animal spiked as its heart rate first raced but then slowed. After two merciless minutes and a last whimper, the vitals indicated the animal's death. A kindness. "Unbelievable," Mira whispered. She glanced at Rain, who appeared to have his head bowed, maybe in prayer. If so, she understood.

The experiment wasn't over. Mira noted while soft tissues were absorbed or transformed faster than skin, sinew, hair, and bone, the non-cellular protein structures were attacked, nevertheless. After what seemed both an instant and an eternity, the body cavity collapsed and the last signs the pitiable piglet had ever been in that deadly place disappeared. The surface was left as undisturbed—flat and featureless—as before the test. A thin wire from one of the sensors attached to the piglet, the sole remnant of the experiment, protruded a few centimeters above the surface.

The observers had all fallen silent. One of them made a remark, Mira presumed a scientific observation. Others voiced questions and postulates about what they'd witnessed. Hushed and somber, they all tried to maintain scientific dispassion.

Jerry stepped closer to Mira. "Dr. Wallace, I'd be interested in your impressions."

"I...I don't know what to think." Her experience didn't help her. Through the fog of horror, she grasped for answers. Answers? She didn't even know the right questions.

A SITREP

Mira hadn't experienced a decontamination procedure so thorough. She and Rain, along with other observers of the experiment, went through a chemical rinse in a portable station near the contaminated site. They repeated the protocol upon their return to the LSF Annex. Mira emerged from the ordeal and couldn't imagine a microbe alive anywhere on her person. She winced. The vast majority of microbes were not harmful—quite the opposite. It was a fact too often overlooked by the scientific and medical community.

Throughout the entire procedure, her mind raced. She had no ideas about the metabolic nightmare she'd witnessed. Though she had perhaps observed more microbes in their habitats than anyone else in the world, the effects of this substance reminded her of nothing else. She could offer little help here.

Rain waited as she emerged from the women's locker room. She avoided his eyes. "I appreciate the situation you're facing here. I'm honored people believe I can help. But the truth is there are plenty of other researchers better suited for this work than me."

"What are you saying?" Rain leaned forward to catch her eyes.

"This case requires knowledge outside of my expertise. As soon as feasible, I want to go back to Berkeley. I need to get back to my own research. The samples we collected at Lake Ellsworth will arrive there soon. I need to supervise the sequencing runs. They may provide important information. Very important."

Rain's demeanor shifted. He was a stern drill sergeant. "You want to leave? After what you just saw?"

"As soon as can be arranged."

Rain stepped closer and pushed his face six inches from hers. "I want you to picture what that poor animal went through." He didn't shout. But if he had, it would have felt the same. She finally looked him square in the eyes. "Picture it good and clear. You got me?"

She didn't want to. She resisted. But when someone commands you not to picture a pink elephant, the request alone breeds compliance.

"Now change your picture. It's not a pig, it's a person. Can you picture that?"

Her face paled as she nodded.

"I don't have to imagine it. I saw it for real. Now I want you to picture that happening to everybody you've met here. Imagine it happening to me."

Mira's lip quivered, and she blinked repeatedly, but remained locked on his eyes.

"You get the picture?" Mira nodded her response. Rain's tone softened, but not the force of his words or the passion behind them. "Don't stop there. If we don't get a handle on this situation, it could spread unabated. Everybody you know; everybody you've ever met, even you, could meet the same fate. We're talking about protecting everybody and everything. None of us have any choice."

"*Atriplex confertifolia.*" The words of her nervous reaction caught in her throat.

Rain placed a hand on her shoulder. The drill sergeant disappeared. "It's all right, Mira. I'm scared too."

Eventually she raised her head and cautiously met his gaze. She saw a tough soldier who looked every bit the part—hard, scarred, with a salt and pepper military haircut. Kind eyes, though. "Can I at least have my phone back?"

He smiled. "As soon as can be arranged, ma'am." He playfully chided, "Come on; now you've made us late."

Mira rode with Rain to the Ditto Area and to the West Desert Test Center HQ building, where he escorted her to a large meeting room. Quon flanked a projection screen on the far end of the room, animated as he addressed the attendees. These included a cadre of scientists, some of whom Mira had seen earlier and some newly arrived.

Quon acknowledged Mira with a quick head bob as she and Rain took two of the few remaining open seats, "Please be advised, SONA is extremely dangerous, but also represents a deep mystery."

"SONA?" blurted one of the scientists, a short middle-aged man with a close beard, bushy eyebrows, and no other hair on his head.

"My apologies. It is the acronym I use to describe the organism— Sudden Onset Necrobiosis Agent. As I was about to say, this agent, SONA, is dangerous in the extreme. It has unusual, possibly unique, qualities. It appears to aggressively attack the cellular structure of any organism. My hypothesis is that by some means it catabolizes carbon from organic material on contact."

Mira's mind worked. Quon's hypothesis left much to be desired: vague description, free-wheeled assumptions. Still, she had to admit she had no better ideas to offer. What specifically had he seen to lead him to this conclusion?

The bald scientist, his defiance still evident, retorted, "Are we expected to believe this SONA simply appeared spontaneously on an Army base known to experiment with the world's most dangerous pathogens?"

Thank you, thought Mira. Someone had to ask the obvious.

"What we know is, sadly, small in comparison to what we do not." A pant-suited black woman with a Virginia-lilt hurried into the room trailing two aides. She joined Quon at the front of the room as her aides stood against the side wall. The woman's hair was pulled back and slightly askew, gray streaks evident among the tight curls. Mira suspected the woman was more about her work than her look.

Good. Her kind of woman. The woman's words were forceful. She expected others to listen. "I realize the circumstances strain belief. Let me clarify for you. The U.S. Army has not worked with weaponized pathogens at Dugway for decades. As you will see, this agent appears to be entirely new to science. Homeland Security assets will continue to pursue this investigation, but in our initial assessment this is unlikely to be manmade."

Quon spoke as though he too had doubts. "Yours is an important question." He looked to the woman at his side. "Dr. Dixon is too humble to emphasize as much, but she is—what? The Deputy Director? At the Department of Homeland Security. She and senior officials of the U.S. Army assure me they have no previous knowledge of this agent whatsoever. Based upon what I have observed thus far, I believe them. The circumstance of its discovery on a military base that happens to work with biological and chemical agents is perhaps a suspicious coincidence. The causes behind it, I suspect, have to do with other factors, probably environmental, such as the salinity of the soil."

This assuaged, at least a little, the objecting scientist and the handful of others who shared his attitude. It had the opposite effect on Mira.

Deputy Secretary Eleanor Dixon's smile had a warm Southern quality. "We must proceed together as a team. We need to operate on a basis of trust. If this was some kind of weapon that got out of hand, or some accident that would further explain its appearance, I assure you I would share that information with you. But that isn't the case." Her smile vanished. "This agent poses a serious danger. It's imperative we develop a way to mitigate it. Dr. Quon, excuse my interruption. Please, continue."

"Of course. May I have the next slide please?"

The slide advanced as Eleanor took a seat next to Quon.

"The properties of SONA complicate research procedures. Sample collection is hazardous and the substance itself is not amenable to many conventional test and measurement techniques.

We have not been able to classify it into any previously known chemical or biological category. As indicated, we do not know its source. Yet through great courage and personal risk, the scientists at Dugway have generated some important, albeit perplexing, data."

The image stimulated and confused Mira with its odd microscopic structure. She'd not seen the like before—notable for someone who has spent a lifetime studying such images. Some elements struck her as familiar—spirals are ubiquitous. But this was unlike those. Mira noted the scale bar at the bottom right-hand corner of the image. The structure was ten nanometers in diameter—one tenth the size of the average virus; one hundredth the size of the average bacteria; and almost one millionth the size of a grain of rice.

Quon surveyed the room, apparently gauging reactions. "Microscopy is the sole investigation we have thus far been able to conduct with success. This electron microscope image shows you the highest magnification of a sample we isolated. Structures like the one you see here are densely packed together. Via extrapolation from these few images, I estimate there are two hundred billion such inclusions in a one microliter sample. They appear uniform in shape, however less than five percent appear complete. Most appear to be fragmented. Whether they are stable or in a state of formation or deterioration, we do not yet know. Now I would like to give you an idea of the difficulty of further study on SONA. We have some video footage of some standard lab work."

The video commenced—footage of Gigi as she removed the PAGE gel cassette. The sequence ended with a series of stills of the shriveled blot. Familiar with the technique, Mira shared the same perplexed reaction about the results as the other scientists.

Quon paused for effect. He met the eyes of the people in the room one by one. "The same phenomenon occurs in spectroscopy. SONA reacts with the matrices we use for this purpose. This property effectively leaves us blind about the nature of the organism."

"Excuse me." Mira could hold her tongue no longer. "You're calling this an organism. Is there something you know we have yet to be told?"

"My apologies, Dr. Wallace. It is perhaps premature to use that term. Thank you for your clarification." He nodded, and the slide advanced. It displayed two images, one the input stage of the Orbitrap mass spectrometer, unblemished. The other showed the damage done after loading SONA.

"For those unfamiliar, a mass spectrometer is used to reveal the makeup of biological samples. The output creates a kind of fingerprint consisting of peptides, digested fragments of proteins, which we can compare to known samples to help us in classification. We hope to identify a protocol that will yield a determinative result. The difficulties we are experiencing with SONA are unprecedented. We attempted various spectroscopic approaches, none of which yielded satisfactory results. We require ideas about how to overcome these complications."

Murmurs erupted around the room and Quon let them play out. "We will, of course, revisit this topic. For those who wish more detail in the explanation, we will address that individually or in smaller groups. For now, I would like to move on with the briefing. Next slide, please."

This slide showed an aerial view of the Proving Ground desert centered on the SONA site. An overlay highlighted a patchwork colored with reds, yellows, and blues of various intensities that bled into one another.

"This image represents recent satellite telemetry data obtained using classified technology, courtesy of advances in climate science. The colored heat map shows the absorption of carbon dioxide within the bottom ten meters of surface air. This region of dark blue here," he circled a smaller area with the pointer, "is the location where SONA was encountered."

Mira heard one of the scientists on the other end of the table gasp and utter a single raspy word. "Photosynthesis?"

The comment caught Quon's attention. "Yes. An astute observation. It is conceivable SONA may have additional carbon absorptive capacities, perhaps from the atmosphere."

The assertion struck Mira. If true, who knows? "Have you calculated a rate of propagation?"

Eleanor stood. "Dr. Wallace, I'm sorry I have not yet had the pleasure to meet you. You've zeroed in on the area of greatest concern." She paused and looked around the room of scientists. "Despite attempts to restrain the spread, it continues to grow. We do not have an accurate rate calculation. It looks to be on the order of ten percent per day or so."

"That's a relief," said one of the attendees Mira had not previously encountered. "I was told the mass doubled inside the containment tent."

"Relief?" Eleanor admonished. "It's an exponential rate. A ten percent per day growth rate may not seem like much at first. Inside a year, assuming the growth rate is unabated, the whole world could be exposed."

The ticking second hand of the analog wall clock reverberated in the stillness of the room for an extended moment. Mira did some calculations in her head. January was almost over. If the expansion was a simple and constant function, and they couldn't find a way to slow it, by the end of April it would reach about a square mile. Scary, but not an existential threat. It would still be contained on the Army base. But by summer's end—it would expand throughout Utah. By Halloween it could conceivably cover the entire North American continent. By Christmas? The whole planet. The knot in her stomach, present since she witnessed the ordeal of the pitiable piglet, tightened. The research that lay ahead was not easily rushed.

After a dozen more ticks of the second hand, Eleanor continued. "But we're going to make sure that doesn't happen. We must succeed. And we will. We're putting together a plan. You will work in teams, focused around your particular areas of expertise. These include a forensic medical team, an earth science team, biochemistry and pharmaceutical team, and a microbiology team. You will be provided with whatever tools and additional resources you need. Dr. Quon will guide the team here at Dugway, but authority over the personnel assignments and the course of inquiry will remain with the appropriate existing authority structure.

"One of the higher priorities is to develop plans to transfer samples for additional study. I'm told these studies should be conducted under BSL-4 containment. Nevertheless, we will work here as we equip teams to work in parallel elsewhere. Currently that includes Army labs at Aberdeen and Fort Detrick, Maryland. I will work closely with the offices of the Secretary of the Army and the Secretary of Defense to coordinate these initiatives. The principals responsible for each of the three facilities will be Colonel Potteiger, Commander of the base here at Dugway, Colonel Constantine Yanoviak, Military Deputy for the Edgewood facility at Aberdeen, and Brigadier General Bridget Higgins who commands the brigade at Fort Detrick. They will be my eyes and ears. Questions?"

The room erupted in an unintelligible outburst. Eleanor gestured and loudly called for order in an attempt to restore decorum.

Mira missed the commotion. She processed Quon's data, placing each puzzle piece together in as coherent a manner as she could. But as she tried to form a useful hypothesis, it occurred to her most of her questions must have already been pursued, at least to some extent. She shouted over the top of the other scientists, "Where are the sequence results?"

Eleanor heard her and, with a look of puzzlement, said, "I'm afraid I don't understand your question, Dr. Wallace. Could you elaborate?"

Mira stood and addressed the entire group. "If this is a biological agent, it will have DNA, or some kind of genetic material. The presence of DNA and the DNA sequences will tell us if it's biological and possibly where it came from."

Quon smiled. "This is what has me both concerned and excited, Dr. Wallace. We have not, as yet, been able to isolate DNA from SONA."

Mira's mind churned with the implications of this new information. "No cellular structure and no DNA? How about RNA?" This made no sense.

"Nothing as yet. We have the spiral inclusions and have not yet isolated any DNA."

"That casts serious doubt on the hypothesis this agent is biological, does it not?"

"That is an obvious consideration," Quon replied. "Yet—"

"I believe that's a discussion for later." Eleanor interrupted Quon. "Let's keep this discussion more general. We'll talk about the particulars in smaller groups. Now is a good time to split up. I'll leave it to you, Dr. Quon, to get everyone situated. Dr. Wallace, a word please?"

Mira, surprised by the request, stood. She followed Eleanor out the door. Yes, there was clearly more to this situation than she was being told.

A BRACELET

Eleanor stopped in the hallway and peppered Mira with questions. None of them allowed quick answers. When Mira told her so, Eleanor suggested they talk over lunch. Mira accepted, aware of the pang in her stomach. The Ditto Diner was a short walk away. As they went, Eleanor drove the discussion with small talk. They agreed to a first-name basis as Eleanor shared a handful of highlights from her past. In sharp contrast to her own preference, Mira learned Eleanor was an enthusiastic sorority alumnus—Delta Sigma Theta. Eleanor's outgoing manner and by-the-book mentality was common in the successful bureaucrats whom Mira encountered.

They entered the diner and Eleanor requested a corner table.

"This won't take long, right?"

Eleanor grinned. "Your file describes you as direct."

Was that a compliment? "I want to participate in the small group discussion. I have questions for Quon."

"I won't keep you any longer than I need. And I appreciate your help, Mira. If I'm going to be effective in my job, I need a crash course in microbiology."

"It's a big topic for a single conversation."

The waiter took their orders. "We're in a bit of a hurry here, if you don't mind, darlin'."

"I'll let the cook know." He hurried to the kitchen.

Eleanor smiled at Mira. "You emphasized the importance of DNA. I didn't follow."

Mira sipped her water. "If this agent is composed of proteins but has no DNA, we face a quandary. Proteins are always derived from DNA or, in the case of some viruses, they start with a similar molecule called RNA."

"I studied engineering. Now I wish I'd paid more attention in biology."

"You probably at least covered the basics of RNA, DNA, and genetics. It's the central dogma of biology."

"My memory is not what it once was, I'm afraid. You're still over my head, sugar."

Mira perked. Her pitch and pace rose and her gestures grew more animated as she elucidated. "We're talking about how living things develop and grow. It's all accomplished through a genetic code. It's a Universal Code, shared by every organism known to science. Here." Mira undid the clasp of her charm bracelet. She dangled it for Eleanor's inspection.

The chain itself was a string of silver balls linked by sturdy silver thread. At every third link, instead of a silver ball there was a smaller one made of gold. Each silver ball had a different charm attached. Eleanor examined them. Some charms featured jewels of various colors connected by silver posts. There were short charms, long charms, and some with hexagonal shapes.

"This bracelet helps me explain." It was the sole piece of jewelry she owned. The gift was the only gesture her grandmother had made that could be viewed as supportive of Mira's interest in biology. Mira had always ascribed the disapproval to the accident that took her parents. What had shifted with her grandmother to prompt her to commission the bracelet? Mira would never know. Her grandmother died within two weeks of Mira receiving it by courier. The accompanying note had read only, 'Congratulations, Mira.' She had no chance to give her a proper thank you. Or goodbye.

"Imagine this charm bracelet as a protein." She laid it flat across both palms. "The chain represents the protein's backbone. A protein is made by connecting amino acids together into long strings. The charms on my bracelet are models of each of the twenty possible amino acids found in living things. A typical protein has two hundred and fifty or more amino acids. A belt wouldn't even be long enough for that. So, picture this," she dangled the bracelet, "only much longer."

Mira folded the bracelet into one shape, then another. Some charms were magnetized, and they stuck together as she manipulated them.

"Now picture the bracelet folded into flexible yet distinctive structures through magnet-like interactions between the charms, like this." She twisted and pulled the chain as it clenched itself into different forms. Mira's mood lifted. This felt like a welcome a return to normalcy; a routine conversation the like of which she hadn't had for months. "Each protein folds into a specific shape. Because this is the molecular level, the shapes are not fixed but are in constant motion. The folded structure becomes a sort of mini-machine that can perform certain biochemical tasks."

"Your bracelet helps me picture what you're saying. Where did you get it, Mira?"

"It was a gift." Mira stared past Eleanor, her eyes unfocused at a confusing rush of emotion.

"It's beautiful. It must mean a lot to you."

Mira noted the clanks of plates and silverware as their waiter bussed a nearby table. The squeak of his shoes followed as he hustled the overflowing bin back to the kitchen. "It's useful, yes. But in the end, it's just metal and rocks."

Eleanor raised an eyebrow. "That's not true."

Mira's face reddened. "'A scientific man ought to have no wishes, no affections—a mere heart of stone.'"

"That sounds like a litany, darlin'."

"In a manner, I suppose. Charles Darwin. To be the best scientist I can be, I strive for dispassion." Attachment leads to bias and bias would prevent her from answering the most difficult question in all of biology.

Eleanor expressed doubt and concern as she muttered, "Hmm." After a moment, she asked, "These strings just form, what, randomly? And they sort of automatically perform biochemical functions?"

"No. Only the rarest combinations are useful. If you made a random string of amino acids, the protein would be unstable and fall apart. As a matter of fact, this is an area of heated discussion among those who theorize about the origin of life."

"Why is that?"

"If you consider the process of how the first building blocks of life must have come together, the required complexity makes it problematic to regard the process as merely random. Scientists theorize the chances of a strand of amino acids producing a functional protein are anywhere from one in ten to the sixty-fifth to as much as the three hundred ninetieth power."

Eleanor leaned back. "It's like that guy in the briefing; he didn't appreciate compound effects—people often struggle with large numbers and small probabilities. The way I picture big numbers is to tie them to the tangible. The number of atoms in the entire Milky Way galaxy is estimated around ten to the sixty seventh power." Eleanor's eyes went to the ceiling. "Randomly building a usable protein is like selecting a single atom from all the millions of stars and planets and other matter in the galaxy. In other words, impossible, because the Universe isn't old enough to provide enough iterations."

"I'm always relieved when I don't have to explain that part."

"If I hear you right, sugar, you're saying the odds of forming a functional protein at random are less than one person playing the Power Ball a bunch of times in a row and winning every one of them."

"The true picture isn't so simple. The complicating factors here are forces we may not recognize. For instance, the reactions between amino acids may be more complicated than we now understand. There could be processes which reduce those odds. So, it's dangerously reductionist to look at odds, perform first order calculations, and reach hard conclusions."

Eleanor quieted, her tone reverent. "Still, God's creation is truly wondrous."

Mira's eyes drifted to the shrubbery outside the diner window. "*Mahonia fremontii.*"

Eleanor sat back; her eyes sparkled with amusement. "My daddy's a preacher, back in Richmond. He's semi-retired now—he doesn't get in front of the congregation much anymore. I guess growing up the daughter of a southern black preacher, well it gets into your bones, is what it does. I see God everywhere, darlin'.""

Mira's thoughts scattered. The local flora. Religious people. The primordial processes that resulted in the creation of the first entity considered alive.

"You're not a believer, are you?"

"In God? Not like you."

"How then?"

"I don't know." Mira took a moment to recall the exact words. "If I may paraphrase Darwin again: 'The whole subject of God is too profound for the human intellect. Let each man hope and believe what he can.' That seems about right to me."

"That's not the loving God I know."

"You believe God cares about what happens to us?"

"I do. More than we can ever know."

"It makes no sense why a God would create this unimaginably vast and violent universe if He cared what happened to us." Mira grew sullen. "If there is a God who cares, I don't know what I ever did to deserve the loss of my parents. I was seven."

Eleanor mused. "I can't answer that, sugar. Like you, I never had children. Oh, I wanted them so badly, too. I would've done anything to have just one. But my body wasn't made that way. I blamed God for many years. One day, I realized that He must feel the same way. This vast Universe is a testament to that. What He did to bring us here, however briefly, was amazing. We cannot know His plan. But we can talk with him. Through prayer."

"Praying didn't help my grandmother."

Eleanor leaned in; her brow furrowed with concern. "What happened?"

"She was a believer. She still lost her daughter."

"Your mother?"

"Yes. My life would've been a challenge in any case. But my mother's death destroyed my grandmother." Her eyes and lips narrowed, solemn. "I don't see how losing my parents helped either one of us."

"There's no way to know that kind of pain if you haven't experienced it. It must have been hard. I don't wish to be indelicate, and I don't pretend to have answers for you, darlin', but this I do know—everything has many sides. And we can't know them all."

"On that, we agree." Mira hung her head.

Eleanor's big, dark eyes glistened. She leaned closer. "I'm sorry. I just want you to know He has a plan for everyone. Everyone. You, too, sugar."

Was that supposed to be kindness? "I've heard that before. It's nonsense." She expected some type of challenge. Eleanor simply looked at her with the same unreadable expression. Mira stared at her plate.

"I'm waiting," Eleanor said at last.

"For what?"

"For your explanation. You said you don't believe like I do. I'm waiting to hear how it is you believe in how the world became what it is."

"I don't know. I'm doing my best to reveal a part of it. With science."

"So that's it, then? You have faith in Science?"

Mira's western egg white omelet didn't look appetizing in the least. "This SONA, I guess we're calling it now, where do you suppose that fits in with God's plan?"

Eleanor paused and took a big bite of her enchilada. "Just because I believe, doesn't mean I've got answers."

Mira's mind went to the briefing. "The way Quon talks. I don't think he shared all he knows about the agent. What haven't I been told?"

Eleanor raised her brows. "Why do you ask?"

"It doesn't make sense. There's obviously more to the story. And nobody seems to want to talk about it."

"If so, it's news to me. But don't worry. If there's merit in what you say, I'll find out. I'll let you know. Promise." Eleanor finished her lunch. After, she picked up where she'd left. "If not God, how do you explain Creation, the existence of Life?"

That was exactly what bothered Mira about religious people. They never seemed to let the subject go. Still, like the few other true believers she knew at all, Eleanor was kind. This whole discussion stemmed from the woman's desire to be as competent as she could in the middle of a crisis. That was admirable. She could trust this woman. "I've got suspicions, but they're not sufficiently developed to consider them hypotheses. This situation has taken me away from work that could give us answers."

Eleanor's smile widened. "Hopefully, not for long. I'd like to better know your viewpoint, Mira. You just explained the near impossibility for life to come about. Yet you don't acknowledge miracles?"

"Miracles." Mira mused. "Interesting word."

"Why is that?"

"I think we use the word for phenomena we have yet to comprehend."

"By that definition, you consider SONA a miracle?"

Mira offered no response. She had to admit; the word did not comfortably fit what she saw SONA do. On the other hand...

The waiter interrupted. "Can I get either of you senoritas anything else?"

"No, that will be all, darlin'. Thanks. I'll take the check." The waiter retreated. Eleanor lowered her voice. "You know this situation, it's the scariest thing imaginable. You understand that don't you?"

"There are too many unanswered questions to be so fearful. Once we find out what SONA actually is, the chances are good we'll find a solution."

"I prefer more than chance, so you won't mind if I pray for us. For you."

"If it makes you feel better."

"And how do you feel right now?" The waiter deposited the check onto the table and Eleanor thanked him again with a warm smile.

"Fine," Mira stated. It was true, sort of, given the circumstances.

"Fine," repeated Eleanor as she signed the credit receipt. "Interesting word." She stood. "I think we use that word for a condition we have yet to comprehend."

A CONTRACTOR

The restoration after the fire damage and halon suppressant was almost done; the analytical chemistry lab was clean and sterile. But the mass spectrometer didn't work.

"Juan!" Gigi exclaimed. They bumped right elbows and twisted in sync to bump their lefts in a familiar greeting. Though she stood barely over five feet, Juan had only a few inches on her. Her frame was slight; his thick and sturdy.

"You'll take over as escort for the remainder of his visit, Miss Patilla?" Corporal Jessica Jenkins' face wore a sour expression.

"Yeah, I got him, Jessica. Thanks."

Jessica left with a strange raised eye at Juan. He turned back to Gigi, his accent a mishmash, "Isa a kong mabu-ting. Kung pa-ano ito ay pag-punta sa iyo?"

"You remembered the Tagalog I taught you! Que bueno, Jumping Bean. I'm glad to know you're doing well. Mahbang panahon, hindi makita. I said 'long time, no see'."

"May ha bon pa na hun, hindi ma keyta."

Gigi's laugh was bigger than her body. "Close, Latino Boy. We'll work on it."

Juan blushed. "I'd like that, chica. I always do." He grinned at her. A moment later, his nose scrunched. "Ay! What's that smell?"

"Something must've burned, right genius? That's why you're here. The damaged mass spec."

"You can't have nice stuff if you don't take care of it. I left it in tip top shape not so long ago. What's the problem?"

"You tell me. You're 'El Maestro de la Electronica,' aren't you?"

Juan's brows raised, surprised and defensive. "Where did you hear that name?"

"People talk."

"You talk about me behind my back, do you?" He brushed a lock of his dark wavy hair out of his eyes.

"What if I did?" She gazed at him, coy.

"I am on the clock, no? Better have a look."

"Ya think?" She indicated the spectrometer. She had cleaned it, but the partially melted plastic ring on the input stage revealed the nature of the damage. "It's right here. I hope you can work your magic on it. It's hung up and our techs don't know what to do. We need to get it going as soon as we can."

A frown swept across his face. "You guys shouldn't be messing with it. We have a service contract. It's a violation of the terms."

She played with him via a mocking face. But he no longer appeared playful. He wheeled his toolkit closer to the mass spec and bent to select the appropriate tools. She smiled at the Bioprospectors logo on the back of his coveralls. "That's the worst looking logo I've ever seen." It was indeed garish; too colorful and difficult to read.

"Yeah, you've said that before. And what do I always say?"

"You say it's not your company. But if you ask me, it should be."

"What can I say?" The compliment made Juan blush. He noted the melt marks on the outer case of the mass spec. "What happened here, Gigi?"

"Sorry. Can't talk about that. Top Secret. I don't know much, anyway. Only what I need to do my job. You can still fix it though, right?"

"You know me. I'll get it working, so long as it has a circuit board. And I can get parts." He used a miniature cordless screwdriver to deftly remove the appropriate screws and lift away the outer case of the auto-sample bay. Next, he plugged his service computer into the mass spec's HDMI port. Rapid fire, his fingers tapped the keyboard as he conducted a diagnostic routine. She marveled at the precision of his motions; the confidence and command he had for troubleshooting. "You had a fire in here, huh?"

"Just to be safe, I'm not going to talk about what may or may not have happened or why. Nothing personal."

"Oh, it's personal." He was again playful. "You owe me now."

"What do you want?"

"How about you come over Friday night?"

She feigned anger. "Juan Jimenez! What kind of girl do you think I am?"

"The kind that eats food. I don't know what you're talking about, but I'm talking about dinner."

"You're going to have to take me out someplace, if I'm going to go on a date with you. Someplace nice."

"For real? This Friday, right?"

"Sure."

"Good. But I want you to see my place. No funny business, for real."

"Alright. I want to see how the 'Maestro' lives, anyway." They regarded each other warmly for a few moments. Juan broke first and refocused his attention to his computer. The diagnostic app indicated complete. There were multiple error messages. The first one read: 'LEAKAGE.'

Gigi leaned over his shoulder. "I hate when that happens."

Juan snickered and powered down the mass spec. He disassembled the sample inlet and noted the charring. "One reason the machine isn't working is because of a compromised O-ring in the sample stage. I replaced it last visit—it was practically brand new. What did you run in here?"

Gigi straightened, serious. "Juan. I told you I can't say. Stop asking. Can you get it working or not?"

"I'm getting all kinds of errors in the input stage. Besides the O-ring I'll have to replace half a dozen other parts. I'll order them today. Probably next week or the week after by the time I'm back."

"Give me the part numbers. I'll have them here for you in a few hours."

"I don't think it's going to work like that, chica."

"But I know magic. You can wait here with me for the afternoon, can't you?"

They again looked at one another for a long moment. Juan smiled. "Give me a piece of paper."

EXCERPT:
THE NECESSITY OF PRECURSOR
COOPERATIVES

Wallace, M. D.[1,2] and Weingartner, J. A.[1]

1*University of California, Berkeley, Dept. of Plant and Microbial Biology, 311 Koshland Hall, Berkeley CA, 94720.*

2*National Interagency Biodefense Campus, Fort Detrick, MD 21702*

Section #2: Energetic Transformation

The genius of Galileo Galilei, the Father of Modern Science, first revealed the mind-boggling extent of the strangeness of our world. It did not come from his famous astronomical observations, insights that led directly to him spending the last nine years of his life under house arrest for heresy. (The Holy Catholic Church was not amenable to the news the Earth was not in fact the center of the Universe. It took three more centuries to acknowledge that particular truth formally.)

Galileo's most important discovery was so strange nobody understood it sufficiently to object. Prior to Galileo, people imagined energy was some kind of outside force that acted upon objects. If a person kicks a ball, that ball keeps going until it runs out of energy. This is common sense: the harder you kick a ball, the further it goes.

But science often reminds us that even the most obvious things aren't always so.

AN EXPLANATION

On the walk back to the WDTC HQ building they spoke no more about creation, miracles, or God. That suited Mira. She was even more pleased when Eleanor returned to Mira's favorite topic. "I'd like to hear more about your work, Mira. I think it's exciting."

"You do? I don't hear that from many people outside of my field."

"What is it you're trying to prove?"

"Trying to prove." Mira smiled. Eleanor was unaware her words were an insult. "Frankly, I try to avoid thinking like that. It's bad science. The scientific method is suited to disprove alternatives." What a job that was, too, since alternatives seemed endless. As she followed those thoughts into a maze, she considered her family history. Her brow unknit as her face brightened.

"What is it, Mira?"

"My great, great grandfather."

"Go on, sugar."

"He was Alfred Wallace. Do you recognize the name?"

"No, but you're implying that I should."

"I mentioned Darwin. Wallace was his colleague—my relative's fieldwork helped formulate modern evolutionary theory."

"Interesting. But why does that amuse you?"

"Despite his words to the contrary, Darwin tried to prove something. My ancestor was an observer. Wallace spent much of his time in the jungles of South America and Indonesia. He wrote his ideas and sent them to Darwin. He was content to take a back seat when Darwin published *Origin of Species*. Wallace lacked Darwin's personal ambition. He cared only about discovery."

Eleanor leaned closer. "And everybody knows Darwin while nobody knows Wallace."

"Only those interested in the field. Wallace would never have put together such a powerful argument for evolution as Darwin," Mira reflected. "Besides, he eventually abandoned the scientific method and resigned himself to spiritualism, accepting that some invisible spirit was behind the origin of life on earth. But back to your question about my work. We already discussed the Universal Code. So, it is safe to assume that evolution of life on earth proceeded from a common event. If all life traces back to a single common ancestor, we should be able to identify it, or at least its characteristics. I want to know what the first organism was like. Sometimes I feel like I'm the only person who does."

"That's probably not true, darlin'. We're never as alone as we sometimes feel."

Mira tried to read the elder woman's face. Did she have some agenda? Why would she care about her? Mira couldn't guess and got no further ideas from Eleanor's warm expression. "There aren't many in my field who focus on what I do. I apparently lack the sense not to bother." Mira's life suddenly seemed more a gamble than a carefully considered career choice. Would she advise somebody else to do as she had? No. So why persist? In her darker moments, the question burned. Her answer was never clear, only a fuzzy feeling that the importance of the question justified the risk of failure. She felt something else now. It was a strange sensation, a feeling like there was something more, some other reason she couldn't grasp. Whatever it was, it certainly wasn't scientific. Was she headed down the same path her ancestor Wallace had? She stopped herself from thinking any more about it.

"I'll agree that you don't seem to have the same sense as others, darlin'. Your work with unusual life-forms; it helps you?"

"Yes." It was a nearly impossible puzzle. But that challenge was a part of the appeal. "They represent distinct pieces. Each unique life-form helps define the borders, the outer reaches of the biological Tree of Life that helps us understand the relationships between all living things, past and present. Extremophiles hold valuable clues about the Source Code."

"You're losing me again, sugar. Extremophiles?"

"Those are the unusual life-forms you just mentioned. They're microbes that live in conditions we consider unfriendly to life—environments with high or low pressures or temperatures. Or under chemically harsh, even radioactive environments."

"This is why you go to all the trouble to drill into a subterranean Antarctic lake?"

"Yes." She had been one barely functioning generator away from sharing a painful death with the team. Where were they right now? Breaking camp? She fantasized about teleporting there right this moment. What would they bring back? Would it be worth all of that risk? If it helped her fill in the Tree, then yes.

"How does the Source Code you mentioned fit in?"

Mira sighed, but quickly regained her focus. "It's what we've talked about: DNA. The DNA from the original life-form provides the blueprint for all others. The coding language is universal. All animals, plants, and bacteria use essentially the same code derived from sixty-four groups of three DNA letters specifying one of twenty different amino acids in a protein, so the trail is there to be discovered. If you want a better picture, I can show you what I'm talking about."

"Please."

"It's easier to follow if I make a sketch."

"All right," Eleanor held the door for Mira, "right over there, darlin'."

They entered the HQ building and stopped at the unmanned security desk. Eleanor grabbed the pen and pulled a napkin out of her purse. "Here." She handed them both to Mira.

Mira drew as she spoke. "As I said before, DNA provides the

information for a living cell to synthesize amino acids in the proper order for each protein it needs. Do you know what the stretches of DNA that encode specific proteins are called?"

"No."

"I think you do." She held the napkin for Eleanor to examine. "Genes." Mira put the napkin on the desk. She pulled out her phone and made some keystrokes. She showed the display to Eleanor. "This is a DNA codon table. It describes how amino acids are assembled into the proper order." She shook her bracelet. "Remember, those are the charms. The order is specified by the DNA sequence itself. DNA is a long molecular string composed of four types of bases. Here we have them represented in four-letter groups using G, A, T, and C."[1]

"Do I really need all of this detail? I'm not going to remember it."

"That's why I'm making you a sketch."

"I'm not yet seeing how this is going to help me better do my job, sugar."

"You expressed your reverence for God and his creation, Eleanor. Follow me here. It's the most amazing thing in the whole Universe. More than planets, stars, or galaxies. If there is a God of Creation, this is His most beautiful handiwork. Do you want to better know your God? Then you should want to understand this. Life is unlike anything else we know of. And it's based on a chemical machinery that is capable of adapting to almost any environment and becoming almost anything. Even people..."

"All right, you sold me." Embarrassed by her own question, Eleanor pointed to the codon table. "All these letters. It's confusing."

"Only at first. Look closer. These three-letter groups, called codons, specify various amino acids. Some codons encode the same amino acid. That's why there are sixty-four codon combinations but only twenty amino acids. The order of assembly is the crucial part. One mistake in the amino acid sequence can cause the protein to be nonfunctional."

"Is that why the chances of a random sequence resulting in a working protein are so remote?"

"Yes. You're following just fine, Eleanor."

Eleanor studied the table. A group of suited people wordlessly passed them by. "So, this code is a kind of shorthand to describe the formation of the chemical building blocks for life. That's what you're saying?"

"Yes. But bear with me. There's a bit more to the story." Mira put away her phone and again drew on the napkin. She added the lines and letters G, A, T, and C to connect the letters to points along the spiral. She labeled the sketch 'DNA.' Next, she drew a blown-up strand next to her first DNA sketch and labeled the new one 'RNA.' "This is how the code works."

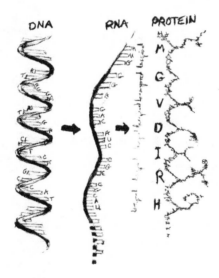

"The DNA sequence for a gene is converted to a sort of mobile version called RNA. It carries the code of the specified protein." She sketched a third figure with corresponding letters to the RNA strand. She labeled this one 'Protein.'

"So, the specific sequence in a strand is what determines the protein the gene makes."

"I'm glad you're getting this."

"You're saying that the genes in a living cell govern which proteins are available. Since proteins are the machines, I think you called them, they shape how an organism grows, what it looks like, what it can do, and so on."

"You know biology better than you said you did."

"No. You're doing a good job of explaining so somebody like me can understand, darlin'. I see your point, it is truly remarkable, this code. God's own language. Can I surmise that this process is how it always works?"

"Yes, for every living thing. Every single creature from the beginning of life on earth uses more or less the same code. Aside from a few minor variations. But it's not perfect. It makes mistakes sometimes." Mira added, "I'm not sure what that says about your God's language."

If Eleanor took any umbrage, she didn't show it. "And if SONA doesn't use this code?"

"If it has DNA, it must. Genetic coding doesn't just appear out of thin air. If you randomly created codon tables, there would be more codes than there are atoms in the Universe. And only a handful of codes are efficient enough to support life. We don't know how it evolved but it must have taken a very a long time."

"Sounds like a miracle to me."

"Miracles again? Supernatural? Let me ask you something, Eleanor. If your God created a universe governed by natural laws, why would He violate them to influence our world? Why would He need to?"

"Fortunately, we don't have to answer that, sugar. We only need to find out what SONA is and where it came from." Eleanor paused, lost in thought. "Tell me more about what it means if SONA doesn't have DNA?"

"It means it's not a living thing."

Eleanor's eyes widened. "Then what on Earth could it be?"

"Good question." Mira had wrestled with that issue since the first briefing. The dilemma was now an itch annoyingly out of reach. "To be accurate, it could employ protein-making RNA, as some microbes do."

"So, we need to find out how SONA makes its proteins."

"If it in fact does. I assume this is why Quon wanted to bring me here. This is how we solve this big puzzle. We use computers to compare the genetic codes of organisms and the proteins they encode. It helps us classify life-forms into groups of related species and determine which came first."

"SONA seems to have unusual strategies."

"It's like nothing I've ever seen."

Eleanor stiffened. "That's why Dr. Quon appears more excited than alarmed by SONA. I suppose I've under-appreciated the scientific discovery implications here."

"You can hardly be blamed for that. A person has died."

"Let's pray he remains the only one."

Mira again grew silent. The piglet's ordeal replayed in her mind's eye. Her horror changed to shame as she recalled Rain's admonition when she asked to leave.

Eleanor grabbed the napkin and held it like a prize. "Well worth the price of an enchilada and an omelet." She put it in her purse. "I don't know how you remember all this stuff, all the letters. And right off the top of your head like that."

"It's what I do."

"Well, I'm impressed, sugar. Thank you. Now I know a bit more about God." She paused as her smile broadened. "And His 'mistakes.'"

---

1. See Supplement for more on the Universal Code and codon table.

A GREENCAR

Quon hastened through the halls of the LSF. Was everyone in this place in slow motion? He would tolerate it for the time being. There was no changing that. Yet. He needed to find a competent assistant; one person who could help him discretely test his hypothesis. He arrived at the mass spec lab and opened the door. "I was told I would find a Miss Patilla here?"

"Present." Gigi jumped to her feet at mock attention.

"I understand we should be able to resume—"

Juan burst from his chair. "Oh my God! You're Wesley Quon—I don't believe it."

"Geez, take it easy, why don't you?" Gigi admonished.

"You don't understand. This is my homeboy." Juan's eyes were glued to Quon as he straightened his shirt and rubbed his hands on his pants to clean them. "I talk about you all the time." Juan rushed over and extended his hand.

Quon wore a bemused smirk. He looked at Juan's hand to consider whether to shake it. He did, his grasp light. "You flatter me, young man. I am pleased to meet you too."

"It's my honor, sir. Your technology is so dope." He spoke faster and faster as he smoothed his hair with his fingers and said to Gigi, "You know about all this, right? How Wesley Quon engineered an algae to harness a battery-charging electrical potential—brilliant." He turned back to Quon. "How did you ever come up with that idea?"

Rain hurried in as Quon was about to respond. "I thought you might be coming here, Dr. Quon." He spied Juan, with whom he'd grown a casual friendship over the many visits the contractor had made to the facilities. "Oh, we have a guest. Hi Juan, here to work on the mass spec, I assume?"

"Good, amigo, good."

Rain and Gigi shared a glance of surprised amusement.

Juan remained on Quon, whose hand was still in his. Juan noticed. "Sorry. I'm just—well, I'm a big fan, I really am. I'm planning to buy one of your AC12s; didn't I say so, Gigi? She'll tell you. I'm impressed with your designs. I'm a real tech junkie, right Gigi? Hey, can I ask you something, Mr. Quon?" The pace of his speech doubled.

"Why, of course." Quon's response was all grace. He could overlook, this once, the young man's failure to address him as 'Dr.'

"I just read an article that talked about problems with the GreenCar: like trouble with repairs and insurance. What's up with that? Is it true? I wanna get one but I don't wanna be stuck, you know?"

Quon's smile faltered. The GreenCar had some issues, he knew that. That information had clearly become too public for comfort. The pressure he'd applied to the major insurers and their actuarial calculations should ultimately keep them in line. Never mind the validity of their concerns. All along, Quon downplayed the fact that mishaps, even the smallest fender benders, resulted in expensive panel replacement to restore the integrity of the algal environment. He would address the issue in time. "I am pleased to inform you those difficulties were misreported. You must know how the media behaves."

"It's hard to know what's true anymore," Juan agreed.

"Yes." Quon's smile returned. "Deliveries of insured vehicles will soon reach fifty thousand. You will not experience the problems they irresponsibly claim. My customers are extremely happy. Trust me; if you invest in one, you will be happy too. You will not miss the expense and inconvenience of constant refueling."

Rain's annoyance showed in narrowed eyes. "I don't know, Dr.

Quon. Can you really assure him of all of that? Most new technologies have problems. Your cars are expensive. He's just a kid; he can't afford to blow a bunch of money."

"I do better than you think, amigo." By the tone of his response, Juan took more offense than Quon.

Quon didn't appreciate the comment, but he maintained his smile. "You make a valid point Sergeant Major. I stand corrected. The mechanism in our vehicles is mechanically simple and should prove more reliable than conventional automobiles. But as with any new technology, it is more expensive for the first adopters and of course many things can go awry. I mean to say we have good people in our company. I am confident we will be able to satisfy all of our customers' needs."

"Course you will." Juan's enthusiasm remained undimmed. "Look at Apple. They had lots of problems. But they always resolved them."

"I suggest you reconsider, Juan." Rain's eyes stayed on Quon. "You'll need your money to buy some lucky girl a ring someday. Maybe sooner than you think."

Juan's response was a blank look. Gigi looked away with a blush.

"I suppose these concerns will not affect you personally?" Quon asked Rain.

"I guess not."

Quon stared at Rain, his smile a constant. "You were looking for me, Sergeant Major? Do you have information for me?"

"It can wait."

"I am disappointed you do not appreciate the GreenCar innovation. But I do hope you will keep an open mind as things develop." After an awkward pause, Quon turned to Gigi. "Miss Patilla, do you have an estimate as to when this lab will be operational?"

"We should discuss this when we don't have a guest," Rain interjected.

"Of course." Quon's tone was ice.

Jessica re-entered. All eyes turned to her. "I believe you expected these?"

"The O-ring," Gigi exclaimed with a light clap of her hands. "Thanks Jessica. Now you can work your magic, Juan."

"Thanks, Jessica," said Juan. The corporal frowned as she left. But she did look back at Juan before the door shut. Gigi let out a harrumph. She handed Juan the parts.

Quon didn't have time for this. "May we speak in private, Miss Patilla?"

"Sure. Rain, you'll babysit our boy here?"

"I can handle him."

JUAN SET back to work on the mass spec as Quon and Gigi left. Most of the replacement procedure was routine for Juan. But he struggled to fit the O-ring in place as the old one had melted, and whoever tried to clean it failed to remove all the residue that gummed up the inlet.

"You want a hand with that?"

Juan started. "Jeez!" Rain stood right behind him.

"You're awfully jumpy, Juan."

"Sorry. No. Gracias, amigo. I got this."

"So, you and Gigi, huh?"

"What? No, man." Juan responded knee-jerk. He settled. "We're going on our first date though."

"About time."

Juan broke into a nervous laugh and Rain grinned back. Juan resumed his work on the mass spec. He thoroughly cleaned the auto-sample bay and the sample inlet, checked the seal on the new O-ring, and ran another diagnostic. "It should work like it's supposed to now."

"Good job, Juan."

Gigi and Quon returned. "You're all set," Juan declared. "Whatever you're doing in here, be careful this time, will ya?"

Gigi responded with playful sarcasm. "We'll try to take your sage advice."

"You have my gratitude, young man," Quon said with exaggerated benevolence. "What was your name again?"

"Juan Jimenez."

"Mr. Jimenez; very well. Take my card." He removed a gold monogrammed case from his jacket and handed Juan a bright green business card. "When you are ready to purchase an AC12 please text me. I will see to it you get one at cost."

Juan froze, his mouth open. He stared at the stylish card. He blinked and looked to Gigi, who smiled and stepped closer. Juan beamed. "Muchas gracias. This is so kind of you, sir. Never would I expect this." Why was the man being so generous? Was he like that with everyone?

"It is my pleasure. Thank you for your work here today. It is more important than you know."

Gigi grabbed Juan's arm. "Come on, Jumping Bean, I'll see you out."

A SETUP

Satisfied with her allotted lab space, Mira inventoried its contents. She frowned at her clipboard-checklist. There were too many items still missing and she said so out loud.

"Fear not; I've got everything a guest star researcher might dream of right here on my Treats Trolley." Gigi wheeled in a loaded cart. "What else do you need Miss Mira?"

Mira's frown disappeared as she inspected the materials. Her enthusiasm rose as she noted the racks of small plastic test tubes, the stacks of Petri dishes, the bottles of various detergents, phenol, both with and without chloroform, and a variety of acids and bases. She ticked each item off her list. "This is a good start. You've brought the rest of the supplies we need. The first step is to prepare the required solutions. It's straight-forward. I can do it, if you have other duties."

"You kidding me? You're my duty today, lady."

Mira raised an eyebrow at Gigi's quirkiness. Was she always like this? If not, why act so casual, almost unprofessional? Their situation was not light or routine. The nature of the agent, the method of inquiry, even the people involved, it all weighed on her. It didn't appear to have the same effect on Gigi: she was jovial, cavalier.

As they worked side by side to prepare the required solutions, Gigi's precision and efficiency eroded Mira's doubt and her demeanor elevated Mira's spirits. Gigi's discordant manner was a palatable price to pay for a practiced, reliable partner. A partner like Jeff or Kyle. What were they doing right now?

After Mira replied to Gigi's questions about how she had arrived,

Gigi joked. "Antarctica, huh? And you didn't bring me any penguins? I only wanted two, you know. Maybe three. One of them a baby. That's all—a little penguin family. Aren't baby birds the cutest?"

When Mira told her where she lived, Gigi sang, "San Fran-cis-co, the Rice-a-Roni treat!"

Mira smiled, not because she knew the reference, nor how Gigi juxtaposed the jingle's lyrics for comedic effect, nor that someone so young would know of a commercial so old, but it simply struck her as silly. She tried to keep conversation light. "Where are you from, Gigi?" It was all she could think of.

"Originally? The Philippines. 'Gigi Patilla from Manila.' That's how I used to introduce myself in college. Catchy, right? I'm not really from Manila, though. I'm from a much smaller town in the north called Jones. But Gigi from Jones doesn't work as well."

Mira regretted asking.

Gigi remained cheerful. "Waddya listening to?" She pointed to Mira's right ear.

"Oh, I'm sorry. I forgot I had them on. I do that a lot."

"It's cool. My jam is hip hop, but I like most music. You?"

"Piano and violin; I keep it quiet. It helps me concentrate."

They worked a while longer in comfortable silence.

"Are you married, Miss Mira?"

"No."

"Ever been?"

"No."

"Good. Men just get in the way."

Mira didn't catch Gigi's joke. "Get in the way of what?"

Gigi laughed. "Good question."

They continued to measure, pour, and mix. Mira's thoughts lingered on Gigi's question. It was one that hadn't come up much. Not in her world. "The main criticism I get is I spend too much time working." Mira frowned. "I don't know why people see that as a problem. I enjoy what I do. How is that negative?"

"You really don't know what they mean; or are you just pulling my leg?"

"I know they don't approve of my work-life balance. I don't know what that means. When I'm not working, I usually wish I was." Mira's eyes were faraway.

"Most people have the opposite problem."

Again, Mira failed to pick up Gigi's humor. "I should be working somewhere else."

"And I should have a family of penguins to cuddle with. All righty, this prep is done. What next?"

"If you could pour the required agar plates, that would save time."

"Stitching, saving nine." Gigi turned to the chore. "So, I guess you don't want an S.O., huh?"

"S.O.?"

"Significant Other. You should get out more, jeez."

"I suppose I'm not an 'S.O.' kind of person." Mira squeezed the plunger of the pipette a little harder. She attributed her discomfort to the separation from her personal work. She was partially right. "I assume you are not like me. S.O.-wise."

"Well, kind of. I got me a straddler."

"A straddler?"

"Yeah, he's got one foot in childhood and one foot in manhood. You'd think his do-dads would be sore from all that fence sitting."

Mira smirked. "Oh. That doesn't sound unusual."

"You said it, sister. There are a few around here who aren't like that, though." She raised a sly eyebrow. "You've met Rain, haven't you?"

"Yes." The flask slipped in Mira's hand. She managed to regain her grip before it fell. "He's been nice to me."

"He's nice to everyone. Unless you don't follow the rules, of course."

"I see." Mira caught Gigi hiding a smile. Was she teasing? "What else do you know about him?"

"Not much. He just saved my life the other day, that's all."

Another joke. Mira allowed herself a snicker.

Gigi didn't smile. "No, for real. I was out of air in decon and he revived me. I got the bruised ribs to prove it."

"Well. That's good. For both of you."

Gigi's demeanor remained serious. "I actually do like my man. A lot. When I was in there, running out of air, he was what I thought about, you know?" She briskly applied agar into the dishes. "I guess it's not right to call him my man. We're going on our first date this weekend."

"What are you going to do?" It wasn't the kind of question Mira typically asked.

"Nothing much, just dinner. He's cooking for me. I've never been to his place."

Mira didn't know how to further the conversation in this direction. "I hope you enjoy yourself." She glanced at her checklist and tended to the next priority.

"Juan—that's his name—he's a genius. He's kind of famous, actually."

"Is he an entertainer? I'm not familiar with popular entertainment."

"No," Gigi giggled. She lit up as she went on. "Nothing like that. He's famous for his work. He can fix anything, as long as it has circuitry. Maybe it would be better if I was a cyborg."

The joke again failed to land with Mira. They worked a while longer. "All right. Looks like we're about done with the prep. I'll load the necessary software. You make sure the centrifuges are balanced."

"I live to balance centrifuges!"

Mira didn't know why, but that struck her as hysterically funny. She chortled. Gigi joined her. The two women shared an extended cathartic laugh.

A BREAKTHROUGH

Mira and Gigi worked side-by-side in the pre-expansion section of Salomon Lothar Life Sciences Facility. The lab's BSL-2 designation meant they needed gloves, face shields, and lab coats, but didn't have to wear isolation suits or manage supplied-air apparatuses. They couldn't work directly with SONA, but could run assays with its separated components deemed safer—if and when those could be reliably produced.

Mira pondered the matter, but came up with no ideas that hadn't already been tried. Her eyes periodically scanned the monitors that displayed a feed from the BSL-3 labs. The team worked feverishly. What about this agent gave it such resistance to detergents? She pictured the spiral inclusions. None of this made sense. Data was missing here. There had to be. Was it being deliberately withheld? Quon. His attitude mystified her. Was it just that he was as passionate for discovery as her? If so, he showed insufficient respect for the scientific method. She saw more figures file into one of the bigger labs and gather around one of the workstations. "Gigi, something's happening in containment."

Gigi looked up from her notebook computer and squinted at the video feed. "Somebody liked the prize in their Cracker Jack. I'll check it out, if it's cool with you."

Mira acknowledged. Gigi hurried out. Maybe they have some definitive experimental results? She pictured the Tree of Life. If SONA was a life-form, where would it fit? Might this help fill in a key gap? Up to this point, she'd considered this recruitment a diversion from her course. But was it really? Coincidence. Was there such a thing? Or was coincidence mere illusion, a product of insufficient perceptive power? Her thoughts drifted to her lunch with Eleanor. A buzz at her door broke her reverie. She pressed the unlock button. In rushed Quon.

He beamed toothily. "I have encouraging news for you, Dr. Wallace." He stopped at an awkwardly close distance and grasped her arm. "At last, we have isolated DNA."

"You did? I suppose you may have been right about SONA being an organism. Did you get sequence?" Mira scowled at his hand on her arm.

Quon released his grip. "Analysis is under way. But it is difficult to obtain useful results with the sequencers available here."

That made no sense. "What's the trouble?"

"The output data is unreliable. I suspect the outdated instrumentation."

That made less sense. "Unlikely."

"The sequencers are giving mixed results. There are too many bad base calls. I am accustomed to greater sophistication in my work."

Mira's brows raised. "Do you regularly conduct genomic studies?"

"Of course. Thank you for the suggestion Dr. Wallace; I should bring specimens to my facility in Seattle."

She'd done nothing of the sort. This man was far too quick to reach conclusions. A dangerous habit. "I wasn't suggesting—"

"I recently acquired a prototype Illumina sequencer," Quon interrupted. "State-of-the-art. Nobody else has one like it. I shall see about using it for these inquiries."

"As you wish." As troubling as Quon's lack of rigor was, he did spur some thoughts. She mused aloud, "If you're having difficulty with assembly, we should employ teams concurrently. Who handles the assembly work for you?"

"I recruit the best and brightest from all around the world."

His answer surprised her. "Genomic work is an important part of your operations?"

"Oh, I go to great lengths to stay in the front of the pack."

"I see." Curious. Quon's speedy thought process may indeed suit his purposes in the business arena. Given the nature of the threat they faced, she also had to admit every moment counted. His pace could be exactly what they needed. Still—her experience taught her jumping to conclusions rarely ended well. Her pace and tone increased with a new thought. "As a result of my Antarctic expedition, I have ample sequencing time scheduled at multiple facilities. I suppose the slots could be re-purposed. Do you think we could use those resources?"

"Given our circumstances, it is appropriate for us to make use of whatever facilities we deem necessary. I will have a word with Secretary Dixon."

"I expect a visit from her shortly. I'll mention this."

Quon paused. For a moment his smile dimmed like a floodlight shadowed by a person walking past. "I suppose you should be able to handle this without me. But if you do not get the permissions we need, please do not hesitate to ask for my help."

She was used to arrogance; she traveled in academic circles. Usually, it didn't bother her. It did this time. "I'll keep that in mind."

Quon regarded her for a moment, without his smile. "Very well." He turned to leave; his steps were slower than they had been upon his entry.

Mira stopped him with a question. "Dr. Quon, how were you able to overcome the problems with the previous DNA extraction attempts?"

His chest puffed as he faced her, his pride intense enough to radiate through his face-shield. "Oh, that. I simply directed them to use the mercury method. I suspected if we eliminated carbon-based molecules from the buffers and matrices, we might circumvent the reactive properties of SONA. My hunch was proven correct."

"Well done." Despite her misgivings about Quon's approach, she had to admit: she was impressed. She brightened with the hope she might return to Berkeley soon.

The door clicked shut behind Quon. Mira looked at the morass of solutions and glassware with a pang of regret for the time wasted. Quon's news changed much of what she had planned for the next day or two. A good problem, to be sure. She sighed and cleaned the lab.

As she put the last bottle into a storage cabinet, Rain and Eleanor buzzed themselves in.

"You are aware of the news on the DNA?" Mira asked.

"Yes," replied Eleanor. "I also understand you believe we lack the resources here to proceed effectively."

Mira shook her head. "What did he say?"

"He said this facility was obsolete compared to his."

"It is true this sort of technology is developing rapidly. No labs have all the important capabilities anymore. Cooperation is essential."

"What kinds of capabilities?" Rain asked.

"It's an over-simplification, but we're talking about constantly improved instrumentation, computational power, analytical tools, and speed."

"Dr. Quon did not explain his rationale," said Eleanor. "Computational speed I understand. I need help with the rest."

"Biology is now as much math as anything else. Complicated math. The keys to understanding organisms are hidden in patterns among oceans of data. The greater the available computing power and the better the algorithms used to interpret the results, the clearer our picture. Bioinformatics. Computational biology. This kind of work is a major part of what I can do for you."

"Then you agree with Dr. Quon. We lack the resources here?"

"Like I said, I haven't yet looked at the process he used. But there are numerous methods for genomic DNA sequencing. This unknown agent has thus far proved difficult to study. Is it unreasonable that we use all available resources?"

"You have a particular proposal?" Rain asked.

"Dr. Quon said he has access to advanced Illumina technology. This method uses a different chemistry than other DNA sequencing methods. It might help us get a better picture." She paused as she cogitated. "And yes. I'm thinking while Dr. Quon uses his sequencer, I could use my own sequencing pipeline. I'd like to re-task my team to help with bioinformatics." The notion again lifted her. She was accustomed to being away from the facilities at Berkeley. Yet she missed the stillness of her lab. Its familiarity.

"That presents a security issue," said Eleanor. "Why don't we just bring the necessary equipment in?"

"You could set up the sequencers. But there is really no need. Dr. Quon and I both have access to sophisticated machines and personnel with the necessary expertise. It would save weeks, if not months. The latest computational servers utilize hundreds of separate processing units. These aren't the kind of equipment commercially inventoried and delivered. They're custom made. They must be installed in a specially cooled room. They require their own dedicated power sources. It's an RFP process. One that will take time. As you've made clear, time is a luxury we don't have. It will be far more efficient to take samples to Berkeley or Los Alamos. We'd only be transporting SONA DNA, nothing dangerous."

"I don't think my superiors are going to go for this idea," said Rain. "It sounds risky."

"Let me worry about that." Eleanor kept her gaze on Mira. "You're convinced it's worth the trouble of sending you to Berkeley?"

"It's easier than dragging me all the way from Antarctica."

EXCERPT: THE NECESSITY OF PRECURSOR COOPERATIVES

Wallace, M. D.[1,2] and Weingartner, J. A.[1]

1University of California, Berkeley, Dept. of Plant and Microbial Biology, 311 Koshland Hall, Berkeley CA, 94720.

2National Interagency Biodefense Campus, Fort Detrick, MD 21702

Section #2: Energetic Transformation, cont.

Galileo showed us the ball is not being acted on after it is kicked. Rather, its motion becomes part of its state of being. It is moving relative to us or it is not. A falling body takes on the property of falling. Riding in a car you don't feel any different when it's sitting in the driveway or when it's barreling down the highway at 80 mph. But in truth you are. When you stomp on the gas pedal, the seat pushes you, at least while you're accelerating. But the energy is transferred to you. It becomes a part of you. You are different. To shed that energy, it must transfer to something else.

It can be traumatic, such as a car crash. Under normal conditions, the friction of the seat or the force exerted upon your body by your seatbelt absorb the energy. But it will, by itself, never run out. At this moment, you are moving through space at a dizzying speed. Assuming you're on the Earth, you are both spinning (at a speed relative to your proximity to the poles, approximately 1,000 mph at the equator) and circling the sun at 67,000 mph. As we increase the frame of reference, our velocities continue to increase. The sun is moving, both speeding around the center of the Milky Way galaxy and moving in dimensions other than a flat circle. The Milky Way is zooming through space as well, at 1.3 million miles per hour. All of this energy is a part of us. Even though we remain unaware of it.

The whole idea is so strange it defies our sense of reality. It would hardly be believable at all if hadn't been for Sir Isaac Newton working out the math. When Albert Einstein, hundreds of years later, calculated a moving object actually weighs more from a stationary point of reference because the added energy has measurable mass, the whole notion of energy became practically incomprehensible to us humans and our limited powers of perception.

Yet this new creation was bound by this reality—a reality that is significant at the molecular scale. The interdependent peptides, nucleic acids, and other organic chemicals had to move energy to one another. Not randomly, but in predictable ways, directing changes in their motion, shape, and their very state of existence. More and more energy flowed through the fledgling system of chemicals. This energy drove it into new states of existence.

A HOMECOMING

The gentle waves of the San Francisco Bay reflected the first rays of the morning sun. Mira absorbed the sight and was strangely reminded of the final approach as she'd flown into Vostock Station, her first stop in Antarctica. That seemed ages ago despite being a mere three months, as she'd traveled there in early November. The waters of her home and of the alien snow sheet, as they captured and redirected light, both transformed into expansive, brilliant, crystalline fields at once inviting and foreboding.

Every time she flew, she battled queasy dread. This time was easier. At least on the plane. This helicopter? Her knuckles ached and her hair felt wet. The prospect of going home after these long, hard months, even if it was for a short while, was a lifeline. The picturesque perspective of the Golden Gate Bridge helped. She still felt sick. But she was glad for the feeling. Like that made any sense.

She had awoken at 0300 hours to make the trip, first by Gulfstream jet to Travis Air Force Base, and the remainder by stealth Black Hawk. Lieutenant Banks led the crew. She'd felt a tinge of resentment when she saw him; he was, after all, the one who yanked her away from her work at the exact wrong moment. It didn't last. Rain had set her straight. None of this was Banks fault; he had his orders. He was competent and professional, qualities she valued. Neither he nor any of the others in the crew spoke to her during either flight. The only conversation was when she questioned the idea of landing a helicopter on the campus grounds. Lieutenant Banks told her not to worry.

They hovered over U.C. Berkeley's campus. Even the soothing mastery of Hilary Hahn's violin couldn't keep Mira's heart from racing when she beheld the iconic Sather clock tower. When the approval for this trip came through, she texted her plans to Jeff. He and their precious Lake Ellsworth microbes awaited. She wanted every detail, including how he was able to return before the revised schedule. As much as that, she craved a return to normalcy—her lab, her office; planning her next expedition. It was all so close, yet so far away.

The grounds were almost deserted as they made an inconspicuous landing in the Memorial Glade. Mira and her escort hurried out through the gaping doors. The squad had exchanged their arctic camos for desert fatigues. They were also accompanied by a man and a woman from Homeland Security. Banks turned to the remaining squad members—the pilot, co-pilot, and three of the detail ordered to remain with the chopper to guard the payload. Mira couldn't make out his words. He used one arm to help hustle her away from the whirring blades. They trotted more than walked University Drive, through the Wickson Natural Area and the Chancellor's Esplanade, and entered Koshland Hall.

Despite the 725-mile journey, they arrived early, before 0730 hours. There was hardly anyone around. They briskly took the stairs to Mira's office; the pair from Homeland Security huffed to keep up with the rest of them. Two soldiers flanked her office door while Banks and the others followed her in.

Mira regarded her desk fondly at first, but with rising anxiety. Normally stacked with printed copies of scientific journals, all dog-eared and highlighted, the clutter would also include numerous graphs, diagrams, dendrograms, and microscope images left by her postdocs and graduate students. Now the surface featured only a barely noticeable layer of dust. Surprisingly, she missed the mess.

But she also knew the cleanliness was illusory. Someone may be managing the papers, but that didn't mean her inboxes, both physical and electronic, didn't overflow. She had fallen way behind. She'd already inventoried the ever-growing thread of requests—from students, fellow faculty, administration, scientific journals, and collaborators both local and far-flung in her email. But she also sighed at thoughts of what else awaited her attention. It would all have to wait, and that was that.

"Where are your sequencers?" asked the Homeland Security IT specialist, out of breath. Mira promptly forgot his name, but noted his appearance: thick black plastic-rimmed glasses, thin patchy facial hair, and comfort-over-style clothes.

"They're handled by Biosciences Divisional Services—Barker Hall, the building next door. We have business before we get to that though." She turned to Banks. "We have some prep work in the containment facility at Hildebrand Hall, a short walk from here. Then we'll have finishing work in Stanley Hall. But we'll have to finalize arrangements for all of that. I wasn't able to get it all done yet."

She called and left a message for the Facility Director of the Coates Genomics Sequencing Laboratory. He would not grant approval to forego the required training, certifications, and approvals for Braden and their military escort without a compelling reason. How much to reveal without breaking confidence? She unpacked her laptop computer from her backpack and chipped away at her to do list.

As she busied herself, she didn't know how long it was before raised voices in the corridor broke her concentration. She looked up to see the guards detain Jeff. She rushed to greet him. "Let him through. This is my associate Jeff Weingartner." She addressed the Homeland Security agent, a woman of nondescript age and even less-descript features. "He's the one you need to clear through the protocol."

Banks signaled, they stood aside, and Jeff rushed in. "Mira—oh my God! Are you alright?" He hugged her long and tight. It was the first time she had ever hugged a professional associate. The reflexive squeamishness was infused with a sensation she couldn't name. It wasn't unpleasant.

Jeff let go and stepped back. "Sorry. I'm just so glad to see you!"

"I'm glad, too." Mira blushed. She respected Jeff. Until this moment, she was unaware of how much she considered him not merely a valuable employee, but a friend.

"I can't tell you how glad I am that you're back."

She frowned. "Not for long."

"Oh, yeah. You texted that. How long do you have? Cause we've got a lot to cover. I gotta know what the Army wants with you." He looked first at Banks, then at the two others from Homeland Security. "Hi," he said sheepishly. "I'm Jeff."

"We'll get to all of that, but first things first." She addressed the woman. "You have some business with, what was your name again?"

"Agent Deming, ma'am." If she took offense that Mira hadn't bothered to learn her name, it didn't show. "I have all the appropriate paperwork to finalize Mr. Weingartner's security clearance. We'll just require a private space."

"You can use my office while we compile the lab work."

Deming nodded.

"All right," Jeff exclaimed, "let's get going."

"It takes a little while." Mira recalled her tribulation. At least Jeff didn't have to deal with the psychologist or DPG's orientation materials. Since he was twenty years her junior and his life story was far simpler, she figured his process to be correspondingly simpler too. "I expect most of the morning."

She started for the door but stopped. "I'm impressed you got everything back so fast, Jeff. I thought another week at best."

"Kyle ran a tight operation. Nobody dared drag their butt. Fortunately, the weather held for us. Everything was much simpler compared to how it was while you were there. Once we finished the collection phase, I figured the less time we took getting the live samples back the better. You might guess—nobody had a problem with the collapsed time line."

"Good thinking. The specimens are intact? Atmospheric integrity held through transport?"

"As good a percentage survived as we'd figured. You'll be happy when you see."

"I look forward to a review of the details with you. Right now, I can tell you this: I want to repurpose our sequencing time."

Jeff's eyebrows rose. "All right. Wow." He paused. "They're running now, you know. The data looks promising."

"What are you seeing?"

"We've got hundreds of new species. Some of them quite unique."

"Excellent. Great to hear."

Jeff's enthusiasm went the other way. "Interrupting the process now is a pain, to say the least."

"I know. You'll understand once you're cleared and I can tell you more. For now, we've got work to do. You can help us set up. After, come back here to meet with—I'm sorry, I forgot again."

"Deming."

Jeff showed no reservation whatever. "Let's do it. Your lab?"

"No. We'll be working in containment."

Jeff's eyebrows rose again. He only half-kidded. "Containment? How worried should I be, Mira?"

She'd tamped her fear under her scientific-mindset ever since the piglet. Now it escaped, evidenced in her widened eyes. "Very."

A COLD RECEPTION

On the walk back to the helicopter, Mira spotted a gleaming GreenCar in the distance as it glided silently along Hearst Avenue. She sighed. Quon worked in parallel to them. How might their results compare? Was he working with the same scientific rigor? If so, it hadn't been evident those years ago when she reviewed his work on the algae that now fueled his Green Cars. It was clear he hadn't lost this tendency to cut corners and jump to unsupported conclusions. Still, she hoped he worked with the same purpose and determination as everyone else. But she doubted it.

The team, with the addition of Jeff, met the others at the Black Hawk. Two soldiers emerged. They gently lowered a 150 lb. climate-controlled storage unit. One grabbed a dolly and strapped the unit in. The entire group of them set off in the direction opposite of the one Mira, Jeff, and the others had come.

Students and faculty looked askance at the group as they passed. Most were puzzled, but some faces were wide-eyed. A squad of armed soldiers was an unwelcome sight to many who taught and studied here. Jeff made eye contact with as many as he could. He smiled. Mira supposed he did so to exude a sense of well-being. She couldn't tell if it helped or not.

Five minutes later, they arrived at Hildebrand Hall. There were the familiar check-in and preparatory procedures for them. The escorts were uninitiated and slowed the pace, so it was forty-five minutes before Mira, Jeff, Braden, and Banks were suited with double-gloves, face shields, booties, respirators, and heavy lab coats, ready to proceed. The others stood guard outside of containment.

Jeff prepared the Biosafety cabinet. He checked the airflow and wiped it with sterilizing Vesphene. Next, he arranged the pipettes, pipette tips, and other supplies. When the staging was ready, Mira asked Banks to unlock the climate control unit.

Mira removed a small tube of SONA DNA sample. Braden noted the skull & crossbones symbol on its cap. "I thought we weren't transporting the stuff itself," he said, nervous. "We're not in serious danger, right?"

"This is extracted and processed genetic material," said Mira. "It's been animal-tested."

"So why all of this trouble with the suits?" Braden remained unsure.

"All of this is classified as a biohazard, and we're operating with an abundance of caution." said Banks.

Mira introduced the sample into the Biosafety cabinet. Jeff took over from there. The DNA sequencing procedure started with the preparation of a SONA DNA library requiring two extended incubation periods. That meant the rest of the morning. When they finished, Mira said to Jeff, "Why don't you get the rest of your clearance out of the way?"

"Will do." Jeff's enthusiasm for the process was a dramatic contrast to hers. "I can't wait to get the scoop." He exited as fast as he could without skipping details.

Mira loaded the climate control unit with tubes and plates that contained the sequencer-ready specimens. She wiped every surface with a 10% bleach solution, autoclaved all the disposables, and they fastidiously completed the exit protocol. Mira helped the inexperienced Braden through decon.

ON THE WAY out of the containment area, an agitated woman approached Mira. "What is the meaning of this? Soldiers on our campus? This is totally unacceptable!"

Mira summoned her patience. Save for the outburst, she could've reacted the same way if their places were reversed. As with all professors outside of those who intersected with her studies, she didn't know the woman well. She did know about her demonstrative reputation, though. "We're working under special circumstances. I'm sorry I can't elaborate. Pretend you didn't see us."

The woman remained unsatisfied. She moved aggressively toward Mira, presumably to continue her rant. Before she could, Banks stepped between the two women. "Ma'am, please move along."

Flummoxed, the woman mumbled about soldier pigs and oppression, but the group paid her no more attention as they left the building.

The campus buzzed with its normal daily activity. At points along the way they encountered sizable clusters of students. Some spat anti-military or anti-war sentiments. The soldiers became more alert. And the encounters tried Mira's patience. On the Chancellor's Esplanade, one bearded, knit-capped fellow blocked their way.

"Step aside please," commanded Banks, polite but firm.

"Please. These soldiers are here to help." Mira lamented; she didn't have time for this.

The instigator didn't budge. "This is our campus. Our home." Belligerent. "Killers are not welcome here."

At a silent glance from Banks, the soldiers who dollied the heavy steel control unit that housed the SONA component stood it up to free their hands. "I'm not going to ask again," Banks said, calm but forceful. "If you make me arrest you, it will be for a federal crime."

One of the fellow's acquaintances put a hand on his shoulder. "Come on, Nathan, we're late, anyway." He pulled him out of the way.

They reached Stanley Hall without further incident. Mira spoke briefly with the director to verify they were all set to use the sequencers.

Mira brightened when Jeff rejoined them. "You're cleared? Already?"

"Yep. Pain in the butt."

"I know." In retrospect, she should've guessed Jeff's case to be far easier to review than hers. She knew he, like her, was an only child. She also knew he'd come to Berkeley at age seventeen where he'd received all of his schooling. One of the brightest graduate students she'd ever taught, she offered him a postdoctoral position upon his graduation. Antarctica was his first trip abroad.

"Time to answer the Big Question, Mira." Jeff bobbed with more than his usual level of enthusiasm.

"Later. Not everybody has been cleared. Please remain here and proceed with the sequencing."

His head and shoulders dropped, but momentarily. He spoke with the assistant assigned to help them at this facility. Mira didn't know her, but it was obvious she and Jeff were well-acquainted. They dove in, slowed only by Braden's continual stream of questions. Satisfied the work was in good hands and nothing remained to do but wait, Mira left.

Accompanied by Banks and one of the soldiers, she went back to her office to chip away at her mountainous backlog.

A DATE

J uan gripped the wheel of his favorite toy, an azure '97 Esprit V-8 twin turbo. He didn't honk the horn. That would be crass. So instead he revved the engine to a loud roar. Capable of 500 hp, Lotus shipped the sports cars with detuned engines that delivered 350 hp to save the temperamental Renault transmission. Juan upgraded his original transmission and re-tuned his engine to deliver its full potential. He had also reshaped the leather dashboard to make room for the latest aftermarket electronics. Despite its age, the car looked as though it could have just rolled off the factory line.

Juan loved his car, but that wasn't what kept him glued in the driver's seat.

Why wasn't she coming out? He couldn't remember ever being this nervous. ¿Lo que es mi problema? At last, he mustered his courage. He turned off the ignition, sauntered to the building, and rang the buzzer for apartment 2B.

Ten seconds later, Gigi skipped through the door. She wore a yellow light-cotton dress with her soft, dark hair pulled back in a flattering up-do. Juan had never seen her other than in her lab attire.

"Wow," he managed.

"Thanks, Jumping Bean. Better than Corporal Jenkins?"

"Wha...what?"

"Don't think I don't notice that stuff. But don't get all worked into a frenzy. I'm just teasing." She raised herself on her toes and kissed his cheek. "You look nice, too. Smarter without those awful coveralls.

If you closed your mouth and stopped ogling me." She half-skipped toward the car. "Shall we?"

"Um, claro." He blushed and jogged to beat her to the passenger door handle. She easily slid her small frame into the low-slung seat. He smoothed his hair again as he jogged to the driver's side and hopped in.

The engine roared to life and Juan zipped away from the curb.

"Nice whip. I've never been in one like this before."

"Gracias. I put a lot of time into it."

"I didn't know you worked on cars. I thought it was just electronics. 'El Maestro de la Electronica.' You've never told me—how did you get that name?"

"It's a long story." He paused. "You really want to know?"

She leaned closer. "I really do."

The drive from Gigi's apartment to Juan's took forty-five minutes. As they sped along I-80, Juan related the details of how he got into his profession. His wizardry with electronics was self-taught beginning at age seven. He worked with his father on weekends selling off-brand audio, video, and radio equipment in Fresno, California. Their wares were mostly junk. Accordingly, they had no repeat business and had no wish to encounter past customers. Every weekend the family drove around to various flea markets and swap meets in search of fresh suckers.

The operation had never set well with Juan. But he had hidden his shame from his imperious father. Most of the time. Whenever his father sensed Juan's 'attitude,' as he called it, his strategy was to beat it out of the boy. But the things the blows had successfully banished were Juan's love and respect for his father. The experience also instilled in Juan a burning desire. He wanted to be as unlike his father as possible. He resolved not to mistreat his family, not to take advantage of people, and to become much more than a conscienceless peddler someday.

Juan could never forget his life's turning point. He shared the incident in vivid detail with Gigi, who remained rapt. One sweltering summer day, an aggrieved customer approached them at a swap meet outside Modesto with his broken-hearted son in tow. The boy, about Juan's age and size, toted a flashy but inoperable portable player. The argument between the fathers left Juan more than a little embarrassed. He might never be able to explain why, but his father's 'All Sales Final' policy didn't sit well. The man cursed at his father in Spanish, threw the unit on the table, and dragged his wailing son away in a huff.

That night Juan stayed up past 3 am, determined to fix the player. He swapped parts from his brother's Sony box until he found the problem. He used one of his mother's few sharp knives and sat at their flimsy kitchen table, pausing as necessary to reheat the blade on their gas camping stove. Meticulously, piece by piece, he re-soldered the tiny replacement components to the circuit board.

The next morning, he summoned the courage to show his successful project to his father. Oddly enough, the unshaven, sunken-eyed man was not upset. "Please Padre, just take it back to them," Juan begged.

He was shocked by how little convincing it took. "Sure, little Chico. We'll deliver it to them together today. First, tell me." His father rubbed his hands on his stained sleeveless undershirt and pointed to the stacks of useless gear that cluttered their modest duplex, a gleam in his eyes. "Do you think you can fix them all?"

By age fourteen Juan had quit school and begun working in the family business full time. At that point, they no longer needed to travel. Customers drove many miles to purchase inexpensive yet high-performing electronics equipment. Juan swapped parts from older name brand equipment and built superior units. By seventeen he'd earned his moniker: those who experienced his prowess referred to him as 'El Maestro de la Electronica.' Almost every Mexican-American home in the Central Valley had one or more of his refurbished a/v devices, music players, tablet PCs, or other gizmos. The large and loyal client base was crestfallen when, without warning, El Maestro disappeared. None more so than his father.

"Is your father still alive? Do you ever see him?"

"Cockroaches die hard." Juan's voice dripped with venom. It didn't last. "I talk to mi Madre, sometimes. The poor woman—she's still with him. She never saw him for what he truly is."

"I doubt that. Women know. It's just what we decide to tolerate." She fussed with her hair. "This is like a superhero origin story. Shame on you for never telling me this before."

He reacted defensively; his voice raised. "When was I supposed to do that? Every time I've seen you, I've been on the clock."

"Kidding." She waited until he glanced at her. "You'll learn as we spend more time together." They drove into an upscale residential area of Salt Lake City. People on the sidewalks craned their necks to watch them drive by. "People like your ride, Bean."

"Yeah. I'm gonna sell it and take Mr. Quon's offer, though. I'd love to not give money to big oil and the government, you know?"

He waited, but she didn't respond. Instead she said, "It's doctor, by the way."

"What?"

"You called him mister Quon. It's doctor. He's picky about that."

"I did that when we met? For real? Oh man, I hope I didn't offend him. I really want that deal."

"A man like him? With his accomplishments? He'll keep his word."

He pulled into the parking garage of his apartment building. He shut off the car and faced Gigi. "Tell me something, chica. What is really going on at Dugway? Everybody's lips are airtight. You can tell me, just me, what you know. Can't you?"

All lightness of mood vanished when Gigi snapped, "Let's get one thing straight right now, Juan Jimenez. If we're going to be together, and it appears we are, you're going to have to respect me."

Juan was taken back. "I respect you, Gigi."

"In your way, yes. But I'm talking about every way. Like this: when I tell you no, and I promise it won't be about much, but when I do, I mean it. I don't expect to be second-guessed or ignored. Do you understand?"

"Si, si!" This was not the reaction Juan expected. "I didn't mean anything by it."

"We need to be clear on this."

"We're clear."

"Besides, they don't tell me much. I don't know the whole story."

Juan got out of the car and opened the passenger door for her. "What if I tell you what I know and you can set me straight where I'm wrong?"

"Juan!" She scolded, but she did so with a smirk. They walked up the stairs. "What is it you think you know, mister grand wizard of all knowledge?"

"Something's up. With the new security protocol—I don't know what, but it isn't business as usual. Like how you got me those parts so fast. Never seen that before. I also know for somebody like Wes Quon—¡Ay caramba! Dr. Wes Quon" (he emphasized the 'doctor') "to be working there, it has to be big. I know it's dangerous. The mass spec—that was no accidental fire. There's some kind of danger—I bet someone died."

"I can't talk about it, Juan. I'm sworn not to."

He caught her eyes. They told him all he needed—he was right.

"Let me just ask you this, chica. If there is danger, don't you think the public should know they're at risk?"

"The public is not at risk."

"Gigi, I hate to argue with you, this our first date and all, but the public is always at risk. Stuff rolls downhill and regular people are always the ones who end up squashed. That's just how it is."

"I don't know about all of that. I just do my job."

"I know—me too. But aren't we obliged to help? To help protect people?"

"I guess so. That sounds right to me. But I don't think about it the same way. I think I help researchers learn. In that way, I help protect people."

They stopped outside of his apartment door. "That is admirable. Noble, even. I wish it were that simple, Gigi, I really do. If I were to tell you about how some of the stuff that affects people is hidden from them, you'd be shocked."

"Like what?"

"Like how most of the reporting you hear through news outlets is contrived to control your thinking, keep you distracted. They use lies of omission, half-truths, and exaggerations—all so the powerful never have to face negative consequences for their selfish actions."

"And how do you know? What makes you sure that the sources you believe don't do the same? Don't tell me you're a conspiracy nut! We can go right back to the car and you can take me home right now." Juan knew she was only half-kidding.

"No. I'm no nut. I'm a knight." He puffed himself up, chest out.

"I admire a man who lives according to his principles. As long as you're doing God's will." Her face told him she was no longer joking.

Juan blushed. "Well, if it's the right thing to do, God is going to help me, right?"

"Yes, if it is His will."

"Maybe it is. Maybe you and I standing here right now, like this, feeling the way we do about each other, is His will."

"Maybe so, Bean."

Juan manipulated his key fob. The door unlocked with a click and swung open.

"Fancy," Gigi remarked.

"You liked my car? I warn you, once you see my crib, it's gonna be game over."

"I'll be the judge of that." She rubbed past him.

The spacious living area looked like a high-end commercial electronics boutique, clean and unmistakably masculine. Everything was hard and angular. Those surfaces not made of glass or brushed aluminum—including walls, ceiling, and hardwood floor—were lacquered black or white. The sofa, chair cushions, and the post-modern area rug shared bold patterned designs, also black and white.

Touchscreen controls on the walls for lights and who-knows-what-else glowed aqua. Everything that operated on electricity was automated by both program and voice command. "Lights at sixty." They dimmed. "Open blinds." The motorized vertical blinds opened to reveal an impressive view of the downtown area of Salt Lake City.

"That's not Alexa."

"I don't recommend using those mass market devices—you give away too much of your privacy. Besides, I had this functionality way before those systems became widely available." He raised his voice. "Play dinner music, volume medium low." A pleasant jazzy samba filled the apartment in crystal clear fidelity. Gigi noted the large inset flat panel monitors. They displayed abstract graphic art in complicated patterns and brilliant colors. The patterns morphed from one to another in rhythm with the music.

"How could 'El Maestro de la Electronica' live anywhere else?"

"I'm glad you're not disappointed. But what really matters is: are you hungry?"

"Starving!"

"Good. I got something special in the crock pot. Wine?"

"A glass with dinner."

Juan poured the wine. Next, he served the food. They enjoyed light conversation with no further mention of the business at DPG or painful memories of the past.

After a wonderful evening, Juan dropped her off. In her doorway, they shared a kiss that bent Gigi's leg and caused drops of sweat to drip down Juan's back. "Night, Bean. Thanks. Better than streaming reality TV."

"Yeah. Way better." She was about to go through her front door. "Best date of my life, if you want to know."

Gigi's face lit up. "Me too."

A PREDICAMENT

S unlight glinted off of the green-tinted glass of the administrative tower. A blinding flash particularly highlighted the conspicuous GreenCar logo atop the building. It had been welcomed by many and resented by a few Washingtonians as a transformative part of the Seattle skyline. Its twin was a massive post-modern sculpture, perched amid an ornate and immaculate garden that served as the hub of the roundabout outside the building's spacious lobby.

Preceded and trailed by black militarized Lincoln Navigators, Quon rolled to his factory complex in Caesarian glory as he rode silky-smooth in a one-off limousine version of his GreenCar. His uniformed driver, who looked and moved like she belonged on a fashion runway, came around to let him out. Quon emerged as if attending a red-carpet event. A squad of soldiers sprang from the vehicles to join him. The makeup of his escort was similar to the one that accompanied Mira, though an observer might easily take this group to be more of a praetorian guard. There were two substantive differences between the two teams. First, Quon's had one representative from Homeland Security instead of two, another IT specialist. Second, Quon required permission from no one for anything he wanted to do here.

Two soldiers carried Mira's secured climate control unit, the one she'd brought to Berkeley. They followed Quon along with the IT specialist who, in manner, expertise, and experience was a clone of Braden. The other armed soldiers flanked as the group entered the building. They marched past the reception desk to the elevators and crowded into two of them.

Quon acknowledged with a slight nod to his employees as he passed and they gawked, though he met none of their eyes. He entered and exited one of the elevators, emerged at the top floor, and went into the executive office suite. His Administrative Assistant rose from her desk and handed him a single sheet of company letterhead with a list, in order, of the highest priorities that required Quon's attention. She didn't speak, not even a greeting. It was how he preferred it.

"These will have to wait." Quon glanced at the list so cursorily it didn't appear he even read it. "Get me Marvin."

His assistant looked Quon's armed escort up and down with a disapproving scowl. She spoke with clinical dispassion. "He's waiting for you in your office. He dismissed the others who want to speak with you."

"Good." He handed the paper back to her and entered his office. To the leader of the military detail accompanying him, he said, "I need to speak about private business matters. Wait here."

The lead soldier was about to protest, but Quon was in his office before the man could give a reason. He settled in to a ready stance, as did the others.

Quon's office was palatial. Though sparse, the few decorative features were post-modern and opulent. He had not one but two brightly colored original Justin Michael Jenkins pencil drawings on the walls, custom acrylic furnishings, black-stained hardwood floors, and a plush area rug custom-made with the GreenCar logo that defined a meeting space.

Marvin Feldman, Quon's Senior Vice President of Operations, sat in one of six leather and steel chairs that encircled the rug and perused a spreadsheet on an over-sized tablet PC.

"Any word on the testing? What is the likelihood of a TPF contract? Like I told you, last month's numbers don't help our situation."

Quon settled in a chair across from Marvin and smiled at his right-hand man. "You worry too much, Marvin."

"It's what you pay me to do." Marvin stood, his posture rigid. He scratched what little hair remained on his head. "Sam and Clairborne are not happy. They believe the early adopter market is saturated and there won't be another wave of purchasers. They want a new design or they're calling in the lines of credit."

"Yes, yes," Quon dismissed. "This I know."

"They may be right. However much drivers may care about the environment; it isn't enough that they'll pay insurance premiums as high as their lease payments."

"Did you not tell them I am addressing that problem?"

"Many times. It's unconvincing, given the circumstances. Do you know about the disposition of the California Department of Insurance? They are hearing from insurers who want to drop us from their coverage. On top of that, there's rumblings of a class action lawsuit. Customers claim they weren't told about the high repair costs at the time of purchase."

"That is why we lease. What do I always say, Marvin?" In stark contrast to Marvin's gravity, Quon was cheery.

"I know what you say. 'Every problem is a gift in the end.' If this is a gift, I want to send it back. Otherwise, it'll be a Christmas without jobs." Marvin stood and walked to the window. He scanned the Seattle skyline. "What about the TPF's, Dr. Quon?"

"I am not here to discuss those. I have other priorities now."

"Good, but we need a contract. I have to have something, some bone to throw, or the banks are going to take action. If I could just have a time frame for the TPF's—"

"Forget about the TPF's!" Quon's cheer transmuted into ire. The reaction was atypical; he rarely raised his voice in anger.

Marvin's head jerked away, mouth open, at the surprising inversion of Quon's mood. Their last time in this office together, Quon had made the case that the solution to their cash flow trouble was the Tracheal Particulate Filter. Marvin had been skeptical of the prospect. Marvin's lips moved, but no words came out.

Quon reestablished his typical decorum. "The new development is more important."

"More important than saving the company?" Marvin's voice was quiet but tense.

"Yes. This could potentially make everything we've done so far look like a street vending operation."

"Well." Marvin put down the tablet and resettled into the chair opposite Quon. "This has got to be good."

"I am not at liberty to discuss it with you at this time. But that is precisely what I need from you. Time. How much can you buy me?"

Marvin's face was neutral. "I know better than to ask for more details. Instead, I'll give you some." He rubbed his forehead, and then his jowls. "It will involve the legal system. That means we won't be able to keep it out of the news. It'll be bad for business."

"As I said, that will be of no consequence. But my facilities must remain in operation. Can you give me a few months?"

"Maybe. Sam and Clairborne are the tip of the iceberg. There's a lot of other people with whom we are in arrears. Holding all of them off will not be easy."

"It need not be easy. I pay you so much because this kind of assignment is not easy. It need only be achievable."

"I'll do what I can."

"That is all I ask." Quon's smile regained its full strength. If Marvin delivered, he might actually achieve his deepest aim to become the most powerful person in the world. All the countrymen who derided him as a 'banana' (yellow on the outside, white on the inside) would regret doing so. "I will need use of our sequencing facilities. If there is a matter that requires my personal involvement while I am in the building, let me know. But only if it is absolutely necessary."

Marvin's scowl contradicted his words. "Whatever you say, Dr. Quon."

A RECONNOITER

Rain found Connie at WDTC HQ. Preceded by a short knock, he stuck his head into the small conference room where Connie kept a temporary office. "Care for some sunshine, sir?"

"You always did have good timing." Connie removed his readers and stretched his shoulders and neck. "My eyes are getting blurry. What do you have in mind?"

"I'm going to inspect the area surrounding the site. To be on the safe side."

"That's the side we want to be on." Connie stacked papers and shut off his laptop computer. "Let's go."

"I want to start at the contamination site. There's a reported breach in the second containment tent." It was his unenviable duty to confirm the alarming development.

"We're not using canvass anymore, right?"

"Right. SONA ate through the original material. We're using a polymer fabric, speaking of which, we'll need hazmats—I brought an extra along for you."

Rain stopped his jeep at the same spot he had with Mira. The two men jumped out to gear up. Rain noticed Connie had no difficulty. "Like riding a bike, right?"

"Been a long time, but I guess so."

Rain's mood was mixed. He felt satisfied to be reunited with

Connie. Dread soiled that satisfaction in proportion to SONA's spread. That fear was in the way of doing his job the best he could. He bit it back. "How's the family, Connie?"

Connie looked away.

It was not the reaction Rain expected. "What is it, sir?"

"It's been a tough ten years," Connie whispered, still faced away.

Rain finished his own prep and inspected Connie's suit. "You're not going to make me guess, are you?"

"I don't like to talk about it."

Rain didn't press. He'd known lots of people who ended up divorced. That was one problem he'd never have. He'd have to be married first.

Satisfied with Connie's seals, they hopped in. As they crested the next ridge, the massive tent came into view.

Rain's eyes widened. In a few short days, a layer of SONA had spilled from under the tent walls. It encircled the tent and turned the ground a dull gray. That formed the most effective moat Rain could imagine. When he had last been here, there was a lone portable decon station, a generator, and a couple of trucks. Now half a dozen other army tents stood with emergency vehicles, satellite antennae, and a score more of hazmat-clad workers. The scene reminded Rain of Syria, when he had dealt with a chemical weapons attack upon a village. It had also been where he sustained the injury that changed the course of his life.

Sweat beaded on Rain's forehead as he brought the jeep to a rocking stop. It's one thing to read a report. It's another to see the reality. The sight of SONA's expansion lit the flame of his fear. The memory of the worst day of his life fueled that fire.

"We lost Steven." Connie's voice quavered.

It took a moment for Connie's words to penetrate. His first instinct was denial. "What was that, sir?"

"Don't make me say it again." Connie's head hung.

The meaning of his friend's words hit Rain full force. "No..."

"Drunk driver. After that, Annie and I, well, it just wasn't the same. She's been gone five years now."

"Connie. I don't know what to say."

"I just work all the time." He blinked. "It's what gets me through my days."

Connie taught him not to make assumptions when he dealt with Chemical, Biological, Radiological, and Explosive exposures. You couldn't be too prepared; things unravel. Often rather fast. One problem begets another. You think you're fighting one battle, then wham. "I can't imagine your pain. I'm so sorry."

"How could you have known?" Connie scanned the SONA site. "That gray band encircling the tent—that's SONA itself?"

"Yes, sir." Rain banished the emotional storm as he entered crisis-mode mentality; the hard-won ability helped him save lives in a crisis. His voice was firm and his face grim. "I want to reconnoiter the entire area to see for myself if there are additional patches. First, let's check in with Jerry."

They approached the site and Rain found DPG's Technical Director at the expanding SONA zone. "Nitrogen didn't work, huh Jerry?"

"Oh. Rain," Jerry's head popped up. "Glad you're here. No. It's still growing."

Rain frowned. The SONA patch was beyond the possibility of containment, at least by any single tent. "How are we going to try chlorine now?"

"That's what I'm trying to figure out."

"What do the results in the lab tell us?" Connie asked.

"That part is promising." Jerry's voice rose, a glint of enthusiasm. "Chlorine slows it to four or five percent per day."

"Is this expansion uniform and consistent?" Connie's face crunched in concentration.

"It looks that way."

"Maybe we can try chlorine gas on an exposed section, see what happens." Connie's manner normalized.

"The main problem at this point is the seal at the base." Jerry exhaled; his exasperation returned. "We're considering digging, but that's easier said than done."

Rain tried to encourage him. "You'll figure it out. Have teams checked the surrounding area?"

"A little. Not as much as we'd like. We're flying drones, but it's not the same thing as being there. Biggest problem is manpower."

"Connie and I plan to drive around and have a look for ourselves. I'll let you know what we find."

"Hopefully nothing." Rain noted Jerry's desperation. He hadn't seen him like this before.

"From your lips to God's ears." Rain led Connie through decon and back to his jeep.

"Aren't you forgetting something, son?"

Rain cleared his throat. "What?"

"Don't we need more air?"

"I think once we get clear, we can unzip. We'll keep the suits on. It'll be safe to break the seals."

"You're sure of that?"

Rain rubbed his forearms. "Do you know something I don't?"

"Just checking. Old habits."

"Yeah."

They lurched and bumped in an expanding spiral as they crept over the ground of the area. "Be on the lookout for a break in the pattern of the brush."

"Yep," Connie replied. "Being out here. It's bringing back memories, Rain." His mood shifted, but Rain couldn't say to what. "Wasn't it over there we conducted our first field exercise together?" He pointed.

"Looks to me there might be a break in the vegetation pattern in that spot."

Rain stopped, and they skulked to the spot. Rain was right—there was indeed a lack of vegetation in the area. He crouched to better inspect the ground, though he wasn't exactly sure what to look for. A gray, nondescript patch, he conjectured. Connie did the same.

"Aren't we near the designated bio-chemical waste disposal area, Rain?"

"No. It's a mile that way." Rain pointed.

"You sure? I thought it was around here. I was here long before you, you know."

Rain suspected Connie of trying to lighten their moods by teasing. He wasn't sure, but he fired back, anyway. "Yeah, I know. You are, after all, ancient."

"If you're trying to cheer me up, you got some work to do in that department, son." Now he was definitely kidding, that was the Connie he remembered.

"I'll keep at it." Rain couldn't remain lighthearted, though. "I don't know what I'm looking for. Something out of the ordinary." He spotted a discoloration in the soil near a flat rock about a foot square. He moved closer and noted the lack of vegetation.

"What is it?"

Rain pulled his hood back over his head and zipped up his suit. "Stay back, Connie." He overturned the rock with his boot. An agitated scorpion scuttled away.

"Is that out of the ordinary?" Connie teased.

"I wish." He bent. The gray spot that had caught his eye was a shadow. "Nothing."

The two men stalked the area, but neither spied anything noteworthy. Connie broke the silence. "Speaking of things out of the ordinary, what do you make of the famous Dr. Wesley Quon?"

"He's smart."

Connie cocked his head. "What do you really think?"

"Does it matter?" Rain trusted Connie. But he also knew how politics too often come into play. He'd learned discretion.

"His priorities seem off. I wondered if it was just me."

"It's not."

Rain knew Connie well enough. He did not bring this up

casually—he wouldn't let it drop. What was Connie saying? What is he after here? Confirmation? Support? They were friends, yes. But Connie was also farther up the command chain. "I don't know. Given our situation—what happened with his TPF tests. He's awfully chipper."

Connie nodded agreement. "That's it. You don't suspect him for anything, do you?"

"I don't know what that could be." He faced Connie and tried, without success, to guess what he meant. "I chalk his enthusiasm up to scientific interest. Those Brainiac-types can be that way. He had no access to introduce the contaminate, if that's what you're thinking, Connie."

"No. I was curious what you thought, that's all."

"I don't get paid to think."

"Me neither." Connie chortled. "Looks like this area is clean to me. You ready to head back?"

"Okay. I'm just procrastinating on my paperwork, anyway."

Connie placed his gloved hand on Rain's shoulder as they walked back to the jeep. "Me too, son. One thing we never run out of in this man's army is paperwork."

Rain unzipped his suit and pulled off his hood. "You got that right, sir."

They bumped and bounced along in Rain's jeep. Rain looked sidelong at Connie. Clearly, the last ten years were hard ones. He saw it in the man's face. Gone was that sparkle, that proclivity for humor at every opportunity. He resolved that he would not neglect this friendship ever again.

AN ACCIDENT

A lone in an observation booth, Rain repeatedly clicked his pen open and shut as he monitored two workers in Lab C in the LSF.

"Poor little guy," he heard Jenna, one of the lab workers, say as she chased a squeaking calico guinea pig with a double-gloved hand. She pinned the animal gently and removed it from its cage.

Her lab partner, Rahim, appeared unaffected by the creature's cries of objection. "You're too sentimental, Jenna. It makes this harder. You'll find out."

Jenna accessed the Biosafety cabinet and grimaced as she placed the guinea pig inside. They needed to determine the LD50 (lethal dose that caused a 50% chance of death.) This experiment called for an injection of 1 ml of a diluted solution consisting of 0.001% SONA and 99.999% double-distilled water directly into a creature's bloodstream. They were to note the effects and the intervals of their onset. The prior experiments used concentrations that were far too high. "Couldn't we have started with this concentration? I won't be able to sleep knowing the number of animals that had to suffer to get us to this point."

"You know we're not hurting them on purpose." Rahim placed a gloved hand on hers. "We need to know the LD50 to determine lethal levels of exposure."

I get that what we're doing is necessary. Doesn't mean I have to like it."

"I don't like it either. Maybe this guy will get lucky. Come on, it helps if we make it a game." Rahim reached through the integrated arm shields and readied the hypodermic. "I say this one lasts less than five minutes. Want to make it interesting?"

His partner shook her head as much as the isolation suit allowed. She raised her voice. "You're sick. You know that?"

Rahim dismissed her comment as he pivoted back to the Biosafety cabinet and held the guinea pig with his left hand. He injected the solution into the creature's neck with his right. "Start recording. It's either laugh or cry Jenna, right?"

"Whatever."

Rain frowned at the monitor. Though he didn't approve of Rahim's attitude, he wasn't going to say anything. He knew the benefit of gallows humor.

"Ow!"

"What?" Her tone shifted from playful disgust to surprised alarm.

"I think the bugger bit me!"

"Not through your gloves." Jenna's voice lowered. "It couldn't have."

He pulled his hand out of the cabinet. Both of them frantic, they inspected the integrity of his glove. Both of their faces paled. There was a puncture mark at the base of his index finger. Rahim cursed.

"You've got another layer. Take a deep breath. Let's get you through decon."

Over the intercom, Rain's voice boomed. "I'll meet you there. Remain calm."

Jenna ushered Rahim to the exit and key-carded the door open. She accompanied him into the chemical shower. While it went through its automated progression, she methodically scrubbed the exterior of his suit and asked him to do the same for her.

Once the chemicals had run, they waited in tense silence for the steam shower cycle to finish. When it did, Rain, now suited, opened the outer door.

"Sergeant Major, thank God you're here," exclaimed Rahim.

"We need to get him to the infirmary," Jenna plead.

"Not yet. His suit has been compromised. He won't be able to leave containment until we know for sure. There's a med team on the way. We'll take care of Rahim. Come on; help me get him back into the lab."

They went back through the chemical shower, now cramped with three people inside. Rahim fought off panic. "Sergeant Somerdale, what if—"

"Don't think like that. It won't help." Their face shields touched as Rain forced Rahim to focus on him. "Jenna will be waiting in the outer room. We've got to make sure you're clean. We'll run some tests. After, we'll celebrate. You pick the drinks, okay?"

Rahim's face shield fogged as his skin beaded with sweat and his dilated pupils darted back and forth.

Jenna's eyes welled. "Rahim? Go on. You'll be all right."

Without warning, Rahim twisted away from Rain's hand on his shoulder. "My hand—it itches!" Frantic once again, he grasped at the zipper on his hazmat suit.

Rain clamped Rahim's wrist in a steel-grip. "Stop," he commanded. "You will remain calm, Rahim. Remember how we trained."

Rahim hyperventilated. Rain let go of his wrist and grasped Rahim's shoulders. "Easy, just breathe." He glanced at Jenna. "I've got this. Get through the other side right now. I'll open the door for you. Run the shower again to be on the safe side."

He guided Rahim, now passive, back into the lab where two suited figures opened a cot. He sat Rahim on it, nodded acknowledgment to the med team and reentered the chemical shower to let Jenna out.

Rain returned to the lab. The two medics held Rahim down. "Cut my hand off! It's gonna spread, I know it." His face was past pallid, blotchy with reddened and bluish patches.

Rain knelt at his side. He again pressed his face close to Rahim's. "Be still Rahim, can you do that for me?"

Rahim showed no sign he understood or intended to comply.

Rain grabbed the man's head with both hands and pressed the pliable plastic against his temples. "Get ahold of yourself!"

That broke through. Rahim ceased his struggle and the two medics used the opportunity to swap Rahim's compressed air canisters. After a few minutes, Rahim regained his wits.

"Nothing's happening," he whispered.

Rain knew what he meant. "We'll keep you under observation for a little while, just to be safe, okay?"

"Okay." Rahim was nearly inaudible.

Rain sighed in relief. The incident with Gigi filled his mind. His jaw clenched as memories of Roberts returned.

A DRUNK

Jeff bounded into Mira's office, Braden in his wake. Banks sat in a chair on the opposite side with his head buried in his hand. Mira focused on her computer as she sat at her desk and responded to messages. "Done already? Findings?"

"Still running; it'll be a while longer. We should begin to see results sometime before midnight." Jeff moved closer. "You know what I'm here for now."

Banks looked up. "He should be told only what he needs to know to do the work."

"He needs to know everything," Mira said. At least everything that intersected with their studies. "He's a gifted scientist; he'll be of great help."

Banks shrugged and relented by returning his attention to the screen in his hand.

Mira covered what she'd learned about SONA. Jeff peppered her with technical questions, most of which she wished she had answers to. Eventually he landed on the scariest topic.

"How much time do we have?"

Her throat constricted. "Simple question. Complicated answer."

"I know. To quote you, 'Life is inconveniently complex.' Still—"

"Current calculations show the rate of expansion could endanger the entire North American continent by autumn." As she spoke, the pressure to get useful results, and do so fast, intensified. "By year's end, the spread could be everywhere else, too."

Evidently, neither Braden nor Banks had previously heard this analysis. Braden gasped and Banks' face was drawn. Jeff exhaled. "I guess we should have stayed in Antarctica."

Mira stood and paced as she talked. "We must keep in mind those projections are based upon many assumptions. For instance, they assume a constant rate of expansion applied linearly over time. The calculation also ignores mitigating forces, both ones we apply and naturally occurring."

Braden still appeared shaken. "That's good to hear." All eyes turned to him and he hung his head, self-conscious. "Sorry."

Mira's attention remained on Jeff. "I believe your question was more about how much time we have to identify a solution before any large-scale damage is done."

"Yes. I work better when I know my deadline."

"I've noticed. If you want a deadline, how about a month? Two at most. Any longer, and it would probably cost the state of Utah."

Jeff swallowed. "That's not a lot of time."

"You want to go check those sequences?"

"Yep." He was halfway through the door when he stopped. "Oh, before I forget, Kyle told me if you've got a minute, he'd like to see you before we leave."

Mira's mouth rounded. "Oh. He didn't go home?"

"No. He decided to hang around, at least until you got back. I haven't seen him much. He's probably in a bar somewhere around here."

"I hate bars."

SHE SPOTTED him at the far end of the bar. The pub overflowed with collegians and intellectuals; he was conspicuously not one of them. The other patrons gave him a wide berth; the barstools on either side of him were empty despite having standing-room only. He waved his arms in big gestures as he shouted, his words slurred, "...that's one more reason this whole world is going right into the big ole' canister."

The close-packed bodies and onslaught of sight, sound, and smell ratcheted Mira's nerves. She pushed her way through as fast as she could. Kyle's demeanor transformed. "There she is, by God! A sight for these old sore eyes. Smartest woman in the world right there, I tell ya! Woman, forget that. Smartest person in the world, I dare claim!"

"Kyle, I'm grateful for all you've done." He stood as she approached. His big wiry beard splayed over his chest as he looked down at her. He surprised her as he easily lifted her off the ground in a smothering hug. It felt awkward; it even hurt a little bit. She amused herself with the notion that somehow, she had become a hugger. Or at least a huggee.

"Good to see you, Wallace." He spun back to the bar and shouted down its length, "Barkeep! Get my friend a flippin' drink already! Somethin' off the top shelf!" His words were stretched by alcohol's effect.

"I shouldn't," Mira protested, but realized Kyle would buy the drink no matter what she said.

The bartender brought something caramel-colored over ice. Kyle grabbed the glass and handed it to her. He raised his own. "We never properly concluded our mission together. We need a toast."

Mira didn't toast. All her concentration went to suppress nearly overwhelming sensory stimuli—a dozen conversations, vacuous lyrics and soulless beat from the jukebox, clinks of billiard balls somewhere in the back, a high-pitched scrape of a sliding barstool, the assault of smells from bar food, drinks, perfumes, and body odor, and the menagerie of people dressed in an array of fashions. She gathered her thoughts, raised her glass, and said, "It didn't go as we planned. It even cost a few fingers and toes—along with twenty-five million dollars. Nevertheless, we accomplished what we'd set out to do. And, in spite of Antarctica's best wishes to the contrary, we all got out of there alive. Here's to a successful venture."

He clinked his glass to hers with enough vigor to almost knock hers from her hand. She took a sip and grimaced. She wished it was a soda, not this infernal liquid that burned her throat and quenched no thirst. She thought of no logical reason for anyone to voluntarily drink it. She glanced at the bar's patrons on either side of her. Everybody was not only drinking, but clearly enjoyed doing so. Why? Why deliberately impair the one thing of most value to you—your mind?

Yet Kyle did that. Nobody had brought alcohol to Antarctica. She had done a background check when she hired him. There was no indication of any problems related to alcohol. She'd heard talk of two barfights in his past. They both ended the same way. Short and decisive. She pitied anyone who received a blow from one of those fists.

"Beauty, Wallace, well said. Sorry ya missed all o' the fun. Ya know—gettin' that show on the road."

"Yes, well. I knew you and Jeff would handle it." She stopped herself. "I didn't expect you to be here, Kyle. I assumed you would go back to Vancouver."

"Oh, that. Yeah. I gotta tell you the truth." He went from jovial to sullen. "There's not much to go home to."

"No?" A pang of guilt forced her eyes to the floor. She knew little about this man but his professional accomplishments. Up to this moment, she hadn't cared to know.

"Nah. Figured I'd hang around here a while." He drained his glass, slammed it on the bar and shouted, "Barkeep! Another Paralyzer!" He lowered his voice. "I had to teach this numb-nut how to make one, do-ya-believe-it?" He added at not-quite-a-whisper, "I wanted to make sure you was alright, ya know, the way you left and all."

"Me? I'm okay, I suppose. Tired." She took a swig and puckered. "I'm sorry I didn't ever ask about you. I'm not good with that kind of thing."

"Wasn't yer job, now, wazzit Doc? That's one of the things I like about ya." He dropped a heavy hand onto her shoulder; some of her drink spilled. "Around you, a body don't never gotta talk 'bout that kinda stuff if he don't wanna." He glanced the length of the bar.

"Where is that drink, anyhow?" He returned to Mira. "What was that nonsense with those troopers, eh?"

"Do you mean Lieutenant Banks?"

"Yeah, those guys. They couldn'ta waited another day or two? Seems awful fishy to me."

"It was legitimate. They're with me here." She lowered her voice. "I hope to get a chance to tell you about it, Kyle. Sometime soon. But I can't right now." Mira's cell phone buzzed, and she checked it in anticipation. Jeff. Good. But the message was not what she expected: *u got 2 c asap.* "I have to go." Excitement accelerated her pace and increased her volume. "I'm leaving tomorrow, before eight a.m. It was good to see you, Kyle. I hope to be back soon."

"Me too," he slurred. He watched her push her way out and shouted behind her, "Make way—let her through!" As she left, he called out to the bartender, "Hey, b'y, where's that Paralyzer?"

A PUZZLING RESULT

The downcast contingent spoke little on their way back to DPG. None were more forlorn than Mira. Eyes glassy, she gazed out the portal of the Black Hawk. San Francisco held none of the charm she'd experienced on the arriving flight. People below went about their lives, blissfully unaware of what lay in wait for them. If not for the remotest turns of fate, she'd be one of them. She turned up her music.

Her thoughts came reluctantly—dull, fuzzy. Almost useless. She squeezed her eyes shut. It made no sense to her. The sequence results from Jeff revealed nothing; just a jumbled mess. She wasn't much for fiction, but during her undergraduate studies she developed a fondness for the genius of Shakespeare. Despite her exhaustion, she recalled with perfect accuracy the words, upon discovering the Queen's death, of Macbeth:

> She should have died hereafter;
> There would have been a time for such a word.
> To-morrow, and to-morrow, and to-morrow,
> Creeps in this petty pace from day to day
> To the last syllable of recorded time,
> And all our yesterdays have lighted fools
> The way to dusty death. Out, out, brief candle!
> Life's but a walking shadow, a poor player
> That struts and frets his hour upon the stage
> And then is heard no more: it is a tale

Told by an idiot, full of sound and fury,
Signifying nothing.

The passage inspired an unpleasant string of thoughts: SONA was full of fury, if not sound. Dusty death? Now it appeared to have no signature. And she was the idiot. Eleanor, the fool. If it was biological, as it appeared, what could SONA possibly be? She shuddered. She detested the feeling of powerlessness.

As they transferred to the posh Gulfstream at Travis, the gravity of their circumstances couldn't keep the enthusiasm from Jeff's face. He plopped next to her. "Stealth helicopter, and now a private jet. I could get used to this."

Distracted as Mira was, Jeff's meaning didn't land. "No reply from Quon to my texts," she mumbled, more to herself than Jeff. "He is supposed to be there by the time we arrive. Maybe he has something." She wished she believed that.

"I can't wait to meet him." Jeff grinned. "Do you think I might get a chance to work in a lab with him?"

"What?" Mira finally noticed Jeff's demeanor. "I don't know. Maybe." His exuberance annoyed her. "I'm going to try to get a nap." She reclined the seat and faced away. On her playlist, Brian Crain's 'Rain' played.

"Okay. I get it. I'll shut up." He only did so for a moment. "It's just—when I came on with you, Mira, I had no idea it would lead to stuff like this."

She wondered how Jeff could be anything other than frightened. She supposed all was not lost. Not yet. She again faced Jeff; this time with a slight smile. She placed her hand on top of his. He looked at it, his brow raised in surprise. "Me neither, Jeff." She spun back to the window and used that same hand to pull down the shade. "Now let me sleep."

"SOMETHING MUST HAVE GONE wrong during the DNA extraction process."

"A worthy idea, Colonel Yanoviak," said Quon. "But I suspect something else entirely."

A vexed group assembled in the large conference room at the Life Sciences Facility at DPG. Connie, Quon, Mira, and Jeff for this progress review were joined by the senior team and via videoconference on screens in front of the room, Aaron Moore from his office at Ft. Belvoir and Brigadier General Bridget Higgins from hers at Ft. Detrick. They expected, hoped, and prayed for answers. Now, they shared Mira's frustration. All they had were more questions.

Quon's results matched Mira's. DNA sequences from thousands of species, mostly known microbes, could be identified no matter what instrument or assembly algorithm they ran. Yet none of the runs revealed evidence of a new, unique organism. There were, however, billions of small DNA sequences that matched nothing, they weren't even identical to each other. It was a molecular mess; like someone took the pieces of a thousand jigsaw puzzles and mixed them together with a billion extra pieces that fit nothing.

Quon was the one person who didn't appear discouraged. "It is likely this DNA disorganization is yet another unique property of SONA."

That seemed a leap to Mira. She looked Quon over. He had a different suit for every day, but only one tie. Or at least one color of tie—his iridescent corporate green. She cared nothing about fashion, but it still struck her as curious. "What does that mean, Dr. Quon?"

His smile lost a measure of intensity. "I simply suggest its DNA may be hidden among the DNA of other organisms."

"I don't know what that means either." She addressed the others in the room. "It's normal to find many types of DNA in any particular sample. If what Dr. Quon is saying has any scientific merit, this agent is unlike any other biological entity."

"Yes, that is it exactly." Quon's energy was discordant with the rest of the room. "I suspect we may have found the second known example of abiogenesis."

Potteiger's face scrunched. "Abiogenesis?"

"This is the word we use for the emergence of life from non-life." Quon explained haughtily. "It happened once. We know that for certain. When all Life began."

"And you believe that's what happened with SONA?" Eleanor's eyes narrowed, dubious, as she pointed in the direction of the containment tent. "This thing just happened to appear in that desert out of nothing?"

"Not from nothing. But abiogenesis remains a fascinating possibility." Quon's voice increased pace and volume. "Dr. Wallace, I believe this is an area of particular expertise for you, is it not? You can better explain the origin of life on Earth than me."

"I don't see how that's relevant. And no one can explain that, anyway."

Quon's smile widened further. "Perhaps not as a factual matter, but there are theories that approach a consensus among experts like yourself."

Was Quon trying to get her to say something in particular? What, she didn't know. "Consensus is not data. Theories are useful to the degree they are supported by data. But there are many such theories. Which one do you deem pertinent? DNA first? RNA first? Protein first? Metabolism first? Which?"

Quon's ruler-straight spine relented as he fumbled for an answer. "I believe the latest postulates claim, well, the exact theory is RNA preceded..." He adjusted his tie. "Let us not get too deep into all of that. Which one do you most favor?"

"I don't favor any of them. They all leave too much unanswered." She looked at Jeff. "Life is inconveniently complex."

He grinned back at her. "That's why she does the work she does." As eyes focused on him, Jeff's self-consciously looked at his feet. "I'm sorry. I didn't mean to—"

"This is Dr. Jeff Weingartner. I've come to rely on him." Her tone chilled as she turned back to Quon. "I'm still trying to understand your point."

"My point? I should think it obvious, especially to you." He looked away from Mira and spoke to the group as a whole. "Of course, we must find a way to contain SONA's spread. That is first and foremost. But this evidence points to one thing." He straightened. "SONA is a new life-form, related to nothing else."

Connie let out a dismissive grunt. "Probably not." Quon scowled as Connie spoke to Mira. "What did your team find?"

"It was essentially the same as Dr. Quon's results."

"Maybe we should explore alternate methods?"

"That was my initial reaction too." Mira paused to sort through the evidence. "The results are consistent across multiple sites and sequencing technologies. It's doubtful the problem is the method."

Moore's voice rose and his face flushed. "You're at a dead end? Is that what I'm hearing? Does anyone have any useful suggestions?"

General Higgins' tone was steady, her manner authoritative over the video link. "Our teams have just begun. Connie's team at Aberdeen is conducting chemical tests while here at Detrick we're focused on contagion mitigation protocol. These, along with the ongoing biological research you're conducting there at Dugway, are going to take time. We are directing all necessary resources to this matter. There is nothing more I, nor my superiors, can ask."

Eleanor stood. "There is at least a sliver of good news. Jerry?"

"We were able to isolate a section of the primary SONA pool. With that done, we applied chlorine gas. The treatment seems to slow the propagation by perhaps as much as fifty percent. Thank you to Command Sergeant Major Somerdale and Colonel Yanoviak for their help on this."

"For the record, that was Mira's suggestion," Rain corrected.

"Thank you to all who have contributed," Jerry said with a head tilt toward Mira. "Though the approach makes a hazardous situation even worse for our people, it could buy us time."

That's a relief. Mira thought out loud, "I hoped to get a definitive result from the genomic studies. We didn't get that. There is something we can do."

"And in your opinion, what might that be?" Moore asked, his tone demanding.

Eleanor leaned toward Mira. "You have an idea, don't you?"

Mira's eyes sparked. "It's a long shot. It's liable to take all the time that Jerry and his people have bought us."

"Well?" Moore grew even more impatient.

"Give her a minute, please." Eleanor smiled, encouraging.

Mira spoke in her professorial mode. "Where I grew up back in Pennsylvania, we were hit with a plague of invasive *halyomorpha halys* accidentally transported from Asia. They multiplied out of control. They swarmed houses. Destroyed crops. But after several years of this, the problem all but went away."

Moore asked, "What are hally morphy halls?"

"Stink bugs," said Jeff. "Brown marmorated stinkbugs. I see where you're going with this, Mira. Bioremediation."

"What are you talking about?" Potteiger's manner mirrored Moore's.

"We should try to identify or engineer a microbe that will use SONA as a food source."

"You mean you want to create another monster?" Harrison's choked words conveyed dubiousness. "But instead of attacking us it'll attack SONA?"

"In time, a parasitic wasp followed the stinkbugs from Asia and brought their population under control." Quon's reaction was the polar opposite of Harrison's. "This is an idea with much merit." He spoke to Harrison. "It is not playing 'Frankenstein,' as I believe you characterized it, sir. Microbes are routinely re-purposed. It is the technology behind my GreenCar."

Mira rose and met eyes in sequence: Rain, Connie, and finally Eleanor. "I'm not ready to conclude SONA is an organism yet. But its behavior is similar to invasive species. This strategy is the most likely to give us positive results." She glanced at Jeff. "If SONA is a living thing, we would call this approach biocontrol."

Eleanor perked. "So, if SONA is a stink bug, we need to find the right wasp?"

Xi, in her subdued manner, said, "This idea makes me think. Might SONA be capable of adaptation? Can it evolve?"

"We have no evidence for this." Mira lectured again. "First, we don't see cellular structure or even a stable DNA sequence. Besides, evolution tends to drive ecosystems towards balance. Even infectious diseases tend to exist in nature as non-pathogenic. They grow at low levels so as to not kill their hosts. It's a more powerful survival strategy. It's when they 'jump' to a new host, one with which they have not co-evolved, does severe disease and widespread death occur. We could be better off if SONA did evolve."

"This is why I suggest SONA is novel," Quon interjected. "If it was engineered and introduced into the environment, that is one thing. Since multiple investigations now appear to rule that out, my abiogenesis postulate remains the most robust explanation."

Eyes naturally returned to Mira. "Either SONA is a living thing or it isn't. If it isn't a living entity, then it also cannot evolve, at least in a traditional sense."

Quon's smile disappeared. He appeared to formulate a response. Eleanor spoke before he could. "Regardless of its nature, does this issue of adaptation mean any solution we find may only be temporary?"

Quon pounced. "No. I believe what Dr. Wallace suggests is worthy."

"How do you find an organism that could eat SONA?" General Higgins asked.

"We screen them one by one," replied Mira. "Millions of them. Maybe tens or hundreds of millions."

"How could we possibly do that?" said Jeff.

Mira spoke to Jeff but her eyes found Eleanor. "It will require specialized instrumentation we do not have here at the West Desert Test Center."

"Our BSL-4 facilities here at Ft. Detrick are state-of-the-art," Higgins offered. "I can offer you the full support of the Integrated Research Laboratory, Dr. Wallace. I'd like to extend my invitation for you to come to Ft. Detrick to conduct your investigation."

"Dr. Quon, can you spare Dr. Wallace if we reassign her to Detrick?" asked Eleanor.

Rain and Mira shared a glance.

"It would, of course, be a detriment to our ongoing inquiries." Quon looked at Mira the entire time he spoke. "However, I believe we can manage without her."

"While that's happening, I'd like to parallel the Aberdeen tests on how to physically or chemically degrade SONA at the WDTC," said Harrison.

"Sounds like a good idea to me," Potteiger added. "Approved."

"I have designed experimentation along similar lines, as energetic studies are another area of specialty for me." Quon turned up the volume of his smile and addressed Harrison. "May I join you?"

Harrison looked to Potteiger and next to Eleanor. In Mira's estimation, there appeared to be no objection in their faces. "I suppose that's okay," Harrison said. "Thank you. We appreciate your help."

Moore remained exasperated. "So we're clear—when I report this through Command, our status is we still don't know what this deadly thing is, where it came from, or how it got there. It looks like it may be an entirely new life-form. We're now looking to burn it up or find a microbe that can eat it. Have I got that right? Anybody else see how this might not put the best spin on what you all are doing?"

"You may emphasize the comprehensive nature of the work, Mr. Moore." General Higgins' tone was calm and even. "We will continue in earnest to get answers."

"I will emphasize to the Director of Homeland Security we are pursuing all pertinent lines of investigation," Eleanor added.

"That is a reasonable stance, Secretary Dixon." Quon spoke as though everyone there reported to him. As Mira understood things, Eleanor, Potteiger, Connie, Higgins, maybe even Harrison, Jerry, and Moore outranked him. She held her objection as Quon went on. "I have additional inquiries in mind. As extensive and well-equipped the resources you all have at your disposal, things are becoming—crowded. I should run experiments at my facilities in Seattle."

"That may be helpful, I'm sure, Dr. Quon." Eleanor's brows rose. "And we appreciate your generous offer. Let's hold up on that, at least for now. We don't need additional risk if it can be avoided. Let's see what happens with our studies at the three Army facilities first."

EXCERPT:
THE NECESSITY OF PRECURSOR COOPERATIVES

Wallace, M. D.[1,2] *and Weingartner, J. A.*[1]

1*University of California, Berkeley, Dept. of Plant and Microbial Biology, 311 Koshland Hall, Berkeley CA, 94720.*

2*National Interagency Biodefense Campus, Fort Detrick, MD 21702*

Section #2: Energetic Transformation, cont.

Unlike the visible objects around us, molecules do not have defined shapes. They exist in a world of probabilities; a range of possible states. The probability of any one state depends on its interactions with other molecules and the amount of energy present. And something else. As Schrödinger pointed out with his famous thought experiment, the introduction of the concept of time inextricably ties the observer to outcomes. Calling this world bizarre is inadequate. It's as though there are countless realities that all exist but only manifest upon observation.

The chemical cooperative rapidly became more and more complex. Long peptide strings, some 30-40 amino acids long, formed. To do so, they needed energy. Thinking of them as strings is a poor description of their shape. It's better to picture them as knots that continually tie and untie themselves in myriad ways. Only when specific and particular knots are formed do the peptides become functional.

It takes energy to convert these peptides from one type of knot to another. Up to this point, the energy was available via high levels of ultraviolet light. This ultraviolet radiation energized either the peptide itself or its target. But energy also came from transmission by other chemical reactions nearby that had themselves become energized by heat or light. The ability to capture light energy and store it for later use as chemical energy would be but one key step in moving from short peptides to the advent of long and highly efficient proteins.

A REASSIGNMENT

Mira wrestled with what her new research commitment to SONA meant. Her lagging work at Berkeley weighed heavily on her. Her life's work. The millions of microbes she spent decades collecting from every corner of the planet. All the deprivations. Years of isolation. The flying, sweating, freezing, bleeding. She was so close now to building the ultimate tree of life. And at its root, finding the oldest living thing and possibly the origin of life itself.

But SONA changed that. Her own work now seemed a selfish pursuit. Instead, she would be screening her microbe collection for a specific use. Quon's kind of work. She had no choice and knew what she must do. There was only one place with the laboratory facilities she'd need. She would relocate to Maryland.

As Jeff and she worked to repurpose her lab, she delayed telling him her decision no longer. "Jeff, I want you to return to Berkeley."

He marked an open bottle for disposal. His shoulder-drop signaled his reaction. "I hoped to go with you."

"I know." Mira's personal vigor was back. For the first time since Ellsworth, her bones didn't ache, and her eyes didn't continually want to close. As much as she would like to have Jeff by her side, it wasn't the right thing to do. "Call it a hunch. I need you to finish the microbial sequencing and complete the informatics."

Jeff remained crestfallen for only a passing moment. "Of course, Mira. I'll be happy to. I'll keep analyzing the SONA DNA data too. Who knows, maybe I'll find something useful."

"I have no doubt you will, Jeff."

A FEW MINUTES LATER, Gigi breezed into Mira's lab bubblier than ever. The mood lift was most welcome. Mira left Jeff and Gigi to introduce themselves and finish the remaining tasks. She planned to spend much of the day in teleconference with her new team at Ft. Detrick to discuss resources, microbes, and supplies she'd need for the assays she wanted to conduct, to establish a timeline, and to assign responsibilities. Two meetings were scheduled before her departure. She realized that before she flew out, she needed a ride to and from the English Village to retrieve her few belongings. Why hadn't she brought them with her this morning? She left the LSF, walked to Rain's office, and tapped on the door. His deep voice invited her in.

"Sorry to disturb you," her voice was uncharacteristically diffident.

Rain's face lit. "It's a nice surprise. To what do I owe the pleasure, Dr. Wallace?"

"Mira, please." Self-conscious, she fumbled for words and shifted her weight from leg to leg. "I have...I wanted to ask...two things of you. First, I'm not sure where Eleanor is—I mean at the moment. Can you help me find her?"

"She's not responding to texts?"

"I didn't try." She tried to look him in the eyes.

"Oh." He grinned and leaned back in his chair. "It's no problem. If she's in, she's set up down the hall. I'll take you."

"Her message said to meet her in her office at this time. It didn't say where that was." She noted a beautiful piece of stained glass mounted on the wall behind him.

He looked up. "We'll get you there. No problem. What's the second item?"

"I don't want to impose." What was this reluctance to ask?

"Don't think twice," he assured. "My duty is to make sure we properly accommodate you."

"I'm flying out this evening. I left my belongings back in the English Village. Stupid oversight."

"It's not like you had anything else on your mind." His eyes sparkled. "I'd be happy to drive you."

"It's not too much time out of your day?" She wiped her brow.

"I welcome the chance." He grinned and stood. "What time do you leave?"

"1930 hours." She wiped her suddenly clammy hands on her slacks. She was no young coed. Why was she acting like one?

"I'm impressed, Mira. We've been able to militarize you."

"Not exactly." She kept one arm at her side and grasped that elbow with her opposite hand. "I lived on that clock for a few months. Antarctica."

"Oh, yeah. Gotcha. A bit late to travel, isn't it?"

"This way I can work a full day tomorrow."

"Right." He scratched the stubble on his chin. "Tell you what. How about I drive you and we leave enough time to have dinner together—does that fit your schedule?"

"I could, I mean, sure." She blushed. "I could make the time, I guess."

"Okay. My place isn't far from you. I planned to grill a steak. It can just as easily be two. Do you eat meat?"

"Not as a habit. But as hungry as I am, I could eat half a cow."

He chortled. "I'll hold you to one good-sized steak. Come back at, say, 1630 hours?"

"Okay." Rain's cordiality, his laughter, the instant materialization of dinner plans; it all made her—lighter. She managed a deeper breath. "I'll do that."

"Good. I look forward to it. Now, let's get you to Secretary Dixon."

THEY FOUND Eleanor in her temporary office. The room was sparse —nothing on the walls and two stackable chairs in front of the clean desk, behind which Eleanor sat in a comfortable leather chair. The handoff took less than a minute. Rain returned to his office. In her warm manner, Eleanor invited Mira to sit. "All set to go?"

"I suppose." Mira shook her head to regain her focus.

"One item I wanted to review with you before you left. I'm not nitpicking. These matters are sensitive, considering there is the question of how this all began."

Mira wasn't there at the beginning. Quon was. Did Eleanor suspect foul play? "Is there something about Quon you need to tell me, Eleanor?"

"No, sugar. But I am interested in the exchange between the two of you in the review. It's an important question. I understood his perspective. I can't say the same for you. You're resistant to his abiogenesis hypothesis about SONA. I want to know why."

"I believe I was clear in the meeting." She dialed into her habitual scientific demeanor. "There is no data to support his assertion. And there are no theories that adequately explain the formation of life."

"Like we talked about at lunch." Eleanor's voice was low and in her eyes was—acceptance? Fondness? "I've thought about that. A lot."

"I hope it was helpful."

"It was. I'm amazed."

"I agree. The mechanisms that define Life are the most fascinating subjects."

"Yes. But that's not what I'm talking about, darlin'. I'm talking about you."

"Me? I don't understand." Mira straightened.

"For one thing, how you're following in your great, great grandfather's footsteps."

Oh. That's what she meant. She relaxed again. "In a manner. His were big shoes."

"You're filling them well. Anyway, something I want to ask you. It's personal. If you don't mind?"

"Go ahead."

Eleanor leaned forward and lowered her voice. "Why do you think you were invited here, Mira?"

"I wasn't invited. I was brought here. Forcibly. I've stayed because people here think I can help."

"It's obvious you were born for your work. Do you think it is all an accident?"

"Every genetic trait is statistically distributed. With sufficient population size, we see a wide but recurrent differentiation. Every person is capable of much, but some cohorts are comparatively better suited for particular roles. I suppose the more specific that role is, the easier it is to identify. Maybe that's why I knew what I would do at such a young age."

"Seems to me you could say the same about anyone, Mira. I surely won't argue with you. But things happen for a reason, don't you think?"

Mira considered the question. "Do you believe SONA happened for a reason?" As she spoke, tendons in her neck tightened and her voice inflected up. "What if we can't identify a remediation solution? Then what? Do you believe a calamity that may claim who knows how many lives in a manner too horrific for words serves some greater purpose?" If she wasn't mad specifically at Eleanor, what was her anger about?

"If I'm being honest, I have to say I don't know." Eleanor sat back as she considered Mira's challenge. "But it hasn't happened yet. I believe God's on it."

"That is insufficient. We must manage this threat—with science. It won't miraculously solve itself. God is not sending help."

Eleanor laughed, hard.

The response wasn't what Mira expected. "I fail to see what's funny."

Eleanor leaned forward and placed her hand on Mira's. "He sent you, didn't He?"

Mira looked at their hands. She didn't pull away. Nobody sent her. Quon recommended her, that's why she was there. Why had he been so keen to get her specifically? She felt forced into this service. She almost said so again. She should be at Berkeley. No, she no longer believed that. It struck her as odd, surprising, this shift in her attitude. "You're saying God created this and then sent me to fix it? I'm sorry, Eleanor, but that's delusional."

"The God I know works through us, sugar. We're his hands in this world. Sometimes we do things so extraordinary we call them miracles. Other times, we do His will in our everyday actions." Eleanor extended her other hand and clasped Mira's in both of hers. Her smile widened, and she held Mira's eyes for an uncomfortable moment. "I'm worried because I'm human, child. And I don't presume to put this all on you." She looked at the ceiling, contemplative. "I try to 'fear not' as Jesus teaches us. I have faith—all is ultimately according to His plan. We only play our part." Her voice became a near whisper. "But you know what? If we're quiet, and we listen, we can know what that is."

"Listen to what?" Mira heard talk like this before. She'd always found it senseless.

"To Him. He's a friend. He whispers to you, hoping you'll listen."

Inner voices? Rubbish. She preferred Vivaldi. Or Amy Beach. "What does He say to you?" She didn't hide the skepticism from her voice.

"Truth."

"Scientists don't have that luxury." Feelings. Anecdotes. It'd be so easy if those had value. They didn't. "We require evidence." Mira pulled her hand away.

"You've never had a feeling you didn't know where it came from?"

"No." Eleanor's faith was the antithesis of what Mira believed.

"If it turns out SONA is not part of the Tree, if it's a new life-form as Quon believes, doesn't that challenge your beliefs?"

Eleanor leaned back. "I don't see how, but do you want to know how I look at it?"

"Alright." Mira's voice was flat.

"Jesus compared faith to a mustard seed. He taught us that faith is so mighty even a small amount achieves wonders. I also picture faith as a connection with God that, once established, grows over time. That's if it's cared for. If not, faith shrivels and dies. But when nurtured, its power is awesome. Literally. It inspires awe. I can't really explain it to you, darlin'. We're talking about something that must be experienced. Maybe it's complex, like the origin of life as you describe it." Eleanor's eyes sparkled as she awaited Mira's response.

Mira's finger traced the deep weather-drawn lines in her forehead. After a few moments, Mira said, "I don't know what to say."

"You need not say anything. Just think about it. I'll add this: my relationship with Jesus Christ gets me through everything. Everything. I shudder to think what I would do without Him."

Mira paused again, then muttered, "Is that all?"

Eleanor looked at her with an expression Mira couldn't read. Concern? Care, maybe? "Here," said Eleanor. She removed a necklace from around her neck. Mira hadn't noticed it before that moment. Calling it a necklace wasn't right—it was a woven cord dyed blue. It held a crucifix formed by four bent nails—the old-fashioned kind with square heads. "I want you to have this." She extended it to Mira.

"You don't have to do that, Eleanor."

"I know."

"I told you I'm not a believer like you." She didn't take it.

"I know."

"So why give it to me? I won't wear it."

Eleanor remained unfazed. She gazed intensely into Mira's eyes. "Why do you wear your bracelet?"

"I explained that to you."

"Explain again."

"It helps people visualize the workings of life."

Eleanor grabbed Mira's hand and pressed the rustic totem into her palm. "Wear this for the same reason, sugar."

Mira looked at the necklace. Its maker probably had a little workshop in a corner of their house; maybe even just a work desk. She pictured the person making dozens, even hundreds of these in a single session. But it wasn't awful looking. It wasn't jewelry, exactly. Not like her bracelet. But they were both objects of deep symbolism. Science and Faith. She could appreciate that. Maybe she would even wear it. Sometime. "Thank you," she said as she put it into her pocket.

A CHANGE OF PLANS

Mira's next scheduled stop was with Wes Quon. She texted a confirmation but got no response. He wasn't in the room in the LSF he'd used as an office. She looked in the lab facilities, including BSL-3 containment. Nobody knew where he was. Why set up a meeting with her if he didn't wish to meet? She had another forty-five minutes until her scheduled call with the Ft. Detrick team. She asked a couple of people if they'd seen him; one told her she heard he was at the Kendall Combined Chemical Test Facility. She had enough time, so she walked there.

She found Quon in one of the test bays. He wore a hard hat, safety goggles, and a white lab coat. She couldn't cross the line on the concrete floor demarked with safety tape to approach him without donning similar attire, so she waved to get his attention. He waved his arms as if to say he'd talk to her later. In response, she pointed to her wrist. He went back to the conversation he'd been in and showed no further signs he had any intention of keeping their appointment. She stared for a few minutes and got no further acknowledgment. What was he doing here, anyway? Fine. If he didn't need her, he didn't need her. She might normally be insulted, even agitated by such treatment. Not this time.

AFTER A LONG BUT productive session with her team-to-be, Mira stopped by to say goodbye to Jeff and Gigi. "You go save the world, girlfriend." Gigi hugged her and they shared a laugh.

That's it. She was now officially huggable.

"You never asked me about my date, by the way."

"I'm sorry." Mira was unembarrassed. She never remembered to ask anybody about such matters. "How did it go?"

"He's climbing down from the fence."

Mira shrugged and looked at Jeff, reluctant to say goodbye. "We'll be in constant communication, right?"

"Right." Jeff hugged her too.

She knew it was time for her to go to Rain's office. She'd looked forward to it all day. But now the time was here, a part of her didn't want to go. A big part. "Gigi, do you think you could drive me to the English Village to get my things?"

"Sure. But wait a minute. Weren't you supposed to do that with Rain?"

"Yes, but... Wait. How do you know about that?"

"I have my ways. So, what's up? He didn't blow you off, did he? He's gonna have to answer to me."

"No, he didn't."

Gigi's eyes narrowed, serious. "You mean you're gonna blow my friend off?"

"Well, I didn't—"

"No, you didn't," Gigi scolded. "You march your butt over there right now—you hear me?"

Mira flushed in shame. Gigi was right. "Okay, I'm going." She left the lab, but before the door shut, she turned back. "Thank you."

"Don't mention it. Now go." As the door shut, Mira heard Gigi say to Jeff, "Weenie."

"YOU'RE the one with the deadline," Rain teased.

Mira scavenged around the townhouse to make sure she'd hadn't left anything. Though in truth she didn't have much to gather. She had one suitcase she'd grabbed the one night she'd slept in her San Francisco home. But she took her time, anyway. "Alright," she said at last, her reluctance evident in her low tone and averted eyes, "I suppose I have everything."

"Are you okay?" Rain asked. "If you're not comfortable with this, we can go back."

She looked at him. Not in his eyes, at him. His short sleeves were rolled up to the shoulder. She admired the sharp creases where his deltoid muscles met his triceps and biceps. She noted his yin/yang and Cross tattoos. Her hand reached for the crucifix in her pocket. What was her problem? She was glad for the opportunity to be with him; to have this little break from the pressure. She'd looked forward to this dinner all day; to her it was more than a casual way to kill a couple of hours. The emotion was akin to a flame; it gave warmth, but you wanted to be only so close to it. "You promised me a steak."

"I did." Rain grinned. "Let's go. I didn't get lunch."

He carried her suitcase for her. The drive to Rain's place took less than a minute. He held the townhouse door for her. Mira hadn't known what to expect about how Rain lived. But it wasn't this. The stained glass in his office now made sense. There were pieces of it, some finished, some in progress, all around his townhome. "Why all the stained glass?"

"Just a hobby." Rain's eyes went to the floor. "I work on these projects on and off. It's been a while now—I've been preoccupied, as you know."

"You make all of this? What do you do with it?" She ran her hand over one of the pieces, a half-finished kaleidoscopic depiction of peacock feathers fanned in a semi-circle.

"People buy it." He paused with a sheepish shrug. "I would've cleaned up in here if I'd known you were coming over."

"It answers one question I had about you."

"What was that?" His chin rose and his eyes widened.

"What you do when you're not working." Mira picked up one of the five books from the coffee table, *The History of Western Philosophy* by Bertrand Russell. "A little light reading?" She noted the others—Nietzsche, Aristotle, Schopenhauer, and the Bible.

"It's either tinker or read, one of the two."

"'The majority of men are not capable of thinking, but only of believing, and are not accessible to reason, but only to authority'—I've always hoped it wasn't true."

"You know Schopenhauer?" Rain smiled. "I'm impressed."

"Don't be. I couldn't tell you anything else about him. Just that one quote. I had a professor who was a big fan, I guess. My reading is mainly restricted to my field." She scanned more of the room. More books and stained glass. A shelf with tools. Glass cutters, pliers, soldering irons, supplies for working with stained glass. A couple of interesting lamps, one on an end table, the other a floor-stand. A plush old sofa and a couple of functional chairs at his work desk. No electronic equipment, not even a clock. "It seems to me most people don't make time to tinker. Or read. It seems everybody expects to be entertained."

"I know. I guess I'm strange. Maybe it's because I grew up on a commune."

She pulled on her ponytail. "I don't know any military people; I mean before I was brought here. But I'm guessing most don't read Schopenhauer."

"Like I said."

She replaced that book and picked up *On the Freedom of the Will*. "I guess I shouldn't be too surprised. Look at your name."

"What can I say? My parents were hippies. At least I'm not Command Sergeant Major Sunshine." They shared a nervous laugh. He related his early life in Alaska and that he'd been in the military for over twenty-five years, primarily at Dugway but also in various hotspots in the Middle East. Rain recounted his father's reactions every time young Rain showed any interest in the army, whether it was his plastic soldiers or Avalon Hill board games years later. It was always derision. When Rain told her that, at age thirteen, his long-haired, bearded father had thrown his Africa Corps game into the trash, Mira remembered her grandmother doing something similar with a corkboard of pinned moth specimens. "Now I'd like to ask you something, Mira." She nodded assent. He pointed to her earbuds. "What do you listen to?"

"Piano and violin music. Not loud, barely audible."

"Not the Ramones?"

"No." She smiled. She guessed he had no Brian Crain on his playlists. "I told you it helps me. Without it, I'm constantly distracted. I don't know the physiological reason. The drip of condensation off of your air conditioner, for example. If I didn't have the music, such environmental stimuli would be even more diverting." As she explained, the lines of tension along her forehead and in her jawline released. "I suppose some see it as off-putting. I don't mean for it to be that way." She removed them and put them in her pants pocket.

"If it helps, it helps. Right?" He pointed to the back door, on the other side of the small kitchen. "If we're going to eat, we better get to it. Time's getting short." He led her out back, where there was a modest patio set, a small fenced yard, and a salsa garden. He lit the grill and offered her a beer. She didn't enjoy beer. But she accepted it, anyway. He went back inside and re-emerged with the beer, food, a knife, and a cutting board. He twisted open one bottle and handed it to her. "Your performance in the progress review yesterday impressed me."

"Why?" She took a big swig and grimaced.

"For one, your research idea." He worked on the bell peppers—green, red, and yellow. He discarded their seeds and stems into the small garden behind him. "You came up with it right on the spot like that. In front of Command and everyone."

"It should have been obvious. I didn't think in terms of having the right equipment being available to me. It didn't hit me until the problem with DNA emerged. What else?"

"Your interaction with Quon."

"What about it?"

"Most people are intimidated by him. Have you noticed?"

"No. People get distracted with such unnecessary things."

"You got that right." He peeled off the outer layer of a Vidalia onion and sliced it. "Not you, though."

"No, I suppose not." She took another big swig.

Rain paused to do the same. "How long will you be at Detrick?"

"I don't know. Weeks, maybe. If we're lucky."

"I'm not sure we have weeks." His eyes watered. Probably from the onion.

"I'll do my best." She blinked a few times.

"I know. It's just, well, what we're facing, it makes you think."

"Tell me about it."

Rain seasoned the steaks and vegetables and drizzled olive oil on the mushrooms, peppers, and onions. Next, he arrayed the food on the grates of the grill. He sat and up-ended his beer. He held out his empty bottle. "Want another?"

"No."

"You don't mind if I do, I assume." He stood. "Water with dinner then?"

"Yes."

"Glad you said that; I don't have much else, anyway." He took the prep materials back inside and came back with their drinks and tableware. He tended the grill.

"Have you always lived alone?" It was all she could think of to ask while he'd been gone.

"Yes." Eyes narrowed in protective reflex from the heat, he flipped the steaks. "I know from your file it's the same for you. A couple of loners, right?"

"I suppose so. People think it's strange."

"It is, isn't it? How do you explain it when people ask you?"

"I don't." She sat back, finished her beer, and unscrewed the cap from the bottle of water. She fiddled with it absently.

"Me neither. How do you like your steak?"

"I don't know. How about medium rare?"

"Music to my ears. I think we're about ready then."

He plated the food, and they both ate so ravenously they didn't talk much. Rain noticed her bracelet and inquired. She answered him the way she did everyone. As they finished and carried the tableware back inside, she thanked him for the delicious meal.

They put the dishes on the kitchen counter and Rain led her to the living room where he invited her to sit. He joined her on the couch. Mira's phone beeped; she checked the message. "They postponed my flight. Something about a weather system. I leave first thing in the morning now."

"Oh. Well, I guess we don't have to hurry."

"Why would they do that?"

"Lots of reasons—not unusual. When you want, I'll take you back to your place."

"Why? All my stuff is here."

"Oh," Rain flushed red.

When Mira saw his reaction, she blushed too. "I'm sorry, I didn't mean to be forward. I didn't mean anything; I wasn't suggesting..." She trailed off, embarrassed. "It was a careless thing to say."

"It's okay, Mira." He turned and smiled at her. "You're welcome to stay here. I'll make up the bed upstairs with fresh sheets. You're welcome to it."

"No, I don't want to put you out."

"I spend more nights than not on this sofa." He patted the cushion. "See? It's comfortable. It's no problem. Really."

"I couldn't."

"It's okay. It gives us more time to talk. I think I might have Honey Nut Chex for you in the morning."

She smiled. "You don't mind?"

"I really don't mind." He smiled back, and they shared an extended glance—she looked him in his eyes. "I'll get your bag out of the jeep."

As he retrieved her luggage, Mira examined the stained glass more intently. "Show me."

"Show you what?"

"Show me how you make your glass."

"You want to know?"

"Sure, why not?"

"Most people aren't interested." He shrugged in self-deprecation.

"Most people watch TV."

A NEW PARTNER

Mira boarded the now-familiar Gulfstream with newfound energy in her step. With all her recent time aboard the airplane, she didn't suffer her fear so acutely. She had slept well, despite the strange bed. She knew that wasn't all of it. She couldn't sort the emotions she felt about the previous evening. She and Rain talked until almost midnight when Rain made the bed and, despite her protest, insisted again she sleep there.

The night was an oasis in the desert of the SONA crisis. But the time to get back to it had come. She deplaned onto the tarmac of the Ronald Reagan International airport. The attending Corporal retrieved her suitcase from the cargo hold, handed it off, and returned to the plane. Mira wheeled it through the concourse. She was to be picked up by one of her new team members at the terminal exit.

Mira followed the throng of travelers through the terminal, alone in public for the first time in longer than she remembered. She descended via a long escalator. When she was halfway down, she saw a man near the landing who held a poster board sign with 'DR. MIRA WALLACE' written with black marker in legible but untidy letters.

By his unkempt gray-blond hair, scraggly salt and pepper beard, and cracked ruddy cheeks, she judged her escort to be in his early fifties. She discovered later that he was, in fact, forty-four. Under a tattered denim jacket, he wore a checkered flannel shirt that hung over a pair of faded blue jeans. Mira waved to him from the escalator, but he looked in every direction but hers. Only when she approached him, gestured to the sign and thanked him for meeting her did he look her in the eye. She surprised herself—she didn't avert hers to break eye contact.

"Oh, Dr. Wallace. Okay, good. Glad to meet you. I hope your flight was good. I'm Randy Foust. I'm a technician with NIAID[1] at Detrick. I was in conference on the phone with you yesterday."

"Yes. Shall we?" She gestured toward the exit.

"Yes, good. Do you have any luggage?"

"Just this one I'm dragging behind me."

"Good, good. Let me get it for you." He grasped the handle. "You have a coat? It's pretty cold out."

"No. I'll be all right."

"Up to you." He wheeled around and walked to the short-term parking area. People considered this cold. She smiled at the thought. It wasn't even below the freezing point of water. Though he struck her as eccentric, she appreciated how fast Randy moved and how little he spoke.

He led her to an unwashed hatchback with a large dent on the rear quarter panel. Despite the appearance, the inside was clean enough. Randy was silent, but as they crept through the heavy morning traffic on the Capital Beltway and turned north onto I-270 towards Frederick, it was as though something flicked an 'ON' switch.

Once he started, he didn't stop. In the subtle but distinct mid-Atlantic accent of native Marylanders, he mostly complained about the leadership at NICBR[2], or lack thereof, and what they should be doing differently. He complained that there were too many bosses and too many mouths to feed. He griped about the politics that blocked approval on a promising new research initiative for his boss, a scientist with NIAID.

Randy shifted to his career history and recapped how he landed his first job as a technician at Fort Detrick almost twenty years ago. He had enrolled in a Master's Degree program at Hood College in Biomedical Science, but dropped out. School, work, and the pressures of his personal life simply hadn't lined up. The reliability of a federal salary was more important.

Mira listened with head nods and a concerted effort to remain attentive. They merged onto U.S. Route 15 and passed a shopping center and a cluster of restaurants. "Hungry?" Randy said. "I could hit a drive thru for you."

"Fortunately, they fed me on the plane."

"Okay, good. I hope you don't mind, but I need to get my son to afternoon daycare before we go to the lab. My mom can only watch him in the mornings. She's getting older now. I'd do it the other way and drop you off, but I've been late a lot and they're on my case."

"All right. How old is your son?"

He exited off of Rosemont Ave. "Five." He answered as though he had to think about it. "He's five now." After a few side streets, they eventually pulled in front of a modest row house. He parked and went to the door. A moment later, he led a young boy by the hand and helped him into the child safety seat behind Mira. She hadn't even noticed it.

The boy spoke. "Daddy? Who's the lady?"

"I'm sorry," said Randy. "Manners—right, buddy? This is Dr. Wallace. She is visiting for some work we need to do together. Mira, this is my son Tyler." He secured Tyler's seat straps and jogged around to the driver's seat.

"It's nice to meet you," she smiled awkwardly as she turned in the seat to hold out her hand. The boy took it without hesitation. He saw her bracelet as it dangled and became transfixed. Mira pulled her hand back.

She tried to think of words to say but came up empty. She'd spent her entire life in the company of adults. Unlike Eleanor, she had never longed for children of her own. She never knew what might be appropriate or not in her infrequent encounters with them. Tyler had no such inhibitions.

"I made a picture of Lucy. Wanna see?"

"Lucy is our cat," Randy whispered as he put the car in gear.

"Sure, I'd love to see it."

Tyler unzipped his backpack and pulled out a blue folder. Rather than open it up, he pulled sheets of paper out from the top. "Here." He thrust forward a ripped and rumpled paper with stick drawings. The figure in the middle looked more pig than cat to Mira. Next to it were two stick figure people.

"You made this picture yourself?"

"Yep!"

This boy sure was enthusiastic; Mira could not guess about what. "It's colorful. Who are they?" Tyler became riled for no reason clear to her.

"That one's my Dad and that one's my Mom." He spoke as if it was the height of ignorance to not know that. "She went away but she'll be home soon."

"Where'd she go?"

"She went on a trip."

"On a plane? Did she go to another country?" In Mira's world everyone traveled.

Randy leaned over and whispered, "His Mom died this past November. I should've mentioned it earlier. Breast cancer. It's been tough for him. For us." He wasn't entirely successful as he feigned a smile. "Tyler, I know you miss Mommy. I do too. But she's not coming home, son."

"You don't know, Daddy!" Tyler slouched back in his seat with a grimace and stared out the window. "Gramma says she's in a happy place now. She'll come back, soon as she misses us enough."

"We've talked about this, right? It doesn't work like that."

The boy harrumphed; his volatile mood disturbed Mira. The story of what happened to the family hit harder. "I'm sorry Randy. I know that kind of pain." She hung her head and covered her face with her hand. Randy's eyes remained on the road.

"Yeah. Sometimes I still expect to see her when I get home." He turned up the music and leaned closer. "I wish I could say it was getting better." A few moments later, Mira assumed he meant to change the topic. "Do you have any kids of your own?"

"Me? No." Her voice cracked. "No kids."

"Too bad. You seem great with them."

She had never been accused of that before. If it was true, it was because she treated them like she did anybody else. She wrestled with alien emotions and kept her face toward the passenger side window. If she couldn't identify a bioremediation solution, and do it soon, how many children would lose parents to SONA?

Unlike Dugway, built in a remote desert, Fort Detrick sat in the middle of town. They waited through two red lights at the busy intersection at the main gate.

When they stopped at the gate, Randy distractedly flipped through the badges on his lanyard as a guard tapped on the window. Randy shouted through the glass, "Window's stuck. Gotta open the door." The guard stepped back and gestured for him to do so. He opened the door and showed his badge. The officer shined a purple flashlight to illuminate the UV authorization code, noted it was in order, and sent them through.

"I put in a request to get this darn window fixed three months ago."

They crept along at 15 mph through the grounds. The place reminded her of a college campus, but with unique infrastructure. Large metal pipes snaked in the strangest places—over the roads, in front of buildings, and down alleys. Water, air, steam, and electrical systems appeared to be all above ground. The place looked like a film maker's art deco vision of an alternative reality. She could easily picture the work of science fiction within those walls.

They passed tan metal buildings reminiscent of her time at Dugway. There was even a street sign labeled Ditto (DPG had a Ditto area too). There was one big difference. They drove up a small hill where she saw a 'CHILDREN AT PLAY' sign. The deadliest pathogens known to mankind were stored at this facility. The picture of children at play nearby, safe as it may be, did not sit well.

They pulled up to bldg. 1776, the Ft. Detrick Child Development Center. Randy stopped and hopped out. Tyler said, his voice louder than necessary, "Bye, nice lady. Nice to meet me." He reached out to shake her hand.

She grinned and took his hand. "Very nice to meet you."

Tyler didn't let go of her hand. He looked at her bracelet, and with his other hand, played with the dangling charms. He again became fascinated. She watched him.

"Do you like this?"

Tyler nodded emphatically. The boy's energy and attitude struck her. She was older than him when her parents' plane had gone down over a jungle. Maybe that was harder, maybe not. The boy clearly didn't grasp the finality of his situation. He would never see his mother again. Just like she hadn't. She could barely picture her mother's face in that moment. Her eyes welled. She reached out and undid the clasp. "Then here. I want you to have it."

Tyler grabbed it from her hand and played with its magnetic qualities, his face lit bright. Randy opened the door and unbuckled Tyler. "You don't have to do that."

"It's okay." She thought of Eleanor's cross. Superstition or faith? "I want him to have it."

---

1. See Supplement for explanations of various U.S. Government agencies in the story.
2. See Supplement for explanations of various U.S. Government agencies in the story.

AN ERASER

M ira marveled at NICBR's laboratory facilities. She inspected the microscopy lab. Was there any product Zeiss manufactured that they lacked? Her eyes widened as she noted the latest super resolution real-time imaging model, a setup she wanted for her own lab. That wasn't feasible any time soon; the $3 million price tag was not in her budget. The instrument sat on a pneumatic shock absorption table to keep objects in focus even during earthquake tremors—a constant problem in her lab at Berkeley. She was familiar with its function. The device scanned a single cell via laser and rendered the subject into thousands of optical slices, whereupon the internal processor reassembled them into a crystal-clear image. The process was fast enough to give researchers 3-D video of cells in action. As the subject microbe moved, the device continually tracked and adjusted focus. But this marvel of engineering wouldn't be necessary for her work here.

Her daydream continued as she inspected the other laboratories: spectrometry, analytical chemistry, nuclear magnetic resonance, and of course genomic instrumentation. The equipment was state-of-the-art. As a result of feverish battles against growing pandemics, NICBR was subject to few budgetary restrictions. At least when it came to equipment.

An administrator whose name Mira promptly forgot hosted her orientation. Though the facilities were designated BSL-2 through BSL-4, they did not enter containment. She peered into the various labs through the never-ending walls of glass.

The administrator struck her as unserious. "We keep our dinosaur eggs in the basement." He had a strange lilting snigger. He made other bad jokes, but Mira was too preoccupied to be either amused or annoyed. She focused on her new exploration and the stakes involved. A few times, her concentration broke with thoughts of Rain.

After the tour she went through a round of required security paperwork and a BSL-4 procedures orientation, mainly on the proper use and care of the isolation suits.

Randy rejoined her on the way to the BSL-4 facility where they'd do most of their work. "Thanks again for being so nice to Tyler. I can't tell you how good it felt to see him like that again."

Mira raised a brow but didn't ask what he meant. "You're welcome. We will begin with a study of cytopathic effects on common cell types. This will help me decide which microbes to screen. Do we have the inventory I specified? There should be several thousand."

He stopped. "Yes, the others and I worked overtime this week aliquoting them into glass cell culture flasks."

"Very good then." Mira walked sufficiently fast that Randy hustled to keep up. They approached two stiffly postured security guards—one male, the other female.

Randy greeted them in a warm, casual manner. "Hi, Shane. Hi, Vanessa. This is Dr. Mira Wallace. She needs escorted into containment." He turned to Mira. "You'll receive your ID and be authorized in the system, probably before the end of today or tomorrow. Then you won't need an escort anymore."

Vanessa gestured to Mira. "Right this way, ma'am." Mira followed her through a short hallway to the Ladies locker room entrance, which required a wave of Vanessa's card. The locker room struck Mira as more country club than government facility. Vanessa indicated a row of lockers and a set of clean chrome shelves that held neatly organized scrubs and socks of various sizes.

"Please remove your clothing, including underwear and jewelry, and place your belongings in a locker." As Mira complied, she noted with mixed emotion both the absence of her bracelet and the presence of Eleanor's crucifix in her pants pocket. Vanessa visually sized Mira and selected medium scrubs and socks. "Put these on, socks over the scrubs."

The escort next snatched one of many rolls of brightly colored bandaging tape from another shelf, "It helps for comfort if you tape your socks up. Do you need help?"

"No, thank you. I can get it." Mira took a role of purple tape and encircled the top of her socks around her calves twice. "Is that right?"

"Yes. Now we do your hands." She retrieved latex surgical gloves from a dispenser and helped Mira put them on. "It's easier if I tape these for you."

Once Mira was set with her underlayer, they left the locker room and went to the adjacent Suit room. A row of white isolation suits with integrated clear plastic head coverings hung from the ceiling along a metal pipe. Stacks of perfectly folded towels and bright white boots lined the wall in racks. Coiled yellow air hoses with brass nozzles hung from hooks around the small room.

Mira closely followed the procedures, including the required check-in sheet. She examined one of the suits for tears or mars. "We've got a special molded face shield for you." Vanessa offered the helmet. "This will facilitate your microscopy."

Mira accepted the headgear. She noted the indents around the eyes and put it on. It wasn't uncomfortable, but the slight pressure near her eye sockets produced a distracting sensation. She zippered the helmet to the suit as Vanessa directed. Next, Vanessa pointed to the stoppers. Mira fastened them inside the suit to block the two exhaust ports. Next, she zippered it shut and connected the air supply through the integrated hose fitting. As the suit inflated, Mira held it up and rotated it to inspect for leaks. "Good?"

Vanessa leaned close to look. "Yes. Now unhook. We'll deflate it and get you in."

Once Mira was suited, Vanessa indicated another door that led to the BSL-4 labs. "Detach your hose." She opened the steel and glass anterior door with a card swipe. "You'll reconnect on the other side."

Mira did so. Randy awaited her, similarly attired. He shouted so Mira could hear him over the white noise of the air supply system. "All set, Mira? Good. I'll show you where we'll work."

Mira found the BSL-4 facility as impressive as the labs she'd seen earlier. It was a significant upgrade from conditions at Dugway. Spacious, it included every conceivable piece of microbiological equipment. She met a couple of their team-members, then followed Randy through two doors and into one of the smaller labs. They both selected air hoses from ceiling hangers and attached. Randy unlocked a freezer. "As you requested, I had the Pandora inverted scope transferred into this containment lab. They made a fuss, I gotta say. You know what the tech said? 'Call somebody else when you want to move it again,' can you believe that?"

Mira didn't know if he joked or not. She didn't joke in return. "This work is important. You know that, right?"

"I suppose." His gaze dropped and his eyes became unfocused, faraway.

"Is there a problem?"

"I have to be honest with you. I've worked with Ebola, Marburg, anthrax, even Smallpox in here. Nobody's ever gone to these lengths before. I know it's not my place to ask, but...should I be scared, Mira?"

She stared at him intently. "No. That won't help. But you should follow the protocols. If you do, you have nothing to worry about."

"Good. Phew. I can do that. It's what they pay me to do around here. Well, if you call what they give me pay."

He pointed to the three small incubators arranged on the long lab bench a few feet away from the microscope. Each one held small glass containers with liquids of various shades. Most were clear, but some ranged yellow to amber.

"The cell counter-stains you requested were added at the

designated times last night. The cells and their parts should light up like Christmas trees."

"Okay." Her voice tensed. "Where is the agent?"

"Yes. We obviously need that. Over here."

She followed him to a tabletop freezer and spied a clear plastic box through the glass door. Inside the box stood a solitary glass vial decorated with a bright red biohazard sticker. The assembly was the only item in the freezer. Not even a trace of frost. Fear widened Mira's eyes. The image of the vial expanded in her mind. It seemed alive with menace and glowered at her with an almost personal animosity.

Randy broke the trance when he removed the box with two hands. Mira closed the freezer door for him. He carried it to the bio-safety cabinet situated behind them and gingerly deposited it. "Okay. What do you want to look at first?"

"Let's start with the *E. coli* bacteria."

He went to the incubator labeled with a 37°C sticker, turned off the shaker, and removed a glass flask. Next, he transferred 0.5 ml of the liquid it held to a quarter-sized glass dish and replaced the flask. He carried the crystal-clear bacteria-containing dish to the workstation.

"Good, Randy. I'll handle the next step."

"You sure?" Randy didn't hide his relief.

"I'm sure." She took a deep breath, opened the clear plastic box, and gently removed the red glass vial. Motions steady, she unscrewed the lid, setting it upside down on the white silicone liner paper covering the work surface. She held out her hand and Randy placed a pipette into her palm. Slowing further, she removed .25 microliters of the gray-black substance from the vial and ejected it into the bacterial solution in the dish. She screwed the lid back onto the vial and replaced it in the box. She also returned the pipette to its rack inside the cabinet.

Mira sealed the plate with the SONA-*E. coli* mixture with clear, soft biopore plastic tape, careful not to occlude the bottom of the dish where the upward-oriented inverted microscopes objective lens would peer. Next, she carried that to the microscope. Randy observed on the video monitor while Mira peered into the binocular eyepiece. She gasped at what she saw.

"Hand me a plate with untreated cells," she commanded with a swallow.

"Sure. Is something wrong? They were all checked this morning." Randy retrieved another dish into which he added the *E. coli* solution but no SONA, and handed it over.

Mira placed the control plate onto the mechanical stage of the scope. Bacterial cells bloomed. They glowed blue from the fluorescent DAPI stain bound to the DNA that filled the insides of the cells. She slid the SONA sample back into the viewer field. Nothing. Mira increased the magnification to 750x. Still no blue— no cells at all. But now the background color had a faint red tint. She zoomed in to 1000x. Barely visible tiny glowing red dots speckled the field of view. She shuddered. "Those are membrane fragments!"

Randy's eyes fixed on the monitor. "Membrane fragments? What happened?"

"The red stain is specific for membranes. The cells have disintegrated. I want to try something else."

Randy carefully removed the toxic glass dish from the microscope stage and placed it back into the transfer hood. "What do you have in mind?"

"CHO cells."

"Okay." He opened a 37°C incubator and removed a rectangular glass culture flask. He swirled it lightly and pipetted several milliliters into a clean glass dish.

"Here you go, Mira. These are healthy." He handed them over. "Never made sense to me why everyone uses Chinese Hamster Ovary cells. What twisted dude even thought that up in the first place?"

Mira was too absorbed to answer. She was about to grasp the red vial again when she pulled her hand out of the cabinet. "I'm not sure what happened to the *E. coli*. But maybe it happened too fast to see."

"It was only two minutes from the time you added that stuff to the time you observed it. How much faster can we go?"

"I want you to add it to the plate while I'm looking."

"You want what?" Randy's voice inflected up. "Wait a minute. You said I had to follow protocol. You said everything would be fine if I stuck to that. Now you're telling me it killed those bacterial cells, every single one of them, in less than two minutes? And I'm supposed to throw the book out in response? I'm sorry, Mira. I can't do that."

"I'll do it then. We'll be doing this hundreds of times, so we better find a rhythm you're comfortable with. I prefer to look through the eyepiece but can manage viewing the screen." Mira wished Jeff was here. No, he needed to be at Berkeley.

Randy stood there, blinking, brows knit in consternation. "No, it's my job—I'll do it. But you need to put in a good word for me. If this all works out, I want to be promoted to support scientist—GS-11."

Mira didn't know what that meant but reasoned whatever they paid Randy probably wasn't commensurate with this work. "I don't know what kind of difference I can make."

Randy found a measure of bravado. "Let's do it."

Mira added the CHO cells to a clean glass plate and placed it in the microscope stage. While she did, Randy nervously reached into the biosafety cabinet. Despite his unsteady hands, he managed to remove another .25 microliters of SONA.

"Ready for this?"

"Yes, bring it over."

He withdrew his hand with the pipette from the cabinet and moved steadily to the scope. He placed the pipette tip into the CHO cell solution and ejected it.

The CHO cells were lit by the four lasers which excited the various fluorescent dyes. This time the outer membrane glowed green and enveloped a web of tiny arrow-straight orange threads which crisscrossed the cell like a network of city streets. In the center, the nucleus that harbored the DNA glowed deep blue. Mira marveled at its beauty. Her eyes widened in horror as she witnessed what happened next.

The green plasma membrane that surrounded the cell dissolved and blobbed out into thousands of smaller spheres. The orange threads dimmed as they twisted and disassembled. The membrane surrounding the blue nucleus likewise disintegrated and transformed into thousands of blue pinpoints. Within seconds, the entire cell was erased from existence.

Randy witnessed the process on the monitor. "What is that stuff? I've seen every kind of nasty virus, bacteria, fungus, prions—I've never seen anything like that. Not even close."

She remained transfixed to the binocular eyepiece of the microscope. Her stomach turned as she envisioned the piglet and grasped for an explanation—something to help her comprehend what she just witnessed. "What could survive such a thing?"

A GROWING THREAT

"You can't catch me!" The elder brother, a worldly ten-year-old, taunted his pursuer, who was a naïve seven.

"Yes, I can!" The younger pumped his pedals with all his might.

They raced their mountain bikes through the desert brush, accustomed to the scrapes to their shins and ankles. The elder brother slowed a little. The chase was no fun if it wasn't at least close. His brother closed the gap, and the game resumed at one of their favorite places: a small gully they transformed into a war zone. They pretended to be soldiers and hurled dirt clod grenades at imaginary assault squads. Other times, when their mood was less pugilistic, the place became the landscape of another planet, usually Tatooine. They dropped their bikes and dove for cover, indifferent to the dirt which smeared their Darth Vader and Yoda t-shirts. They lay prone in anticipation.

"Incoming!" The elder shouted.

"I'm gonna take 'em out this time." The younger brother searched for a dirt clod at the bottom of the gully. He got one, scrambled back up, and tossed it over the edge.

The elder shouted as they both plugged their ears with their fingers. "Fire in the hole!" They rolled down the slope, thrown back by the imaginary explosive shock wave. "Good work, Corporal. You got 'em all!" He pulled his beaming brother upright, and they made their way along the gully. They paused now and again to inspect the odd piece of refuse. At other points in their journey, they tilted big rocks up to see what life they hid, occasionally sprinting away from made-up or real critters like scorpions or rattlesnakes.

They came upon a small dark gray patch of ground unlike the surrounding area. It looked soft but was otherwise featureless. "What is that?" mused the elder.

"Quicksand! I'm gonna get stuck in there so you're gonna have to pull me out to save my life!"

RAIN SPENT the bulk of the last hour flicking his pen open and closed as he stared at the inscription. *Ever vigilant.* It was the most necessary, and difficult, thing about life. You never know what might happen. SONA, for instance. Mira, for another. He smiled as he recalled their time together. He took off his reading glasses and sat back in his chair. A uniformed woman broke his reverie as she popped her head into his office.

"CSM Somerdale, I'm afraid I have some bad news."

He sprang to his feet. "What is it, Corporal?"

"Another outcropping of SONA. This one off-site. There's been an incident." As the significance of the words sunk in, Rain admonished himself for being in a good mood amid this crisis. He pushed past the soldier and bolted down the hall.

LESS THAN AN HOUR LATER, Rain, clad in an isolation suit, stepped past the yellow caution tape. He approached one of the many similarly clad servicemen posted around the area. "Sitrep?"

"Two boys from Terra were reported missing yesterday. Their friends located their bicycles a quarter-mile that way," he pointed east. "As you commanded, we monitored the Utah State Police radio and heard the missing persons report. Lucky that civilian searchers didn't get this far before we got here. Our team swept the area and found the patch."

Rain frowned. "Evidence the boys fell victim here?"

The soldier pointed. "Over there."

Rain noted a few objects inside of clear plastic baggies strewn on the ground. He picked up one of the bags. His consternation intensified into a scowl as he examined a plastic light saber. He picked up another bag that held metal buttons, maybe from blue jeans or a shirt. He kept his eyes on the evidence but spoke to the soldier. "Cordon the entire area, two-hundred-yard radius. Keep it discrete—same procedure as the first one. No sense in fueling flames. Get roadblocks up and more security. No one gets near here. Clear?"

"Clear, Command Sergeant Major! The remediation team is on its way. They should arrive in twenty minutes."

Rain knelt by the patch's edge. It was tiny compared to the original. "Get a team to sweep the desert. At least two miles in all directions." He threw the evidence bag to the ground and ran as fast as he could manage in the suit back to his vehicle.

A PROTEST

"That does it. I'm ordering an evacuation of the entire area."

"Just a minute, Colonel. Let's not get ahead of ourselves." Eleanor remained calm, diplomatic. "We need a detailed statement and a media strategy."

"I don't care about any of that. Every single person on or around this facility needs to be evacuated. Until we know how it's spreading, there's no telling where SONA will pop up next." Potteiger's voice increased in force and volume. "I want everyone not absolutely essential out of here today."

"I appreciate your point of view, Colonel, I really do—and I agree with you. In theory. But as a practical matter, we have to avoid panic and chaos. If this news isn't properly handled, we'll have conspiracists crawling all around this desert. You know that, right?" She turned to Rain. "Command Sergeant Major? What do you say?"

Rain stood, walked to the window of Potteiger's office and scanned the goings-on below. By appearance, all was normal. Uniformed soldiers and civilians scurried about; if not on foot, then in vehicles that ranged from silent golf carts to noisy Humvees. The day was picture perfect: 65°F, not a cloud in the sky. He turned back. "I'm afraid I'm with the Commander on this. There isn't a moment to lose."

Eleanor stood. Rain sensed her attempt to maintain her demeanor. "Look, I'm not against you. We must agree on how we proceed. First, we need to know precisely how SONA spreads. We must have coherent messages about what's going on and what is being done."

"I'll tell you what's going on, Deputy Secretary." Potteiger's voice remained loud. "Our scientists don't know jack about any of it. We almost lost one of our research technicians. Now we have civilian casualties. I'm responsible for the safety of almost two thousand people, many of them women and children. I cannot allow anyone to remain in harm's way if it can be avoided. Not for another second. Am I clear?"

Eleanor looked him in the eye for a long moment. She returned to her seat in front of him. "Colonel, with all due respect, I'm afraid this is not your call. I don't even believe it's mine. This is a Commander-in-Chief decision."

Potteiger slammed his fist on his desk. But he remained silent for prolonged seconds. "You know, it's common to curse the chain of command in the military. I have done so on plenty of occasions. But it's the way it has to be, isn't it? I will agree I do not have the authority to order an evacuation of the civilian population." His tone geared down, almost gentle. "I defer to those higher up than me on that part of it. But as the commander of this base, I do have a say over what goes on here. We're going to essential-personnel-only status."

"That may be subject to some interpretation, sir," said Rain. "Do we shut down the cafeterias, the gas station, and the cleaning services? Dealing with SONA will require a lot of infrastructure. More services than we have in place right now."

"That's a good point." Eleanor paced. "We have to think things through a little more. I think we can all agree nobody should remain unless they are needed to support the SONA remediation."

"Fine." Potteiger sat back in his desk chair. "I'm canceling all unrelated projects, effective immediately."

"Makes sense to me," said Eleanor.

"Sir, if I may make a suggestion?"

"What is it, Somerdale?"

"We can conduct a safety drill. It'll move us in the right direction without causing undue public attention. I'll work with Arnie on it."

"Arnie?" asked Eleanor.

"Garrison Manager Arnie Goodling. Safety drills fall under his responsibility. I assume he's been fully briefed?"

Potteiger stood to signal the end of the meeting. "Yes. I've ordered him to keep a tight lid on things; the last thing we need is for people to panic. After the past couple of days, I don't know how well he'll be able to do that." Potteiger's manner normalized—resigned and authoritative. "Very well, Command Sergeant Major. See to it. Let's just pray nobody else gets hurt while we're looking for ways to explain ourselves."

Rain and Eleanor shared a glance. He appreciated the gratitude in her eyes. "Already on that," Eleanor said.

MANY LONG-TERM RESIDENTS of the region distrusted the West Desert Test Center. Though lethal agents had not been tested at Dugway in decades, people remembered incidents such as the "sheep kill" of 1968, where many blamed large-scale VX gas tests for the death of thousands of sheep in neighboring Skull Valley. Whether it was true or not didn't matter. Fear squelches reason. Not long after the disappearance of the two boys, a crowd gathered at Dugway's main gate. Many of them were prepared to camp out. As the hours passed, their numbers grew. Inversely proportional to their number was their willingness to cooperate with the guards. The result was predictable—escalated tension.

Several dozen marched back and forth outside of DPG's main gates in the desert heat. There were family-types of all ages; mostly poor, mostly of Mexican or other Native American descent. One woman wielded a megaphone and stoked the crowd with chants of "NO MORE SECRETS!" and "WHERE ARE THE DIAZ

BOYS?" Their signs echoed their complaints: THE U.S. ARMY KILLS—IT KILLS AMERICANS! And STOP BIOLOGICAL WEAPONS RESEARCH!

An 18-wheel tractor trailer approached. The protesters, their boldness at a peak, rushed into the road to block the way. Until then, the ranking guard had been impeccably professional. The crowd blocking an important delivery vehicle changed his attitude. Sweat trickled over the bulging veins at his temples; his powerful 6'3" frame was tense and ready to strike as he glared at the offenders.

His colleague, half his bulk, noticed. "Easy, Ron. It won't do us any good."

"I've had enough of this," Ron growled. "If I have to tell them one more time to stay out of the darned way—"

"I know, I know." His friend stepped forward and called to the protesters, his tone professional. "Please remain on the side of the road."

Some complied, but others remained defiant. "Screw you!" shouted one woman. "We will be heard! We want answers! My nephews are missing—you know where they are!"

She moved toward the two guards as others nearby held her back. One whispered, "Martina, let's keep it peaceful. We agreed."

Martina relented. But others didn't. The loud blast from the delivery truck horn stopped conversation for long moments as it rolled to a stop inches from the protesters in the road. Some turned and faced the truck and pressed their chests against its grill.

Anger spiked amongst protesters and guards alike; their fury intensified under the unsympathetic desert sun. Ron leveled his weapon and racked a round. "I'm not going to tell you again. Move aside. Now!"

The protestors were unsure and shared glances amongst one another. One chanted, "Heck no, we won't go! Heck no, we won't go!" Others joined, and the chant grew. The intensity attracted a few bystanders who bolstered the line. Now twenty or so blocked the truck's path.

"Last chance." Ron glowered.

The chant went on, unattenuated. Ron opened fire with a staccato burst. A 3-round volley of rubber projectiles slammed into two of the protesters, a woman and a man. The chants broke as loud shrieks of pain and anger filled the air. Four of their fellows knelt to their aid, the others scrambled to the side of the road opposite Ron.

Ron's associate stepped forward. He raised his voice but projected as much empathy as he could. "Everyone, remain calm. We don't want to see anyone hurt. We are armed with less-than-lethal munitions—they'll be okay and will be attended to. Please, everyone. Remain on the side of the road. You're free to express yourselves. But this driver must do his job. If you block the road again. You will be forced to disperse."

Martina crouched to the sides of the two hit by the foam projectiles. Satisfied they weren't seriously hurt, she looked back at Ron, who stared cold daggers as his rifle now pointed at her. "Just do what they say, everybody," she spat. "We'll stay right over here as long as it takes to get them to listen."

The woman with the megaphone held it high and shouted. "NO MORE SECRETS!" Others took up the chant as they slowly merged with the crowd at the side of the road. The truck lurched forward and pulled to another stop at the gate. The driver flipped his middle finger at the crowd as he passed them. Some of them spit on the ground in the wake of the desert dust and black exhaust.

While two of the six-guard detail processed the truck through the gate via inspection of its undercarriage with curved mirrors on poles, a fifth guard picked up a base phone in the booth. "Sir, we have a development out here. The situation is unstable." He looked out at the angry crowd. A teenage girl caught his eye. Tears streaked her cheeks. She held a sign: "U.S. ARMY RANGER SERGEANT ED ROBERTS WAS MY FATHER. WHAT REALLY HAPPENED TO HIM?"

POTTEIGER AND ELEANOR shared the podium in the WDTC auditorium in front of a crowd of local and national news reporters. The format was two short statements followed by a Q and A session. Potteiger spoke first.

"An investigation is underway into the disappearance of two young boys at the eastern boundary of the Dugway Proving Ground. The area has been declared unsafe. We have officially designated the surrounding areas as restricted zones. They will be so designated until further notice.

"It's with great sadness," the lump in his throat choked his words, "we've confirmed the worst. The two Diaz boys encountered a toxic substance. At this time, we do not know the particulars of how it came to be in the place they played, outside of the base perimeter. The substance is of a classified nature. Therefore, I can offer no additional details. I can tell you that I'm personally committed to remedy the situation. For an abundance of caution, Governor Hauser will order an evacuation of the surrounding areas."

His last words triggered an eruption in the room. Most reporters shouted questions. Those who didn't pecked furiously at their digital devices.

Eleanor stepped to the podium. "Ladies and gentlemen, please. Sit down. I have a brief statement. After, we'll address your questions." The reporters settled, and the din hushed enough for Eleanor to be heard. "I am Deputy Secretary of the United States Department of Homeland Security Eleanor Dixon. Homeland Security is coordinating all federal resources to provide support to ensure everyone's safety. Efforts are ongoing. As Commander Potteiger indicated, in concert with Governor Hauser's office, we will be evacuating the surrounding areas. This base is remotely located. This means the evacuation will not affect many residents, fortunately. A few hundred people. For those without a better option, The Department of Homeland Security is working with FEMA to provide temporary accommodations in the Salt Lake City area. I believe Governor Hauser will be making a similar announcement shortly. We're prepared to take a few questions at this time."

Reporters shouted out once again and waved their hands. Eleanor selected one and invited her to speak. "The family of the missing boys has requested they be allowed to take custody of their remains so they may have a proper service. Why deny them?"

Eleanor spoke over Potteiger. "We are not denying the family. We are concerned with their safety. The nature of the accident has created a situation where there is no good solution. I, we, are deeply sorry for their loss. It is the worst kind of tragedy. Of course, we sympathize with the suffering of those who loved them. We appointed a special liaison to work with the family and provide them information as it becomes available." She paused, then indicated another reporter.

"We've received reports there has been increased attention by high officials here, such as you, Secretary Dixon. Why is Homeland Security involved? Is this terrorism? Can you speak to that at all?"

"Not much. I can say the United States Army is mobilizing all available resources to control the situation. This Administration is doing all it can to avoid any further risks, both to civilians and to military personnel. The appropriate authorities are acting in concert and the situation is under control."

Another reporter shouted, out of turn, "Why are there tents, drilling gear, and such on the testing range? Can you explain that?"

"No. As some of that information is strategically sensitive, we cannot elaborate further at this time. One more. Yes?"

The fashionable young woman she pointed to said, "I understand Dr. Wesley Quon is assisting. What is the nature of his involvement?"

"I'm not at liberty to comment on that." She looked to the wings, and an aide came and whispered something to her. "Thank you everyone." She walked away.

Potteiger followed, but turned back to the reporters. A few of them vied for his attention. One succeeded. "Colonel—protesters at your gates claim they've been fired upon. Your response?"

"We addressed the concerned citizens who gathered at the gates. Because it is not safe to remain in that area, we have asked them to relocate. That's all for now. There will be additional announcements soon." He followed Eleanor out.

A DRILL

The exercise proceeded as planned. Rain deployed three squads, one per designated area. Two of them went to Dugway's main base, one of those for the residential areas and the other for the commercial facilities. The third squad attended the Michael Army Airfield and the WDTC/Ditto area nine miles to the west.

The soldiers took attendance, systematic and polite. They gathered names, occupations, places of residence, names of family members in their households and, if not currently with them in person, their whereabouts.

It sounded straight-forward, but Rain knew these kinds of operations have a way of becoming complicated. It was easy to miss people, especially in an installation with a couple of thousand employees, family members, and visitors all spread over a massive area and busy with activities as varied as life had to offer.

Arnie objected to Rain's suggestion to assign soldiers to conduct the exercise. He believed handing out forms to be simpler. As Garrison Manager, Arnie had also voiced concern that Rain's oversight was an encroachment on command protocols. "And I won't be the only one who sees it that way."

"I'm sorry, Arnie. I'm not trying to do your job." Rain's manner was warm and his attitude supportive as they discussed the issue in Arnie's office. "I know most of the people around here. And whether they're supposed to or not, they know about the danger too." Arnie relented with a slight nod.

Rain sped from group to group in his jeep. The professional and courteous manner of his troops pleased him. He heard a few objections to the procedure, mainly from guest contractors who had paid for the use of the facilities and had tight schedules. He took a few minutes out of his review to calm the more aggravated of one such group, a private sector team who were anxious to test their drone prototypes.

"This delay is totally unacceptable—we should already be at the airfield!"

"I'm sorry, sir. The schedule will be changing. You will be asked to suspend your work and you and your team will be leaving this afternoon. We'll do our best to get you rescheduled soon."

The news further riled the man. As he ranted, Rain spied Juan in a nearby group. Juan beckoned, so Rain walked away from the contractors. He did not respond to the angry demands hurled at his back.

"Rain. I wanted to let you know. I'm gonna do what you said." Juan's manner was that of a grade-schooler showing a parent a successful report card.

"What's that?" Rain half-listened, preoccupied with the drill.

Juan beamed. "I'm gonna ask Gigi to marry me."

He caught Rain's attention. "Really—just like that, huh? Listen, Juan, I'm glad for you, and I want to hear all about it, but not right now." He walked briskly away.

"Yeah, sure, I get you." Juan called after him. "I got you to thank, amigo! You're gonna be in the wedding party—plan on it!"

Rain imparted calm as he spoke with more of those assembled on the walkways. He overheard push-back from one more person, an older DPG employee who questioned one of his team about the orthodoxy of these procedures. Rain knew the man. He was the kind who jumped to conclusions. But Rain didn't intervene. Instead, he listened from a few yards away to hear how his soldier handled the situation. She did as well as could be expected, even though after their exchange the man grumbled and grilled those around him about what Command wasn't disclosing.

The soldiers instructed the groups from each building to assemble in the marked locations. Rain's concern concentrated on the civilian population. He made them his personal priority. He checked in at the English Village and was pleased by the cordial attitudes of most. He got a report from the airfield where those using the Biological, Chemical, Explosives and Ordnance, Unmanned Aircraft, and other test facilities congregated. Over the radio, Corporal Jessica Camarillo reported some concerns, but had the procedures there well in hand.

Rain jumped from his jeep and joined the group from the administrative building. He chatted with Jerry. Quon was upon them before Rain was aware of his approach. "It is good to be careful, but delays are costly too." Quon was testy but polite. "How long do you suppose this interruption will last, Sergeant?"

"It's Command Sergeant Major," corrected Jerry.

"My apologies. I mean no disrespect. When can we expect to resume our important work? I am in the middle of a new line of investigation. This exercise is more than a little inconvenient."

"I'm sorry, Dr. Quon. I estimate you can be back in the labs within the hour."

"Sooner is better than later. Is there some way you can hurry your men along?"

"Our people are doing their best right now. Won't be much longer. Now, please excuse me."

"One more matter, if you please, Sergeant Major."

Rain took a breath to summon his patience and quell his feeling Quon was like something on the bottom of your shoe you can't wipe off. "What?"

"I have two concerns. Perhaps you can help me. I was told of a decision coming to approve my use of the Whole System Live Agent Test Chamber."

Rain sighed. "Walk with me, Dr. Quon. This sounds like a sensitive matter."

"Oh, yes. Of course." They walked a few yards away from the group.

"What is your difficulty?"

"The way resources are managed here is perhaps well suited for managing disparate lines of study. But the bureaucratic process is slowing me down. Perhaps it is because I am used to being in charge. But I can tell you these continual delays for every new experiment are counterproductive. I have had to be driven three times between here and the Test Center already. I have not yet had the opportunity to discuss this matter with your Commander, as we both have been occupied, as you know. But whatever you might be able to do to cut the red tape to accommodate my work would be invaluable in achieving our ends."

"Have you spoken with Jerry and Bob?"

"Yes." Quon glanced back at Jerry as he conversed with fellow researchers. "They have priorities of their own. I assure you the studies I propose are mission critical."

"I'll see what I can do. There are good reasons for their decisions."

"I am sure. However, no one understands the priority of my work here better than you. I should not have to further explain—"

"No, you don't." Rain stepped away to resume his oversight duty.

"One more thing Sergeant Major?"

Rain bit back his irritation. "What?"

"I have questions to explore that require the use of the Materiel Test Facility. Dr. Harrison has been, let us say, less responsive than hoped for. I require a time allocation for experimentation in the explosive containment chamber."

"Tell you what, Dr. Quon." Rain hoped he could shut him up with a promise. "As soon as this safety drill is concluded, I'll drop by there to help with the arrangements. As you can see, I'm a bit busy myself. Will that be all?"

"Yes. Thank you, Sergeant Major. Your help will be most appreciated."

AN EXPOSURE

"Rain—just one thing! Real fast, amigo!"

Rain walked back to his jeep when he heard the shout. Juan again waved at him. Though he was happy for Juan and Gigi, now was not the time. He mouthed the word 'later' as his radio crackled to life.

"Rain! Emergency at the Ditto muster station. Come quick!"

He snatched the radio from his hip as he trotted to his jeep. "On the way." He grimaced. "What is it, Camarillo?"

"It's SONA! There are casualties!"

Rain's heart skipped as he sprinted and jumped into the jeep. Tires squealed in protest as he slammed the accelerator pedal and peeled away. He reached again for his radio and saw a figure hanging halfway into the vehicle. "Juan! What are you doing?!"

"Helping, amigo." He gritted his teeth as he strained to pull himself in. "You think...you think you could give me a hand?"

"No." Rain slowed, leaned over, and with his right hand, pushed against Juan in an attempt to make him let go. "You stay here." Juan wriggled past Rain's reach and hoisted himself inside. Rain glared at him. "What you're doing is not help. I'd stop and kick you out, but there's no time." Rain accelerated again. He glanced back and forth between the road and Juan as his anger gave way to admiration for his willingness to run towards danger. Juan may have been an electronics technician—uncleared, unbriefed, and untrained in the circumstances they now faced—but he was able-bodied, quick-witted, and could at least help him herd people away from harm. He mentally reviewed the protocol most appropriate for this situation. "You should be aware of the risk. It's worse than you know."

"You're going, aren't you?"

"You just told me about your intentions with Gigi. You've got to think about her."

"Why do you think I'm doing this, man? She's out there. I heard that bit about casualties. You know as much as me—she'd do the same thing."

Rain softened. "You want to be helpful? Hold the radio for me."

Juan did so. Rain first dispatched additional emergency services. When he heard someone, not one of his troops, order an immediate evacuation of the area, he shouted. "Disregard that order!"

"*Sergeant Major?*" returned a voice.

"Allow nobody to leave the area. I'll be there shortly."

"*What about our team?*"

Rain didn't yet know enough to issue a high-quality order. What was the manner and method of the exposure? Where and how widespread is the affected area? How many victims? "How many of the team are wearing Class Four hazmat suits?"

"*None, Sarge.*"

He glanced at Juan, who shared his wide-eyed alarm. He spoke on the radio as Juan shifted to hold it steady. "Get as many as you can suited up. Stay away from the victims. Under no circumstances does anyone not wearing a Class Four hazmat suit approach any of them."

"*That's a problem, Rain. We have people refusing to leave the side of their afflicted coworkers.*"

He stomped the accelerator, but it was already pressed to the floor. The classic jeep could go no faster than 80 mph. "I'm two clicks away. Have a suit ready for me." He scowled at Juan. "Make that two suits."

"*Roger that.*"

Rain's demeanor belied his inner turmoil.

Juan's mouth hung open. "What's going on, amigo?"

"I'm afraid you're about to find out." Empathy infused his voice, but it didn't diminish the force of his command. "When we get there, stay back. Don't go near anyone."

"Hey, man, I want to help! I'm not afraid."

Rain recognized Juan's attempt at bravado. Common in crises among the untrained; it was a dangerous attitude. "You should be."

Less than two long minutes later, they skidded to a stop into chaos. Camouflaged soldiers and white-shirted businesspeople rushed helter-skelter, most in panic. Two large groups huddled in one of the muster stations. Numerous people lay on the ground. Some screamed in pain, flanked by others who knelt helplessly at their sides with no clue about what to do. Some of the figures made no sound. They didn't thrash about. But they weren't entirely still; their flesh disappeared. It flaked and oozed away in an odorless gray mass.

The same thing happened to the shoulder and neck of a woman in her late twenties. A spout of blood erupted from the ruptured flesh and sprayed in a wide arc as she shrieked in pain and horror. Juan doubled over and retched. Rain, too preoccupied to respond, scanned the entire area to assess. Some members of his squad tried in vain to restore order. Two men attempted to enter a nearby sedan. "You there," Rain shouted. "You are not to leave this area. Get over there right now!" He pointed to the muster station. They complied.

Corporal Jessica Camarillo ran to Rain. "Not sure what happened, Sarge. Screams started coming from that area, over there." She pointed towards the water tower and airfield. A cluster of a dozen bodies dotted the ground thirty yards away.

"Hazmat suits," Rain demanded. "Where are they?"

"There's a crew getting them from the test facility." She indicated the building.

"Let's go."

The three of them sprinted there. A man stumbled toward them, blank-faced and zombie-like, numb from shock as half his arm crumbled away. Juan struggled to keep pace with Rain and Jessica. "Gigi!" he called as he turned this way and that amongst the chaos.

Some of Rain's squad, now geared up, ran to separate infected from non-infected. Rain stopped one. "Get more med kits. Make sure we have tourniquets." As the man complied, Rain grabbed his arm. "And saws if you can find them."

Juan blanched. Rain helped Juan into a suit while Jessica donned one herself. Once they were set, he donned his own. "I've gotta find Gigi," Juan said to Rain.

"We will. But you're here to help, right? That means you do as I say. Got me?"

Juan nodded as Rain zipped himself in. Robert Harrison jogged over. He appeared disheveled and wide-eyed but was nevertheless coherent and resolved. "Rain, I'm glad you're here." He tried to catch his breath.

"Do you know how this happened, Bob?"

"No. There's nothing on the desert surface; it's not like before. At least not that we've found. It came from nowhere." He teetered on panic. "What are we going to do?"

Rain steadied Harrison with a tender squeeze of the man's shoulder. "We're going to be systematic. One thing, then the next. Got it?" Harrison nodded. Rain went on. "We will set up test stations and determine as fast as we can who is exposed and who isn't. Can you help with that part of the operation?"

"We don't have to screen." Harrison sunk, crestfallen. "When someone is exposed, the symptoms always appear right away."

"Roger that. When you're satisfied people are clear, isolate them and transport them back to the LSF for further examination. Also, alert the clinic—they're gonna be busy. I'll get some buses out here."

"Okay."

The soldier returned with the medical supplies. Rain took them. "Good work soldier—distribute all you can." He returned to Harrison. "You'll help him with that?"

Harrison nodded, and the two dashed off.

Jessica challenged Juan. "What are you doing here?"

"I'm looking for Gigi—have you seen her?"

"No."

Rain turned back. "Juan. You wanted to help. Now's your chance. Come on." They ran toward the screams. Two people who helped the exposed now shrieked themselves, transfixed in wide-eyed disbelief as necrosis consumed their fingers. "Corporal, you ever train as a medic?" Rain was composed but urgent. She shook her head no. "Alright. You and Juan will need to hold the person while I work. It won't be easy. Put all of your weight on the chest."

She gulped and shared a glance with Juan as Rain laid a panicked man prone.

"We'll do our best to save you. Close your eyes." Incoherent, the man writhed in pain. Rain put his knee on the man's shoulder and indicated where the others do the same—Jessica on his chest, Juan on his legs. Rain set a tourniquet, pulled out a saw, and set upon the gruesome work.

"Juan! You're not supposed to be here."

Juan was soaked—blood on the outside of his suit, sweat on the inside. "Gigi, thank God!" They embraced, hard and long.

"Well?"

"Helping." His shock broke, his face relaxed a little. "Looking for you."

"Since when is that your job? You shouldn't be here."

"I should be wherever you are."

"You're on the way to decon, right?" She took his gloved hand in hers. "Me too. We need to keep moving."

THEY HUSTLED to the LSF and went through decon. Juan pulled her aside as they exited. "This is some kind of biological weapon that has spun out of control, right?"

"Not quite." Gigi frowned. "We're working to eliminate it."

"That's why Quon is here. It makes sense now."

"Now you know how important it is. Dr. Quon is studying it, yes." She looked up and away, contemplative.

"What? You were about to say something else."

The nascent tears in her eyes glistened in the florescent light. "Maybe she won't either." Gigi's eyes widened.

Juan didn't understand, but didn't care. He embraced her and they held each other for a long while. It helped. "I came for another reason." He gulped and let go. "Doesn't matter now. Those people. What happened to them? What did I see?"

"I don't know, Bean. I know it ate the mass spec."

"I figured." His hand went to the box in his pocket. This changed everything. He embraced Gigi again. He tried, without success, to keep his tears from dampening her shirt.

EXCERPT:
THE NECESSITY OF PRECURSOR COOPERATIVES

Wallace, M. D.[1,2] and Weingartner, J. A.[1]

1 University of California, Berkeley, Dept. of Plant and Microbial Biology, 311 Koshland Hall, Berkeley CA, 94720.

2 National Interagency Biodefense Campus, Fort Detrick, MD 21702

Section #2: Energetic Transformation, cont.

As from the onset, continued dependence on random events meant rapid extinction for the fledgling entity. It needed a stable source of energy to persist. But as fate had it, again, a new, energy harvesting chemical began to accumulate. The amino acid glycine and another organic molecule, succinate, reacted to form porphyrin, a square snowflake-shaped molecule that had the ability to absorb energy from light. When hit by light in the wavelengths within the visible spectrum, porphyrin molecules became excited and resulted in physical separation of positively charged protons and negatively charged electrons, creating an electrochemical proton gradient. This gradient powered the formation of another molecule. This chemical, called Adenosine, was a close relative of the original Cytosine and Thymine that made up the nucleic acid polymers stabilized by the peptides. The porphyrin-transferred energy caused Adenosine to bond with phosphate molecules. This modified Adenosine Triphosphate (ATP) could stably hold large quantities of energy that in turn could be readily released by interactions with certain peptides. The

Porphyrin family's ability to create an electrochemical gradient for ATP formation would indefinitely fuel the collective. It had food.

A REUNION

The flight back to DPG departed from Hagerstown. Mira was less tense about the flight than usual, grateful for the time she would have lost in capital beltway traffic. Randy had wanted to drive her, but despite the constant failure and her growing doubts about the approach, Mira insisted he and the rest of the team continue the biocontrol screens. She opted for a taxi app instead. She slept a little on the Gulfstream, but her slumber remained fitful and sporadic. Her anxiety about flying was there, as always. Most of her consternation came from the results, or lack thereof, from the SONA assays. Mira had selected thousands of microbes known to be among the most durable, and none of the 1,200 she and Randy tested over five exhausting ten-hour days could withstand SONA's cell rupturing effects. Mira now suspected if there was a biocontrol solution at all, finding it would require new ways to carry out millions of assays in parallel. They simply knew too little about SONA to make educated guesses. She suspected that her massive extremophile collection would offer the best hope. But they lacked the technology to screen it. She grimaced in frustration at the thought.

There was another matter on her mind—the cryptic message from Eleanor summoning her back: *We have a situation. Return to DPG. Report to Commander ASAP.* Mira couldn't concoct a good reason why she had to drop the research at Detrick and return to Dugway. What more could she do? Why no explanation? What situation? Had something bad happened? If so, to whom? She didn't permit herself to dwell on the last question.

The impact of the landing shook her awake. She rubbed her eyes and glanced out the window. They weren't at the Michael Airfield, but Salt Lake City International.

"Why are we here?" This would add two plus-hours to her travel time.

"We were re-routed. They gave no details; just that Michael Airfield was unavailable."

Ominous news. She shuddered as her mind searched for potential explanations. Her fingers worked furiously as she texted Rain, Eleanor, and Quon in turn. The lack of a response from any of them only fueled her fear.

Dugway was a different place than she had left mere days prior. What struck Mira first was how deserted it was; gone were most of the cars, both moving and parked, as well as the normal throng of people who milled about the place. The handful of people she did see wore hazmat suits. Not a good sign.

She reported to Potteiger's office. An unknown spike of emotion jabbed her when she saw Rain. Relief? Joy? Something else? With them were Harrison, Jerry, and Eleanor. She smiled at Rain and he at her. She noted the dark circles under his eyes. It robbed them of their usual warmth. At least he was okay.

"Welcome back, Mira." His voice was tired, hoarse. "Tell us you've got good results at Detrick. Please."

"I wish I could." The words tasted like defeat.

"Nothing?" Potteiger asked like he might change her answer by force of will.

"I'm sorry." Her eyes dropped, and she struggled to maintain her scientific dispassion. "We haven't yet been able to identify a biocontrol solution. Every test was negative."

As she noticed more about the people in the room, they appeared as worn, borderline broken, as Rain. His state became even more dreadful in response to her news. His spine was no longer straight. The angle of his chin tilted down. The vibrancy in his deep voice was dead. "I can't tell you how sorry I am to hear that."

"What happened here?" As disappointing as the last few days were for her, it was worse for these people. She braced herself. She didn't want to hear the answer. But she knew she must.

Eleanor stepped closer. "SONA appears to be spreading in a new way. Some theorize that it has gone airborne through wind or perhaps as debris stuck to flying insects or birds, but nothing has been confirmed."

The picture of what must have happened to the victims formed in her mind and struck her like a physical blow. "How many?" she managed.

Potteiger spit out his response. "SONA has now taken thirty-four lives, including two young boys outside of the Dugway perimeter. The base is now on 'Essential Personnel Only' status. Large sections have been cordoned off. Until we know what happened out at Ditto with this outbreak, everybody in the area must wear protective gear. We'll get you equipped before you leave the building."

Mira's eyes welled. "I'm sorry."

"Our hands are being forced here, Mira. We don't have much more time." Eleanor's tone was grave and her hair mussed; gray and black strands protruded at various angles.

"The work is going to be what it's going to be." Jerry was adamant in a way Mira hadn't seen from him before. "No matter what you all decide to do, we're looking at an extensive subterranean survey."

"That will take time we don't have." Potteiger struck Mira as angrier and less sad than the others. She hadn't seen him unshaven. The graying stubble aged him.

"I've heard the rumblings too." Harrison was even more wretched than Rain. "No matter what command decides, the investigations must continue."

"Where's Quon?" Mira asked.

"Good question." Was that frustration in Eleanor's voice? It was probably typical Quon. He would do what he wanted; he assumed he answered to no one.

Rain said, "He's in the chemical and explosives test facilities. He was very intent."

"He hasn't answered me." Mira felt a flicker of hope. "Is he on to something?"

"I don't know," Rain said pessimistically. He and Eleanor appeared to be in accord when it came to Quon.

Eleanor looked Mira over as though she judged a farm show event. "I have an important question for you, Mira. I want you to take over for Quon and run the biological research. Will you do that for us?"

Mira didn't want more responsibility. Her reflex was to decline. But apparently, Quon's leadership was inadequate. From the beginning, his approach raised doubts; primarily how he jumped to conclusions. Such leaps are never advisable. Yes, in the present circumstances time was of the essence. But that didn't mean you should disregard scientific discipline. "I don't think Dr. Quon will like this."

"I'll worry about that, Mira," Eleanor assured.

"The work we're doing at Detrick is going to take time. We've screened a couple thousand microbes. None showed promise. It may still be possible to identify a biocontrol solution, but we need to find a way to screen millions. Many of those will require specialized equipment. It will take a miracle to screen that many in time."

"I have faith in you." Eleanor smiled.

"Me too," said Rain.

"If there is an answer, you'll find it," Eleanor continued.

"Hmmm," Mira replied, doubtful. "I'm no miracle worker." Her mind raced. She could allocate more lab space and screen more candidates against SONA. But she had to face an undeniable reality here. The tools she needed didn't exist. She knew little of the other sciences trying to find a solution. For the first time since she had been brought into this crisis, she considered the most expedient answer might lie somewhere outside of her purview. Eventually, she said, "Surveying, you say? Can I make a suggestion?"

A PROBLEM SOLVER

"Kyle, you're squishing me," Mira gasped. Despite the discomfort, Kyle's presence sparked a welcome rush of relief. She supposed it was her confidence in his abilities.

"Sorry Doc." He let go, and she fell back in a chair in front of Rain's desk. "Just good to be here, I 'spose. Tired o', I mean—I've just been sittin' round—you know, nothin' much to do." He wiped sweat from his forehead with the back of his hand, then he leaned close and whispered, "Sorry I was all snocked."

"Think nothing of it." Mira indicated Rain with a glance. "Meet Command Sergeant Major Somerdale, Kyle. He oriented me. He'll do the same for you."

Rain rose from his desk, approached Kyle, and extended his hand. Kyle's hand engulfed Rain's strong grip. "Pleased to meetchya."

"Likewise. Mira speaks highly of you. I hear you're cleared already. Good. Follow me—we'll get some chow and I'll give you the rundown." Rain turned to Mira. "You two can use my office as long as you like."

"Thank you, Rain. I have a few matters to discuss with Jeff. We'll be at the LSF after that."

"Be careful, okay? We still don't know how those people were exposed."

"We'll follow all the protocols." To Kyle, she said, "We'll catch up more later."

"Sure, Doc, sure." His bushy beard and eyebrows shook with his animation. Rain opened the door for him and he and Kyle left.

Mira turned to Jeff. "Thank you for bringing him."

"You kidding? I wanted to come back."

"How is our sequencing proceeding?"

"It's going very well, Mira. It's nearing completion." Jeff was upbeat.

Mira stood, uplifted by Jeff's news and spirit. "That's great to hear. I needed you here again because things have changed. I'll tell you about it on the way to the labs. First, we have to suit up."

Jeff's eyebrows raised as they left Rain's office and exited the admin building.

"WE MIGHT HAVE A SLIGHT PROBLEM."

"What's that, sonny?" Kyle's manner was uncharacteristically jovial.

Rain didn't wish to be impolite. "I don't think we have any suits that will fit you."

Kyle chortled. "I'm used to that sorta problem. When yer boys told me I needed one, we got one ordered. They said it'd be here before me."

"Good. I'll track it down and have it delivered to us." He texted his contact at Army Materials Command. "Mira tells us you're a wizard with subterranean structure. I gotta tell you, I don't know anything about that. But we'll confer with experts from the Army Corps of Engineers, along with a few private contractors. They said they're bringing assets down from Boise."

"They bringin' down thumper trucks?"

"I don't even know what that is. I recall something about 'vibroseis' trucks. Does that make sense to you?"

"Yep. That's them. Makes the job of mappin' fast and easy. Not like the old days—lots o' drillin' and samplin'. Not to mention drawin' and calculatin'."

Rain shared what little he knew of the current geological

activities. Once they had their protective gear on, Rain drove them to the danger zone—the Ditto Area. When they went into the WDTC HQ, they removed the headgear but kept the suits on. The meeting was underway when they entered Harrison's office. The room was laid out perfectly for how Harrison operated—large, utilitarian, and arranged for team meetings.

Rain indicated two empty chairs on the far side of the table. He and Kyle took seats as Harrison addressed the group, all similarly clad in hazmat suits. "...so you can see this will require more of us than any prior military geological operation." He acknowledged their arrival, "Ah, welcome, gentlemen. May I present our Installation Command Sergeant Major Rain Somerdale? And I have not yet met his guest. I'm Robert Harrison. I direct the West Desert Test Center."

Rain spoke. "This is Kyle Newman. He has most recently worked with Dr. Wallace. Mr. Newman is here based on her recommendation. He has extensive experience working in extreme environments."

Kyle was unusually chary. "Pleased to meetchya."

"Thank you, Mr. Newman. Let me introduce our Technical Director Dr. Jerry Griffin and our guests from the U.S. Army Corps of Engineers, Sacramento District Commander Colonel Dennis Ramon, Deputy District Engineer for Project Management Ms. Tricia Heller, and Dr. Yolanda Fisher, Senior Engineer." Everyone nodded acknowledgment.

"We know each other," said Colonel Ramon. "I'm glad you're on this project, Kyle."

The team spoke about the available assets, risk reduction, special technical challenges, and estimated timelines for their survey of the region. Yolanda finished her summary.

"That's skookum and all," Kyle responded, "but you're leavin' a few things out of your thinkin' there, missy."

Tricia raised her brows, "Like what for instance, Mr. Newman?"

"I'm just talkin' off my head here, but by what everybody's been sayin', this ain't no Bob's Your Uncle kind o' deal. We're not gonna get a good picture by knockin' on the ground a few times, eh?"

Harrison broke the tense pause. "What are you saying, Kyle?"

"This stuff is spreadin', right? Ain't likely it's just seepin' like, let's say oil, might do. It won't just be flowin' along a path of least resistance, collectin' in cavities or migratin' from dense to less dense rock formations. Maybe it's doin' somethin' else—you could fool me about what it is. Bottom line—we might not be able to place concentrations in the way we're used to, at least with any confidence."

"What are you suggesting, Kyle?" asked Ramon.

"We're gonna have ta drill holes—lots of 'em. Only way we'll be sure to get the seismology right. We'll use acoustics to make a good map. You're gonna need to order up a bunch o' rigs. Gonna need a bunch o' Rig Pigs, too, if they're all gonna give'r at the same time. And not just any old ones, neither. We're gonna need Barber rigs."

"What are Barber rigs?" asked Tricia.

"Sorry, they ain't called that no more. I'm talkin' about Foremost dual rotary drills."

"Might that pose greater risk of exposure?" asked Jerry.

"That mayhap be. That's one reason why I say the DR rigs are the ticket. They don't use percussion and they drill dead straight—don't matter what they hit into. Less stirrin' things up."

"It's also going to mean more time," said Harrison.

"Probably. If we got to wait for the rigs ta get here." Kyle spread his long arms out on the table to either side. Rain had to lean away to avoid his beefy elbows. "But there's two ways to do jobs like this." He held one hand up and extended his index finger. "Fast," he extended his thumb, "or right."

THE DUGWAY DESERT looked like an industrial circus. The original white canvass tent over the first SONA outcropping gave way to a monstrous half-acre covering that featured a special ceramic-fiber cloth, one that did not have an organic binder susceptible to SONA. The tent was flanked by a dozen or so smaller siblings pitched around the vicinity, all the same near-white color. Those were in turn encircled by encampments of special equipment—power generators, pumps, and hoses of all kinds. Scores of rounded gleaming metal storage tanks filled with either liquid fuels and disinfectants or gaseous chlorine, nitrogen, or oxygen ringed them.

Spaced throughout this menagerie were dozens of mobile drill rigs. They all extended their masts, strong steel scaffolds of red, yellow, or blue which extended anywhere from thirty to a hundred feet into the air. Tanker trucks and dozens of hazmat-clad workers flanked the rigs. Space-suit clad operators tripped pipe, monitored rotary drill progress, or adjusted platforms. Other personnel tended risk-suppression—they drove tanker trucks, managed hoses, and sprayed surfactants into the holes and on the crushed rock and mud that issued forth. Yet another small army managed air supplies and helped workers through isolation prep or decontamination. Lines formed at these and the flanking outcroppings of red plastic portable toilets.

Rain ferried Kyle between work-sites in his jeep. They approached one where the drilling had come to a standstill. "What's the problem?" Rain shouted through the protective equipment and over the drone of the engines.

"We keep key-seating," said the crew chief.

Rain gave a curious glance to Kyle. "Once you free the pipe, circulate water for half an hour and decrease yer rotational speed."

Pipe jammed at another site. Rain let Kyle inquire. Once he heard the report from that crew's chief, Kyle instructed, "You need to reduce yer hydrostatic pressure, eh? Use some nitrogen to gasify the mud."

At yet another, the rig resonated wildly on the verge of failure. Kyle's advice was different this time. "It's a problem with yer differential pressure, eh? Place a packer in that quiggly. That'll equalize it."

Rain gained more appreciation for why Mira wanted Kyle here as the day went on. Many of the drill operators, especially the more senior ones, knew who Kyle was and were happy for his advice, even when he gave it in a gruff, vulgarity-ridden manner.

They drove to the temporary supply depot to get more air charges. Kyle expressed satisfaction with the crews. "Them Barbers are the ticket, right? No trouble with 'em."

"How much more drilling do you think we'll need to do?"

"We'll see where we are with the samples, eh? A few of the crews reported trouble with hole integrity. That could mean subsurface degradation." Kyle deliberated. Whether that is caused by yer nasty down there or a natural formation, I can't say 'til we get the survey results."

"Are we done out here?"

"Looks like yer boys are on top of it now."

"Good. I could use a break."

On the way to decon, Kyle said, "There's something I gotta say to you, sonny." He paused to face Rain. "This whole show. It's futile. You know that, don't you?"

Rain's brow raised in surprise. "What do you mean?"

"We ain't gonna be able to dig all of that stuff outta there, and there ain't no way we're going to be able to stop its spread. It's too far gone now. But you know that. I can tell you do."

"We do what we can. That's all we can ever do, right?"

"I 'spose that's so. We'll have a lookie at the results they give us. But I can tell ya sure as you please, our laundry is blowin' away in the wind."

"That's one thing I hope you're wrong about, Kyle."

A REALIGNMENT

Mira helped Jeff and Gigi re-purpose their lab. "Our first priority is to determine if SONA has indeed been spread by an airborne factor."

"Makes sense, Mira," said Jeff.

"They're continuing to pursue a biocontrol solution at Detrick." She gained clarity as she spoke. It often helped her to talk things out, especially when she did so with Jeff. "We could work in parallel on that. Even though we lack the equipment and resources they have, there are millions of species I'd like to run. I wish we could run our extremophile library. It isn't technically feasible, though." She paused. "While I was there, I had the chance to view what SONA did to cells in real time. It was remarkable. I'd like to get as close to that setup here as possible. Two labs are better than one."

"Music to my ears." Jeff removed bottles and supplies from a crate.

"There, we worked in BSL-4 level containment. This lab is BSL-2. We're going to have to take extra precautions, and we're going to have to take some shortcuts. Much of the work will have to be conducted in containment, so you'll have to work both here and in the BSL-3 facilities. Any objections?"

"If you're good, I'm good."

"I'm good, too, in case you were wondering," said Gigi.

The door buzzed open and Quon flew in. Under the hazmat suit everybody was now required to wear in the Ditto area, he wore the same hardhat and goggles Mira had last seen. He did not wear his normal smile. "I don't want to disturb you, but I need to speak with you, Dr. Wallace."

"Yes, I was concerned when I received no responses from my many texts."

"I was busy on a new line of inquiry." He addressed Gigi, "Miss Patilla, I require your help on some experiments." He faced Mira. "If that is acceptable to you, Dr. Wallace. I understand you are now in charge here and I no longer enjoy that privilege."

Mira preferred that Gigi assist Jeff. She was clearly competent, knew the facilities, and helped them work efficiently. She looked Quon over. Something was different about him. His manner was calmer, his voice less boisterous. What did it mean? Clearly, he was not happy about something. Maybe it was the shift in their positions.

"Is there a reason it needs to be her specifically?"

"I was informed Miss Patilla has worked extensively in the Materials Testing Facility. The other technicians there have been assigned to other priorities. I need to work fast. With your permission, she will provide me with a capable set of hands for some of the energetic studies we need to conduct."

This was definitely out of the norm for him. He was never this deferential. This wasn't even his sticky sweet false humility. She looked back at Gigi, whose expression revealed her preference. Gigi wanted to remain and work with Jeff. But Quon's request was reasonable. She didn't ask about his studies, but she didn't doubt it was important. She met Gigi's eyes. "If it's acceptable to her."

Gigi scrunched her face. "If I must," she said, her verve absent.

Mira noted the reluctance. She reconsidered, and almost voiced it, but instead said, "Very well, Dr. Quon. She's at your disposal."

"We shall get started right away, Miss Patilla."

Jeff nudged Mira, who slowly understood why. "Dr. Quon, I'd like you to meet my fellow researcher at Berkeley, Dr. Jeff Weingartner. I didn't have the chance to introduce you earlier."

Jeff stepped forward and extended his hand. "It's an honor to meet you, Dr. Quon."

Quon looked at Jeff's hand. "Yes." He spun around and dashed out of the lab.

Jeff looked at Mira, dumbfounded and dejected, his unshaken hand still extended. "Did I do something wrong?"

"It's not you," said Gigi. She said to Mira, "See why I wanted to stay here?" She gathered a few things and was about to leave the lab herself when she turned back, with no attempt to conceal the snark. "Thanks for this."

The hair on Mira's neck raised as she watched Gigi go. Again, she felt a reluctance to let her go. She almost stopped her. But she and Jeff would manage. Besides, Gigi could handle herself, even with Quon. Mira held her tongue as she joined Jeff in their work.

A DISTINGUISHED GATHERING

M ichael Army Airfield reopened for the Strategy Summit. Exposure risk required that all personnel wear Personal Protection Equipment until they were inside the West Desert Test Center HQ building. VIPs arrived in a steady stream and jammed the tarmac with jets.

Rain and Kyle drove past them on their way back from another morning of survey oversight. They efficiently went through the decon station in front of the HQ building and entered. Rain's feelings were mixed that the building was deemed safe. Until the Ditto contamination was better understood, how did they know for certain? Nevertheless, he was glad to be out of the isolation suit. By Kyle's relieved grunt, the big man agreed. The two men hung their gear on the portable racks in the hallway while a group of uniformed generals, high-level officials, and their retinue did the same.

Kyle looked down at his stained steel-toed boots, grimy logger pants, and well-worn gray flannel shirt and let out a grunt of a different type. Rain stretched to place a hand on Kyle's shoulder. "Come on, big guy," he said softly. "Us working men are invited too."

Kyle grunted a third time as he extended his thumb. "Those types don't think much o' guys like me, eh?"

Rain grinned. "It won't be like that. They appreciate the work we do." Kyle grumbled unintelligibly as they followed the stream of attendees to the amphitheater.

By the time Rain and Kyle arrived, nearly a hundred people milled about. On the wall behind the podium was the WDTC logo, flanked on one side by the flag of the United States of America and the blue flag of the state of Utah, and on the other the white background flag of the U.S. Army and the blue-green and gold-lettered and fringed flag of Dugway Proving Ground.

Rain smiled when he spotted Mira across the room. He glanced at Kyle, who smiled at her too. She didn't see them as she spoke with a cluster of scientists and bureaucrats. Around that group stood many of the upper echelons of military and civilian governance.

Included was the entire leadership team of the DPG, along with Connie, Eleanor, and Quon. Much of the leadership of the U.S. Army Corps of Engineers was there too, which included two of its top generals. They joined the other USACE officials, Tricia and Yolanda among them, who had already been assigned to DPG. That loud contingent dominated the far-left side of the room.

Other areas of the Defense Department attended. Notables included DTRA Director Darryl Cambridge (flanked continually by Aaron Moore), the Major General Mark Charles who commanded ATEC, Director of the Defense Information Systems Agency Lieutenant General Adam Fillmore, and Secretary of the Army Jonathan Agnew.

Since SONA had claimed dozens of lives and imperiled more, the most senior members of the Executive Branch of the U.S. Federal government were now involved. Circled by members of their staffs, Secretary of Defense Carson Gallagher, Secretary of Homeland Security Rodrigo Vega, and Chief of Staff of the U.S. Army General Miles Marcus—the Army's highest-ranking officer—were absorbed in a vibrant discussion.

The federal authorities had also invited Utah State Governor Gale Hauser to this forum. He and his senior staff had come from Salt Lake City, a modest 90-minute drive compared with the treks of the others. Other attendees included lower officials and subject matter experts in public and private sector roles. The room buzzed as the appointed hour arrived.

Potteiger and Eleanor called the meeting to order. It took a few minutes for everyone to settle into their seats. Potteiger finally spoke. "Welcome to the United States Army's Dugway Proving Ground and the West Desert Test Center. I'm Colonel Garrett Potteiger, Base Commander. With me is Deputy Secretary of Homeland Security Dr. Eleanor Dixon. Our objective today is to evaluate the situation and make some difficult decisions. I regret to tell you our options are limited. We face significant cost and risk no matter what course we take."

Potteiger reviewed the time line of the SONA crisis. He briefly described the fatal encounters, their effects, and a few of the details of SONA's spread. Tension and fear were palpable in the room as he yielded to Eleanor.

She cleared her throat. "Going forward, we have three options. I will outline them. The appropriate experts are here to fill in details as needed." Her slide deck advanced to display the words OPTION #1: HOLD THE LINE on in-wall flat screen monitors to her either side.

She read the words and paused. "This is the strategy we've used since SONA first appeared. We isolated the original area of contamination. Numerous others continue to appear, and those have been treated similarly." A bullet point appeared on the screens: ISOLATION AND CONTAINMENT.

"We've set up containment tents and filled them with lethal concentrations of chlorine gas. This has significantly slowed the propagation of SONA once it is manifest in these signature outcroppings. This method, however, does not stop it. SONA has spread, anyway." Another bullet point flew in: TEMPORARY SOLUTION.

"This approach can be compared to putting our fingers in a cracking dike. And like that approach, the measure is only temporary. The hope has been to develop an effective mitigation process before the agent becomes impossible to contain. Despite the efforts of some of the best scientific minds in the world, it looks less and less like we will be able to do that. It's not realistic to expect work that takes years to be completed in days or weeks. But days or weeks are what SONA is giving us."

The slide advanced and the next title read: HOLD THE LINE: RISK ASSESSMENT. "The risk of continuing on this course is now untenable. We know SONA is spreading underground. The tents are not effective and represent no small risk because they are unsatisfactory vessels for the long-term storage of such quantities of concentrated deadly gas. We have also had a major incident that involved much loss of life. We don't yet know how that particular exposure occurred, but the indication is that SONA is now spreading in ways we don't know."

"I want to know where this stuff came from." The formidable baritone voice of four-star General Miles Marcus echoed.

Before Eleanor could respond, Quon stood. "That is a matter in some dispute, General." He strode to the podium. "The truth is SONA is an entirely new organism. I know that because I discovered its DNA. It is unrelated to any other on the four-billion-year-old Tree of Life. It represents a second event for the emergence of life on earth. This suggests SONA is one of the most important discoveries in our lifetimes. It proves the theory of abiogenesis."

"What does that mean?" Marcus demanded. Potteiger and Eleanor looked at each other.

Quon smiled and puffed himself to his full height. He gazed purposefully around the room to catch the eyes of many in the audience. He returned his gaze to the eyes of General Marcus. "It means stories of an otherworldly Creator, such as in the Judeo-Christian Bible, are now provably false."

A DECISION

A cacophony of comments and questions ensued. Mira stirred in her seat. Why would Quon make such a claim at this time and place? It had nothing to do with science or the scientific method. He was pushing an agenda. But what? Why?

Potteiger pushed past Quon to reclaim the microphone. "Ladies and gentlemen. Please sit. Let's have order."

Eventually the crowd complied. Eleanor bit her lip, smoothed her hair, and reestablished herself at the microphone. "Dr. Quon's speculation notwithstanding, let's return to our original agenda and the decisions ahead of us."

She clicked to advance the slide, and the screens displayed OPTION #2: EXCAVATE AND REMEDIATE. "Consider our second option. With the help of the Army Corps of Engineers and many others, we conducted extensive seismic surveys and geologic analysis to better evaluate where we are with regard to the subterranean spread of SONA."

The slide advanced to show a multi-layer cross-sectional view of the geologic structure underneath the surrounding desert. A moment later, a sinewy blue blob superimposed and extended throughout the various layers of rock. "This is the agreed upon minimum boundary of SONA's current spread."

"Show 'em the real one, why don't you?" Kyle shouted with no attempt to hide his irritation.

Eleanor's eyes widened in surprise. "Yes, Mr. Newman. We've included your evaluation. This next image shows Mr. Newman's estimate and displays what we believe is the maximum current boundary."

She advanced the slide. The blue tendrils expanded both outward and downward by a factor of five.

Mira gasped at the sight. She pictured Medusa's head, buried upside down and at an impossible size. Its reptilian locks snaked down and out and even broke the surface in numerous places. She had been, to this point, plenty fearful. But those fears were tempered by her work. The monstrous image shattered that gauzy defense. She was not the only one flushed and breathless.

Eleanor paused to allow them a moment to refocus. "If Mr. Newman is right, excavation would not be an effective option. If the more conservative estimates prove to be accurate, the job would be monumental. But the Army Corps of Engineers' official position is it remains viable."

Lieutenant General Thompson spoke. "My people believe much of what is shown there are water wells and natural cavities."

"Bull," spat Kyle.

General Marcus conjectured. "What if we excavate and find Newman's model is the right one?"

Potteiger answered. "We make things worse. We expose more of SONA to the air with no hope of deploying isolation structures. It could spread widely before we could incinerate."

Marcus stood. "I've heard enough. I don't want any more slides and I don't want to hear arguments. Just give us the third option Madam Deputy Secretary."

"As you wish, General. Option Three is remediation through incineration." She did not advance the slide. The inverted Medusa head pulsed, ominous. "Calculations are underway to establish the incendiary requirements to eliminate SONA."

"What are we talking about here? Thermite? Napalm? Tactical nukes?" Marcus pressed.

"Those won't suffice," said Thompson. "We're looking at strategic-level devices."

Governor Hauser stood, incensed. "Am I to understand you're considering the use of nuclear weapons in the state of Utah? This close to Salt Lake City? I oppose this notion absolutely." The rest of the Utah contingent voiced similar objections.

Potteiger gently nudged Eleanor to the side and leaned close to the microphone. His voice was loud and distorted as he overdrove the input, but his words remained intelligible. "I assure you, Governor, I feel the same way. This decision means closing this base. It means cordoning large swaths of the surrounding areas." He paused as more comments and concerns erupted in the room. He resumed when the chatter waned. "The only thing worse is if SONA continues to spread. In that case, you won't have a state to govern. Here's the hard truth. We don't know how to stop it. SONA could spread everywhere."

More gasps skittered throughout the auditorium. Potteiger continued. "Yes, that's right. We must have the courage to see this threat as it is. SONA could destroy every living thing on Earth."

This news didn't hit Mira the same as many of the others. Hers was a fear that remained ever since she witnessed what happened to that poor piglet—and Rain's admonishment thereafter. She looked around the room to gauge reactions. Rain was grim, as were the other DPG leaders. Connie's face was pasty. Among the visitors, some in the room were blank-faced, shocked. A few unsuccessfully fought back tears.

Quon reasserted himself to the microphone. "The stakes are indeed high. But I can assure you this doomsday scenario will not happen. Biospheres do not work like that. We will find a solution. This is not to say there is no chance we might experience the worst. But nature will balance itself. I strongly suggest you allow the scientific team to continue our work. It is a mere matter of time before we validate remediation solutions. In the meantime, I recommend you allow the Army Corps of Engineers to proceed with their plans."

Thompson stood again. "Thank you, Dr. Quon." He faced the room. "We are confident we can at minimum buy time for him and his colleagues to do their work. I ask that my men and women be allowed to do the same."

Secretary Vega spoke next. "This strikes me as the most prudent approach. But let's hear arguments against before we come to a final decision."

"You'd be a pack 'o morons to dig that infernal stuff up now." Kyle's voice delivered as much force as the authority figures. "I don't care what these engineers say. I've seen too many of 'em get it wrong." He stood; his 6'8" height and physical bulk added to the weight of his words. He pointed to the Medusa head that represented his map of the body of SONA. "See that?"

"Newman has a good point, sir," said Yolanda, with a deferential glance to Thompson. "See how many tendrils are forming from not only the source pool but also additional concentrations? They could break through to the surface in places we can't predict."

Kyle went on. "They'll make their way into yer sewers and yer water supply. It'll happen at times nobody can guess. This is a whopper of a problem. I'm a digger. Believe you me, I'd like nothing more than to dig it all out. But I tell ya, it's gonna buy us nothin' but trouble."

"What are you suggesting, Mr. Newman?" asked Eleanor.

"This whole area's already a goner. You just don't know it yet."

General Marcus stood and strode toward the exit. "Get me the analysis of the yields necessary to vaporize the pool as mapped by Newman. Commander Potteiger, work with the Governor and whoever else is appropriate to evacuate as large an area as is necessary. I want detailed plans within forty-eight hours."

Quon again leaned in front of the microphone in front of Eleanor. "General, I do not believe this is a good idea. Give us more time. Please."

The Utah contingent, along with many of the Corps of Engineers, the leadership of DPG, Higgins and Dr. Fitzgerald, and a handful of others, voiced agreement. Secretary Vega stepped to the front of the room. "I cannot recommend to the President the deployment of nuclear weaponry on American soil, General Marcus."

"When a leg or an arm is irreparably wounded, you must cut it off or risk losing the man." Marcus' resolution gave his voice an even harder-than-normal edge. "If you wait too long, you lose him, anyway. We must cut off this arm. This much is clear. I will speak to the Joint Chiefs. And the President."

Mira glanced first at Rain, then Kyle. She could see on their faces their agreement with General Marcus. She wanted to agree, too. She squirmed as she recognized she was for once on Quon's side of an argument. It sat less well after his unscientific claim, irresponsible really, regarding SONA and the Bible. Her gut knotted. She thought she might get sick as she rushed from the room.

AN INSIGHT

The process of entering containment—meticulous, systematic, tactile—settled her. Procedure. The known. You disinfect a thing, it's disinfected. You place a barrier between yourself and danger, you're safe. Not everything was like that. She daydreamt about an all-powerful barrier, something that would protect you no matter what. Silly fantasy, she chided herself. Despite her deliberation and fear, she entered the lab neither nauseated nor dismayed.

She hadn't checked in on Jeff as much as she'd wanted to over the past couple of days. Pulled in too many directions, she pined for her former life. The fate of many now depended on results for which she was responsible. It wasn't a position she relished. Jeff worked an EVO Cam in a Biosafety cabinet on the far side of the lab. He busily manipulated its floating stage and adjusted its focal parameters. Absorbed, he didn't notice her enter. She stopped behind him and watched as he examined the image on the monitor. The sample was much the same as the many she'd seen while at Detrick.

At last he noticed her presence. "Mira." His gaze remained on the monitor. "Is it over already?"

"I suppose it is." She was more interested in Jeff's work. "Nothing?"

"Not yet." He was undaunted. "This thing is a freak, Mira. Like, indestructible. Even the most aggressive microbes are transformed by it. It consumes everything cellular, really anything living. Those inclusions you told me about? They are a unique byproduct produced when SONA attacks cells. I spent all last night looking into pinwheel inclusions."

"Anything in the literature?"

"Some plant viruses form them as they infect cells. But not much is known about them. These are obviously different. Much smaller. I'll keep looking."

The tension left Mira's face. This young man had the will and ability to find an answer, given enough time and sufficiently sophisticated tools. "It doesn't matter. I think we're done here."

"What? No way." The force of Jeff's objection flummoxed her. He spun to face her. "Why?"

"We're out of time. They're not going to wait for us, whether we find a biocontrol option or something else." Mira's cheeks flushed.

"So that's it? You stop trying?" Jeff was wide-eyed, incredulous.

"It's not up to me." Her hands fell limply to her side.

"You're calling the shots around here, aren't you?"

The position sounded glamorous. It wasn't. "Biology is a small part of it."

"This isn't like you, Mira." Jeff settled. "You don't stop because somebody doesn't agree with you. Nobody ever agrees with you—at least at first. When you want an answer, you go for it. What other people think is not in the equation."

His words failed to move her. "It's different this time."

"How?" Jeff's tone was insistent. "How is it any different?"

They both jerked their heads, startled, when the door opened.

"Eleanor," Mira said, "I'm surprised to see you in containment."

"Consider it a visit to the front line." Eleanor glanced at the monitor. "How's it going in here?"

"Nothing new to report." Jeff glanced at Mira. "Yet."

He managed to sound optimistic. What allowed him to always remain so?

Eleanor addressed Mira. "I noticed your reaction to General Marcus's declaration." She glanced to Jeff. "Maybe you'd like to discuss this, just you and me."

"We can speak freely. I don't keep anything from Jeff."

Eleanor looked at him, then spoke to Mira. "All right. What's going on with you?"

"That I object to the destruction of this entire region surprises you?"

"Well, no, darlin'. It doesn't."

"This is a unique ecosystem. It all stems from the combination of the salinity of the soil and the high desert climate. The lakes, mountains, and plains in this area do not merely give us beauty. They have much to teach us about life. My heart breaks at the prospect of obliterating such a treasure. But its uniqueness gives me pause. This microbial troposphere is only partially understood. We are making assumptions here. For instance, it may be that SONA will be unable to spread much beyond this environment. We may have more time than we think we do."

"I hope you're right. But that's not why you ran out, Mira."

"Many microbes are unimaginably rugged. And by what we've seen thus far, this one is much more so. If it can even be truly considered a microbe. In any case, SONA has numerous properties we do not yet understand."

"And?" Eleanor pushed.

Mira's tone hardened. "And we still don't know how it came to be here."

"No. We don't. And this is what you're upset about?" Mira didn't answer right away. Eleanor glanced at Jeff.

Jeff shrugged. "It's either a spontaneous occurrence as Dr. Quon suggests or the military created it. Either way, it's troubling. The latter implies some or all of you are lying to us. Frankly, that's the scenario I find plausible."

Eleanor's charm returned. "Mira, look at me." Mira did so. "I'm telling you, right now, as God as my witness, I am not lying to you, sugar."

"I often can't tell. I assume people are truthful, because lying is not a smart thing to do. But people do it. All the time. Even people

I've come to trust." She looked at Jeff. His eyes reassured. "Do you believe her, Jeff?"

He responded with a quick nod.

"Good." Eleanor's pace increased. "We must work together." Her eyes narrowed, serious. "Now, I've learned over my career to read political tea leaves. I'll tell you what's going to happen." Mira and Jeff leaned closer. "The Administration will claim success no matter what course of action they take or what the outcome. It may even take the official position that the danger has been eliminated. That means there will be no reason to divert significant resources to the remediation of SONA. There will of course be academic work, but it will have a tight lid."

"That is not reassuring," said Mira.

Eleanor placed her gloved hand on Mira's suited arm. "No matter what happens, we must seek better solutions. I want you to stay on this, Mira."

"How?"

"Don't worry about that. I'll help. I have a feeling; I can't explain, darlin'. But I believe you're going to find the answer."

Mira's brow raised. "Faith again?" Her forehead furrowed. "We do science."

"It's not a matter of comparing faith vs. science. I've learned to trust, that's all."

Mira's brow unknit as she gazed upwards.

Eleanor noticed. "What is it, Mira?"

"Hmm. I wonder."

"What?" Both Eleanor and Jeff waited in anticipation of Mira's reply.

Mira glanced at her computer screen. "You said it's not about comparing. Makes me think. I want to see something. We've been looking at the DNA results all wrong. What looks like noise might be transitional states." Mira bent to use the computer. The thick gloves rendered her motions with mouse and keyboard no less deft. After a few moments, she adjusted the monitor to show the others. "See these two files? Keep your eyes on the screen." She enlarged the view and flipped between the two of them. "Notice anything?"

"What am I looking for?"

"Think of each sequence of letters as a genetic 'word.' Keep looking at them."

"Okay. I see the differences between them."

"Now watch this." She introduced a third FASTA file and toggled between the three files. "Anything?"

"I still don't know what I'm supposed to see, sugar."

"Just keep watching." She added a fourth, then a fifth, and finally a sixth file. She increased the pace of her transitions from one file to the next. "How about now?"

"Okay, I think I see. The individual 'words' as you call them, which I believe are individual lines of genetic code, keep changing their placement. But the sequence is similar each time."

"Holy smokes!" Jeff snapped. "You think SONA is doing this, Mira?"

"Yes."

Eleanor frowned. "I'm lost here. So what?"

Mira took her eyes off the screen. "Let me explain it this way. Let's say we're reading text. If we swapped one word in a paragraph, you'd still get the general meaning?"

"Of course."

"But the more words we swap out, the less sense the paragraph makes, right? At some point, the content—and therefore the meaning —of the paragraph are lost. It would bear no resemblance to the original whatsoever."

"Sure." Eleanor frowned as she grappled with the concept. "Nope. I still don't understand, darlin'."

"If we took different paragraphs and swapped out the words, we'd have a bunch of gibberish. Say we did millions of these swaps. And let's also say the swaps were done according to a defined set of rules. What might we expect to see?"

"If you knew the rule, you could predict what might happen to the next paragraph."

"Exactly! Good, Eleanor. You'd have made a pretty good scientist, I think."

"Yeah? I still don't see how this helps us, sugar."

"If we can identify this pattern, it could lead us to the rules of this swap. If we're right, SONA is responsible for making the rules."

"And that means what?"

Mira's grin widened. "SONA is not what Quon thinks it is."

"Still lost, darlin'."

Mira looked Eleanor in the eyes. Normally, that gave her a shiver of discomfort, however slight. Not this time. She took her time and eased her breathing. "Quon believes SONA is an example of abiogenesis, that it is a new life-form. This evidence suggests something very different. It appears SONA is a DNA-editing agent. It's not replicating like normal cells do, it's editing the DNA of other living things to make copies of itself. Essentially erasing their genetic information and rewriting its own."

"Doesn't sound reassuring." Eleanor was rapt.

"It's both good and bad. The good is we've learned something. Something very important. It brings us closer to a remediation solution."

"Mira, doesn't this mean SONA is engineered?" Jeff offered.

"Perhaps."

Eleanor's excitement shifted, and she frowned. "You're suggesting somebody made it. If that's true, it follows that somebody put it there. Who would do such a thing? Who could have? Why?"

The three of them looked at each other. Nobody had answers. Jeff spoke first. "How is SONA being a DNA-editor bad, Mira?"

Mira's eyes narrowed. "No living thing that we know of has a defense system against this kind of DNA-editing pathogen."

Jeff swiveled back to his computer and once again tapped away at the keyboard. "Fortunately, we don't know of everything yet."

EXCERPT:
THE NECESSITY OF PRECURSOR COOPERATIVES

Wallace, M. D.[1,2] and Weingartner, J. A.[1]

1*University of California, Berkeley, Dept. of Plant and Microbial Biology, 311 Koshland Hall, Berkeley CA, 94720.*

2*National Interagency Biodefense Campus, Fort Detrick, MD 21702*

Section #2: Energetic Transformation, cont.

As the interdependent relationship of the nucleic acids and peptides grew more sophisticated, particular patterns began to emerge. The complex chemistry, now driven by large quantities of energy, became subject to extremely rapid selection. This was exacerbated by the fact that the light-absorbing porphyrin molecules emitted highly reactive oxygen molecules as they were bombarded by the abundant UV light. This reactive oxygen was highly destabilizing but had the side effect of stimulating chemical reactions. Millions of new nucleic acid-amino acid partnerships began to form, most of which were short-lived. The handful that accumulated functioned as stabilizing subgroups, twenty or so. Each consisted of a small group of nucleic acids bonded to a singular amino acid.

The persistence of these subgroups prompted a tremendous advantage—they interacted to link amino acids together into precise strings. Some nucleic acids in the group took on this function—encoding the first proteins. The sea of chemicals had self-organized into an interdependent system that could now store information. The resulting code was an arrangement representing one of 10^{84}

combinations. Given that only a handful of possible codes had the necessary properties to sustain the collective, it was a practical impossibility to arrive at one. But it was not necessary to try all codes at random. The most efficient codes happened to be those that were also the most chemically stable, a sort of inherent property of the molecules themselves. It was fortune driven by an underlying property of the chemicals themselves—that is if the glass is half-empty.

AN EDITOR

Rain clicked his pen repeatedly. "Explain this again so a grunt like me can follow."

"Viruses replicate their DNA by using the host cell's DNA copying machinery." Mira sat on the edge of the chair in Rain's office. Her excitement accelerated her words. She even gesticulated as she elaborated. "But SONA is different. It's not a virus. Our evidence demonstrates it doesn't use the host cell machinery to copy itself."

Rain shared a puzzled glance with Connie. "SONA kills indiscriminately?"

"Not exactly. It's worse than that. SONA edits the DNA of living things to match a specific pattern. What we thought was noise in the DNA sequencing is actual caused by incompletely edited DNA strands. The pattern is so unexpected that our analytical algorithms were never designed to detect it. SONA rewrites the genetic sequence of its host DNA. It doesn't make copies of itself; SONA converts every living thing it contacts into itself."

Connie's face flushed and his head drooped. Rain pressed. "Why is that worse?"

"Viruses take over your cells but they remain your cells. This entity edits the host DNA to match its own. Then it cleaves the new strand to replicate further. This explains what we found at Detrick. It erases the victim like it never existed."

Connie's cheeks remained flushed. His eyes narrowed and his tone was skeptical. "I mean no insult, Mira, but this seems implausible. You have proof?"

Mira was not insulted. "First, we disproved the alternatives. If you come to the LSF, I'll show you what I showed Eleanor earlier. We calculated the patterns in the sequences resulting from SONA's DNA editing functions. The patterns are distinct. The statistics indicate near certainty."

"I will. Later." Connie's tone remained challenging. "Say for a minute you are right. How does that change the remediation effort?"

Mira was initially baffled at Connie's attitude, but it didn't extinguish her enthusiasm. "We need to focus on disrupting SONA's chemical processes."

"So how does this help us? What do you want to do differently?"

Connie was still oddly antagonistic, or so Mira perceived. Her mind churned as she spoke. "That is not yet clear. We still need more data. We need to figure out how SONA is carrying out the editing and what proteins are involved. Then we can look into screening for inhibitors."

"You'll be able to narrow the subjects for your screens?" Rain's enthusiastic tone contrasted Connie's. His hand absently grasped the crucifix at his neck.

"Yes, that's one benefit."

"I suppose that would work the same way for our chemical research at Aberdeen."

"Yes. There's one other thing implied by the hypothesis that SONA is not in fact an example of abiogenesis."

"What?" Rain asked.

"It would follow that SONA was likely man made. That would suggest that it was put there by somebody—intentionally or not. How or when would be speculative too."

"Put there?" Rain scratched his stubble. "That area is not a disposal site. Never has been. That implies sabotage or some kind of intentional attack. Moore suspected as much from the get go. He first assumed I did it, because I was the only one known to be alone in that area prior to the test. I think my mask brought suspicion too."

"Why would you put it there?" The idea sounded ludicrous to her. "How would you obtain such a substance?"

"That's why Moore dropped it, I guess. But if not me, who?"

"It sounds ridiculous to even say it." There was nobody else who even remotely fit. "Could Quon have done it?"

"I don't see how," said Rain. "He was never in that area. If he is responsible, he could not have acted alone. He had to have somebody help him."

"In fact, I don't suspect him. If he knew what it was, he wouldn't be acting the way he has." Mira glanced at Connie. She couldn't read his reaction, but his silence struck her as strange.

Rain seemed to sense her thought. "Connie, what do you think?"

"If what you're saying is right," Connie's voice cracked, "the implication is SONA resulted from something done in the labs here."

"Most likely," Mira replied.

Connie again stared at his knees. "I have no idea what it could be."

Rain appeared pensive too. "My memory is fuzzy, but when I was first assigned here, I remember talk of a terminated research program. Maybe half a year before. I don't know anything about it, but maybe it was related to what you're talking about." He turned to Connie. "You were here then, sir. Does this ring a bell?"

"There were a lot of programs." Connie was dismissive.

"It was classified, so there wasn't much talk. I only caught passing references. Not enough specifics to know anything about what I heard. Nothing, Connie?"

"I just said I didn't know!"

Rain physically recoiled, befuddlement evident in his raised eyebrows.

Connie's reaction didn't strike Mira the same way; she was consumed by what Rain suggested. "This could be important, Rain. Think. What else can you tell us?"

Rain turned away from Connie to Mira. "Nothing." He shook his head. "But I could dig around in the archives."

"Please do!" The prospect of more information, maybe even definitive answers, energized her. Anger followed. "I can't believe this hasn't been done already."

"I can." Connie's normal decorum returned. His eyes met Rain's. "But then again, we've spent our careers in the military."

"I'll get right on this," said Rain. "But I still don't know what I'm looking for."

Mira encouraged him. "Your keywords will be 'virus,' 'viral,' 'editing,' 'recombinant DNA,' and 'gene sequences.'"

Connie was still less enthusiastic about this revelation. His eyes narrowed, not angry exactly, but surely not positive. "That might not be sufficiently narrow. It's going to bring up a ton of documents." His voice was soft. "Tell you what. I'll take point on this. Leave it to me."

Rain and Mira shared a questioning look. Rain said, "Okay. Thank you, Connie."

Quon joined them in Rain's office forty-five minutes later. "My apologies for your wait. I am about to begin a potentially breakthrough experiment. As you know, time is short. What is so important?"

"I applaud your attempt to convince General Marcus to give us more time." What breakthrough? Mira made a mental note to follow up. "We have evidence that might help."

"I am happy to be kept in the loop."

This was a different Quon. What caused such an attitude shift? "We believe SONA is a DNA editing agent."

Quon's smile blossomed bigger than ever. "This is good news indeed. I suspected this myself. It should be straightforward to interrupt such a process. This will allow us to—" He stopped mid-sentence to stifle his smile. "We must inform your team at Aberdeen at once, Colonel Yanoviak."

"Already done. But there is something else we need. As you

know, in the wake of General Marcus' decision, there is considerable momentum building for the use of explosives. You opposed that. Would you be willing—"

"To take up the issue with the White House and buy us additional time?" Quon interrupted.

"Well, yes. They may listen to you."

Quon considered the request. He made a show of the process as his brow furrowed. He used all the little available space of Rain's office as he paced back and forth while he clasped and unclasped his hands. "I shall see what I can do."

A PRECIPITANT

Quon nettled with impatience for the time-consuming procedure required by the latest safety protocols. He jammed his legs and arms into the pants and sleeves of an isolation suit and didn't bother himself with the required visual inspection. He zipped up, then hurried from the WDTC HQ to the LSF and to Baker lab.

Gigi awaited. Her gloved fingers drummed a complex rhythm on the lab table. "Dr. Quon. I figured you blew me off." Gone was her light-hearted manner. "The centrifugation is done, and the separation looks clean. I would have done the fractionation, but you never confirmed the band you wanted."

She held one of the clear thermoplastic tubes to the bright fluorescent lights in the Biosafety cabinet.

Quon pointed to the tube. "Do you see those lighter bands at the top?" She nodded. "Then the darker one? That is the fraction I require."

Gigi used a high-speed hand drill to make a tiny hole in the bottom of the plastic tube. The modified sucrose solution gathered and bulged at the hole. Each droplet held for a brief moment before it swelled, and surface tension gave way to gravity. When they broke free, they fell into the collection flask below. Quon and Gigi watched intently as the unwanted part shrank, barely perceptively so, with each droplet.

After a while, Gigi spoke, reflective. "My boyfriend, Juan—you met him, he fixed the mass spec—he was with me out at Ditto."

"What? Yes. How nice," Quon replied absently.

She shot him a befuddled look, but went on. "It was such a nightmare. All those people." She shuddered. "I really hope what you're doing is going to help get rid of this stuff."

"Yes." Quon's attention remained on the separation process. "What we're doing is very important."

She glanced at him. His eyes remained on the dripping tube. "You know, you might be super smart and super successful, but you could use some work on your listening skills, Dr. Quon."

"Yes. How much longer will this take?"

Quon didn't react to the mocking face she made at him, if it registered. "Almost there." With dexterity that defied the bulk of her puffed up sleeves and protective gloves, she grabbed a sterile storage vial.

Beads of sweat dripped from both Quon's and Gigi's brows and splashed onto the inner surface of their face shields. The sounds interspersed with the drops into the flask and created a spasmodic rhythm. The targeted band crept ever closer toward the hole.

At last, the next droplet that formed was darker. Gigi smoothly swapped the new vial in the place of the collection flask. The next three dozen drops shared that same darker color. The fortieth drop was clear again. Gigi removed the storage vial and replaced it with the collection flask. She snapped the plastic lid shut, removed the vial from the cabinet, and handed it to Quon. "That wasn't so bad, was it?"

Quon remained preoccupied. He regarded the vial with an incongruent smile.

"Dr. Quon?" Gigi prompted. "What next?"

He kept his eyes on the vial. "Since this procedure has gone so well, my dear, please scale up and prep more sample. I shall want to repeat these experiments."

"I can do that. How much do you need? You want me to use the remaining seven gradients? Since we didn't load any sample in them, they should still work fine."

"That is acceptable. You may load the same quantity in each. In the meantime, you may find me at the CCTF[1] preparing for our experiments." The Combined Chemical Test Facility sat nearby.

"No problem. Don't worry about it."

"Good. Speed is of the essence now. Excuse me." Quon sealed the vial in an insulated protective container and placed that on a wheeled cart. He guided his precious cargo to the exit. He chafed that the container had to go through a gasification decontamination process before he could transport it. He found the inconvenience of it intolerable.

To begin, the assigned Test Director, a forgettable man (to Quon, at least—the man was popular among DPG staff for some reason) who in his estimation wouldn't be fit for the lowliest job at his company, resisted Quon's requests. He had the gall to require Quon to continue his experimentation at the CCTF, where most of the desired equipment sat. It would have been far more efficient to equip the containment lab properly: going back and forth between the CCTF and Baker Lab in the LSF was unacceptable. It took far too much of his valuable time. In light of General Marcus' decision, there was no telling how much time he had left. Not much. He had to push.

The Test Director also insisted Quon be assigned a test team including lab assistants, data recorders and analysts, and other personnel—all of whom would be more than a nuisance to him. That was one battle Quon had won, though he'd had to escalate all the way to Robert Harrison to do so. "I must not be hampered, tripping over all of these people," he said as he barged in. Harrison had wearily replied he didn't wish to argue.

In the far corner of one of the many labs in the CCTF sat a benchtop SpeedVac, a specialized centrifuge that spun in a heated vacuum to dry samples quickly. Quon removed the vial from its container and placed it in the white plastic rotor, and closed the lid. He struggled with the black rubber sealing cap on the vacuum chamber, but managed to get it off, ease out the lining material, and make sure the collection bottle was clean. He replaced everything, punched in the parameters he desired for this evaporation cycle, and pressed the START button. The rotor hummed as the sample whorled around inside the device.

Based on the volume of the liquid inside the vial, Quon calculated 20 to 30 minutes for the solution to dry in the heated vacuum chamber. After 25 minutes, he stopped the machine and paused to let the vacuum release. He eagerly pulled on the cap but it remained sealed by the vacuum. After four increasingly frustrated attempts, he got it free with a pop. Quon next lifted the centrifuge lid, removed the vial and held it to the light. All that remained was a dark crusty film at the bottom of the tube.

He took it to a digital balance where he placed an empty but otherwise identical tube on the metal pan and tared the scale. Once the readout settled at 0.0000, he replaced the empty vial with the encrusted sample. The readout settled at 0.1273 grams.

Quon clapped his hands with pleasure. This was a better yield than he dared to hope.

---

1. See Supplement for explanations of various U.S. Government agencies in the story.

A PUZZLING PROCEDURE

Quon inspected the odd contraption. The sooty stainless-steel device looked part wrecking ball and part desktop computer. A large steel sphere hung from an integral fixture over a cavity in the main body. Cables and hoses tethered the device to a number of cylindrical tanks and adjacent instruments. For Quon to have had this heavy device requisitioned and relocated from Picatinny Arsenal was a coup. The Test Director argued against him, citing manpower and safety concerns. But Quon countered that his work was mission critical. Nobody could make a convincing case against him. As usual, he had gotten his way.

He inspected the instrument and found the bolts of the 20-liter explosive chamber. He unscrewed them and peered into its interior.

He jumped, startled, when Gigi loudly burst into the lab as she pushed a fully loaded cart. "Now, Dr. Quon," she teased as she wheeled the cart to the instrument, "you know you're supposed to wait for a certified technician to play with that toy."

He didn't laugh. "I am merely preparing for a wide array of testing. You are here to assist, are you not?"

"Sorry—that's an explosion chamber. I'm not certified to work with it." She examined the controls, the various attached gas canisters, and the computer screen attached to the bulky metal instrument. "It looks pretty complicated. We should get somebody over from Dissemination and Explosives at Kendall if we're going to use it."

"Most of those personnel have been reassigned. I perused the appropriate manuals last night. The operation of this device and the analysis of the data is straightforward. I wish to first establish the minimum temperature to ignite the extract. I should also like to record energetic outputs from both combustion and detonation as well, so that we might extrapolate the expected results of the proposed incendiary action. I can do it alone, if I must."

"Jeez. No need to be so touchy. I never said I wouldn't help."

"You can begin with a simple measure of the caloric content of my substance."

"That I can do. Calorimeters are old hat." Gigi wheeled the cart to the other side of the room where that device, a mini version of the explosion chamber, sat. In sequence, she turned on the printer and the calorimeter. She opened the valve on the attached oxygen tank and verified that the pressure read 450 psi.

The touchscreen display on the calorimeter illuminated. Some button options remained grayed out. Gigi scrolled through the machine logs. "Good news. The Kendall boys were kind enough to calibrate the instrument for us before they left. Sorry I missed them— I'd have made them some of my world-famous brownies." She toggled the HEATER AND PUMP button to ON. "It'll take ten minutes or so to stabilize."

Quon scribbled calculations. He remained on the other side and didn't react to anything she said. "I guess I'm talking to myself. Don't worry, I'm getting used to it." She went to the attached nitrogen tank and twisted the valve shut.

Next, Gigi returned to the calorimeter and removed the red cap on the water reservoir. She craned over the bench. The level was full. She checked the pressurized rinse tank and released the pressure valve. The level was optimum; three quarters full. She replaced the lid, closed the release valve, and reopened the valve at the nitrogen tank. She looked at the control screen. The temperature was still stabilizing. "I'll print bar codes for these samples."

"You need not at this time."

Gigi shrugged. "So, your ears do work. We should probably still run a control or two with benzoic acid pellets first."

"Time is the greater factor. Prepare 100 milligrams of my sample and run that."

"It won't do any good to stress the protocol, will it?"

He didn't respond. She harrumphed and asked, "Use spiking material to catalyze combustion, do you think, Dr. Quon?"

"That will not be necessary."

She looked once again at the main menu of the control screen. The bar turned green. She opened the lid, checked the seal of the bomb head, closed the lid, selected and ran PRETEST.

While the instrument cycled, she went to the sample preparation station. She placed a clean capsule on the integrated balance and tared the scale. She opened the insulated container. Next, she removed the tube with the experimental particulate. With a small lab spatula Gigi doled out the contents into the capsule until the display read 0.14 grams. She dumped the substance from the capsule into the pelleting form, secured that in the adjacent pelleting press, and pulled with all of her 95 lbs. She released the handle and removed the form. With the integral removal mechanism, she popped the pellet out into the capsule and placed that on the balance. The readout settled at 0.10 grams. "Am I good or what?" Quon said nothing in response.

As she cleaned the pellet form, the pretest run finished and the calorimeter automatically idled. Gigi opened the lid, removed the bomb head, and placed it in the preparation fixture. She snipped 10 cm of cotton thread and wrapped it around the heating element suspended between the two electrodes. She placed the capsule into its holder and verified good contact between the thread and the newly formed pellet. "Looks like we're good to go."

She gently replaced the bomb head into the calorimeter and closed the lid. She selected STANDARDIZATION on the Calorimeter Operation menu and then typed 'SONA0213201' to label the run. After she entered the sample weight, she called to Quon, "Ready, Freddy?"

"What? Yes. By all means, proceed."

The START button was no longer grayed-out. Gigi pressed it and the stirrer motor and pressurization cycles whooshed into action. A red progress bar and a countdown clock appeared on the display along with readouts for JACKET and BUCKET temperatures.

The instrument sounded a series of short warning beeps. "It's gonna trigger." A muffled pop sounded and the screen flashed an ERROR message. "Well, poop. Not to worry. That can happen."

"I do not have time for this." Quon strode over. "Please make sure the next run yields successful results."

Gigi stuck her tongue out at him but again Quon either missed or ignored the mockery. Once the instrument idled, she opened the lid. The emergency pressure release valve on the bomb head was open. "That's weird," she puzzled. She twisted open the locking mechanism and sensed the heat from inside the canister even through the isolation suit. "Holy smokes! It shouldn't be that hot."

Gigi used a padded cloth to remove the hot bomb head and placed it in the preparation fixture. They both leaned in to inspect the capsule. Nothing remained inside, not even black residue. None of the cotton string remained either. Moreover, something had severed the heating element. Only small stubs remained on each electrode. "There's one problem, right there. Heating element failure."

Quon looked into the bomb canister in the calorimeter. "Interesting. No residue or fragments here either." His lips curled, satisfied. "Run 10 milligrams this time."

Gigi found a replacement element in a drawer and attached it to the electrodes. "Okeydokey. I can't pelletize so small an amount, but we can run it as a powder."

The next run resulted in another error.

So did the one after. Though the emergency pressure release valve did not blow, the results were inconclusive. But the water was hot. Gigi ran a dozen more tests until they ran out of sample. Not a single conclusive trial.

Quon was beyond frustrated. He complained with every result. He aimed most of his derision at Gigi, though she had faithfully executed the procedure consistently. His mood reversed as a strange smile appeared on his face.

"What are you so happy about all of a sudden?" Gigi asked.

"It is nothing. Run another one."

"Sorry, Dr. Quon, all out. Nothing more we can do here now."

He frowned for a moment, then said, "Fractionate more and have it ready for tomorrow." He eyed the explosion chamber across the laboratory. "We shall use a different approach."

GIGI SCRUNCHED HER NOSE. "This can't be right."

"I prefer my assistants do as they are told, not debate, Miss Patilla."

"Okey dokey, but based on yesterday, maybe we don't run this much sample?"

"Unfortunately, we learned little yesterday." Quon's mouth smiled, but his eyes didn't. "Perhaps I should request a new assistant."

"Oh. Now it's my fault, is it?" She knew she was his sole option and consequently the threat was an idle one. "You can't do any better than me and you know it," she laughed. "But sure, Mr. Big Boss, whatever you say." She used a spatula to add five grams of the dark gray powder into the sample vessel, essentially a smaller chamber tethered by hoses on one side to the explosion chamber and on the other to a compressed air tank. "Now what?"

"Make sure the temperature in the chamber exactly matches room temperature."

She checked. "It's two degrees warmer."

"Increase the water flow."

"How?"

"Never mind. I will do it." Quon impatiently bumped past Gigi to adjust the appropriate control. "Vacuum the chamber pressure to minus six bars." He pointed out the control and stood upright. "Once that equalizes and stabilizes, let me know. This experiment will generate a pressure-time curve on this computer. That information is vital to understand the energetic properties of my substance."

"You know, Dr. Quon, I'm not so sure Uncle Sam thinks of this stuff as yours."

Quon's manner shifted, almost apologetic. Almost. "Yes. Of course. A figure of speech. I suppose, being a businessman, I have an ownership mentality."

The temperature stabilized; the chamber pressure settled: -0.6 Mpa. "Looks ready."

"Yes. Excuse me a moment, I have an important call coming in."

She didn't hear his phone—he wasn't even supposed to have it in there. Quon stepped away, but she overheard him. "Yes. I am in the middle of it now. No. I am not available... Marvin, I can barely hear you. Hang on..." He looked back at Gigi and signaled for her to continue. He held the phone away and said to her, "Simply press the DETONATE button. The computer will record the result. You may, if you wish, observe through the port there." He pointed at the small but thick safety glass window on the explosion chamber.

"That's okay. I'm good over here." Her eyebrows raised as she eyed the button.

Quon exited the lab, unzipped his headgear and held the phone to his ear. "Marvin, listen to me..."

She shook her head. Quon should not have taken that call and should not have unzipped. He wasn't the first eccentric person with whom she'd worked. She zeroed in on the DETONATE button. Five grams. She wasn't sure why, but that seemed an awful lot. Something in her made her hesitant to press that button. She adjusted her protective gear. Then she crossed herself and pointed her gloved finger upward. She moved that same finger to the button. She leaned away, still maintaining contact. "Here goes nothing."

A TERMINATION

M ira yearned to be back in the lab. There, facts ruled. Opinion, perspective, rank, organizational priorities, politics, egos, or any other counterproductive, confusing factor, she could ignore. Her focus would be where it belonged—on the true; on the real.

Instead, she spent the day at HQ in unending conferences. This was probably why Alfred Wallace spent so much time in the hazardous jungles of South America instead of the comfortable wood-paneled British centers of learning. Better to send his findings to Darwin; let him publish, speak publicly, receive the ire of skeptics and the accolades of those whose minds remained open to discovery. Alfred wasn't suited for nor interested in such intellectualizing. In that at least, she connected with her forebearer.

General Marcus' decision had been straightforward. But execution was not so simple. Mira figured the number of opinions about timelines and priorities equaled or exceeded the number of installations, agencies, and bureaucrats involved in the emergency. It made zero sense to her to halt or slow any line of research at this time. And she said so. More than once.

The conference included, either in-person or streamed, DPG's senior team, three Generals, an agency director, and a cabinet member. During the fourth hour, Mira turned up the volume on her playlist. She had to. It was just too much—too much talking over each other, too many opinions, too much sensory input. Eventually, Eleanor noticed and came over.

"Are you all right, darlin'? Do you need a break?"

Mira nodded. "I think so. Looks to me I'm done here, anyway. I can't seem to communicate the significance of the agent's DNA editing characteristic."

"It's not that."

"Whatever it is, I can't seem to get through to them." Mira's frustration imparted an unusual harshness to her voice. "If they don't care to hear the science, I don't know why I need to waste my time."

Eleanor guided Mira to the door. "Let's talk out here." They walked a short distance down the hall. "I think I understand where you're coming from, Mira." She pointed back to the room. "This isn't working for you. Am I right?"

Mira stared at the heavily scuffed laminate floor. Distracted, she briefly speculated about how long it had been since a cleaning crew had been through. The thought of leaving didn't feel right. She also felt relief, though. "I belong in the lab, not in conferences."

Eleanor stepped closer and lowered her voice. "I suppose it's time to relieve you of your duties, sugar. Your recommendations have merit. I'll do my best to express them. But I also want to know something. You seem to be at continual odds with Dr. Quon, scientifically speaking. I want to know why."

The question surprised Mira. She hadn't thought of it like that. But since Eleanor said it, she knew the answer. She half-smiled. "Strictly speaking, science can prove nothing. It can only disprove hypotheses. Scientists are all taught that, but we too often fail at it. In fact, too many are like Quon. They suspect something, something they want to be true for whatever reason, and then they look for ways to confirm their belief. These are human tendencies. But it is not science."

Eleanor's smile matched Mira's. "This is why science can never answer all of your questions, Mira." She looked at Mira's wrist. "Your bracelet. Where is it?"

"Oh, that. I gave it away."

Eleanor's eyes widened. "For a good reason, I hope?"

Mira shrugged.

"Do you still have the necklace?"

Mira pulled it out of her pocket and extended her hand.

Mirth appeared in Eleanor's eyes as she examined the bent nails and blue woven cord in Mira's palm. She put her hand on top of Mira's. "This may be the end of our time together here, sugar, but I hope it's not the end of our time together."

Mira looked into the woman's caring eyes. "You've been kind to me. More than anyone else." That wasn't exactly true. "Almost anyone else. I want to know why."

"I think I told you." Eleanor still held Mira's hand. "I read your file. I know your history. You're more important to more people than you know."

Mira doubted that. But she smiled, anyway. "Thank you for saying that. But that's not an answer."

Eleanor released Mira's hand. "A brilliant mind is not enough to get things done, is it? There are lots of brilliant people who for one reason or another never get to use their gifts. Despite your—social difficulty, let's call it—that doesn't describe you, does it?" She turned and went back to the meeting.

When Gigi pressed the DETONATE button, the device injected a blast of compressed air which forced the SONA-derived substance into the explosion chamber. A dust-cloud formed instantly. The cloud was simultaneously mixed with fuel and air and subjected to an electronic spark.

The mixture ignited and expanded. That explosive force pressed against the strong steel walls of the 20-liter chamber. It was built to withstand forces of up to 40 bars and remain intact.

The 60 bars of pressure from this explosion ruptured the chamber along the seams of its observation portal. Pieces flew, like grenade-shrapnel, propelled by a force of over 100 kilojoules. They tore through all they hit—walls, floor, and ceiling. Glass shattered. Shards and other debris punctured hazardous equipment, including tanks of compressed gases. They hissed loudly as their contents mixed with the expanding fuel. The mixture exploded into a super-heated fireball.

Gigi stood less than two meters away. As she pressed the button, she reflexively leaned away. The conflagration, flying metal, and concussive wave ripped into her left side. Her left hand, forearm, bicep, shoulder, hip, and thigh all received third-degree burns. Fragments tore through her left triceps, buttock, and hamstring. The force damaged most of her internal organs. As she was thrown into the shelving units along the closest wall, she broke thirteen bones, including ribs and vertebrae in her neck. She noticed none of it. Unconscious, she crumpled to the floor, bleeding and battered—barely alive, as the fire spread.

The klaxon alarm sounded and the automatic fire suppression system engaged. Gigi lay there, enveloped by spray and the noxious cloud.

Quon was the only other person in the vicinity. At the moment of the explosion, he was seven meters away in the adjacent hallway. The distance and the wall provided a measure of protection. Still the blast knocked him off his feet. His head struck hard against the far wall. The fall to the floor also bruised his tail-bone and sprained tendons in his wrist and shoulder. Disoriented and shaken, the noise of the multiple explosions rang in his ears. Smoke issued from the room and into his lungs. He coughed uncontrollably.

He remained in this state when two strong arms lifted him to his feet. "Dr. Quon? Can you hear me?"

Quon tried to speak through his coughs, to no avail.

"Don't try to talk." Rain addressed the other man with him. "Let's get him to medical."

"Right-o." He lifted Quon, but Quon waived him off as he doubled over.

Quon tried to get words out between coughs. "Miss...Pat..."

"Oh." Rain's eyes widened in alarm as Quon's meaning sank in. "Hang on. I've got to go in there."

Kyle placed his massive hand on Rain's shoulder to hold him in place. "You can't. These suits ain't gonna protect ya from that."

Rain pulled away and lurched toward the shattered door. "Take Quon. I'll catch up."

Kyle easily scooped Quon and rushed away while Rain steeled himself and disappeared into the smoke.

A DISMISSAL

"Yes, that may well be Dr. Quon. But the facility is still being shut down." Eleanor's patience dangled by a slender strand.

"That is unacceptable. I must be allowed to continue my inquiries." He lay in bed in Dugway's clinic and struggled to pull himself upright.

"There's nothing that can be done now."

"I must disagree. I await a return call from the President of the United States. The call was about a related matter—the delay of the demolition. There is no need for a shutdown at this time."

"You are entitled to your opinion, of course."

Quon's smile vanished. "I would greatly appreciate it if you did not patronize me, Secretary Dixon. With Dr. Wallace's recent discovery, we can realistically expect a chemical solution that halts the spread of SONA. This needs due consideration."

"It has been considered and has been rejected."

Anger darkened his face, and he raised his voice. "Listen to me. I paid handsomely for the use of these facilities for my TPF. That program has been utterly compromised through no fault of my own. I have generously donated time, resources, and my expertise to this remediation. I ask this small consideration."

Eleanor fought to maintain her professional demeanor. "We all appreciate everything you've done. But there are other factors."

"Again, I must respectfully contradict you." Though he regained his composure, the rise in his heart rate on med-set betrayed him.

"The more elegant and less dangerous biological solution is the right course. An effective chemical suppressant may become available at any time now. This military solution will prove disastrous."

"How can you be so confident of that?"

"SONA has properties we are just beginning to grasp. You people do not understand what you are dealing with."

"Us 'people' understand there are risks either way." Her patience was gone along with her charm. "There is no arguing that. Look—the decision has been made. The President has signed off. It's final."

"That will not do. I must insist I be authorized to continue."

"You're in a position to do no such thing." Her voice raised further. "And not because you're heading for the hospital. Regardless of how it happened, you destroyed an entire laboratory, Dr. Quon. The assistant assigned to you is in critical condition. It looks bad for her. There will be an investigation."

"As well there should. I shall be happy to cooperate." Quon appeared immune to admonishment. "I hope Miss Patilla pulls through. But this accident teaches us—"

"It teaches us you will conduct no more unsupervised and unapproved experiments, Dr. Quon." Eleanor regained her composure, but remained stern. "Your time at Dugway has come to completion."

A slight frown darkened Quon's face as he silently stared into space. Eleanor stepped towards the door. "One more moment, Secretary Dixon." He sat up with exaggerated difficulty. "Please, reconsider my position. My corporate facilities are capable, as you may know. May I have your personal support in my cause to be authorized to continue my research there?"

"At this point, Dr. Quon, it's best we leave our inquiries in the hands of the Department of Defense."

Quon restored his signature smile. "I could be allotted a small sample of SONA and conduct a separate inquiry. All billed at cost, of course."

"With what just happened to you and Miss Patilla, not to

mention the outbreak at Ditto we have yet to explain, there's no way to authorize that." She turned to leave but paused in the doorway. "I wish you a speedy recovery. You're going to be helicoptered to Evans at Fort Carson later today. I won't see you again before you leave, so on behalf of the people of the United States of America, thank you for your service. God bless you."

"That is good of you. But I am fine. I shall not require an extended hospital stay. I will be ready to resume my work tomorrow. So, as I was about to explain—"

"I need to go now. As far as your return to work, that won't be happening in this or any other U.S. government facility. And you'll be discharged when the doctors believe it is safe to do so. Thank you again." She grasped the door handle.

"Eleanor, one more thing?"

She responded back through the doorway. "There's nothing more to discuss."

"Please ask Dr. Wallace to visit me before I am taken from this place. It is important."

She reopened the door as she summoned her last bit of patience. "I'll see what I can do. Goodbye Dr. Quon." She closed the door harder than necessary.

RAIN AND KYLE joined Mira and Jeff, who packed to leave their lab.

Mira's spirit lifted. "It's a relief to see the two of you." By their expressions, the feeling was not shared.

"I'm afraid I have some bad news for you, Mira." Rain's voice was flat. "There's been an accident in the CCTF."

Mira's gut knotted. She knew the answer before she could ask. "Gigi?"

"Yeah."

"Bad?" Her voice quavered.

"Yeah." Rain struggled to get the words out. "She's comatose. In critical condition."

"Only reason she's alive is this man ran into hell to pull her out," said Kyle.

Rain turned to Kyle. "Thanks for your help."

"Told ya." Kyle shook his thumb in Rain's direction. "Mr. by-the-book didn't want me to go. You're welcome."

Mira grabbed the table edge to steady herself as she plopped into a lab chair. "I assigned her there."

"It's not your fault, Mira," said Jeff.

Rain said, "No. it's not. Accidents happen. There's nothing any of us can do to change that fact." He put a gloved hand on the isolation suit covering her upper arm and offered a squeeze of reassurance.

Mira sat still and impassive. Jeff was pale. The four of them were silent for a long while. Tears filled both Jeff's and Mira's eyes.

"You should see the lab where the explosion happened," Rain whispered. "That she's still alive is a miracle."

"I'll say," added Kyle.

"Gigi is a woman of faith," Mira murmured.

"Yes, she is," Rain confirmed.

"Like you."

"Yes. I suppose so."

"Like Eleanor." Mira's head hung.

"Yes," Rain confirmed.

Mira sat quiet for a while. She said, softer, "Look what it got her."

Rain met her eyes. Neither could hold the glance.

Jeff asked, "You said Dr. Quon was there too?"

"Yes," said Rain. "He was apparently out of the room when it happened, but was close enough to be injured by the concussion of the blast. He's going to be okay."

Mira and Rain again looked at one another. Words eluded her. What was he thinking? How did his faith make his view of this tragedy different from hers?

Rain's voice stiffened. "Eleanor told me he asked you to visit him. He'll be transported to a hospital in a while. I can take you to the infirmary now, if you'd like."

Mira wished she could wipe her eyes. The constant wearing of isolation suits unnerved her. "Yes. Okay. I must speak with him."

A BARGAIN

"If you don't mind, I'd like to speak with him alone."

"I don't mind." Rain turned to leave but stopped. "I don't know if I'll see you before you leave."

"Oh." Mira didn't know how to respond.

Rain's voice had a melancholy note. "You'll be heading back to Berkeley?"

"Yes. I guess so." She couldn't think of any better words. "How about you?"

"I'll be here a while yet. There's a lot to do."

"Yes. That makes sense. After that?"

"Wherever they tell me."

"Oh." Her eyes dropped.

Rain lifted her chin with two fingers. "I think we'll see each other again."

She grasped his wrist. "I hope so." She held it a moment. She rocked back on her feet and even stumbled as she walked towards Quon's room. The movement, unsteady as it was, helped. With each step came a clearer picture of what happened to Gigi. And where fault landed. She'd seen enough of the way Quon worked to know how he valued expediency and speed over care and caution. She also knew who put Gigi in that vulnerable position. Inside, guilt and anger battled.

"Dr. Wallace." Quon brightened. "I appreciate you coming to see me."

The moment she saw him laying comfortably with a clean bandage around his head, her anger won out over her guilt. Her voice trembled. "Maybe not. What did you do to Gigi?"

"What I did to her? Did someone report to you what happened to us was somehow avoidable? It is not true. Look where I am right now; even though I do not wish to be. They are keeping me here; ordering I be taken to a hospital. Ridiculous. It is unnecessary."

"It's good you're not seriously hurt. The same is not true for Gigi. What happened?"

"I should like to know the answer myself." His face wore surprise and innocence.

"Hypotheses come to you readily, Dr. Quon." She managed not to shriek at him. Barely. "Give me your best one."

"My hypothesis is that a fault in the equipment or the setup, perhaps something that happened during transport, was liable for the explosion."

"That's the best you can do?" Mira couldn't say how, but she knew it wasn't the full story.

"What are you suggesting, Dr. Wallace?"

"Your experiment, whether cautiously conducted or not, may have gotten Gigi killed. I'm told she's hanging on. We have that to be grateful about."

Quon did not react in the defensive manner Mira expected. Instead, he was almost reflective. "Gratitude. Yes. We could use more of that around here."

"What is that supposed to mean? You're denying responsibility?"

"Let us not do this. We learn and move on; the past has passed." He grimaced and made a show of his attempt to sit upright. "I am more interested in what happens next. What are your plans now?"

Her inclination was to argue and press for details about the accident. Argue armed with what? Feelings? "I'm going home. Other than the short visit to conduct the sequencing, I haven't been there in a long time." What did the future at home, or anyplace else, really hold? "You'll be going back to your business, I suppose?"

"Yes. But I must confess. My preference is to continue to work with SONA."

"It's over, now. They won't allow you—us—to continue."

"What if you could?"

"I can't."

"Assume you could. Tell me, what would you do?"

Since her discovery that SONA edited DNA, she'd dwelled on ways to expand the bio-control screens. Her extremophiles. They represented the best chances for success. But screening them all was not possible, at least not within the timeframe SONA gave them. Extremophiles required extreme environments to thrive. There just wasn't enough time to requisition, maybe even build, automated incubators to recreate the wide spectrum from near boiling to Antarctic cold, from absolute darkness to intense ultra-violet light, not to mention many other parameters. Her lab had a few such devices, but they were wholly inadequate considering the sheer size of her library, samples from thousands of environments. Her sequence count of distinct species approached two billion. She frowned as she considered how little she knew about how those microbes lived and behaved in their natural habitats. She pictured the work of screening them. A daunting task. It would require thousands of man-hours. To do it in containment? In close proximity to the deadliest substance ever known? "At Berkeley, we store a large collection of the most rugged microbes on the planet. I suppose it's possible that under the right conditions one or more could break SONA down..."

"But you lack the necessary equipment. You need the capacity to culture and sequence microbes in an environment in which you may dynamically regulate pressure, temperature, salinity, humidity, acidity, alkalinity, and both UV and ionizing radiation, and do so over atypical ranges."

She was taken back. "How do you know that?"

His smile broadened. "I told you I have followed your career Dr. Wallace."

"You didn't get all of that by reading the literature. Why the interest in me particularly?"

"Why, indeed." His smile remained as he regarded her for a few moments. "You do not know your own value, my dear."

He sounded like Eleanor. Mira hadn't considered how others might view her—she simply followed where the science led. She never considered they held any commercial value. Now she was not only disgusted by Quon, she also grew self-conscious and turned away. Her value. How much was that now? Gigi might die. How many others weren't far behind? Despite her contributions, she hadn't stopped SONA.

"Your work has validated my decision to bring you in." He wore the wide version of his perma-smile.

Her spirit sank further. She noted the contents of a nearby shelf. A jar of tongue depressors. Cotton balls and swabs on long wooden sticks. On the wall opposite of Quon's bed, a biological schematic of the human respiratory system and the negative effects of smoking. "Eleanor says I'm here because it's God's will. Not yours."

Quon let out a derisive snort. "People like Secretary Dixon are deluded. Surely you know there is no mystical force that can save us. Our fate is in the hands of people like you and me, Dr. Wallace; people with the ability to see the world for what it is and the will to use our creative capacity to shape it as we will."

His words made sense. So why did they bother her so much? Was it the way he was so dismissive of Eleanor? And by proxy, Rain. And Gigi. And her grandmother. Were they all deluded? "You talk as though you have something specific in mind."

"We must work together, Mira."

His use of her first name struck her and she spun back to face him. "You don't believe the incineration is going to work."

"We both know the likelihood of that. There is also the very real risk of spreading it a great distance. Perhaps through the air."

Muscles in her back spasmed. She didn't relish the thought of continuing to work with him. But that mattered not a bit. This area would be demolished. The authorities would claim victory. But Quon was probably right. SONA would continue to spread beyond this desert. How long did any of them have? Was it even the rest of the year? "What do you have in mind?"

"I have similar needs for my algal research as you do for your studies."

"What are you saying? You have equipment that can recreate harsh conditions for microbial cultures?"

"I do."

"What, exactly?"

"I recently commissioned the construction of an environmental nanocycler. It is state-of-the-art; one of a kind. It will perform the tasks we require."

"At a scale that would make a comprehensive screen feasible?"

"Yes. You may populate each chip with as many as 20 million samples."

"And you want to use my library of extremophiles?"

"Does it not seem prudent?"

She perked, but was still held down by the practical constraints of such an endeavor. "Screens involving SONA need to be conducted in containment."

"Yes. That does pose a challenge." Quon's smile faltered.

"It would be quite difficult. And dangerous."

"You are no stranger to such conditions."

Maybe it was possible. It was preferable to doing nothing. "If I make the request, I'm sure I could continue to work at Detrick. Is it possible that your instrument could be transported and installed there?"

"Difficult, to be sure. But we do not let the difficult stop us, do we Mira? The chip preparation must be done at my facility. That equipment is not portable, and that portion of the procedure would not involve SONA. You will need to send your library there."

His suggestion felt unpalatable. Quon seemed eager, enthusiastic. How long had he considered this course of action? Why wait until now to suggest it? "I have to discuss all of this with my Department head. And Eleanor. And General Higgins."

"Of course. I find myself reinvigorated by our conversation, Dr. Wallace. Thank you for your time and consideration. I look forward to continuing our work together."

Did she just make a deal with Quon? To trust this man with her library, to return to Detrick and work long hours under uncomfortable and dangerous conditions? These were unwelcome choices. But there wasn't really a choice here at all. "Okay." Quon's smile widened. She left in a hurry. Every moment mattered again.

A DEAL

"Please, amigo, I beg you. Nobody's telling me nothing."

"Visitors are not allowed, Juan. Even family, which you're not."

"I am. I mean—I'm gonna be. I told you—I'm gonna ask her to marry me." Juan's eyes teared as he fumbled in his pocket.

Rain noticed and glanced at the clock on his desk. He liked Juan. But time was short. "What are you doing here, anyway? Non-essential personnel and contractors have been dismissed."

"There's a bunch of equipment they need me to work on. But I just can't. I can't do anything; I can't work, I can't sleep, I can't eat. Not until I see her." He extended his hand. He held the black velvet jewelry box. He opened it. "See? I gotta give this to her."

Rain pocketed his pen, took the box and examined the ring inside. He knew nothing of such things. But the diamond looked large and expensive to him. Juan's state pulled on his heart. The young man's earnestness and love for Gigi made Rain want to help him. "Juan, I don't mean to be insensitive. I can't know what you must be going through. I've prayed for her; I'll pray for you too. I received a report from the University of Utah Hospital where she was Medevac'd. I'm sorry to tell you this. She's comatose—she won't even know you're there."

"She'll know." Juan plea was more emphatic as tears ran on his face. "I'll know."

Rain looked again at the impressive emerald-cut diamond. It caught the bright light and sparkled. He glanced at Juan, who shifted from one foot to the other as his lips quivered and eyes pleaded puppy-style. "I'm sorry, Juan. It's not my call." Rain handed the ring back.

"I know she's in bad shape. I have to see her." He held the ring up to Rain's face. "I have to. You're my friend. Her friend. Please. Help us. It could be the difference."

Rain checked his calendar; no meetings for the rest of the day. Things calmed considerably since the incident at Ditto. That didn't mean he had nothing to do. Reports and plans awaited. With staff reduced to essential personnel, there was nobody to whom he could delegate. He sighed. This whole place, his home for almost two decades, was over. "Alright, Juan. I know there's an escort from here stationed with her. Let me make some calls and see what can be done. Give me fifteen."

"Gracias, amigo. That's all I ask. I just need a chance to see her." He threw his arms around Rain. "I won't forget this."

Juan returned and knocked on Rain's office door fourteen minutes later. Rain was still on his phone. "I get all of that, Cathy. This is a special case. You could do me this one favor, couldn't you?"

Juan crept closer in the attempt to hear the voice on the line. Cathy told Rain to wait while she retrieved someone with the authority to grant his request. A few moments later, a man's voice came on the line. His tone was clinical and dispassionate.

"Yes, Juan Jimenez. No, he is not military; he is a private contractor."

That made Juan freeze, his brow knitted with fear and disappointment.

"Yes. He will have an authorization with Commander Potteiger's signature."

Juan's frown reversed itself and he rushed around Rain's desk. Rain raised a finger to stop him. "Yes, I'll just finish up with her. We at Dugway appreciate your help with this, sir."

Juan danced from leg to leg, back and forth.

The female voice returned on the other end of the line. "Thank you, Cathy, I owe you one." Rain waited as Cathy spoke, then replied. "Yes, a big one." He ended the call.

"Gracias amigo." Juan exclaimed and clapped his hands together.

"It's fine, Juan. I already talked to the Commander. You'll need to stop by his office to get the authorization before you leave."

JUAN TAPPED ALL the ungoverned power of his Lotus to race to Salt Lake City. He squealed to a stop at the hospital and rushed into the burn unit. "Dios mio!" He exclaimed. The right side of her face was exposed, the rest of her covered or bandaged. Traction secured her body so she couldn't move even if she was able. She was also connected to an IV drip and a battery of portable machines. "Oh, Gigi."

"Five minutes," the military liaison, Cathy, said.

"Si. Gracias," Juan replied absently as Cathy withdrew. He crept closer to Gigi's bed. "Chica? It's me. It's your Bean."

No response.

He lowered his voice. "We gotta make another deal. You get better and I do whatever you want, si? How's that sound?" He moved closer still. "Can you hear me?"

The beeps of the monitors were his answer.

"I got something to ask you." He pulled the velvet box from his pocket. "I changed my mind and spent the money I was gonna spend on a GreenCar. Don't worry about it—this matters a lot more than any whip ever could. Check it out, chica." He opened the box and held it close to her uncovered eye. "See?"

He stretched two fingers toward her as though if he touched her cheek, she might awake. But he stopped and withdrew his hand. "If you open your eye, you'll see a diamond so big you won't believe it. I guess that means you'd know my question."

Could she hear him? Did she know he was there? "You need to wake up if you want to pick the colors for the decorations. If you leave it up to me, you'll hate them. I'll pick a green brighter than Quon's tie."

She didn't move. Tears flowed on Juan's cheek as he rose and stepped away from her. In the doorway, he indulged a last look. There. A small flutter of her eyelid. He rushed back to her side.

With obvious effort, her eye half-opened. Her iris circled around like a searchlight. She appeared distant, confused. Her lips barely moved. She tried to speak, but couldn't.

"Gigi! I'm here. I'm right here." Juan leaned close.

Her eyelid fluttered again with the struggle to speak. She managed a garbled whisper Juan heard only because he was an inch away, "Bean. Prayer. Answered. One last time."

"Hey, hey. Don't talk like that, chica. They're going to take you to the best hospital and the best doctors are going to fix you."

"Plugged in...you fix."

A soul-soothing snicker escaped him. "Only you, Gigi. Nobody else could joke at a time like this. That's one of the reasons I love you." A crow's foot formed at her eye and a slight curl appeared at her upper lip.

"Bean," she struggled even more and Juan leaned even closer. His ear touched her lips. "Wanted..." Her eye closed as her voice failed.

"Gigi," Juan exclaimed, alarmed. He called, "Doctor!" To Gigi, he said, "Hold on, chica. A doctor is coming."

The monitors indicated weakened blood pressure and unsteady pulse. Juan fought back his panic. "Somebody!"

Gigi's head moved slightly, and Juan's heart skipped a beat. He leaned close. "Stay with me, Gigi. Por favor."

Her eye remained closed, but her lips moved. Juan didn't comprehend. It sounded like 'kwanu.' "Kwanu?" he whispered, puzzled.

"Quon. Knew," she managed. She went still and the heart monitor flat-lined.

A STRAY REPORT

Rain visited Arnie, Jerry, Harrison, and Lyden as he collected their evacuation plans. As he placed each folder in his briefcase, his mood sank further. The same disappointment sullied each man's face. Of course, the top priority was safety. But this marked the end of an important part of all of their lives. None of them talked about that, nor what lay in store. They lingered on the incidental, on personal topics. Bob asked Rain about his stained glass. Rain asked Jerry about his daughter's dissertation and Arnie about his son's Little League baseball team. They all inquired about Gigi and whether Rain thought she'd be all right. His voice trembled when he reported he didn't know.

Rain was half out of Lyden's door when the elder man stopped him. "Rain, I almost forgot. That program you asked about? Connie said he found nothing."

"Yeah, me too. I must've misremembered."

"No. What you mentioned rang a bell to me too. So, I poked around a bit. Nothing was there. That's irregular. The best explanation is the records were deleted."

"Deliberately? Who could do that?"

"Somebody with a lot of authority."

Rain's brow furrowed deeper.

Lyden rummaged through his attaché case. "I looked in my own files. It isn't much—nothing technical—just overall program information. Here." He pulled out a faded, musty-smelling manila folder and handed it to Rain. "I hope it helps."

"What is it?"

"It's an old report. Just a summary. You say Mira suspects it's relevant to SONA?"

RAIN TEXTED and found Mira at the LSF making final arrangements for her departure. He zipped his headgear and hurried out of the WDTC HQ. On his way, he waved to Leigh, a security guard with whom he'd shared beers and watched Brigham Young football on numerous occasions. Probably never again. He spotted Hank, one of his go-to crewmembers when they had to clean up noxious chemicals. They would never work together again.

He entered the lab and Mira's eyes lit. "Rain. I didn't think I'd see you before I left. Any news on Gigi?"

His face remained solemn. "Yes. Not good. She clinically died, twice, before they were able to revive her. Now they have her on life support in an induced coma." He pulled out Lyden's file. "I have to show you this." He handed her the file. "Something weird is going on. This is the only record of the project. I got my hands on it only because Victor had it in his personal files. All the other reference material is missing."

"That is odd. Why?" She took the file and opened it.

"No idea."

She read the pages as Rain spoke. Her lips straightened, severe. "You lied to me all along?"

Rain stepped back. "What? No, I haven't."

She shoved one of the pages close to his face, a cover letter with the Dugway logo.

"So?" He struggled to make sense of her reaction.

"Look at the signature, Rain." She hadn't spoken to him like this before.

Rain looked at the place she indicated. The writing was angular yet flowing, the first letters of each word oversized, but legible: 'Major

Constance Yanoviak.' Rain sank into a chair. "I didn't know. I brought it straight here."

"You're telling me you knew nothing?"

"No. Connie said nothing about this to me."

"Where is he?" Mira returned to the file and again perused the pages as she flipped them furiously. She no longer pointed her anger at Rain.

"He went back to Aberdeen. But he's supposed to come back today or tomorrow." He stood and went to Mira's side and they examined the report together. "You think—"

"Missing records," she interrupted. "Connie denied knowing about the program. I was right there when he denied it." She stabbed the page with her finger. "That's his signature. What am I supposed to think, Rain?"

"You're supposed to think the same thing I do." He shook his head, back and forth; his lips pinched tight. "But I can't believe it." Some pages had parts too faded to read and other parts that were redacted. But sufficient legible text allowed them to discern the subject of the study. Entitled 'Special BioProtection Division Study 2829EA,' the executive summary indicated it had been deemed ineffective for DNA repair in response to cellular damage resulting from over-exposure to radiation.

Rain read aloud. "Samples were devitalized and disposed onsite." He massaged his neck. The tendons were tight enough to twist his head to one side. "That means burial." He pointed. "These numbers are the coordinates." The blood left his face. "I know this location, Mira," he whispered. "That's where Roberts died."

Mira thumbed through the remaining pages. She stopped and dropped half of the stack on floor.

"The scope of research statement explains." Her voice was loud and her pace quickened. "They delivered bacteriophage DNA repair enzymes to human cells using a modified Lentivirus vector."

Her words meant nothing to Rain. "Why dispose of this waste in an area not marked for that purpose?"

Mira sat as she read further. "This is advanced stuff. These guys were successfully gene editing twenty years before anyone else. They tried to develop a treatment for radiation exposure incurred by soldiers." She grew more animated. "Do you know what this means, Rain?"

"It means we did this." Rain was visibly shaken. His voice choked.

"Not on purpose."

"Connie..."

"Is it conceivable he didn't know all this time?"

His face went blank.

"Rain?"

"My dad never understood me. Once I left for the Army, well—we never talked much after that. Connie made it hurt a lot less."

Mira put her hand on his arm. "Rain, listen."

"What?" he muttered.

"Could Connie have known all this time?"

"No," he managed. "He's a good man. He's a hero. He's dedicated his life to protecting people." His chin dropped; his eyes faraway.

"But is it possible?" Mira appeared unmoved by Rain's obvious distress.

"I don't know," he whispered. At last, he raised watery eyes. "Yes."

A PARTING

Mira ran late. She was supposed to report to the MAAF and should have been comfortably settled on the Gulfstream by now. But she couldn't just leave in the wake of recent developments. Not without talking with Eleanor and Potteiger. Rain couldn't stand in for her, not on this.

She could have been more sympathetic to Rain. His pain was a kind she knew; worse than hardship such as she faced in Antarctica. What might she have said to help him? She had no idea. But she should have said something.

She couldn't reach Eleanor. Mira assumed that she was on a plane. The inability to speak with her added to Mira's frustration, and she felt even more on edge. She needed to get clearance to perform the extremophile screen immediately. She started to send an email, but abandoned the draft. The logistics were complicated. It required a conversation.

During her exit interview, Potteiger indicated he'd be in his office on a scheduled call at this time. She knocked on the outer door. No answer. His admin must have gone home for the day. No, unnecessary personnel had been dismissed. She tried the door and found it open. The inner door was ajar. She heard the Commander inside, presumably on the phone. She stuck her head in.

Potteiger held up a finger. "One moment please, sir," he said to the person on the line. "Dr. Wallace, aren't you supposed to be on a plane by now?"

"I'm sorry to interrupt, Colonel. There's been a development."

"I'm on an important call right now. Let's discuss it after."

"Like you said, I'm supposed to leave."

"I'm sorry. Can't you take it up with Eleanor?"

"She's already gone."

He said into his phone, "Sir, I apologize. Dr. Wallace is reporting she has some news that won't wait. Permission to hear her out?" He paused to listen. "Two minutes, yes sir." He ended the call.

"You heard. Talk."

She placed the folder on Potteiger's desk and opened it to the signature page. He perched his half-moon reading glasses on the end of his nose. "What am I looking at?"

"This is a program that was terminated two decades ago. All records of it have been removed. All that remains is this one file."

"Okay."

"This program is likely the precursor for SONA. It was secretly disposed, and that disposal was covered up sometime later."

"Covered up? By who?"

"Look at the signature."

"So?"

"Connie knew about this and said nothing."

Potteiger sat back. "Maybe he did and maybe he didn't. Signing off on this kind of document is routine. It doesn't necessarily mean wrong-doing."

"No. But this was not routine. This was breakthrough technology, advanced even by current standards. The report indicates disposal at the site of the SONA outbreak."

"Have you talked to him about this?"

"He's not answering texts, calls, or email."

"He may be in transit. Tell you what. Leave the file with me. I'll talk to him and take whatever action is appropriate."

"But Colonel, what about the missing records? That suggests—"

"Thank you for bringing this to my attention." He picked up his phone and redialed. "Have a good trip home."

She hadn't known what to expect, but Potteiger's reaction was not it. She stared blankly, frozen.

He waved her out of his office and swiveled away when his call connected.

"General Marcus," Potteiger said, "my apologies."

Puzzled, she backpedaled. She hesitated, and left.

EXCERPT:
THE NECESSITY OF PRECURSOR COOPERATIVES

Wallace, M. D.[1,2] and Weingartner, J. A.[1]

1University of California, Berkeley, Dept. of Plant and Microbial Biology, 311 Koshland Hall, Berkeley CA, 94720.

2National Interagency Biodefense Campus, Fort Detrick, MD 21702

Section #3: Strategy

A stable food source and electro-chemical fortune, while vital, was alone insufficient for its long-term viability. Up to this point, it remained shapeless. Just like the occurrence of the nucleic acid code, the transition to form was likewise driven by inherent properties of the chemicals themselves.

Some components of the growing collective were not water soluble. The porphyrin that harvested light energy was one of these. Porphyrin persisted within bubbles or fragments of bubbles of sorts, formed by chemicals called lipids. Some amino acids catalyzed the formation of phospholipids that assembled in tandem, producing stable bilayers. The phospholipids self-assembled into microscopic fluid, flexible, and self-repairing membranes not unlike soap bubbles. The collective began to segregate within discrete bubbles. Every bubble contained all the chemical ingredients necessary to ensure its persistence. At last, the amorphous collective had become individual entities, each one slightly different and competing for their individual survival.

AN ANCESTOR

M ira's pre-Antarctica activities at Berkeley resumed. She worked long office hours, attended a few meetings, caught up on correspondence, and analyzed data that had piled up over the past year. But her life was anything but normal. The discoveries from the Antarctic survey, results she'd sacrificed years of her career to obtain, barely crossed her mind. Her thoughts centered on the work that lay ahead at Ft. Detrick. Sure, it was a longshot. But she'd spent her career on longshots.

The daily, sometimes hourly, calls from Quon were not helping. Irked by his pestering, Mira nevertheless marveled at the man's tenacity. When he wanted something, he did not stop until he got it. After a few days, she dodged his calls and did not respond to his messages. She didn't like doing that, but he left her no choice.

It was always the same conversation anyway—he wanted an update. She had nothing new to report. Preparation of her extremophile library for transport continued around the clock. She'd recruited nearly every grad student and postdoc in the department in order to collapse the time frame. They would be done soon.

She didn't wish to inform Quon about the origin of SONA and the suspicious behavior of Connie, even Potteiger. The matter clearly required discretion. Discretion Quon lacked.

Her phone buzzed. She smiled when she saw the screen. "Yes, Jeff?"

"You better come to the lab, Mira."

"The final batch of Lake Ellsworth sequences are done? The

Tree is complete?"

"*I'll show you. Come down.*"

SHE FOUND Jeff glued to a computer monitor, a handful of grad students circled around him. They moved aside to let her through. She studied the display. Over 20 years of work was about to come to conclusion. Her heart raced and her fingers felt electric.

Jeff spoke to the students as much as to Mira. "After 14 hours of run time, we've finished phylogenetic analysis of 27.8 billion microbial genomes, almost two billion of which were sampled from particularly harsh environments ranging from a subterranean lake to volcanic undersea thermal vents. There seems to be a single microbe at the base of the tree. It has a significant bootstrap value."

A student said, "I'm sorry, Dr. Weingartner, I'm not clear on what you mean."

Jeff faced him. His gestures were animated and fast as he explained. "As you know, we're aligning microbial sequences. We can tell how each is related to one another by how similar their sequences are. We also look at the rate of change. We calculate that from the sequences too. This is another way we sort which ones predate others. So, we order the position of the microbes' relatedness over time to determine which begat which. Again, you all know very well how difficult this is. It's messy. We don't have all the data. Big chunks of the picture are missing. It's kind of like trying to connect a person to their great, great grandfather but not having any information about the mother, father, or grandparents. The DNA sequence allows us to build the timeline, but only if the gaps aren't too big. The more info you have, the more reliable the relationship predictions are. When I say significant bootstrap value, I mean that the gap is reasonably small enough for our confidence to be high."

Mira examined the genome map, her brow wrinkled in concentration. She found herself unexpectedly calm given the momentous occasion. At 378,879 DNA base pairs in length, the genome was small and simple—a good indicator. It was primitive. "What is this one? Does it have an ID?"

Jeff beamed. "Nope."

"This is from Ellsworth?"

"Nope."

She looked Jeff in the eyes, her eyebrows raised.

"One of the atmospheric surveys from last summer." Jeff almost bounced with excitement. He couldn't sit still. "Above Longyearbyen."

"The Norwegian samples?" She had almost forgotten them among a sizable batch of atmospheric samples that she'd sampled using drones several years ago. She returned to the sequence and stared as if she might grasp something deeper in so doing. "What elevation?"

Jeff opened a database file on his phone and searched for the sample reference number. "Let's see. Says here 'lower stratosphere— 36.04 kilometers.' That can't be right. There's almost nothing up that high, the atmosphere is too thin. Ultraviolet radiation is too intense— the chances are too remote. Maybe the samples got mixed up?"

"It's possible, Jeff, but not likely." Plenty of microbes were known to exist in the atmosphere, yet relatively few had been sampled and sequenced. Mira reasoned out loud. "Maybe this makes sense. The atmosphere shortly after Earth's formation was a thousand times denser. It was a product of volcanic outgassing; a mixture of water vapor, carbon dioxide, methane, ammonia, and other gases similar to those produced by volcanoes today. The environment was hostile, but also good for complex chemical formation."

Jeff's squint indicated he was not convinced. "What about the atmospheric changes that have taken place across the eons? More UV light, less water, additional pollutants, and almost no food sources to sustain a particular species over time. It would have to use sophisticated strategies for nutrient consumption. Unlikely for such a simple genome."

Her expression neutral, Mira turned to the students. "Thoughts?"

One of them said, "Well, the data says it's up there no matter what we think about it."

Jeff scratched his light stubble. "Point taken. Let's take a closer look at the DNA sequence." He took the mouse from Mira's hand and opened a search box. He typed a short search code followed by the long numeric sequence ID. A folder with a dozen files opened. He identified and opened a text document which featured a series of headers with notes beneath them.

Jeff summarized the data as his finger traced the screen. "According to the BUSCO[1] scores, the gene complement is incomplete. This could be an artifact. A fragmented assembly."

"What's the N_{50}?"

"Single contig. Gap analysis indicates the genome assembly is highly accurate and complete. All the ribosomal RNA sequences are there, but many of the core ribosomal proteins are missing. This doesn't make sense. The RNAseq data shows the presence of ribosomal RNAs, but many have no corresponding DNA sequence." Jeff gained speed. "Mira, this is an incredibly primitive microbe. The protein synthesis machinery is extremely reduced. The other biosynthetic pathways in this microbe are also simple. Only three hundred seventy-five protein-coding genes."

"How about the molecular clock algorithms?" Mira asked. The students around them looked at one another, curious and anxious.

Jeff typed in another series of codes followed by the organism ID. "Running now. Should be done in a few seconds." He attended the computer and opened the appropriate window. The readout on the screen indicated the age: 4.339 bya (billion years ago.)

Another graduate student spoke, her manner demure. "Over four billion years? This is one of the first living things on the planet?"

Mira answered matter-of-fact. "In a manner of thinking. The species has been around a long time and predates all other known organisms. In the literature, it's referred to as the FCA—the First

Common Ancestor. I really didn't expect we'd find it in the sky." Was this what she'd searched for all her life? Why wasn't she more excited? Was she hoping to find something else? She struggled for dispassion. But it wasn't excitement she tamped down. It was disappointment. She had always pictured finding some kind of hybrid organism, one that blurred the line between something inanimate and something considered alive. She'd hoped to find some life-form with a simplified version of the Universal code that would move her closer to explaining the origin of life. This one struck her as too...normal. Yes, it was simple. But it wasn't really very different. What could she take from that observation? "We hoped to find something this old and primitive, but the odds were always against it being found or even still existing. It's hard to take this in, Jeff."

He beamed back. "I know, right? This really opens things up. Before long, we'll have a much clearer idea of how Life emerged."

She wished she shared his sense of triumph. Her thoughts drifted to SONA and the screens ahead. And what awaited them in their likely failure. Her gaze returned to the genome on the monitor. She observed before her one of the biggest discoveries in the history of biology. All of that work, the risks, the sufferings, the good fortune— what did it really matter now? Her face slackened.

Some of the students tittered, excited. Nobody noticed Mira's shift. Except Jeff. He leaned close. "What will you name it, Mira?"

Mira felt lifted. Of course, this mattered. It mattered to Jeff. That was enough. Amid the clouds of fear and doubt, she began to feel something else—gratitude. "You found it, Jeff. You name it."

Jeff flushed as he smiled broadly. "Really? You're sure?"

"I am."

"This one is easy. You've had me thinking about this since I was an undergrad in your senior seminar. This is *Primum viverea*."

She smiled at him. "First life... Perfect."

---

1. See Supplement for explanation.

A TRANSITION

"Dr. Wallace. I am gratified you finally returned my call."

"I apologize. We've been preoccupied. We've made a discovery."

"*Something related to our upcoming SONA screens?*" Quon's voice raised.

"No. Something else. Related to my ongoing research."

His voice fell as fast as it rose. "*Congratulations.*"

Clearly, he wasn't going to inquire further. She leaned back in her desk chair. "We are almost ready to transport my library. I plan to deliver it personally. We have some important issues to discuss."

"*Normally, that would be fine. I would of course be happy to have you visit us. But current circumstances complicate the matter.*"

"How so?"

Quon hesitated. "*I will see what can be done. We may be able to accommodate you alone. Are you willing to work with my technician?*"

"I suppose."

"*I shall have my assistant help you with the arrangements.*"

"I appreciate that." Without warning, he placed her on hold. Quon's attitude change struck Mira as odd, even for him. After all, he was the one who pushed for this partnership.

Mira spoke to the technician, a thick-accented man named Ji. Best she could tell, this part of the process would not take a long time. That was a relief, in stark contrast to this first phase which finally drew to a close. She assured Ji her library was carefully arranged, in strict accord with their instructions, on the micropore plates they had sent. It had required many hands to get that laborious task accomplished in just over a week.

Not long after she ended the call, the Vivaldi melody of her ringtone sounded. Maryland area code. "General Higgins, thank you for the callback."

"I'm glad to hear from you, Mira."

"I wanted to inform you of the timeline. We're near completion of the prep of our inventory here. We've selected samples from 90 extreme environments. They represent 1.8 billion extremophile species. I will take it to Quon's facility in Seattle personally. I fly out in the morning. There, we'll conduct a transfer from the storage format to one compatible with his environmental nanocycler. I'm hopeful that I can get that done by the end of day tomorrow. I will accompany the sequencer as it is delivered to you at Detrick. It will take a team to install and ready the device, but the plan is to be operational by late the day after tomorrow."

"That's good news. Excellent work, Mira. Time is even more critical. I'm told preparations for the demolition are almost done. It may be only a week or two now."

"Oh." The news sobered her. A week or two? The blink of an eye in biological research timelines. From the little she'd gathered from Ji, it would take hundreds of hours to complete the screen. They'd have to proceed at a breakneck pace. "Once we're set up there, it will still be time-consuming. We'll have maybe two hundred chips to run, each one will take hours."

"I can press, but I don't believe I'll be able to move the deadline. Assume you have a week."

Mira sighed. "We'll do our best, General."

"I know you will. I look forward to seeing you when you arrive."

They ended the call. Mira didn't know how to feel. They'd just made the biggest discovery of her life. She should be celebratory. She wasn't. *Primum viverea* didn't feel like the crowning achievement she'd always anticipated. A solution for SONA, one that might save uncountable lives, that mattered far more. Quon had given her the means to find it. But was there time? That made the remote odds of success even longer. Still, she had hope. All was not lost. Not yet.

MIRA EXITED Quon's private jet and anxiously watched the steward emerge from the hold with her cargo—the specialized case that contained her nearly two billion extremophiles, less than 10% of her total collection, which was in turn less than 3% of the estimated microbial species on the planet. Still, hers was by far the largest collection of environmental microbial samples in the world. And perhaps not large enough, she worried. She checked its seals for integrity. Satisfied, she followed the man to Quon's stretch-limo GreenCar. He placed the case into the front of the spacious passenger compartment, then opened the rear door and invited Mira to enter. They whisked away without a sound.

She shook her head at the ostentation of the GreenCars corporate HQ—the glints off of the tinted windows, the big, bright neon signage, and the verdant shrubbery that marked the grounds all around the factory and the tall office building. Quon must fancy himself the Wizard of Oz; he built the Emerald City as proof.

The steward stopped at the front door and wheeled the library as Mira followed him into the building. He led her through security and upstairs to Quon's executive suite. Given the size of the complex, she didn't expect to see so few employees. Aside from her not-so-talkative attendant, the only people she encountered were the lone security guard at the front desk and Quon's administrative assistant who barely uttered a word. She waited another eerily silent fifteen minutes before the admin signaled her into his office.

"Dr. Wallace. Please do come in." Quon turned up his charm to full strength as he welcomed her, but he remained at his desk. He wore his customary uniform—an expensive, tailored suit and his GreenCar-colored necktie with matched pocket square. In contrast to the rustic crucifix in Mira's pocket, his ostentatious jewelry appointments included an oversized gold and green watch, two emerald cufflinks, a GreenCar Logo pin, diamond and emerald rings, and of course his gold-rimmed glasses. His bandage, crownlike, remained on his head even though the explosion happened two weeks prior. Not a hair exposed above the wrap was out of place. "Please forgive me for not rising. Unfortunately, I remain in some pain. I must also apologize for the state of our operation here. As I said to you, now is not the best time for us to receive guests. We are in the midst of a significant corporate transition."

"I see." Despite the generosity of his travel arrangements and the considerable show he made of her welcome, she didn't hide her irritation she'd had to wait. What could he think might be a higher priority than this?

"It is all very exciting but I am afraid I cannot yet share the details. I trust your travels were pleasant?"

"Fine. Time is important now, Dr. Quon. I'm told—"

"The jet was to your liking?"

"Yes. Anyway, as I was saying, I should begin the transfer right away."

"The steward sufficiently accommodated you?"

"What?" She felt her patience ebb and took a deliberate breath to stop it all from getting away. She was here to work with Quon. Not that there was much of a choice. She couldn't deny his courtesies. He'd sent his personal jet and limo for her; the only price he appeared to want was appreciation for the gesture. "Fine, yes. Everything was fine. Thank you for your generosity. I've always been afraid to fly. Lately, it's been—better."

"Yes. Commercial travel is a nightmare by comparison." He spied her case. "These are the extremophiles?"

"Yes. As I was about to tell you, I should get started right away. But there is one matter—"

"I should like to inspect your library, Dr. Wallace." Quon made a show of the difficulty as he rose from his desk, limped over to the case and reached out with both hands. As soon as his fingers made contact, he pulled them back. His brows rose. "It is cold."

"Yes, it is." Protective, she edged past him and opened the outer case. Cold vapor billowed from the seams. Inside was another metal case. "There isn't much to see. Just a bunch of micropore plates in racks."

"Of course." Quon stared at the case for an extended time.

Mira closed the outer case. "I need to attend the transfer process. But I need to talk with you first."

Quon hobbled back to his desk and waved for her to sit. "I hoped to give you a personal tour of the facility, but that is not a possibility at the moment."

"That's fine, Dr. Quon. Time is of the essence. Your technician was not clear about how long the prep may take. I'd like to finish before the day is over."

"The plane will be available whenever you are ready to depart." Quon pressed a button on his intercom to alert his assistant.

"One more item. You should know that we now know where SONA came from."

"You do? That is good news indeed." The steward came back. Quon addressed him. "Please escort Dr. Wallace to the sequencing lab."

"Ready, Dr. Wallace?" That seemed the extent of his mastery of the English language.

"You don't want to hear more?" Mira surmised that nothing Quon did could surprise her. She'd been wrong.

"My apologies. Of course, I do. I have much that requires my attention. I will try to visit the lab before you leave. Please excuse me."

Quon buried himself in his computer monitor. Mira shrugged. Why the lack of curiosity? She followed the steward as he wheeled her library out. With the seal of the outer case now broken, clouds of vapor enveloped her legs as they walked through the near-deserted complex.

The steward opened the lab door and motioned her to enter. The glass on two walls had been hastily papered over. Part of the construction process, Mira surmised.

Ji was as Mira pictured him when they'd spoke on the phone—a diminutive Chinese man of indistinct age. "Welcome. Honored work with you. I am Ji." He spied the case, its handle still in the steward's hand. "This is library? Bring, please." He pointed to a workstation.

The steward complied and left without a goodbye. Ji eyed the library. "You open?" He pantomimed the motion to open the case.

Mira exhaled in relief at the opportunity to get to work. She noted the nanocycler, the specialized environmental DNA sequencer. How likely was it Quon possessed this one-off device? Why did he have it built? By recreating the conditions of their natural habitats, her extremophiles would remain viable during the screens with SONA. She pictured a machine much larger and more complicated. But this instrument was both nondescript and about the size of a large refrigerator. It was not ready to run, but was already packed on a palette for shipment.

Ji's English was broken, but Mira understood what he told her: they would arrange the prepped micropore plates and the target chips, and the transfers would happen at the robotic assembly station that took up most of the space on the far right of the room.

Mira examined the station. On one end was a control panel with two large video monitors. From there, a long metal work surface at navel height ran the entire length of the wall. Above the surface, a series of robotic micro transfer units hung from the ceiling. A sliding plexiglass shield, currently raised to allow access to the space, separated occupants from the mechanism. She noted the blank chip array set into integral recessed holders in two groups along the surface.

Ji pointed to the clear spaces between them. "Trays here."

"Gloves?"

"Sorry." He crossed the room, opened a cabinet and provided Mira with lab gloves and eye protection.

Once she had them on, Mira reached to remove the first rack of trays from her library, but stopped. "Remember, we discussed the samples must be kept cold. Once the chips are loaded, how will they be stored for transport?"

"Thank you. Special freezer." He indicated he'd get it and hurried out.

Mira scowled as Ji left. For a scientific procedure, especially one as critically important as this one, this was sloppy. She speculated about what other important details might be missed. She hoped the transfer protocol was more robust than what she'd thus far witnessed.

Ji pushed a portable freezer smaller than her library case in front of him as he returned.

"Ji, may I double-check the sample layout for transfer?"

He looked at her, puzzled.

She made motions like she unloaded trays and placed them on the unit. "Layout? Transfer?"

Ji beamed as he understood her meaning. "Yes. Very important."

"Let's have a look. Do you have the data I sent with the environmental conditions for each sample? ASCII format, as you requested. Were you able to load them?"

"Yes." He went to the control station and typed. Mira peered over his shoulder as he worked. "Okay?"

She pointed at the appropriate clear space. "The first plate goes here?" She next pointed to the corresponding space under the second robot arm. "The second there?"

"Yes."

"Shall we?" She manipulated a small lock to open the metal inner case of her library. A cloud of mist encircled her hands as she removed the first prepared tray. Inside were millions of individual samples, each one suspended in dimethyl sulfoxide and frozen to -80°C. She extended the tray to Ji, but stopped. "It's cold. You'll want to put your gloves back on."

"Yes." He was unembarrassed.

Once thirty-two of her trays were set in two four-by-four grids,

Mira closed her library and Ji pulled down the plexiglass shield. Ji typed in a few commands on the computer to initiate the robotic transfer. Nothing happened for an extended time.

"Is there something wrong?"

"Robot looking." He observed for a while, then pointed.

As Ji indicated, a loud click echoed as the transfer arms shot to life, a blur of reciprocal motion. First the arms removed individual frozen samples from their trays, a thousand at a time. Next, they deposited the samples into nano-sized depressions on the chips far too small to see with the naked eye. Mira felt both disconcerted and amazed at how many of her samples, a large percentage of which she'd toiled and suffered to collect, fit into these tiny chips. She marveled again at how abruptly the procedure came to a halt.

"Next one?" asked Ji.

Mira retrieved another set of trays and they repeated the procedure until her entire library was loaded. The samples were transferred in triplicate which meant that rather than 900 chips that roughly corresponded with the various environment types, they populated 2,700 of them. This tripled the time, but was not optional. Repeats were essential for success. Finding one successful biocontrol option out of millions could always be an error. Finding two of the same thing out of millions could not. And a third set provided a necessary backup in the event of a malfunction or equipment failure. Mira reminisced about the trips she'd made as she considered the range of natural habitats of the microbes at their fingertips. There wasn't a single excursion that hadn't also come with hardship, sometimes even danger. Her sense of claustrophobia in her first deep sea dive nearly panicked her. Her mouth dried at the thought. It was the same story with the tight, hot volcanic caves she'd squeezed through. She remembered the failed carabineer that compromised the rope while she abseiled into an active volcano on a remote south Pacific island. She'd managed to grip the rock surface, but barely. And not before she'd been badly scraped. So many deserts. So many ice sheets. Never had she imagined they'd lead to this moment.

After two hours, Ji loaded the last of the chips into the portable freezer. "Next time slower. Different robot."

She understood. The next phase, the introduction of SONA in containment at Ft. Detrick, involved more steps and more complication. This was just the beginning. She nodded. "Are we ready to go?"

He pointed at the freezer. "Right back." He rushed from the room and returned with another freezer, identical to the first one. "Third set stay here."

"What?"

"Dr. Quon insist. Back up."

It made some sense to Mira, scientifically speaking. But it didn't feel right. The thought of leaving a copy of her library with Quon unsettled her. She did not trust him.

Ji transferred the third chipset as Mira texted Jeff. His opinion was that it was okay. He added that he'd be on the first available flight out of San Francisco and would meet her at Detrick.

"Now I take you to Dr. Quon," he said as he shut the freezer doors. His smile faltered. With the culture difference, she was unsure what that meant.

He led her to an open area outside what she assumed to be the GreenCars factory floor. Quon approached in a bright green golf cart. He looked at Ji, who bowed and loped away the way they had come.

Quon remained in the cart. "I trust the transition went well? You are set to leave for Detrick?"

"Dr. Quon, we didn't discuss my leaving a copy of my library here."

"What is the problem? It is prudent to back it up, just in case there is a mishap in transport, is it not?"

"Yes, but..."

"Let us not worry further about it. It is secure here, I give you my personal assurance on that. Please keep me apprised of what you learn with my nanocycler."

"Of course. Thank you again for the use of your instrumentation, Dr. Quon." Her gratitude was heartfelt. "If we find a biocontrol solution, it will be because of you."

"I am grateful to be able to help." Despite his attempt at humility, his chin and chest rose.

"I started to tell you earlier I've seen documentation that outlines a research program at Dugway. They attempted to use a virus to edit DNA to confer better resistance to radiological damage."

"Interesting. And?"

"The documents show the subject materials were disposed at the site of SONA's first appearance."

"You have these documents?"

"No. Potteiger has them."

His reaction was a frown that, to Mira, didn't match the words he spoke. "This confirms what I theorized: abiogenesis from a primordial soup. Just like the first life."

"I conclude the opposite."

"We shall have to agree to disagree."

"No, this isn't a matter of simple disagreement," Mira insisted. "SONA resulted from an improper disposal. This is wholly unlike the process that resulted in first life." Even as she spoke, she recognized that Quon had a small point. SONA wasn't entirely created. It did arise from a primordial soup of sorts—one where the ingredients were man-made, not natural. But not intended either. In a way, it could be considered analogous to the process that resulted in first life—if you ignored the roles of existing complex life-forms that apparently recombined to create it. However, it differed in a more important way. It arose from life's components, yes, but it was not life. It threatened to wipe out life. SONA and life were made of the same stuff. But life had a unique property. It could evolve. Life was powered by an elegant, balanced machinery driven by mistakes—a kind of imperfect perfection. Living things moved towards a balance between vigor and adaptability. If they survived, they eventually settled into a relatively harmonious state with their surroundings. SONA lacked this balance. It could only destroy.

Quon's signature smile returned. "I do not wish to argue with you. I would like us to continue to work together. I hope you find my plane comfortable for your journey east. If things go the way I plan, you will continue to have the opportunity to use it for your travels. I wish you good fortune with the screens, Dr. Wallace. I know you will make good use of the nanocycler." Without waiting for a response, he drove away.

AN OPERATION

The seismic survey gave the demolition team important knowledge about the SONA formation and its environs. The drill placements Kyle suggested became useful pilot holes for this new purpose. Still, widening the bore diameters of the selected shafts from a maximum of 15 inches to up to 6 feet was risky work. The initiative strained the ample resources of the U.S. Army Corps of Engineers and the labs of both Los Alamos and Livermore, along with personnel from dozens of private firms and various related government agencies. The CDC provided hundreds of hazmat suits and the infrastructure for field decon stations.

Crews worked around the clock for weeks straight. Personnel constantly rotated in and out, but the pace did not waiver as the work shifted from preparing the boreholes to lowering the munitions into place.

There were complications. SONA saw to that. Fourteen additional surface outcroppings had to be controlled with chlorine gas tents. Two of them were so close to bomb placements they had to abandon those drill operations. That was a setback. But not the biggest one. Two workers, their suits torn during the heavy and hard work of tripping pipe, became exposed to SONA and died in agony. The incidents caused fear throughout the workforce.

Despite the tragedy, the operation didn't slow. To the authorities unfamiliar with the technical challenge, the operation looked like a tortoise race. Lowering munitions into each shaft, the variables being depth and the dimensions of the ADM's (Atomic Detonation

Munitions), took three to five days. Stemming each shaft took another couple of days. To do so, they installed six or more sanded-gypsum plugs, each one separated by 50 feet of gravel and 10 feet of sand. They also had to seal the holes for the cable core that ran through the middle at each plug. ADM placement depth varied anywhere from a dangerously shallow 600 feet (which safely allowed a yield of only 8 kilotons) to almost 2000 feet (which allowed a blast up to thirty times as powerful.)

Additional workers, also sworn to confidentiality about every detail, installed equipment bunkers. The remediation did provide the authorities and nuclear scientists a small windfall. After all, this was the most comprehensive deployment of nuclear explosive technology in history. This incineration would include explosives that had never before been tested with live detonations. Accordingly, seven bunkers were placed outside the blast zone perimeter and hardened against both physical shock and electromagnetic pulses. Placed within them was sensory equipment which would capture the internal dynamics of each blast.

Hot debate swirled around the types and potency of the ADMs. Ultimately, they selected an assortment: thermo-nuclear fusion/fission hybrids, an Oralloy thermonuclear design, and pure fusion devices, the existence of which was officially denied by the U.S. Government. Pure fusion promised a large blast force along with an intense spray of neutrons, but few radioactive remnants. Some argued non-nuclear incendiary devices were preferable for both political and safety issues. But the majority of the experts, including a few recruited out of retirement who had worked decades prior on underground nuclear tests in Nevada, disagreed. They pointed out that the aftermath of the incineration would include disposal of large volumes of residual debris, mainly rock. Powerful explosions would minimize the scope of that phase. Because of the program's extensive experience with previous detonations (over 1,000 nuclear tests conducted over the course of more than 40 years), those experts were confident they could minimize radioactive fallout.

THE NEUROSURGEON WIPED the sweat from her brow. The patient should not be alive. The damage to her spinal column was too severe —the worst she had ever attempted to repair. The systemic trauma from the extensive burns alone should have exhausted the patient's metabolic energy. Yet the doctor and her team spent hours in the OR, meticulously repairing what they could. The patient stubbornly held on to life; none could explain how. Despite multiple complications, the doctor and her team did the best work in their careers. There was hope yet.

A COVER-UP

National and international reports about the events at Dugway were well-managed. Three arrests had to be made for breeches of confidentiality; none of those unauthorized disclosures were particularly damaging. The public relations campaign worked. Eleanor became the go-to spokesperson. She attributed the deaths to an accidental, improbable, and tragic chemical spill. She explained the evacuation and the unavailability of the facilities at Dugway Proving Ground were necessary because of the nature of the clean-up operation. She even included the factual detail of the deployment of deadly chlorine gas as a necessary step. That justified clearing the vicinity of all residents. The stories went through the 24/7 news cycle for a few days and faded away.

Residents were relocated to FEMA facilities in Salt Lake City. No protests were allowed near DPG. The angriest of them established a support group, active on social media. There had even been a few stories about their outrage at being displaced in the Salt Lake Tribune and the Deseret News. But those stories weren't picked up after an initial wave of interest. The reporters who had previously grilled Eleanor and Potteiger moved on. The only off-site discussions about the SONA crisis were sporadic hearsay, a smatter of unsubstantiated social media claims, and occasional rants by several habitual conspiracy-theory kooks. Their boy-who-cried-wolf warnings of dire and imminent disaster fell on deaf ears.

WES QUON ARRANGED another phone conference with the President of the United States. "Mr. President, as always I appreciate your time and consideration."

"You're welcome, Wes. As supportive as you've been, it's the least I can do."

"Yes. Well, as you are undoubtedly aware, we remain unable to stop the spread of SONA. Nevertheless, I need more time."

"That's what you said last time." The President spoke to Quon as someone who had his good will. Nevertheless, his manner was severe. "My people tell me there is no more. Do you have new information?"

Quon paused. He had to be cautious here. He needed more time, true. Much work lay ahead. Best to attend it with minimal attention. He couldn't reveal too much, or his opportunity might be lost. How bad was the situation, anyway? "We have a better appreciation for the exact nature of SONA and have identified a new line of inquiry."

"Good. Keep at it. I'll put you on speaker." The President did so. In the Oval Office with him were his Chief of Staff Patricia Engel, Vice President Margot Pinkerton, Secretary Gallagher, Secretary Vega, and a handful of senior advisors.

Quon went through a cursory explanation of Mira's imminent work at Ft. Detrick. He didn't mention her name. "I cannot offer you a guarantee we will identify a biocontrol solution, at least one available within the critical window. But there is a non-zero chance. There is a much greater chance the incineration will not end the crisis either."

Patricia Engel stepped forward, animated in response to this information. "You should grant Dr. Quon's request, Mr. President. You know my position on the demolition plan." She paused, looked the others in the eyes, and landed on the President. "We've always abided the treaties that prohibit nuclear testing. We haven't run one since 1992."

Secretary Gallagher looked past her at the President. "It's not a test, sir." Patricia raised her eyebrows. "Not technically," he clarified.

"And the United States is not a signatory to the CNTB treaty," said Vega.

"The previous agreements were never ratified by Congress." Vice President Margot Pinkerton appeared sympathetic to the members of the Cabinet. Conviction underscored her words. "We are under no legal restriction in this matter. Aside from that issue, it's all too clear we can delay no longer. I'm not arguing against the biological research. Continue to do what you can, Dr. Quon. But every day we wait, our chance to end the crisis decreases. We must move forward with the incineration too."

"Do not sign it, sir. I implore you." Patricia was pallid as she fell back into her seat. Her voice softened. "At least until it stipulates the operation to be less than 1.5 megatons, as outlined in the 1974 Test Ban." Two of the other advisors nodded and mumbled agreement.

"The engineers all agree—that small an amount won't fix the problem," countered Gallagher. "Vega, Pinkerton, and I are scheduled to leave for Utah, sir. We need your decision."

Quon's voice permeated the Oval Office tension. "I request a two- to three-week delay. By then, our options will clarify." Quon frowned, relieved he didn't have to hide it behind a smile. This was not going as he wished. If he lost this argument, it would be inconvenient, but a potential calamity of any sort shouldn't derail his plans. He would press on regardless. If not commercial markets, there was always the defense industry. In this country or others. There was always a path. One way or another.

The President addressed his Chief of Staff. "I'm sorry, Patty." He looked at the speaker on the desk. "And you too, Wes. Thank you both. I appreciate your perspectives and your valuable feedback."

"What about Russia? China?" Patricia's voice weakened in defeat. "As you yourself acknowledged, they won't sit idly by."

"We'll do what they would do." The President, his lips set in two parallel lines, picked up the pen and executed the order. "We'll do it and claim we didn't."

RAIN FRETTED about the end of DPG. He went through the motions of his work. He attended the requisite meetings and performed duties as ordered. But it was all passive, a mere carrying out of orders. His proactive leadership style had been short-circuited. He'd even stopped trying to reach Connie. He'd see him soon enough.

He worried about Gigi. And Juan. He needed to reach out to him, but he had nothing new to say. Gigi had a battery of operations to go through. As frustrating as it was, neither he nor Juan could do anything now. Gigi's fate was in God's hands.

Rain prayed for her. That was one thing he could do. He also prayed for Connie. His prayers included Juan, and Mira too, that she'd find a solution and find it in time.

Rain signed some papers and left his office. He zipped his headgear and walked to the MAAF. Connie would arrive any minute. As he walked out onto the tarmac, he spied an outsized suited figure near the hangar. Kyle.

"They're givin' me the boot. Guess I'm non-essential personnel now."

"It's no reflection on the work you've done here, Kyle. On behalf of the U.S. Army—no, everybody—thank you."

"Glad I could help, fella." He put a massive arm around Rain's shoulders. "Been good ta work with ya."

Rain struggled with what now lay ahead for this installation. It was in the process of being overrun by a microbe. "How much volume do you think SONA has reached now?"

Kyle frowned. "I don't know."

"Your best guess."

"The main mass? Probably over a million cubic meters."

Rain's expression matched Kyle's. "Sounds like an awful lot."

"Darn tootin' that's a lot."

A soldier approached. "We're ready to depart, sir. Please come with me."

Kyle nodded. He looked at Rain. "Mayhaps our paths will cross again."

"I hope so."

Kyle followed the soldier to the plane. Another jet, this one much bigger, taxied closer. Rain's eyes narrowed as he regarded it. Connie was there. He'd find out what his mentor really knew and when he knew it. For better or worse.

A dozen dignitaries deplaned. Rain recognized most of them. But among the senior leaders, no Connie.

A PATTERN

"Mira—I'm so glad you're back! I'm excited to work with you again."

The Randy she remembered was forlorn. He'd been talkative, but not like this. She found him outside BSL-4 containment, observing through the glass as Ji and a host of other iso-suited technicians busily installed the environmental nanocycler. "It's good to see you too, Randy." He looked better, too—clean-shaven, a fresh haircut, and unwrinkled, unfaded clothes.

"I've got something for you." He pulled a shiny object from his breast pocket.

Mira froze as she saw glints of gold and silver.

He held the bracelet out. "Here. Don't say no."

The sight struck her hard enough for her breath to catch. She focused on the sparkle of the multi-colored charms as they refracted the bright fluorescent light. "It was a gift, Randy," she said softly as she remembered to breathe. "I didn't expect it back."

"I know." Randy beamed. "Tyler played with it for a while and moved on. He doesn't even know it's gone. You know how kids are."

She didn't. At Tyler's age, she had every one of her belongings neatly catalogued and organized. The few toys she had were classified by size and weight. If anything went missing, she knew immediately. She held out her hand. "Oh," she whispered. Randy placed it in her palm. "Okay."

The bracelet felt heavier than she remembered. Though it hadn't been that long, it seemed a lifetime since it last adorned her wrist. She felt a rush of relief for its return. A memory of her grandmother flooded her mind. She'd steamed corn on the cob and half a bushel of blue crabs, Mira's favorite, for her tenth birthday. They had spent a lovely evening feasting and laughing; cracking the crabs open over spread newspaper and making a big mess. Mira remembered the little cuts on her fingers from the shells and how it stung when the Old Bay seasoning rubbed in. She recalled the lingering crab smell. They cleaned up together and sat on the porch swing to watch a meteor shower. Mira didn't recall what they talked about, just that they'd talked. The memory contrasted with her perception about her grandmother being distant, inattentive, and judgmental of Mira's pursuits.

"I know it's important to you. Thank you again for your kindness to my son."

"You're welcome." Mira ran her fingers over the bracelet. She formed it into two interconnected loops, one where the alanine charm magnetically connected to the cysteine charm and the lysine charm attached to the aspartic acid charm. She stared at that combination for a moment. Patterns. That's what it all came down to. Not random, but intricately crafted patterns. Patterns created function and significance—meaning. Patterns were everywhere, everything. She straightened the bracelet and clasped it around her wrist. "Thank you, Randy."

Randy's smile melted away as his mien became serious. "I wanted to ask you about what we're doing, Mira. Forgive me for saying so, but it seems impractical. Do we really have to screen so many species? I mean, why not continue what we were doing before and pick the ones you think will have the best chance for success?"

"That didn't really work out so well."

"But these are different. Your collection is unique, right?"

"I know only that these are unique microbes and where they were collected. How these organisms live and behave, and what characteristics would give them a higher chance to metabolize SONA, I have no idea. Our best chance is to screen them all. There are more than a trillion or so microbial species on the planet. These extremophiles are only a fraction of them."

Randy seemed hopeful despite his fear. "But because they live in harsh environments, they have the best chance, right?"

"That's the working hypothesis."

Randy glanced, furtive, down either direction of the hall. "It's still almost two billion samples, and you said in replicate. That means four billion individual screens."

"Closer to three and a half billion."

"Oh, only three and change billion. I guess we're good then." They shared a smile in response to the levity. It didn't last. "But seriously. That many. In containment. How can we possibly do it?"

She pointed to the nanocycler on the other side of the glass. "The miracle of modern technology, Randy. Provided courtesy of Dr. Wesley Quon. That, and a lot of careful work. I hope you got a good night's sleep. It's going to have to last. Ready?"

Randy swallowed and gave her a sheepish smile. "See you on the other side."

"Okay." Mira's phone indicated a text message. Jeff, right on schedule.

JEFF TOOK notes as he watched the technicians load the materials bays in the environmental nanocycler with double-distilled water, purified salt, and other solutions. Mira called him over to join Randy, Ji, and her. "These procedures require us to be meticulous," she instructed. "But to get through so many we'll also have to be efficient and fast. Randy is the only one of us who is acclimated to work in BSL-4 containment. I spent time here recently. Jeff, you have a little experience. Ji, have you worked in containment?"

"Work, yes. Fast."

"In containment?" His expression told her he didn't understand.

She grabbed the hoses that tethered them all to their air supply. "You've worked like this before?"

"Work, yes. Now."

She shook her head. "We must revitalize the samples by slowly thawing to their native conditions, introduce SONA, incubate, denature the wells, and process the DNA sequences. It will take hours for each chip. There are almost two hundred of them. We have to do this in less than a week. We have to be precise and not confuse the order of the chips, so as to maintain the proper environmental alignments."

"There are one hundred sixty-eight hours in a week and you just described five hundred to a thousand hours of work," Randy said.

"There is overlap," said Jeff. "While some chips incubate, others can be screened while others are sequenced."

"It won't be easy," said Mira. "But it's necessary. I have worked under these kinds of conditions with many different people—long hours of concentration, no sleep, and no room for error. You can do it. I know you can." Mira's thoughts turned to the collection. It felt like a part of her. What an incredible variance among the life-forms. She had a good understanding about the survival strategies of many of them. But not most. She wondered about *Primum viverea.* They all traced genetically back to that microbe. She knew nothing about it, other than how surprising was its very existence. Like SONA. "Jeff, which chip houses *Primum?*"

"I could come up with a search algorithm to answer that, but it'll take me some time. Why?"

"Never mind, then. I was just wondering, that's all."

Randy nodded. Ji smiled, obviously not comprehending much of the discussion. He pointed to the technicians as they finalized the calibrations. "Almost ready. Take long time. Start now."

Ji HAD some difficulty adjusting to work in containment. He tangled air hoses with the others as they prepped SONA sample and loaded it into the nanocycler. Randy had to put his hands upon Ji's shoulders and physically guide him to sort the lines out numerous times.

Yet he was no liability. He played an instrumental role in maintaining alignment between the atmospherics of the nanocycler and the chips. He and Randy remained on the automated, repetitive tasks while Mira and Jeff revitalized the extremophiles and prepped them with SONA.

As time was more crucial than hygiene or comfort, they wore adult diapers. Going in and out of decontamination to use the restroom would take up too much time. They did need to stay hydrated and nourished, so Mira insisted on no more than ten hours without a hard break, back through decon. She restricted each such break to fifteen minutes. After the first one, Jeff returned to the monitor station. The first sequencing files began to appear in a designated folder. "Mira, their finished," he called.

She rolled a lab chair next to him and examined the screen as Jeff opened the files. "This looks like the same mixed up genetic jumble we've seen in all the SONA sequences, Jeff."

"It's just the start," Jeff said, sunny. "It means the method and machine are working, at least."

She patted his arm and returned to the task of revitalizing the next batch of chips.

They continued for two more exhausting ten-hour shifts. During that time, none of the results varied. Doubt began to gnaw at Mira's hope. Ji nearly dropped a chip on the fourth shift. "It's been nearly 48 hours. We need to break and sleep." She glanced at the wall clock. "It's 0400. Let's come back at 0800."

Randy's bleary eyes showed gratitude. "You're an angel."

A BATTLE

Mira awoke in the same townhouse from her last stint in Frederick, only now she had Jeff and Ji as house-mates. Groggy and unrested after what was essentially a long nap, the image of the sequence of *Primum viverea* nevertheless filled her mind. Since the discovery, the organism never seemed to leave her thoughts. What did it tell us about life and how it first came into being? How did this relic of the past persist all these millennia? It had to have evolved from something. What? What could that process be and how long had it taken? Though primitive and simple, the genome still wasn't all that different from the numerous other microorganisms she'd studied. It shared the same basic functions. It was amazingly complex for something so ancient. So many unlikely chemical events had to take place before it. What had she expected? A simple genetic code? A lack of proteins encoded by the DNA? Something that stretched the definitions of living vs. nonliving? A transitional state? She'd finally found the object of her lifelong quest—it left her with more questions than answers. It was perhaps the greatest biological discovery in a century—yet she still felt painfully unfulfilled. As the tension in those last thoughts eased, another feeling lingered. There was no rational basis for it, at least that she could identify. She felt that *Primum viverea* meant something more. She recriminated herself. That thought was not scientific dispassion. It was bias. Bias was the enemy of science.

THE THREE RESEARCHERS returned to the lab at precisely 0800 hours. Mira excused herself to report in with an increasingly anxious Higgins, but was back before 0830. The others were already busy with the unending SONA-extremophile screens. The nanocycler hummed and emitted periodic clicks, thuds, squeals, spurts, and whistles as it re-created the full spectrum of environmental conditions. The relentless hours robbed them their ability to concentrate. For the next three days, it was only the enforced habit of repetitive motion that kept them going. The conditions were unforgiving. The continual whoosh of forced air and the constriction of the suits (and the smell inside them) combined with a lack of sleep to diminish their faculty. Randy had to be dismissed for a full night's sleep. Ji carried on in his absence without slowing too much. But he eventually required an extended break himself, and Randy picked up when Ji left. Jeff was resolute. Mira marveled at him. If he hadn't been here...

She took the depravations in stride too. At least the physical ones. Her nerves frayed. She snapped at Randy when he came back after his eight-hour absence. "About time."

Randy reacted, hangdog. "Sorry, Mira."

She immediately regretted her words. "No, Randy. I'm sorry. It's not you. It's me."

Randy half-smiled. "I totally understand. It's okay."

Her anxiety grew with every result. Her eyes strained with the task of examining the stream of genetic information that resulted from each microscopic well. It was always the same. Every result, millions and millions of them, displayed SONA's genetic gibberish. Each line of the offensive code felt like another inch closer to apocalypse.

AFTER ANOTHER 10-HOUR stint in BSL-4 containment, Mira felt the effects of true exhaustion. Despite the last message from Higgins that informed her that she was now out of time, she felt a sense of calm overwhelm her. Maybe it was delusion, her mind giving way to the strains of the past days. But as she examined the scrolling code, a slight smile curved her lips. It felt almost like looking at the first Ellsworth samples. Without evidence, with nothing but a hopeful hunch, she knew what would happen.

Jeff noticed and joined her. "You okay? Maybe it's time for a real sleep. It helped the others."

She didn't answer. She just kept staring at the screen.

"Mira? I'm getting worried."

She whispered, almost too soft to be heard over the forced air, "Look, Jeff."

He squinted, then jerked back. "That's not randomized!"

"No, it's not," Mira's smile widened.

Randy wearily shuffled over. "That's good, right?"

"Yes, it's good Randy." Mira swelled with newfound energy. "It's microbial. Begin the sequence assembly and analysis for that sample. I want to know what that species is." She twisted her air supply hose free and rushed towards the exit.

"You're leaving? Now?" Jeff asked, incredulous.

"I've got to tell Higgins, hopefully Marcus." She grabbed the handle of the door that led through decontamination. "We might yet stop the demolition."

A MENTOR

Rain assisted Potteiger as he packed his belongings in advance of leaving his office for the last time. The two men wrapped Potteiger's framed photos in bubble wrap and lined them vertically in two clear sealable plastic containers.

Potteiger plainly knew no more than Rain about Connie's conspicuous absence. "He's scheduled to be here, that's all I know, Sergeant Major."

"Permission to speak freely, sir?"

"Of course."

"What do you make of BioProtection Study 2829?"

Potteiger took another photo off of the wall and held it out, wistful. It was an old one, maybe his graduation photo from West Point. "Look at that kid, huh? Handsome devil, right? What I wish I could have told him back then."

"Sir?"

"You're talking about that old file Dr. Wallace brought me? Now we know what happened. That's good. What else is there?"

"The matter of Connie's involvement? It doesn't concern you?"

"Why should it? All we have is an old signature on an old program summary. That doesn't mean much."

Rain almost dropped the photo of Potteiger and his family posing with an ex-Governor of Virginia and the last President of the United States, but caught it. "He might have warned us; it could have made a big difference."

"Careful with that," Potteiger snapped and grabbed the frame from Rain's hand. "You think he hasn't helped? From what I've seen, he has been instrumental."

He wanted to give Connie the same benefit of the doubt Potteiger gave him. He had done so; at first. "What about his insistence he knew nothing about any of it?"

Potteiger wrapped the photo. "It was a long time ago. You don't think he might have honestly forgotten? Or signed a program summary he didn't fully grasp? I've got news for you. I've done the same thing myself. We all do."

"I wish I could just leave it at that. But it doesn't explain his behavior now. He hasn't returned a single one of my messages."

"We're all busy. You know that as well as anyone."

Potteiger's attitude troubled him. Giving someone, especially a respected career man like Connie, the benefit of the doubt? Rain understood that. But evidence was evidence. "The missing archives? What about them?"

"Does that matter now?" He packed the frame into the container and put the lid on it. "Dugway is closed. We can only hope it isn't forever."

"You don't find the unauthorized erasure of important program info a problem?"

"Who says it was unauthorized?"

That gave Rain pause. He hadn't fully considered the possibilities. Maybe he lacked all the pertinent information. Did Potteiger know something he that for some reason he wouldn't share? "Why is he suddenly too busy to help us?"

Potteiger's answer was a blank stare. The sound of the outer door preceded his next words. "Ask him yourself."

Rain spun to see Connie right behind him. He didn't know if he wanted to slug or hug the man. Both. He didn't know what to say either. Too many things. He managed one word. "Why?"

"Why what?" Connie acted as though nothing was out of the ordinary.

"That's the best you've got? You've been avoiding me."

"I'm sorry about that. I've been busy with the research at Aberdeen. I should have at least told you that."

"And you don't think we need to talk about Study 2829?" Rain looked over to Potteiger and searched for support. He received none.

"We've done that. There's nothing more to say. We don't have time to linger on the past, anyway. We need to deal with the here and now."

"The Colonel's right," said Potteiger. "Let's get to it. The way I see it, we should get as much distance as we can and still be able to observe when they light this cake. That means the west range—Ibapah Peak. Agreed?"

Rain didn't answer. He felt as though he was in a room with two strangers.

"Command Sergeant Major. I expect an answer when I ask you a question."

"What was that, sir?"

"I want your opinion on the best point of observation for us. If something goes wrong—I've got a family to think about. I want to be far away. But we still need to view the operation. West range best, right?"

After a lengthy pause, Rain mumbled, "The west range. Right."

"Somerdale!"

"Yes, sir. Sorry, sir."

"How about Ibapah?"

Rain struggled to focus. Potteiger ignored the implications of Connie's behavior. Connie acted as though he owed Rain no explanation. Were they right? Had he overreacted? "That might be okay. Maybe something slightly to the north."

"It's tough sledding up there," said Connie. "Vehicles can only go so far. Can Bob and Jerry manage?"

"They both want to be here. This has been their home a long time. We'll leave plenty of time and take it slow. I could use a good hike." Potteiger said to Rain, "Looks to me like you could too, Somerdale."

Rain didn't respond. What would Mira say if she was here? Am I supposed to just let this matter go? He was a soldier. These men were his superiors.

"Sergeant Major," Potteiger barked. "I told you to acknowledge me when I speak to you."

"What? I'm sorry, sir. What was that?"

"Never mind. I don't need you to tell me. You need some fresh air and exercise. North of Ibapah Peak it is. We'll finish here and coordinate with the others."

"Sounds good to me," said Connie. "I'm tired of being cooped up."

A VANTAGE

"So that's it then? You've got nothing to say about going dark on me?" Rain huffed from the climb, but not as much as the four other men with him, especially Bob and Jerry.

"I had nothing else to say." Connie was in impressive shape for a man approaching retirement. "You had your assessment; I told you mine."

They followed the trail, if one might call it that, a while longer in silence. It stretched along the western side of the range, a rather lengthy drive to the point at which they'd taken to foot. The path seemed as much vertical as it was long. Jerry and Bob were in no shape for this. Each man carried his own gear and water. Rain offered to carry both of theirs, but neither man allowed him. Rain made sure they took frequent breaks on the steep climb and kept well hydrated.

About three quarters of the way, the five men found boulders to perch themselves, give their feet a rest, and break out their canteens. "Your glass artwork, Rain," asked Connie. "All squared away with it?"

"Yeah, I shipped the good pieces along with my library and a few lamps to my family's compound. Alaska. I don't have much else I care about, so I left it in the townhouse."

"Might be awhile until they let you come back, you know," Jerry managed to gasp. Sweat streamed and the man's face flushed. He poured some of his water over his head. "Where are you going? You know, after?"

"If you want, I can get you assigned to Aberdeen," Connie offered.

The sense of betrayal lingered in the form of a tightened throat and heat at his temples. "I suppose."

He lost track of how long it took them to reach the summit. But reach it they did. Rain worried about Jerry and Bob and the hike back. Nevertheless, now the five men stood together in a row on the ridge ten miles to the west of the place where Roberts died. Where it all started. It felt a lifetime ago. Rain gazed through high-powered binoculars. Even from this distance, he could see the crews had already removed the drill equipment. The last few of the containment tents were being disassembled by crane and helicopter.

Thick cable bundles, some containing over 250 separate feeds, snaked their ways from each of the shafts to the equipment bunkers. To Rain it looked like the valley suffered from varicose veins. He counted a couple of dozen hazmat-suited figures who shuttled around the expansive field. It wouldn't be long now.

With the tents and equipment gone, the desert surface was a desolate gray wasteland. It wasn't like the surface of the moon—that would be far more interesting, with craters and rocks strewn hither and tither. This was like large swaths of desert had been erased. There was nothing on the valley floor. The sight unsettled him.

Potteiger dropped his binoculars to his chest and glanced at Rain. A few moments later, Rain spoke. "Your wife and kids, sir. They're good?"

"They're at her mother's place. San Diego. Thanks for asking." Potteiger's cell phone, its ring tone the intrusive one of the old-fashioned rotary-style, broke the moment. Potteiger answered and listened for a short time. "Roger that." To the four other men, he said, "It's time."

"Are you sure we're safe up here?" Jerry gulped and his eyes darted back and forth from man to man.

"There's a whole lot more people a lot closer than we are right now." Potteiger's manner was sure and soothing. "If what they said is true, it won't be much to see. They say maybe we'll see some craters form. They called them subsidence craters, or some such. Maybe it will be immediate, maybe it will take a while."

"We'll feel and hear it, sure enough," said Rain. "Better gear up."

"I think I want a transfer," said Jerry.

"I don't think we have a choice now," said Harrison.

"Shut up." Potteiger played. It was an unsuccessful attempt to lighten the mood. Nevertheless, they snickered as they augmented their protective clothes with earplugs and a lead-lined outer layer.

Rain efficiently got himself ready. Next, he checked the other men.

Connie required no help. But Rain approached him, anyway. Connie placed his binoculars to his eyes and viewed the operation below. "I guess it doesn't much matter now," he whispered. "I didn't put it together until Mira said something. But this whole mess is my fault." Tears welled in Connie's eyes and his voice cracked. "I didn't know how to deal with that, Rain."

"You signed that summary, and the coordinates were wrong. You had to know."

Connie flared. His voice remained hushed, but now his words and gestures were animated, wild. "You don't understand how things were back then. It's a lot different now. Better. Back then, everything we did was under suspicion. You remember the VX gas leak, the sheep kill?"

"Of course."

"There were other mishaps. Some worse. Everything we did was under so much scrutiny. Mistakes were not tolerated. The disposal didn't end in the predetermined area. But it was remote. The contents were autoclaved and properly treated. But there was no known danger in that case. It was easier and more cost effective to just let it be. Nobody could have predicted this..."

Rain looked at Connie who did not meet his gaze. His heart broke with disappointment. "You're the one who removed the records from the archive? To cover your mistake?"

Connie looked up, a guilt-laden apology in his eyes, but not on his lips. He put in his earplugs and put his headgear back on.

Rain stared at the man for a moment. His gut knotted.

Potteiger came over. "Here we go."

Rain turned away and walked to the other side of the ridge. He spied the Humvee, far below near the base of the butte.

Jerry called to him. "You're going to miss it, Rain."

"Yeah," he said as he sat on a boulder and put on his headgear.

GENERAL MARCUS DROPPED his binoculars to hang from his neck and caught the eyes of General Thompson to his immediate right. He was about to signal when his cell phone rang. He did not recognize the caller, but recognized the number as a government phone.

"Marcus," he barked.

"*It's Higgins. I haven't yet been able to reach the President. We've had a development. I'm calling to ask you to suspend the order to proceed, sir.*"

"I'm sorry, Brigadier General, it's a little late for that."

"*We've made an important breakthrough. One that may lead to a viable solution.*"

Marcus frowned as he noticed the other leaders looking at him. "You have something ready to go now?"

Higgins dreaded the question and had gone through the answer in her head a dozen times. "*No, sir. There are some technical hurdles ahead, the challenges of production and application. But we will handle those. We demonstrated success in the bioremediation of SONA in the laboratory. We can certainly surmount these last few barriers.*"

"That's good, Higgins. But it changes nothing. You should see the desert here. It's like a different planet. I'm sorry. I am. But there's no more time."

"General, please. Dr. Wallace just left my office. I can get her back to explain—"

"Not necessary. Thank you for your efforts, General. I'll see you in D.C." He ended the call and replaced his phone to his belt. He retrieved his binoculars and scanned the desert one last time. His phone rang again. He didn't answer this time; rather he tipped his helmeted head forward.

Thompson radioed the final warning and reports came back from the bunkers and observation posts. One by one, they all reported ready. "That was the last one," said Thompson.

Marcus commanded, "Go."

The assignment of the trigger person had been a matter of considerable discussion. A few viewed it as an honor to be vied for; most the opposite. In the end they concluded it best not to delegate. It was Vice President of the United States Margot Pinkerton who said a silent prayer to herself and depressed the black button.

In less than half a second it was all over.

A BLAST

Almost 2000 feet down the shaft nearest to the main SONA formation, the first ADM ignited.

It was a miniaturized version of a fission/fusion hybrid design, often referred to as thermonuclear and colloquially as an H-bomb. The full-sized version of this particular design yielded more than 10 megatons. This skinny version—less than a meter in diameter, yielded a little over 200 kilotons. Fifty times smaller, it was still an order of magnitude more powerful than the bomb that demolished Nagasaki and helped bring the Second World War to a sudden end.

The stage one fission reaction ignited first. That implosion sent intense X-rays into the lead and uranium-238 tamper. As this shell burned away, it exerted tremendous pressure on the lithium deuterate fuel core, compressing the gas volume to one thirtieth its original size. The compression shock waves triggered fission in the hollow plutonium-239 rod in the center of the device. Radiation, heat, and an intense spray of neutrons drove into the compressed lithium deuterate fuel. Neutrons combined with the lithium and formed tritium. Tritium combined with deuterium as did deuterium with other deuterium molecules. This fusion reaction was the main source of the explosive power. It gave off tremendous energy without forming radioactive byproducts with lengthy half-lives. As this concentrated energy expanded, the enclosing vessel ruptured and the whole assembly exploded. These processes were done before the first microsecond was half over.

Around this time, all the other devices triggered too. Some were the same, others differed with various fuels and designs. But they all resulted in massive energetic bursts. During the second half of the first microsecond, these energies transferred into and through the subterranean environment.

Over the next few milliseconds, the rock that surrounded the explosion epicenters superheated and vaporized. Twenty-seven bubbles of gas and steam, with temperatures measured in millions of degrees and pressures greater than several million atmospheres, created melt cavities 30 to 200 meters in diameter. As planned, the melt cavities intersected the SONA formation. At those junctures, the energy propagated into and throughout the SONA concentrations.

The heat and force were presupposed to break the molecular bonds that held SONA together. And that's what happened. Mostly.

It did something else too. It ignited SONA's concentrated-carbon byproduct. Though not purified as Quon had done in the laboratory, it still contained explosive power roughly 400 times that of TNT. When the force of 27 nuclear explosions blasted into this material, a second—unexpected—reaction occurred.

It was an explosion that made those of the ADM array seem like firecrackers.

THE MEN on the ridge saw none of it. Before their minds could register anything, the flash burned through eye protection and retinas. Disoriented, in the half second it took for the shock wave to hit them, they sensed something had gone terribly wrong. When the concussive heat reached them, none remained conscious to consider what that could have been.

The hydrodynamic front, propelled by an explosion terrestrially rivaled in force only by the Earth's all-time largest volcanic eruptions and meteor impacts, raced outward faster than the speed of sound.

The wave swept out over the equipment bunkers and crushed and melted the concrete, lead, and steel and reduced them to rubble. The people inside had no conscious perception of what happened. Their bodies were incinerated faster than the speed of their thoughts.

Destruction continued outward to the safety perimeter. The personnel who observed from there, among them the entire Advisory Panel, a significant contingent from the Army Corps of Engineers—including Colonel Ramon, Yolanda and Tricia, numerous scientists and technicians, also never knew what hit them. Along with Generals Marcus and Thompson and Vice President Pinkerton were no few additional senior government officials, Aaron Moore, Director Cambridge, Secretary Agnew, Secretary Gallagher, Secretary Vega, Governor Hauser, and EPA Administrator Steve Pabst—accompanied by many of their staffs. The protective gear every single person on site donned in precaution was useless. Their bodies vaporized.

Eleanor Dixon was among them. Her last thought, a prayer to God.

DPG sat empty save for the security personnel who guarded the gates and a cadre of emergency responders. Those soldiers barely had time to flinch. They perceived something had gone awry as they died. Buildings throughout the base crumbled under shock waves.

The blast zone continued its rapid expansion, propelled by a force equivalent to the explosion of a gigaton of TNT. Anything combustible anywhere on Dugway Proving Ground ignited. Blast effects, in essence a raging inferno, raced out over the valley. It slammed into the tiny evacuated village of Terra to the east and set every modest dwelling there ablaze. Fiery force splashed against the base of the Dugway mountain range, which stopped its spread further east into the populated Rush Valley. The Cedar Mountain range did the same thing on the western side.

The explosion was thus refocused along a north-south axis. It covered almost entirely the Utah Test and Training Range 13 miles to the north. Windows on the cars and trucks bound in both directions on I-80 shattered and a dozen or so motor vehicles crashed. The damaging effects also shot south and southwest into the salt flat wilderness. Since the entire valley was off limits, nobody was in that direction, only the sparse vegetation and natural wildlife of the area. All of it was crushed and burned.

A SHOCK

As Higgins tried to reach the President, Mira sat in the General's office and texted Eleanor, then Rain. Neither responded. After a few minutes, Mira said: "General, I'm sorry. I really need to get back to the lab. I don't even know any of the details yet. With your permission—"

"Go," Higgins said. "I'll keep trying. I'll talk to Marcus. But I might need you to explain, so be available, okay?"

"Okay." Mira rushed out. On the way to the lab, her head felt light. The next thing she knew, she opened her eyes to see recessed ceiling lights. Disoriented, she said, "Where am I?"

The unfamiliar but kind and caring face of a young woman bent over her. "I think you fainted, ma'am. How are you feeling?"

Mira blinked and shook her head. "I've got to get to BSL-4 containment."

"Why don't we work on sitting you upright first," the woman said. "I got you some water. Here, let me help you up." The woman did so as Mira discovered she'd been laid on a sofa in a break room. Her head swam, and she fought a wave of dizziness and nausea. The woman must have noticed. "I think we need to get you to the infirmary, ma'am. I'll call for transport."

Mira struggled through the mental haze. "That's not needed. Please, may I have that water?"

"Of course."

Mira gulped it, previously unaware of just how profound her thirst had truly been. "Refill?"

"Sure, just sit tight." She turned and went to the sink across the room. Mira struggled, unsteady, to her feet. She was out the door as the woman called after her, "Ma'am? Wait!"

SHE FOUND JEFF AND RANDY, their faces slack, unreadable, glued to one of the monitors. "What's going on?" No response. "What's the microbial species?" Again, no response. "Why aren't you working?"

She moved closer and reconnected her air-hose. "Where's Ji?" Still, neither Jeff nor Randy acknowledged her. They watched the screen, spellbound. Displayed there was not the data Mira expected, but a news broadcast.

There was no sound other than the whoosh of the lab's forced air system. She looked at the screen and read the closed captions as they scrolled. Bit by bit, the gist of the report sank in. A catastrophic event. An explosion of some kind. Utah. The broadcast didn't say, but she knew the story—SONA. More accurately, the demolition of the SONA formation. She sank as she realized their discovery had come too late. Higgins either didn't get through or she'd been ignored—the demolition went ahead, anyway.

But this wasn't right. There wasn't supposed to be a national news story. Something had gone terribly wrong. She joined Jeff and Randy in stunned silence.

Though reports got the location right, they were rife with misinformation and, as far as Mira was concerned, irresponsible speculation. One "expert" interviewee claimed a meteor impact. Another postulated detonation of an experimental doomsday-type weapon. Yet another implied the United States had been attacked by one of its nuclear adversaries, China most likely, and World War Three had begun. The broadcast cut back to the second "expert," who argued the Dugway Proving Ground, the likely epicenter of the blast, was an experimental facility, not a strategic target and consequently, the explosion was therefore accidental, the result of an ill-fated weapons test by the U.S. Military.

Interruptions of power and communication services were reported throughout large swaths of the western United States. No official reports issued from the Dugway Proving Grounds environs or even from Salt Lake City.

The Administration's Press Secretary was ill-prepared. She did not confirm or deny any of the speculation. All she could substantially do was confirm the President would address the issue sometime later that evening.

Rain! Eleanor! Mira froze in fear for them, and then the others she knew to be at DPG. Her throat closed and waves of nausea wracked her frame.

"They did it, anyway." Jeff's face was ashen. "They didn't listen to you, Mira. What happened?"

Nobody expected it would really come to this. She considered the matter for a long while. The demolition was supposed to be controlled. The deliberations of the experts she'd heard suggested little of the incineration would be visible. Her thoughts drifted to her interactions with Quon. His strange talk during their last encounter. He planned something. The state of his company. Quon had blown up the lab. The realization struck like a physical blow.

"SONA itself combusted. That's why the blast was so big." Her mind raced as she thought out loud. "Quon knew this would happen. To be fair, he argued against the incineration. But he never warned them of this. He didn't want anyone else to know what he knew. He wants to use SONA for himself." She unhooked her air-hose.

"Now where, Mira?" Jeff said, shaken.

"Can I help with something?" Randy said, confused.

She didn't answer. She rushed to the exit as her temper flared. She calmed herself by following the containment exit procedure properly but rapidly. Dripping wet, she rushed back to Higgins' office.

THE GENERAL HAD LEFT. Mira demanded of her Administrative Assistant, "When will she be back?"

"She rushed out. She didn't say anything." His stoic manner was different. He was wide-eyed and worried as he nervously stapled and filed reports. "There was talk among the agencies of an emergency meeting of the leadership."

"I'll wait." She collapsed onto a thick leather chair in the waiting area. Her thoughts swirled. She tried Rain's phone. The response was the annoying call fail signal followed by the robotic voice: *Your call cannot be completed as dialed.*

Her fingers trembled as she texted Kyle. *You ok?* That message indicated undeliverable. Maybe he was okay. Maybe. Her spirit fell. Her anger receded, elbowed aside by a fear she couldn't deny or banish. She fingered her bracelet.

"You heard the news, then." By the way Higgins' AA's voice and lip trembled, he was as upset as she.

Mira nodded.

"Do you have any idea what happened?"

"I can't say."

He started, stopped, then spoke. "The General. I've never seen her like that."

"I bet."

"She threw things. Broke things. What is happening, Dr. Wallace?"

"I don't know."

He hung his head. Time stretched as they both fidgeted with their fingers. Mira supposed he fought his fear the same as her.

"My wife is pregnant."

"Congratulations." Mira could manage none of the requisite enthusiasm.

"Do you think? Is this the time to have a baby? What if this really is nuclear war?"

"It's not."

Mira dozed off in her chair. The next thing she perceived was someone gently shaking her shoulder. She turned. It was General Higgins. "Dr. Wallace, you're not well. This week's work, you've over-done it."

Mira felt as though lead blankets were laid on her body. She struggled to straighten. "General, listen. I've got to tell you something."

"I'm supposed to be at the White House in—" she looked at her watch. "I'm late already. Can it wait?"

"No." She looked at the AA who returned a silent plea. "Just a quick word in your office?"

"I apologize for the shape of things in here," Higgins said as they went in. The desk was the only tidy surface in the room. Everything normally on it was somewhere on the office floor. Books littered the office floor. Mira stared at the gaps on the shelves. There were gashes in the drywall. An expensive floor lamp lay on its side, the porcelain of its body cracked.

"Your office looks like how I feel," Mira said. The two women looked at one another. Mira recalled the reason she'd stormed here. "The disaster—it was SONA itself that combusted. That's what went wrong with Quon's experiments. He knew this would happen."

"That's a serious charge, Mira. You're sure?"

"I am."

"I need more than that. I'm sure you can understand."

"Quon focused on the energetic studies. He insisted he work in relative isolation; he allowed one assistant when protocol required a team. The explosion in the lab—it had to do with SONA. To my knowledge, he never provided reports to the team. Shall I go on?"

"And now you think there's something I should do about it?"

The response caught Mira off guard. "If not you, who?"

Higgins grasped the door handle, about to leave. "My next meeting includes the President. I'm in no position to make any accusation, but I will pass the information along. Fair?"

"I just wanted to make sure you knew."

"I appreciate that, Mira. I'd also appreciate it if you would go get some rest." She opened the door and hurried out.

AN ANNOUNCEMENT

Measured as a percentage of the population, viewership ratings doubled Neil Armstrong's first step onto the surface of the Moon. Over three billion people—more than a third of the people on the planet—were glued to a video screen of one sort or another. Some did so by themselves, viewing their personal devices, either at their places of work, holed up in an apartment, or a room in a house either too-empty or too-full. Many more were gathered in groups—family, friends, and strangers—and conjectured about what the President of the United States of America might say. In Times Square and other cities around the world, throngs pushed shoulder-to-shoulder to experience the broadcast.

After a few blessed hours of sleep, Mira joined Randy and Jeff along with many others who worked at Ft. Detrick in a large auditorium to watch the broadcast together. Chatter in the room abated as the President took the podium at 9 pm EST sharp.

"My fellow Americans, and my friends around the world, I come before you in this time of crisis and mourning with news both tragic and hopeful. It will be difficult to hear. We experienced an unprecedented cataclysm. This was not a meteor or a volcano, as has been speculated. It was also not a test gone wrong of some fictional Doomsday device. America has never and will never develop such weapons.

"It was also not a nuclear test gone awry, at least not in the way many are speculating. Yes, nuclear devices were involved—"

Shocked mumblings and outbursts swept through the rows in the auditorium. Mira shifted in her seat to gauge reactions as the others returned their attention to the President.

"This explosion was a result of an effort to control a previously unknown threat. Somehow, this substance, about which we will talk more in a moment, tragically ignited and exploded in a way our scientists could not predict.

"Many of the heroes who undertook this perilous remediation were tragically caught in this terrible disaster. That included dedicated people who had given their lives to public service, people who were invaluable to our nation and to me personally, and who conducted themselves in an exemplary and distinguished manner. Their loss is nothing less than a national tragedy. Three days from now, I will come before you again in a nationwide remembrance in order to honor these good people, among whom were members of my Cabinet, including Vice President Pinkerton—"

Another wave of shocked mumbles erupted around Jeff and Mira. Her worry spiked. Rain? Kyle? Eleanor? Potteiger? Connie? Were they all lost? The President continued to speak, and the murmur died.

"Other good public servants, perhaps not as well known to you as our Vice President but certainly known and valued by me and many others, were lost too. My thoughts and prayers go out tonight to their loved ones and to the communities directly affected by this disaster.

"Now, it is difficult to talk about a silver lining in such a dark cloud. But my friends, there is one. While we lost almost three hundred precious souls: scientists, the security team, first responders, and public servants in my Administration, the United States Army, and the State of Utah—we especially send condolences and support to those folks who lost their terrific Governor Hauser and members of his support staff—these talented people had the good sense to evacuate the surrounding area before they took this action. Had they not done so, the losses would be far worse."

More reactions peppered the crowd. Mira hung on every word the President said.

"Damages as a direct result of the blast were primarily to the military property on the U.S. Army's Proving Ground at Dugway. There was damage to the sparse private properties in that vicinity. But the populated areas to the east, including Salt Lake City and its surrounding communities, were protected by the mountain range between them and the epicenter of the explosion.

"Aftershocks did, however, cause considerable damage to those areas. Some of the earthquakes were quite destructive. I regret to tell you many people were hurt in building collapses and other secondary calamities. More people, at this time we don't know how many, have died in these disasters too. The good people of that area continue to need our prayers and our help. They don't have power, and many homes, even if they still stand, are nevertheless too damaged for the homeowners to continue to safely live there. I have dispatched FEMA and the National Guard to assist them. More help is arriving to help afflicted communities by the hour.

"Earthquakes have also been reported as far away as Las Vegas, Boise, Albuquerque, and Denver. First responders are also busy there and we will send support wherever it is needed.

"Some have expressed fear about the risk of exposure to radioactive debris. Investigators are working on this, but they assure me there is every reason to believe that such fears are unfounded. While it is true radiation levels in the disaster zone have risen, it is only by a little. I'm told it's like having a couple of extra chest x-rays over the course of your lifetime. Again, I must stress this was not a nuclear test. It was something else. And that means, as bad as the things I have just outlined are, we face bigger difficulties ahead, my friends.

"The explosion made a large cloud of dust. It covers the region. The cloud is growing and it will move. This will result in additional difficulties. We'll see changing weather patterns. We'll see crop failures in the American mid-west that provides food to the nation and the world. I am continuing conversations with the appropriate leaders to form a cooperative approach to food production and distribution. It's going to be hard—very hard. But if we can foster a *spirit of cooperation and togetherness, we can minimize the hardship."*

The crowd's reaction was more than murmurs. Some used their phones to text or call people. Mira couldn't hear the next few sentences the President said.

"...when markets reopen. More announcements about financial matters will come over the next few days. We will stabilize trade so that the damaging effects of this tragedy do not multiply.

"Now to the good news I can report. There are indications that they achieved their objective. The original threat has been mitigated. And it may be difficult to understand, but this was far more dangerous. To explain further, I would like to invite Dr. Wesley Quon, one of the great scientists who has worked to contain the threat, to speak to you. You know him as one of the world's leading innovators. He identified the new life-form that has caused this problem. Dr. Quon?"

Mira's jaw dropped. Quon joined the President in his gliding manner. He still wore gauze bandage wraps amid his otherwise perfectly styled hair. He stepped up to the podium in the White House Briefing Room as the President stepped aside to make space for him. Gone was his customary smile. In its place was a grave tone.

"Thank you very much Mr. President. Not for this invitation, but for your courageous leadership in this moment of crisis." Quon gazed into the camera and paused for dramatic effect. *"I have firsthand knowledge of the events leading to this cataclysm. Frankly, I hoped to avoid this course of action, but that is not how it happened. Anyway, I can tell you the danger has been eliminated. The President invited me here to give you a detailed explanation. He feels you deserve that.*

"Ladies and gentlemen, a mysterious and toxic agent spontaneously appeared in the area surrounding the Dugway Proving Grounds. I named this substance SONA, an acronym for Sudden Onset Necrosis Agent. It was very aggressive and very dangerous. Every living thing that has come into direct contact with it has not survived the encounter—plants, animals, birds," he paused, *"...people, even microbes in the soil and in the air. It had been spreading at an*

alarming rate and we can thankfully only speculate now about how far that reach may have been had we not successfully acted.

"I led a team of our best scientists to not merely understand what it was and where it came from, but also stop its spread and keep it from escaping the region. That would have been a much bigger problem, I assure you. In that research, we gained important information. Innovations will result from these discoveries. The most profound revelation we can take from SONA is due to it being an entirely new form of life. The implications of this are far reaching."

Mira reddened. She wanted to storm to the White House right then and there. But she remained in her seat. And she continued to listen. And steam.

"One of the longest and deepest debates that has pitted scholars of science against scholars of religion is the matter of the facts regarding the origin of life. The discovery of SONA puts the issue to a final rest. All life on our planet, from the most primitive microorganisms to advanced species such as Homo sapiens—you and me—evolved from a common ancestor that emerged over four billion years ago. Thus, we are ultimately all related in a very fundamental way. We use the same chemical building blocks to grow and function, the same genetic code that came into existence at the beginning. Up to now, there has been no definitive answer as to how this happened. But because of the appearance of SONA, there is. We now know life does begin spontaneously. This means we are very likely to find other life-forms as we increase our capacities to explore other worlds that circle the stars all around us. It means life is an innate feature of the Universe. It also means stories of a Creator, while perhaps comforting, are in fact no more than mere myth."

The crowd around Mira sat in stunned silence. The President moved in and uncomfortably excused Quon from the podium. He made further remarks along the lines of thanking Dr. Quon as he smoothed over what Quon suggested. Mira didn't listen. She was already on her way out. Jeff jogged to catch her.

"Higgins didn't talk to the President, obviously." Mira seethed.

384 | TOM DARDICK & CHRIS DARDICK, PH.D.

"We can't just let him get away with this, Jeff. We have to do something." Jeff's grin contrasted with her scowl. She noticed. "How can you be amused at a time like this?"

"You're a scientist."

Perturbed by his cheer, she spat, "So?"

"So, do what scientists do." Mira faced him. He smiled despite her scowl. Her eyes narrowed as confusion sprinkled her anger. Jeff remained undaunted. "Publish."

EXCERPT:
THE NECESSITY OF PRECURSOR COOPERATIVES

Wallace, M. D.[1,2] and Weingartner, J. A.[1]

1*University of California, Berkeley, Dept. of Plant and Microbial Biology, 311 Koshland Hall, Berkeley CA, 94720.*

2*National Interagency Biodefense Campus, Fort Detrick, MD 21702*

Section #3: Strategy, cont.

The consolidation of a genetic code along with the formation of discrete entities engendered the final, and most critical property. Competition for energy and food among the individual entities or 'cells,' each of which were slightly different, became a driving force. Some were less competitive than others. They, and the uniqueness of their makeup, went extinct. Others accumulated changes that permitted them to grow in new environments—free from competition. Others formed chemical weapons to kill competitors.

This process was driven, in part, by spontaneous variations in the strings of nucleic acids; mistakes of sorts that occurred during the DNA copying processes. These mistakes led to small differences in the proteins they encoded. Sometimes, the mistakes were detrimental. But in rare cases they begat new properties, such as tolerance to saltier conditions, or the ability to withstand colder temperatures. This imperfection would become an enduring property that enabled the entities to adapt and change.

Millions of new kinds of relationships arose. Some lived off of each other in mutualistic or parasitic relationships. Others became predatory. They lost the ability to capture their own energy from the sun and used that of other cellular systems.

Just like the interactions among the various chemicals at its very inception, these complex relationships between the new types of entities were cooperative, leading to the formation of entire ecosystems that were more stable than any single entity could ever manage alone. It was from this moment that natural selection drove the collective into millions of different sizes, shapes, and forms that could adapt to the harshest of environments. Within an unfathomably vast and lonely universe, companionship emerged, and with it eventually came love between its children.

A COINCIDENCE

To Jeff's and Mira's surprise, Ji and Randy awaited them in the analytics lab. The screens were now complete, and the next phase was to interpret the results. Randy had taken upon himself to transfer the voluminous data files so that they didn't have to continue to work in containment. Though this was Jeff and Mira's area of expertise, they were both thankful. "Randy, you didn't have to do that. You need rest just as much as any of us."

"I can't rest until I see what we found."

Mira smiled at him and turned to Ji. "Where were you, Ji?"

"I work here, with you, now on?"

It amused her; a welcome relief. "I'd like that. Did you tell Dr. Quon?"

"Send note. Not care what Boss say."

"I'll see what can be done."

Mira and Jeff sat at adjoining stations. "You want to stay, Ji? We need to run more computational tools to analyze the sequence data from the surviving samples."

Ji nodded, but his words said something else. "Very tired."

"Yes. I know." Mira hadn't even considered the time, but it was now almost 2300 hours. She'd planned to call Kyle an hour ago. They'd texted and arranged to talk. She was relieved he had left before the disaster. But she'd also been too preoccupied to find out the details. She couldn't rectify that now. Tomorrow. "Jeff, how many surviving samples did we detect?"

"Only two out of 1.74 billion."

"What are the IDs? Are those two the same or different?"

Jeff typed a command script into the prompt and two numbered IDs appeared in a column. "Awesome. They're the same. It's statistically impossible to pick up the same thing twice by random chance in a library this size."

Mira didn't respond, fixated on something. She whispered in disbelief, "Jeff, cross check the reference number against our catalog. Does this sample have a name?"

Jeff found the ID. His face flushed. He double-checked, and checked a third time. "I don't believe it! If this is some kind of prank, it's not funny, Mira."

"What is it?" asked Randy. "Nobody's playing tricks at a time like this."

"Then it must be an error." Jeff looked Mira straight in the eyes. "*Primum viverea.*"

Mira knew the answer before he spoke. "How could this be?" she whispered. Mira's life played in her head like a choppy montage in a black and white art film. Her ten-year-old self, running along a stream, the pinch of a hellgrammite on her toe, cutting her foot on a sharp rock. A cold bowl of thin chicken celery soup served by a colder grandmother. Now a young woman, sitting in a biology laboratory late at night, refusing to accompany her classmates to a party. A bout with heatstroke in the Death Valley desert. Curled and freezing, calculating the odds of everyone surviving the frigid, sun-drenched Antarctic night if the generator didn't come back on. Trusty Jeff smiling at her when she told him he was hired. Kyle's big hurts-so-good bear hug. Rain's tanned, smiling face as he introduced himself. The DNA map for *Primum viverea.* Eleanor mouthing the words in slow motion, "He sent you, didn't He?"

She fought to make sense of it all. The result and her earlier hopes were not within the realm of the rational. The odds of *Primum viverea* being the oldest surviving life-form, one that had persisted through billions of years of radical environmental change, just to be discovered and identified now as the one biocontrol solution for

SONA were incalculable. The voices around her faded as she recognized the irony that her discovery had come too late.

"Mira, please help me here." The quaver of Jeff's voice revealed he had the same struggle as she to process it all. "How can this be?"

Randy's brow knitted in confused frustration. "What are you guys talking about?"

"We believe this is the First Common Ancestor, Randy," said Jeff.

"Yes, I remember you talking about it. What I don't know is why that is making you guys act so weird." Randy scratched his scalp. His lips widened to a grin as he saw the implications.

"*Primum viverea* is nearly as old as the Earth itself," Mira mused in response. "We collected it in the uppermost atmosphere, where it is exposed to high levels of ultra violet radiation. Of course, UV damages DNA."

"Like water purification systems," said Randy.

"Yes. It'd mean *Primum viverea* needs to be extremely resistant to DNA damage or editing. It just like you said Jeff. It would have to be incredibly resilient to survive up there all this time. It must have DNA repair mechanisms to cope with the constant UV damage. That must be why it's resistant to the DNA editing effects of SONA. And it also requires the ability to metabolize lots of different carbon compounds because food in its environment is extremely limited. It can probably eat almost anything."

"That would explain why it can break SONA down," offered Jeff.

Jeff and Randy talked over each other as they raised questions and offered explanations. To Mira, their words faded away as she unclasped her bracelet and gently rested it across her palm. She stared at the glinting metal and sparkling jewels.

Essentially, the gems that comprised the charms were no more than simple chemicals. Just like the amino acids they represented. But the combinations of those building blocks provided the blueprints for uncountable life-forms. The genius of the system that provided for all of that was beyond reckon.

The bracelet had a purpose beyond the symbolic. She now recognized how attached she was to it emotionally. She also used the token to communicate, to teach, to help people see the majesty of Life.

Her eyes welled and her cheeks grew hot. The enormity of the moment—a product of countless threads, each one explainable and readily understood, but connected in incomprehensible ways washed over her. The bracelet was only one such thread. As was her family lineage. Her career track, yet another. Sever a single strand and the fabric of her life would unravel. Mira's mind unfurled with awareness beyond her ability to explain. She could merely feel it and know it to be true. Eleanor's words echoed again, "He sent you, didn't He?"

She pulled out Eleanor's crucifix. She caressed it and examined it. Simplicity. She looked back at her bracelet. Complexity. An image of the tattoo on Rain's arm filled her mind. She was left with a single thought—the pathways of her life's experiences were as varied and magnificent as the life-forms she'd always admired. She clasped the bracelet to her wrist. And clutched the crucifix in the same hand. But why? Why had the solution come too late? Her thoughts turned once again to Rain, Eleanor, and the others. Her eyes welled with tears. What had become of them? Her limbs felt numb. It was an emotional pain she had not felt since her parents died. A pain she recognized in the eyes of Randy's five-year-old son. A pain she had steeled herself against. The emotional dam Mira had created as a child burst open. At that, her sorrow gave way to another long-suppressed emotion. She gripped the cross so tightly its blunt nails cut into her palm.

A SURVIVOR

W hen the strands of his consciousness re-knit, Rain's first thoughts were for his colleagues. He opened his eyelids, but all he could see were blurry shapes of dark gray. He tried to stand, but his legs wouldn't work, either. He pushed himself to his knees. Shooting pain throughout his entire lower body was his reward. He fell back onto his stomach.

He rolled over onto his back and explored his torso with aching fingers. Wherever he touched, it hurt. Burns, bruising, maybe some bleeding. Suit intact? He reached for his headgear. No holes. He worked his way to his shoulders and arms. Everything intact. All ten fingers worked, though they responded as though he'd stacked hot, heavy rocks for hours. He returned his attention to his torso. Though every touch on his chest and abs was agony, he found no gaping wounds. From what he could tell, his back was a different story. So were his legs. He found holes in the fabric of his suit, but couldn't stand to touch the skin of his legs and feet. He knew one thing, though. He was exposed.

He thought again about Harrison, Jerry, Potteiger, and Connie. "Colonel?" he tried to call. He had no voice. He tried again, "Connie?" Nothing but eerie silence. Ear protection. He wrestled the headgear off and removed the ear plugs. He could still hear absolutely nothing.

Rain tried to sit up, but that was too painful. All he could manage was to flop from his back to his stomach. He propped himself up on his elbows. The exertion and the contact with the rock hurt. But it was pain he could tolerate. "Connie? Can you hear me?"

A spike of relief energized him when he heard his voice, weak and raspy as it was, echo down the slope. He may have been blinded, but he could still hear. The feeling was short-lived, shoved aside by concern for his friends. He inched his way on his elbows as he dragged his torso and his useless legs up the slope in the direction of where they observed the detonation. He'd been maybe twenty feet from them. The slope of the ridge. Cover. The others didn't have such protection. Maybe they were unconscious. He reached around to find their bodies. Panic rose as he did so. But it didn't stop him. His lifetime of training kept him focused and active. He used his hands to explore the terrain along the line of the crest. Nothing but rocks.

"Commander?" Again, no responses. He rested for a moment. Every movement sent fresh waves of pain through his body. His exhaustion alarmed him more. He reasoned the shock wave could have thrown their bodies in the direction from which he had just crawled. It was the direction of their vehicle too. That meant water. And a way out, if he could call for help or drive blind. His fingers became his eyes. It was much easier to drag himself down the hill. To expand his search zone, he zigged and zagged as much as he dared, which wasn't much, because he did not dare lose his spatial orientation.

He reached out again and his fingers finally found something not rock. A sole. Laces. "Connie? Jerry?" Hope fueled his fingers as they gently followed the boot up the leg. Revulsion, fear, and despair seized him when he reached the end of the fabric—he had found half of one of his friends' legs. He recoiled, as much as possible on his belly. After a moment, his training again won out. He fought for calm, then resumed his situational assessment.

They were fully exposed to the force of the blast. What happened? The incineration wasn't supposed to be anything like that. Whatever it was, they faced the full force of an unthinkably massive explosion. Chances that any of them were still alive? Near zero.

Chances of him staying alive? Not much better. He estimated those odds, however remote, would improve dramatically if he could get himself to the Humvee. He pictured its location. It was the last thing he saw at the moment of the explosion. He was in that position because of Connie. It was why he hadn't been exposed to the full force of the blast. He thanked God at the same time he grieved for the loss of his friends. His prayer ended with a plea for strength. He would need that if he was to get himself down to the vehicle.

He crawled down the hill. They hiked a considerable distance for their vantage. It was all Jerry and Harrison had been able to manage. Their path hadn't been a straight line, either. And it had been along no established trail. He stopped crawling. This would take some doing.

What time of day was it? He had absolutely no idea. Rain focused on the skin of his face in an attempt to detect warmth from the sun. Nothing. There was no change in temperature, or the brightness of the blurry gray images, no matter which way he turned his neck. He concluded that it was nighttime.

He hoped to orient himself based upon the position of the sun. It would rise at some point. When it did, he'd know, at least in general terms, both the time of day and which direction was east. He had a decent mental picture of where he was at the moment, within, say, a ten-meter radius. But he was depleted. His muscles didn't work, his body was one big wound. Despair for what happened to not only his friends, but everyone in the entire area threatened to sap all of his remaining willpower. Maybe he should wait for the dawn. He found what he thought to be the boulder upon which he last sat and curled next to it. He prayed again for strength and guidance, and passed out shortly after he uttered 'amen.'

When he awoke, he again had no idea how long he'd slept or what time it was. He detected no change, no tactile evidence of sunlight. He faced a choice. Wait a few more hours for the sun so he could follow his plan, more hours where he'd continue to bleed, continue to thirst, and continue to lose energy; or set out now and take his chances. Resting longer would be a literal dead end. At least it was all downhill from here.

He reevaluated what remained of his vision. There were hints of brown and red in the gray blurs that filled his dark field of view. He turned his head to face the direction he believed led to the Humvee. He knew there were no cliffs between him and that place, but there were some big rocks and steep grades. He doubted he had the strength to manage with just his tired and aching arms and hands to propel him. But it was all he could do. He crawled forward.

Three hours later, Rain was again on the verge of passing out from the exertion and his internal injuries. The Humvee had to be around here somewhere. Where was the sun? It had to be over a day now. But it wasn't hot and there was no discernable direction for what little warmth he could sense. He expended the last of his energy as he groped around for the vehicle. He recalled Roberts' last words—*But...she needs me.* He lay motionless on the rocks, knowing the Humvee could be just outside his reach.

A NEW FUTURE

"He won't even look into the matter?" Mira fumed. She felt like tearing Higgins' office apart like the General herself had.

"Quon told the President he had adamantly warned General Marcus. He claimed he was disbelieved and ignored."

"But it's not true," Mira plead. "He never warned of a secondary explosion."

Higgins' appeared sympathetic to Mira, but there was an edge to her words, almost a scold. "You're not going to convince the President. Quon is trusted by this Administration. Neither you nor I have the ability to change that, especially since Marcus and the other senior leaders aren't around to contradict him."

Mira stared at Higgins in disbelief. "It's not right," she muttered at last.

Higgins was measured, businesslike. "You're dealing with Washington. Lots of things aren't right. I'm afraid you're going to have to accept this."

"I don't know if I can do that." Mira spun and left Higgins' office. Her mind did what made her most comfortable—focus on science. The enzyme that powered SONA not only catalyzed reactions with carbon molecules, it produced a high-energy carbon bond. That was what gave it the energy needed for DNA editing. A side effect was extreme volatility. The lab blew up for the same reason the catastrophe happened. Quon saw this early on. Everyone else saw peril; he saw something else. Opportunity? She didn't know what to do about it. She had no illusions—other senior officials would share Higgins' reaction. But he had to answer for this. Didn't he?

QUON SHIFTED, giddy with anticipation as the final test commenced. His head-wrap gone; his hair resumed its normal perfection.

"This had better be as good as you say, or we'll both be in jail." Marvin peered over Quon's right shoulder.

"Marvin, you worry too much."

"Maybe if we didn't have to lay off seventy percent of our workforce and file Chapter Eleven, I might worry less." Marvin's forehead glistened with perspiration.

In contrast, Quon's manner was a boy's with a pony on his tenth birthday. "Hush. Observe." They observed the technicians through the thick glass. The subject of this test, a fuel cell the size of a roll of quarters, would drive an electric motor on a suspension mount. The motor had been configured to drive a shaft connected to a dynamometer. It spun at a dizzying 15,000 rpm. "What you see here, Marvin, is a measurement of the power capacity of one of my new fuel cells. Think about what we can do with these. We can extend the range of drones. We can scale these cells down to give people devices they never have to charge, or scale them up for a radical performance improvement for GreenCars. We will not need the algae anymore - it will be revolutionary in any application that requires a power source."

"But how will we produce it at scale? This substance is too dangerous. We'll never get this approved." Marvin's skepticism didn't dampen Quon's enthusiasm.

"Maybe not by this government. There are others."

Marvin's eyes widened. "China?"

"That is my concern, not yours. Observe."

A large display showed the expected miles traveled for a typical vehicular configuration in average driving conditions. The motor ran faster than it would in practice to condense the duration of the test. It slowed and wound to an abrupt halt.

The meter read 442 kilometers.

"I may just be a finance guy, but that's pretty good, isn't it?"

"Yes, Marvin. It is. And I have not yet been able to develop and test my next innovation. We lack the required resources for that. It is not something we can sell to a consumer market, anyway. But do not worry; I spoke with some old family friends. Rest assured, there is much interest. And an ability to pay. Handsomely."

"What? Who?"

Quon put his hand on Marvin's shoulder. "It is best if you do not know."

Quon's phone rang. Mira. "Excuse me Marvin, I want to take this." He waited as Marvin walked away. "Dr. Wallace, to what do I owe this pleasant surprise?"

"Let's not pretend, Wes. I know what you're doing."

"If you had seen what I just have, my dear, I believe you would be excited."

"I don't think so."

"Suit yourself. But you will find it more rewarding on my good side."

"Is that supposed to be a threat?"

"Of course not. I want to remain allies. You and I both know SONA isn't gone. Some undoubtedly survived the blast. We can work together to prevent it from ever hurting anyone else."

"I can't do that. You're responsible for all of their deaths!"

"I do not know what you are talking about, Mira. Frankly, I am beginning to worry about you. We have all been through such trauma. Are you okay?"

"Don't play games with me. You're insane. I know you have it. It's far too dangerous. You must know this."

"Why, Mira, I am surprised by your attitude." Quon's smile widened. "After all, it was you who made all of it possible. You and

Primum viverea. Such impressive work. You do not know the benefits you have unlocked. I would prefer you participate in the fruits of these innovations. If you prefer otherwise, I suppose I will just have to live with it."

Even though it was just a voice connection, Mira's anger was palpable—short breaths, vitriolic words. *"I can't let you do this. You're abominable."*

Quon's smile vanished. "Abominable? No. I am courageous. Take a moment to reconsider, Mira. The innovations SONA can give us; the world will be a much better place. Climate change? Pollution? Sustainable food supply? They shall be concerns of the past. Near-unlimited battery life for every conceivable device. We need these things now, before it is too late. We can save humanity together. You could have near unlimited resources for your work. You would be instrumental in bringing about the next green revolution. We'll save billions of people who have not even been born yet."

"You're delusional. SONA is too dangerous."

"It is such a disappointment to hear you speak like this. It would be much better for you to have me as a friend. We have so much in common. We are both guided by science. We are not deluded by notions of God. We know we are responsible for making the world what it is."

Mira's voice grew cold. *"You and I have nothing in common. And I know you don't care about notions of God or a creator. What was all that nonsense about anyway?"*

Quon's smile returned. "Have you ever read Sun Tzu?"

"No."

"I have."

"I don't follow."

Quon measured his answer. "No? I am not surprised. I will just say this—one of the principles in *The Art of War* is to distract your enemy. Never let them know what you are really doing." He disconnected the call.

A REUNION

For nearly a week, Mira relentlessly tried to get an appointment to see Higgins. Not knowing what became of her friends and colleagues tormented her. The memory of Rain's kind eyes. The sound of Eleanor's soft southern accent. She appreciated the pressures on the General. They had to be enormous. The aftermath of the disaster was chaotic. Leaders in all sectors, public and private, were overwrought, even frantic. Pandemonium was a hair's breadth away. But still. "Not again," she said, jaw clenched, to Higgins' AA as she stopped by Higgins' office for the third time.

"I have barely seen her myself. This time she did leave some instructions for you." He found the note. "She moved your meeting. You need to report to the Barquist Health Clinic, Room 304, as soon as you can." Mira's frustration morphed to concern for Higgins' health.

"Is she okay?"

"As far as I know."

That was a relief.

MIRA WENT BACK to the lab and had Randy drive her to the clinic.

"Just text me when you want to be picked up," he offered, his voice full of sympathy.

She thanked him, jumped out of his Civic, and hurried to Room 304.

The door was ajar. She knocked lightly. "General?"

"Nobody in here with that pay grade," came the gravelly reply. "But please, come on in."

A bandaged man in a wheelchair faced away from her, toward the window. The hospital bed was freshly made and the room immaculate. The man grabbed the wheels and spun the chair around.

Mira gasped. "Rain!"

Tinted glasses obscured his eyes, but did not dampen his broad smile.

"Hi Mira. I'm glad to see you. Well, I don't see well, but you know what I mean."

Her eyes sparkled, and she beamed. She felt electric, like a power surge recharged her nervous system. The emotions were what? Relief, surely. Joy, yes. And others she couldn't name. She choked on her words, "Rain? I thought... How?"

"Turns out I'm kind of hard to get rid of. Remind you of anything?" She couldn't stop herself; she rushed over and hugged him. He winced, but his chuckle indicated he considered the pain worthwhile. "Easy, there. I've just come from a ringside seat to the biggest explosion of all time."

"Sorry." She released him. "I don't understand. I mean, I'm glad, but how?"

"Long story."

"I'm listening." She still beamed, but as she took in more of him, she perceived the price the experience exacted on his body. Her grin dimmed.

"Truth?" His left index finger pointed to his right triceps. "I had help."

Mira stared at the faded symbol on his arm. Not long ago, such a notion would seem at best naïve and at worst delusional. No longer. "Yeah? Look." She held up Eleanor's rustic crucifix.

"What is it? I can't see too much, you know."

"I'm sorry. That was thoughtless." She grabbed the lone chair and dragged it over to Rain, sat and leaned in. She dangled the necklace a few inches from his face.

"If I didn't know any better, Mira, it looks like you have a Cross there."

She pulled it back. "It doesn't mean I believe what you do." She paused a moment and considered the man in the wheelchair in front of her. "But I have come to appreciate it's good you believe." His cocked eyebrow revealed his surprise she had the crucifix. "Eleanor gave it to me." The sting of remorse hit her. Hard. Eleanor was...her friend. After a moment, she managed to speak again. "Did anyone else get out with you?"

He shook his head as his chin fell.

She knew Eleanor died with the others the President had specifically identified during his address. It felt surreal, like if it happened at all, it was long ago, remote, like a nightmare-inducing story. But now, with Rain here, the losses felt all too real. Tears flowed on her cheeks. Potteiger, Connie, the others. They were all gone. She reviewed her memories of each one. Many of the relationships had been professional. That didn't diminish her pain at all. Another name came to mind. "Gigi?"

"I don't know, Mira. She was Medevac'd to the University of Utah Hospital in Salt Lake City." Rain's lips constricted with sadness. "The plan was to complete a long series of operations, and when they could, revive her and relocate her. Ft. Hood is my guess. What the explosion has meant for all of that, I don't know."

Her emotions promised to overwhelm her. Hope and fear for Gigi, remorse for Eleanor, and the others. Elation that Rain was here. Sadness at his condition. "Oh, Rain. I'm so sorry. Your eyes, your legs."

He raised his head. His voice regained strength. "Docs say I have a good chance to walk again. I won't get back my eagle eyes, but I can make out faces. They say it should get better in time. All things considered; I'll take it."

"I'm still baffled by how it is you're here."

Rain explained. He emphasized the feelings of disorientation, thirst, exhaustion, and pain. Mira marveled at his strength of will. How would you crawl, bleeding, broken, and blind, down the side of a mountain? Especially given the trauma of the circumstances. There was one word she could use to describe his story. Miraculous.

Another wave of emotion arose. It watered her eyes and momentarily clouded her mind. It felt good. Gratitude. "I'm so glad you're okay," she whispered.

Rain's therapist entered the room. "Time for PT, Command Sergeant Major."

"We've got a lot more to talk about, Rain."

"I'll be an hour or so."

"I'll be in my lab."

"Dinner? They'll let me eat in the cafeteria here."

"Okay." She pulled the chair aside to let him past. He stopped and removed what looked like a small paper from his shirt pocket. "I have something for you. She insisted I keep it and give it to you if anything bad happened." He handed it over.

Mira wiped her tears and took the napkin from his hand. She recognized her handiwork from their lunch together. It was the diagram she had drawn to explain DNA to Eleanor. On the back Eleanor had written a note:

Dear Mira,

If you are reading this, it means my role or yours has ended. I want to encourage you to keep searching. Your mind, your ability with the scientific method, has done much for you. Really, the world. I just want to remind you. Those tools, your mind and science, they will only take you so far. I pray you will someday come to know you are not alone and never have been.

God bless you,

Eleanor

"Is it something you want to talk about?" Rain asked.

"No." Tears again flowed on her face. Her voice cracked. "Later."

A TREATISE

M ira arrived well before Rain as she planned to use the spare time to write. She opened her computer and tried to peck away, but couldn't stay focused.

She started in surprise as she sensed someone behind her. She turned to see Rain pretend to read the screen over her shoulder. "You snuck up on me. That's not nice."

Rain snickered. The orderly who had silently wheeled him in said, "Are you good here, Command Sergeant Major?"

"Yes, thank you." The orderly retreated and Rain turned back to Mira. "What are you working on?"

"Just a summary of my life's work, that's all."

"Was that sarcasm?" Rain made a mocking face of disbelief.

She grinned. "You remember I've spent my career in search of the First Common Ancestor? Not only did we find it, it turned out that same microbe is the biocontrol solution we sought. It didn't come in time. But we're still going to need it. I just can't digest the irony of this."

"Don't look at me for help, Mira, I'm still trying to understand why I'm still alive. What do you mean we're still going to need it? I sure hope not. I suppose it might still be out there, but they're saying nothing could have survived the blast."

"Quon still has it. He plans to use SONA for commercial purposes. He needed my work to do that, to give him a way to control it. He knew what would happen with that incineration, but didn't tell anyone. How could somebody be so self-interested and callous?"

Rain seemed to take this news in stride. "What do you think?"

"I only know that he is focused on his interest. He even expected me to help him."

"Not really out of bounds for him, right? So, what are you writing about, then?"

"You read Eleanor's note?"

"No. But we did talk."

"And you agree with her, this is all a God thing?" Mira leaned forward, anxious to know his answer.

"What else could it be? Luck? I don't believe that, do you?"

Mira knew her answer. She had not arrived at it lightly, or easily. "No."

Rain leaned in. "I'm all ears; how do you explain all of this?"

Mira looked at the bright white lights in the ceiling above them. "When we discovered *Primum viverea* remediated SONA, we were all so dumbfounded. The coincidence is beyond measure. That it persisted for all those millennia. That I spent my life looking for it. Not ever really knowing why. Eleanor was so convinced that everything was going to work out. It did and it didn't."

Rain pulled up the loose sleeve of the hospital gown he wore to reveal his taijitu. "You know what this means, right?"

"Yin and yang? Complimentary forces? Exergy and entropy, male and female, positive and negative, life and death, that kind of thing?"

"You get the gist. We have experiences in life. We label them good or bad based upon our perspective. All things serve a purpose, even though we never fully understand how."

"As a scientist I operate under the assumption that I can understand things. That which we can detect and measure, that is."

"So, finding this Ancestor thing, that it eats SONA, this helps you understand?"

Mira looked at Rain's bandaged legs. She whispered, "It makes me think." She glanced back at the screen, which displayed:

On the Origin of Life and the Necessity of Precursor

Cooperatives

Wallace, Mira D.[1,2] and Weingartner, Jeffrey A.[1]

1University of California, Berkeley, Dept. of Plant and Microbial Biology, 311 Koshland Hall, Berkeley CA, 94720.

2National Interagency Biodefense Campus, Fort Detrick, MD 21702

Rain rolled himself to the other side of the table. "Why don't we get our food? Then I want you to read it to me since I can't do it myself."

"It's just my first draft."

"Doesn't matter."

"It's technical. You'll think it's boring."

"I doubt that. I want to know what you're thinking, what you want to say to people. What better way than your paper?"

His interest warmed her cheeks. But she remained squeamish to share. They got their meals. Mira helped Rain with his.

Rain took a bite. "Well?"

"Any word on Gigi?"

"No communications. I tried her fiancé, but haven't gotten through. Last I knew she was in the hospital in Salt Lake City. There were power outages, but the hospital has backup, of course. Hopefully, they've been able to keep her stable. I'll keep checking."

"Let me know."

Rain took a drink. "I know you're stalling. It's not going to work. Let's hear it."

"It's a little embarrassing."

"Why? It's just me here."

"It's the scope of what I'm doing. It's like I'm trying to write the Origin of Species or something."

"Darwin?"

"Yes. The whole thing is a bit—presumptuous. But Jeff thinks we need to do it. He's helping me."

"Now you've got me interested, Mira. Come on. Get reading."

"I'll just give you the Summary. I'm still working on the individual sections."

"Give me what you got."

"Okay. Remember, you asked for it." Rain listened intently as she took in a big breath and began. She went through much of the technical material and paused. "Do you really want me to continue?"

"I do," Rain said, "as long as there's no quiz at the end."

Mira chuckled and went on. She finally reached the concluding paragraph.[1]

"...because the spontaneous generation of life required multiple unlikely synergisms to form among randomly occurring chemical reactions that occurred under special conditions present during early planetary formation, it is predicted that the occurrence of life is an incalculably rare event in the universe, if not unique."

Rain shrugged, but immediately winced in pain at the movement. "Correct me if I'm wrong, but if I understand you right, Mira, you're saying you think there might be no life other than here on Earth in the entire, huge Universe."

"I don't know that. Nobody does. But the science suggests that is just as likely as not."

"That's what many Christians believe."

"Belief again."

"Not your M.O., is it?"

"I've tried to avoid it." As she said those words, she saw how that would no longer be true. "But that was self-limiting. I learned that from Eleanor. Science is about theory, discovery, and expanding our understanding about how things work."

"But there's more to life than just knowing how things work."

"I know."

He reached across the table and squeezed her hand.

---

1. For Mira's conclusion to her paper, see Supplement.

SUPPLEMENT

AGENCIES – Several federal government agencies are mentioned throughout the story. These are described here:

DTRA: Pronounced *dē-trah*–Defense Threat Reduction Agency. From the official website: "The Defense Threat Reduction Agency enables the DoD and the U.S. Government to prepare for and combat weapons of mass destruction and improvised threats and to ensure nuclear deterrence.

ATEC: Pronounced *ā-tech,* U.S. Army Test and Evaluation Command. From the official website: "ATEC plans, integrates, and conducts experiments, developmental testing, independent operational testing, and independent evaluations and assessments to provide essential information to acquisition decision makers and commanders."

NIAID: Pronounced "nigh-aid," the National Institute of Allergy and Infectious Diseases. The mission of NIAID is to pursue progress in understanding, treating, and preventing infectious and immunologic diseases.

NICBR: Pronounced 'nick-burr', the National Interagency Confederation for Biological Research. NICBR is a consortium of eight federal agencies to create synergy among their common goals of achieving a healthier and more secure nation. The eight agencies include: National Cancer Institute at Frederick, National Institute of Allergy and Infectious Diseases, U.S. Army Medical Research and Development Command, U.S. Department of Agriculture, Agricultural Research Service, National Biodefense Analysis and

Countermeasures Centers, Centers for Disease Control and Prevention, Naval Medical Research Center, and the U.S. Food and Drug Administration.

GreenCars – Dr. Wesley Quon built his company and glowing reputation on a clean energy technology that he applied to automobiles. The technology is theoretically possible but as far as the authors know, not yet developed in reality. Additional background on his (fictional) invention is provided here:

As a graduate student, Dr. Wesley Quon exploited a peculiar property of an algae species that lived only in Utah's Great Salt Lake, forty miles north of Dugway Proving Ground. There in its natural habitat the algae bloomed seasonally in drifting globs, like slimy balloons. Inside the algal balloons was fresh water. The algae created it by pumping salt from the inside out—creating a life-sustaining oasis inside the balloon. It was a rather ingenious adaptation to survive the extreme saline environment.

Shortly after graduating, Dr. Quon developed and patented the algae along with a semi-permeable conductive membrane which provided the algae essential nutrients to grow. The algae rapidly transfer salt from one side of the membrane to the other. Osmosis then causes the salt to rush back across the membrane, creating an electrical potential that his design exploits. The electricity produced continually charges the vehicle's battery packs. This invention by Dr. Quon was the cleanest form of energy ever known. Photosynthesis using sunlight, water, and carbon dioxide was all the algae needed to fuel its highly efficient cellular salt pumps. GreenCars were true to their name, unmistakable on the winding motorways from San Diego to Seattle: under their clear plastic outer casing, the algae made them a highly reflective iridescent green.

BIOSAFETY LEVEL – In the story, the scientists must work in safe work spaces designated as BSL-3 or BSL-4. These are official designations for working with dangerous pathogens. Detailed information about each biosafety level is provided here.

BSL-1: Agents that have been well-studied and are not a threat to humans or the environment. Requires devitalization prior to disposal.

BSL-2: Agents that have been well-studied and pose only a minimal threat to humans or the environment and they are not readily transmissible through aerosols. Requires laboratory personnel to have training. Laboratory access is restricted to certified personnel who must take specific precautions when handling. Safety equipment such as emergency showers, eyewash stations, and specialized disposal containers for sharp items are required.

BSL-3: Agents known to be a serious threat to humans and are transmissible through aerosols. Requires the use of specialized ventilation hoods or biosafety cabinets and personnel must wear protective clothing. Laboratories must be fully contained, sealed, and access restricted by double sets of doors. Exhaust air must be filtered or sterilized and all materials exiting the facility must be decontaminated.

BSL-4: Deadly agents that are readily transmitted through aerosols and/or for which no effective treatment is available. Facilities are highly secure and access is even more restricted than BSL-3. All effluents and exhaust air are filtered and sterilized. Workers must wear positive pressure suits and follow strict protocols. Facilities are equipped with airlocks and personnel must pass through chemical decontamination showers to exit. All materials exiting the facility must be decontaminated. The world's most dangerous pathogens are housed in BSL-4 facilities. Only a few dozen such labs exist in the world.

SDS-PAGE Procedure – This procedure is performed in the story in an attempt to study SONA and whether it is composed of proteins. The acronym is short for Sodium Dodecyl Sulfate—Polyacrylamide Gel Electrophoresis. Electrophoresis is a process whereby molecules are separated according to their size. It is commonly used to separate DNA fragments or proteins. For DNA, gels are made by melting agarose (a type of polysaccharide from seaweed) in a buffer solution. When the gel cools and solidifies it forms a three-dimensional matrix with very small pores. When placed in an electric field, the naturally negatively charged DNA will migrate to the positive pole. As it migrates, the smaller DNA fragments move faster through the pores and larger ones move more slowly—thus separating the fragments by size. For proteins (where the procedure is properly called PAGE), a gel made from acrylamide is used due to its smaller pore sizes when solidified. The smaller the protein, the further it migrates from one electric pole to the other. In order to assess the size of each protein or DNA fragment, a "ladder" of proteins or DNA of known sizes is loaded in a control lane to provide an index. Since proteins fold into structures of different three-dimensional sizes, a detergent (called SDS) can be added to unfold them first and ensure they separate by the molecular weight of the protein. After separation, the separated proteins or DNA can be stained to visualize the various bands in the gel. In the story, this technique would give the researchers the means to gauge the protein profile of the subject.

Q Exactive HF Hybrid Quadrupole-Orbitrap – In mass spectrometry, Orbitrap is an ion trap mass analyzer consisting of an outer barrel-like electrode and a coaxial inner spindle-like electrode that traps ions in an orbital motion around the spindle. The image current from the trapped ions is detected and converted to a mass spectrum using the Fourier transform of the frequency signal. Part of the process of this analysis involves the methods of preparation for the sample. In this story, it is imagined that gas chromatography is utilized, but it is implied that all approaches are ultimately attempted.

Universal Code – In the story, Mira tries to explain the universal code to Eleanor by making sketches on a napkin. The Universal Code represents the central dogma of biology. It is the basic system by which all living things function. Therefore, it is strong evidence that all living things are related to each other and can be used to study those relationships. Mira's life's work is based on understanding how life started by identifying the most primitive and ancient microbe. Below is a brief explanation and a representation of the code itself:

DNA is composed of long strings of chemicals called nucleotides commonly referred to as bases. There are four different nucleotides designated by the letters A, T, G, or C. The DNA of a typical bacteria cell is a single strand (connected on the ends to form a circle) consisting of about 4,500,000 letters. A human cell has 23 pairs of chromosomes, each harboring a strand of DNA that is on average 130,000,000 letters. Parts of the DNA encode instructions to make individual proteins capable of carrying out cellular functions. These sections of the DNA are called genes. The DNA of a typical bacteria has about 5,000 genes. All 23 human chromosomes collectively contain about 20-25,000 genes.

The proteins encoded by genes are strings of chemicals called amino acids. Living things use about 20 different amino acids that, like DNA, can be designated by single letters (F, L, I, M, V, S, P, T, A, Y, H, Q, N, K, D, E, C, W, R, or G). The codon table below shows how cells decipher the DNA to determine the correct order for each amino acid in the protein. For example, the DNA sequence T-T-T specifies the amino acid phenylalanine (F). So, every three DNA bases encode one amino acid. Because there are 64 possible codons (all possible combinations of A, G, C, T in groups of three), some codons encode the same amino acid. In addition, there are 'start' and 'stop' codons that provide the information about where the coding part of the gene begins and ends. Each cell has machinery to read the DNA of each gene and stitch together the amino acids in the proper order to make a functional protein. Viruses, bacteria, fungi, plants, and animals all use this same codon table or universal code with a few minor variations.

TTT	Phenylalanine (F)	TCT	Serine (S)	TAT	Tyrosine (Y)	TGT	Cysteine (C)
TTC	Phenylalanine (F)	TCC	Serine (S)	TAC	Tyrosine (Y)	TGC	Cysteine (C)
TTA	Leucine (L)	TCA	Serine (S)	TAA	Stop	TGA	Stop
TTG	Leucine (L)	TCG	Serine (S)	TAG	Stop	TGG	Tryptophan (W)
CTT	Leucine (L)	CCT	Proline (P)	CAT	Histidine (H)	CGT	Arginine (R)
CTC	Leucine (L)	CCC	Proline (P)	CAC	Histidine (H)	CGC	Arginine (R)
CTA	Leucine (L)	CCA	Proline (P)	CAA	Glutamine (Q)	CGA	Arginine (R)
CTG	Leucine (L)	CCG	Proline (P)	CAG	Glutamine (Q)	CGG	Arginine (R)
ATT	Isoleucine (I)	ACT	Threonine (T)	AAT	Asparagine (N)	AGT	Serine (S)
ATC	Isoleucine (I)	ACC	Threonine (T)	AAC	Asparagine (N)	AGC	Serine (S)
ATA	Methionine (M)	ACA	Threonine (T)	AAA	Lysine (K)	AGA	Arginine (R)
ATG	Methionine (M)	ACG	Threonine (T)	AAG	Lysine (K)	AGG	Arginine (R)
GTT	Valine (V)	GCT	Alanine (A)	GAT	Aspartic Acid (D)	GGT	Glycine (G)
GTC	Valine (V)	GCC	Alanine (A)	GAC	Aspartic Acid (D)	GGC	Glycine (G)
GTA	Valine (V)	GCA	Alanine (A)	GAA	Glutamic Acid (E)	GGA	Glycine (G)
GTG	Valine (V)	GCG	Alanine (A)	GAG	Glutamic Acid (E)	GGG	Glycine (G)

BUSCO — Benchmarking Universal Single-Copy Orthologs. This provides measurement for assessment of a genome assembly, gene set, and transcriptome completeness.

Hypothesis on the Origin of Life – Our story concludes with Mira reading an excerpt from her paper describing her hypothesis on the origin of life. She arrived at this hypothesis based on her analysis of *Primum viverea* and its unique properties. The portion of the document Mira reads to Rain is provided here. It is written in a typical scientific scholarly manner. To summarize, her discovery of *Primum* as one of the first life forms leads her to conclude that living things were complex from their very inception. She hypothesizes that all life on earth arose from a single event. This event began as cooperation among complex chemicals that accumulated during early formation of the planet. Such a model would require numerous unlikely events to happen coincidentally in series—much like the events of Mira's life described in the story.

The Necessity of Precursor Cooperatives for the Origin of Life

Wallace, M. D.[1,2] and Weingartner, J. A.[1]

[1] *University of California, Berkeley, Dept. of Plant and Microbial Biology, 311 Koshland Hall, Berkeley CA, 94720.*

2National Interagency Biodefense Campus, Fort Detrick, MD 21702

Models for the origin of life are confounded by the interdependent and non-reducible relationships between nucleic acids, proteins, and other organic and non-organic molecules that comprise living systems. The prevailing theory, postulated by numerous researchers, suggests self-replicating nucleic acids, specifically RNAs or a derivative thereof, were the precursors of life. Such theories are attractive because RNA can store information and, under some circumstances, can also catalyze simple chemical reactions.

Recently, RNA-only models have come under criticism since RNA by its nature is inherently unstable, and logical stepwise mechanisms to explain how the central dogma evolved from an RNA world have been elusive. In light of this, protein- or metabolism-first models have also been proposed. These models suffer from the reciprocal problem: proteins (as well as non-protein metabolic pathways) are stable and capable of complex enzymatic reactions, but unlike nucleic acids, they cannot store information and are exceedingly complex. As such, the odds of sustained spontaneous formation defy plausibility.

Here, we describe an ancient microbe, *Primum viverea*, herein postulated to be the First Common Ancestor (FCA) evidenced by extremely primitive genomic features and a substantially reduced ribosome. FCA was discovered in aerial samples collected from the lower- to mid-stratosphere. The organism is a scavenger, living in a volatile environment with limited carbon resources and subject to intense ultraviolet light. To cope with these rugged conditions, it has robust DNA and RNA repair mechanisms to reverse UV damage and stores chemical energy through a set of UV absorbing molecules that show similarity to cyanobacterial pigments. The cell membrane is composed of a simple phospholipid monolayer as found in some archaea. Phylogenetic analysis of 22.8 billion independently isolated microorganisms positions FCA at the root of both the bacteria and archaea kingdoms, and molecular clock analysis dates it to ~4.3 billion years ago; suggesting life originated in the atmosphere, which at that time would likely have been 1,000 times denser than it is today. The primitive genomic complement of this organism consisting of large numbers of small, non-coding RNAs, and a simplified genetic code implies both small RNAs and simple proteins were available at the inception of life.

Based on these features of FCA, a cooperative model for the origin of life is proposed herein. According to the model, life began as a consequence of synergistic relationships that spontaneously developed between nucleic acids, amino acids, lipids, and energy storage molecules. Not unlike other models, the cooperative model starts with an environment in which large numbers of nucleic acid oligomers had spontaneously developed through synergistic chemical relationships with other organic molecules that both polymerized nucleotides and stabilized them; the so-called primordial soup. These cooperative relationships led to the enrichment and persistence of all contributing members of the group.

Amino acids were probably essential to these early synergistic interactions by providing stability to some nucleic acids via physical interactions, or in other instances serving as catalysts for nucleic acid driven reactions. These molecular cooperatives favored increased complexity as natural selection at this stage strongly favored the retention not of individual biomolecules, but entire groups. Some members of the group likely had simple peptide biosynthesis activities. This was necessary for the selection of functional peptides which can only form under a relatively high rate of trial and error (as opposed to their simpler nucleic acid counterparts). Nucleic acids capable of producing peptides that aided in RNA stability and/or replication would have been strongly favored.

This process led to specific nucleic acids "encoding" specific peptides; the basis for modern protein biosynthesis and the central dogma of biology. As more and more nucleic acids in the cooperative adopted the ability to synthesize proteins, many of the primitive enzymatic roles carried out by RNAs were replaced by proteins, as is the case in modern cells.

Based on the genome structure of FCA and its large number of apparently self-synthesizing non-coding RNAs not encoded within the genome, it appears the storage of RNA as DNA copies likely occurred later, after DNA-RNA-protein cooperatives had already formed. While the cooperative model provides a basis for the development of the modern genetic code, several additional concurrent factors must also be considered.

First, sets of DNA-RNA-peptide cooperatives must have formed within lipid membranes—which also must have been provided spontaneously by the environment. Such simple membranes have been identified in diverse environments, and it is accepted that their presence in the primordial soup is plausible. It is anticipated that these lipids were necessary and actively participated in these early codependent chemical relationships, particularly the establishment of electrochemical gradients by energy capturing porphyrin-like molecules.

Because the spontaneous generation of life required multiple unlikely synergisms among specific groups of randomly occurring, renewable organic molecules that formed under special conditions present only during early planetary formation, it is predicted that the occurrence of life is an incalculably rare event in the universe, if not unique.

ACKNOWLEDGMENTS

First, we'd like to thank our families for gracefully allowing us the uncountable hours away from them over the past decade of its creation. That includes Chris's wife Emmy, and their home-schooled children Liam, Ian, and Lilah, as well as Tom's wife Kathleen, their son Collyn, and daughter Geneva. Emmy and Liam read early drafts and offered valuable feedback. So did the authors' parents Steve and Necia Dardick. The manuscript received scrutiny from the eyes of professionals too. One was the authors' aunt, Karen Dardick, herself a professional author. We were fortunate for the work of Terry DiDomenico, a professional editor, who also provided much guidance.

Years later, the manuscript landed in the hands of Tessa Shaffer. She showed us, in her tactful and insightful manner, the huge opportunity for improvement, and conducted a complete developmental edit. Her firm had an intern, Rebecca Emerick, who as part of her schoolwork, performed a subsequent line edit pass. Tessa also recommended that we go through a beta reader phase. During that time Arwa Abbas, who we do not personally know, and Joanna Roberts, a well-read and dear family friend offered valuable feedback.

All of that was before the novel reached the attention of the folks at Immortal Works. Their team has been excellent and significantly improved the product. We're particularly thankful that Staci Olsen was interested enough to like a Tweet during a Twitter Pitch day, and the acquisition staff who deemed the work IW-worthy. John Olsen was assigned as editor, and we could not have asked for his better. John has an in-depth understanding of the science and faith issues raised in the story. Others contributors have included Holli Anderson, Beth Buck, Ashley Literski, Rachel Huffmire, and Jason King, all of whom have performed their respective duties admirably. Immortal Works is truly a great home for aspirational authors.

ABOUT THE AUTHORS

Tom is a student of the human condition. That's the commonality between his various projects, of which he maybe has too many. Maybe too many. He has two businesses, one a consulting practice in which he helps organizations with culture and people strategy. The other is an R&D company that aspires to bring a technology invented by his grandfather to the marketplace. He also plays drums and sings in two rock bands, as well as various worship ensembles at his church. His hottest passion these days is writing, with multiple book projects in varying stages of completion. When not pursuing these passions, Tom enjoys time with family and friends (and fits in reading and studying via online courses whenever possible.)

Chris is a lifelong scientist with a deep curiosity about the inner workings of living things. He received his PhD in Molecular and Cell Biology from the University of Maryland, College Park in 1999 and has since published over 100 scientific papers, reviews, and book chapters on the topics of virology, microbiology, evolution, genetics, and plant biology. His research goals as a Lead Scientist for the United States Department of Agriculture are to help achieve a globally sustainable, healthy, and affordable food supply. He is blessed by his gifted wife with a passion for literature and his 3 amazing homeschooled children. Together they enjoy learning, exploring nature, fishing, and spending time with friends and family.